THE DEADLY SILENCE

EVA HUDSON

–VENATRIX–

THE DEADLY SILENCE

EVA HUDSON

First published as The Third Estate 2013 by Two Pies Press
This edition published by Venatrix

ISBN 978-0-9926357-4-9

THE DEADLY SILENCE

The woman drove a sharp finger into the soft flesh above the waistband of Trisha's jogging bottoms.

Trisha gasped and grabbed her back.

'Liar! You stink of fags.' She was shouting now. 'Give them to me.'

A prison guard Trisha hadn't seen before, wide as she was tall, ambled up the corridor towards them. 'What's the problem here?'

'Nothing, miss,' Trisha's tormentor said in a childish voice. She smiled sweetly at the guard.

'You want to watch yourself, French. Don't think you can bat those eyelashes at me and get away with anything.' The guard wagged a finger at her.

'But I haven't done nothing wrong, miss.'

'Make sure you keep it that way.' The guard leaned back on her prison issue Doc Marten shoes and glanced along he straggly line of restless inmates queuing the length of he windowless corridor. 'Why must you argue over every tle thing?' She walked slowly down the line, scrutinising ch woman's face as she went. Some women looked away, hile others defiantly stared back at her, straightening up d rising on their toes as if readying for a fight. The guard ook her head, tutted and made her way to the locked gate far end of the corridor.

The woman behind Trisha tugged on her ponytail. isha half turned and snatched back her hair, trying not to e her baseball cap in the process.

'Do I know you?' the woman said.

Trisha pulled down the visor of her cap. 'Just got one of se faces,' she said.

As the woman ahead of her returned the handset to its lle, Trisha inched forward. The rubber soles of thirty s of trainers squeaked in unison on the vinyl floor as the r inmates shuffled along behind her. Trisha lifted the iver and punched a number she had memorised into the

For all the heroes at UCH.
Thank you.

ONE

Trisha Collins was second in line for the phone her eyes to the floor and concentrated on k breathing even. She counted to five as she t breath in through her nose. Then one to five a long breath out through her mouth. In he rehearsed her speech for the hundredth time.

'Give me your fags.'

Trisha Collins blew out her breath quickly a A tall muscular woman was standing behind h scars across both cheeks, a nose ring disappe left nostril through an inflamed hole.

'I don't have any,' Trisha said and turned the payphone.

'Liar.'

Trisha edged away and bumped into the of her. She raised her hands in apology a gaze once again to the scuffed vinyl tiles ben

'For Christ's sake – watch it,' the wor pulled the phone from her ear. 'I'm trying conversation here.'

'Sorry.' Trisha winced.

'Give me your fags,' the acne-faced prodding Trisha in the back.

'I don't have any,' she said in a whispe

keypad. The phone rang out five or six times before it was picked up.

'Angela Tate,' a voice at the other end finally said.

'Angela, it's me.'

Tate let out an impatient sigh. 'Who is this?'

Trisha cupped her hand around the mouthpiece and mumbled her name. 'I need your help, Ange. I've got to get out of here.'

'You should be talking to your solicitor.'

'He's useless. I've got no one else to turn to. You've got to help me.'

There was a long silence at the other end of the line.

'Ange?'

'I'm sorry, Trisha. I really don't see what I can do.' Tate said something away from the phone.

'What was that? Ange, please. I can't spend another night in this place. It's not safe.'

'Put the phone down right now and call your lawyer. You're wasting your time talking to me.'

'But I told you – the solicitor Gary got for me isn't any good.'

'Maybe it's time you stopped listening to Gary.'

'Can you get me someone better?' Despite her best attempts to control her nerves, a pleading whine had crept into Trisha's voice. 'I'll pay you back as soon as I can. Please, Ange. I really need you to help me.'

Tate exhaled, the blast of air reverberating noisily in the earpiece of the phone. 'I'll see what I can do.'

'Thanks, Ange. I knew you wouldn't let me down. Go back too far, don't we?'

Tate didn't answer.

'Ange?' Trisha squeezed the handset tighter in her fist.

'I'm not promising anything,' Tate said after a long pause. 'I'll make a few phone calls, put out some feelers. But I doubt a top-flight solicitor will have any more luck with a bail application than Gary's did.'

'I can't stay in here.'

'The police think you're a flight risk.'

'That's just stupid. Where would I go? All I want to do is get back home to be with my kids.'

'You know you can't go back to the estate?' It sounded to Trisha as if Tate was losing her patience. 'The mood's changed there – people are angry with you. They feel duped.'

'But I haven't done anything.'

'I'm only reporting what I've heard.'

The woman behind Trisha yanked on her ponytail again. 'Hurry up, will you?'

'All right!' Trisha snapped.

'What's going on there?' Tate asked.

'Don't speak to me like that. Who do you think you are?' The woman shoved Trisha hard in the ribs.

Trisha threw a glance over her shoulder. The guard at the end of the corridor was busy chatting with a colleague on the other side of the security gate. 'I'm sorry,' Trisha said to the woman behind her. 'I won't be long.' She edged away and turned back towards the phone. 'You know I've got nothing to do with…' She lowered her voice to a whisper. 'With Casey going missing, don't you, Ange?'

Tate didn't answer straightaway. Her silence felt like a slap in the face. Trisha closed her eyes and leaned her head against the painted breeze block wall. 'Christ, Ange – you can't give up on me. Not now.'

A vicious tug on her ponytail jerked Trisha's head back.

'Haven't you finished yet?' The acne-faced woman had wound Trisha's hair around a fist. She pulled on it again. 'Why don't you say goodbye and piss off back to your cell?' Another hard yank.

'Ow!'

'Trisha? What's happening?' Tate said.

Trisha snatched at her hair, but the woman held on tight. 'Just give me a couple of seconds, will you?' she pleaded.

The woman shrugged and glanced towards the guard at the far end of the corridor, her grip on Trisha's hair holding firm.

'Look, Ange, I've got to go.' An unexpected sob erupted from Trisha's mouth. 'Promise you'll get me out of here.'

'You know I can't do that.'

'You kept your promises before.'

'What?'

'You didn't let me down when I needed you before.'

'Christ, Trish, that was over thirty years ago.'

'You've got to help me now.'

Another sudden tug on Trisha's hair knocked her cap onto the floor. The phone fell from her hands and she dropped to her knees, scrambling frantically to retrieve the baseball cap before anyone got a proper look at her face.

'I do know you.' The acne-faced woman pulled Trisha's head towards her. 'I've seen you on telly.' She hauled Trisha to her feet by her hair and shoved her hard against the wall. 'I know what you're in here for.' Her nostrils flared in disgust. 'How could you do something like that? To your own kid? You evil bitch.'

Trisha squeezed her eyes shut as the woman's fist slammed into her face.

TWO

SIX DAYS EARLIER

Tuesday 7th February

'Do you know you're the only member of staff who still has an expense account?'

Angela Tate stood in the middle of the room and stared at her editor without commenting.

'Even I don't have one.' Harriet Fowler took off her glasses and pinched the bridge of her nose. 'For God's sake, Angela. I'm just asking you to ease up a bit. I'm the one who has to account for excess expenditure.'

Tate folded her arms.

'Have you any idea how difficult it makes things for me?'

Tate exhaled.

'Just don't take the piss – is that too much to ask?'

Tate didn't answer, refusing to dignify the conversation by participating in it.

'You must be single-handedly keeping the black cab trade in business.'

Tate turned towards the door.

'Can you at least think before you spend?'

Tate stepped into the corridor.

'I haven't finished. Angela!'

Maintaining her silence, Tate closed the door firmly behind her, resisting both the urge to slam it shut and to tell Fowler where she could shove her expense account.

Harriet Fowler had taken on the job of editing the *Evening News* just over eighteen months ago. When she replaced her disgraced predecessor, Fowler had promised a new regime, one based on accountability and transparency. At the time she'd assured the staff she had the full support of the board of directors, who had apparently welcomed her fresh approach. But the new order lasted all of three weeks. No one blamed Fowler – twenty-two years at the BBC hadn't adequately prepared her for the backstabbing world of Fleet Street. On occasion, Tate had almost found herself feeling sorry for the woman. Not that she would ever admit it. Editors were management and Tate was firmly on the side of the workers. Which was why she never had any ambition to become editor of the *Evening News* herself, even though the job had been offered to her enough times over the years. Tate knew where she belonged and was more than happy to stay there.

After a visit to the car park for a cigarette, she returned to her desk to discover the paper's only staff photographer sitting in her chair, resting his feet on her desk.

'Shouldn't you be out harassing celebrities with that long lens of yours?' she said. 'You know, making yourself useful to society?'

Frank Carter sat up straight and dragged his feet to the floor. 'Just taking a breather.' He stood up and offered her the chair.

As she sat down, Tate noticed a large manila envelope propped up against her computer monitor. 'Is this something to do with you?' She picked the envelope up and inspected it front and back. There was no name on it.

'Nothing to do with me,' Frank said.

'Why are you here?'

He reached into his jacket and retrieved something from his pocket. He thrust it at her.

'What's this?' She glanced down to discover the card he'd shoved into her hands was a theatre ticket for a West End musical she had so far happily managed to avoid.

'Do you fancy it?' Frank said, an uncharacteristic embarrassed expression on his face.

'Why would I want to—?'

'It's for the fourteenth.'

'What's special about the fourteenth?'

'Where's your sense of romance? It's Valentine's Day.'

She stared at the ticket. 'Are you actually asking me out?'

'Don't get your hopes up – it's just a couple of mates taking in a show. That's all. It's not as if it's a date or anything.'

'Thank God for that.' She thrust the ticket back at him. 'I'm busy.' She turned away from him and grabbed the manila envelope from her desk, tore it open and peered inside, then shook out the contents. A handful of newspaper cuttings landed in a heap on the desk. 'Did you see Rita leave this here?'

Frank didn't answer. Tate looked up and was surprised to see a crestfallen expression on his face. She felt an unexpected stab of guilt and the need to say something kind. Nothing came to mind. 'Maybe if you'd given me a bit more notice.' It was the most charitable thing she could think of.

'Don't worry about it. It's not as if you were my first choice.' His tone was flippant, but he still sounded bruised.

Tate decided it best to ignore him and started sifting through the small pile of cuttings on her desk. She recognised a piece she'd written years before, when she was still the paper's crime correspondent. 'You haven't answered my question, did you see Rita?'

'She doesn't still work here?'

'You ask me that every time I mention her name.'

'Why do we need a librarian at the paper when we've got no library? Google seems to be more than adequate for most people.'

'Promise me you'll never say that to her face.'

The landline on Tate's desk started ringing. She picked it up, brusquely offered her name and waited. There was silence at the other end, then an intake of breath. Then the dialling tone. She hung up.

'Heavy breather was it?' Frank's features had recovered their sarcastic sneer.

Tate shrugged. 'Not sure a single breath qualifies.'

'Watch out, enemy fire coming in at one o'clock.' Frank ducked behind her chair.

'Fowler?'

'Nooo. Much worse than that. Your favourite intern has just flounced through the doors.'

'Shit.' Tate shoved the cuttings back into the envelope. 'Why did she have to latch on to me?'

'What? The legendary Angela Tate? Uncoverer of corruption and slayer of despots?'

'All right.'

'You're her role model, Ange. Maybe you should take your mentoring job a bit more seriously.'

'And maybe you should sod off.'

'Oh… hang on a sec. You may have been given a reprieve. Looks like she's been distracted by something sparkly on the sub's desk.'

Tate released the breath she had trapped in her lungs. 'The girl won't leave me alone. Every time I turn around, there she is. Waiting to pounce.'

'She just wants to learn from the best. Can't blame her for that. You should think of it as a compliment. It's your chance to influence the next generation.'

'Next generation? The rate we're going, there won't be any papers left for them to work on. Why can't she just start a blog that no one will read, like everybody else?' Tate clutched the envelope of cuttings to her chest, slipped her cigarettes and lighter into a pocket and headed for the exit.

'Where are you off to?'

'Beating a hasty retreat while the coast's clear,' she called over her shoulder. 'If she asks where I am, tell her I've just shipped out to cover a natural disaster in Outer Mongolia. Or deepest darkest Peru.'

Before she reached the exit, Tate's landline trilled again. She watched Frank pick up, say hello, then pull the handset from his ear and stare at it accusingly. 'I think that was your heavy breather calling back,' he said. 'He hung up on me.'

'Shame – you could have asked him to chum you to the theatre.' Tate slipped through door quickly, without giving Frank the chance to muster a barbed retort and, deciding to forego a nicotine hit until after she'd spoken to Rita, made her way to what the librarian laughingly described as her office.

Since its creation in the first half of the last century, all that was left of the *Evening News* library was the information Rita held in her not inconsiderable brain and the paper's comprehensive database. Rita's physical domain had been reduced from an open plan office taking up half of the second floor, to a tiny room on the third.

Tate tapped on the small window set into the door. The librarian looked up and scowled at her over the half-moon glasses perched on her nose. She grunted a hello as Tate entered. Tate waved the manila envelope at her. 'Look familiar?'

'Should it?'

Tate shook the contents onto a vacant portion of Rita's desk. 'I'm assuming these are from you. What I can't understand is why you needed to be so bloody mysterious about it.'

'I don't know what you're talking about.' Rita gingerly picked up a cutting by its corner, as if it might be toxic, and silently read the article.

'Well?' Tate asked.

'From the quality of the paper and the style of the writing, I'd say it was mid to late 80s. 1989 if I had to be specific.'

'Very impressive.' Tate forced a grudging smile. Rita really knew her stuff.

'Of course the date written in pencil in the top right hand corner helped considerably.'

'What? How did I manage to miss that?' Tate snatched up another cutting and was relieved to discover there was no date. Rita just got lucky. 'I didn't request them.'

'So?'

'So why did you send them to me?'

Rita regarded Tate over the top of her spectacles and sucked in a breath through her teeth. 'Nothing to do with me. We stopped offering a cuttings service in 2001. Obviously something that passed you by.' She prodded the pile of paper scraps with the end of a pencil. 'I can assure you, we'd never have presented anything in this state.'

'But if they're not from you—'

'Is there a note?'

'Of course there's no bloody note.' Tate realised she hadn't actually checked. She peered inside the envelope. No note.

Rita dropped the cutting and watched as it floated back to the pile. 'Now if you wouldn't mind taking your detritus away with you.'

'But my name's not on the envelope,' Tate said. 'If you didn't send it, how the hell did the post room know it was meant for me?'

THREE

Detective Inspector Natasha McKittrick picked her way through the discarded chip paper and crushed fizzy drink cans littering the fourth floor exterior landing of Montague House. When she reached Trisha Collins' front door she took a deep breath.

This was her first investigation for the Homicide and Serious Crime Command and she didn't want to get off on the wrong foot. After only two weeks in the Met she felt just like a rookie starting out on her first case, having to prove herself all over again. She exhaled slowly and drew in another lungful of the raw February air.

She'd lost count of the number of missing person cases she'd investigated, but this was only the second to involve a child under twelve. The first one had turned out badly. She took another deep breath and steeled herself for a difficult conversation with the girl's family. She dreaded this part more than any other. Even after twelve years on the job she was yet to acquire the knack of faking optimism.

Reaching for the doorbell, she noticed for the first time that the door was ajar. It opened suddenly and a uniformed PC appeared in the doorway, carrying a handful of evidence bags. McKittrick spotted a hairbrush in one, a pink, fur covered notebook in another and a toothbrush inside a third.

'Can I help you, miss?' the officer asked her.

'DI McKittrick, MIT seven.' McKittrick reached into her bag to retrieve her warrant card.

'Afternoon, ma'am,' the uniform said, before McKittrick's fingers had managed to locate the leather holder. 'The DCI not with you?'

'He's not inside?' McKittrick said, with more uncertainty in her voice than she'd intended.

'Just me, ma'am. My colleagues have already returned to the station.'

McKittrick wondered if it was worth introducing herself to the family ahead of her superior's arrival, or whether she'd be better off lingering outside to wait for him. 'How's it going in there?' she asked.

The constable let out a long sigh through pursed lips and shook his head. 'It's a bloody madhouse.' He slipped past her and onto the landing. 'Good luck, ma'am.' He gave her a nod and hurried away.

A fierce wind picked up and whipped along the walkway. Eager to retreat from the cold, McKittrick stepped inside the flat and found herself standing in a narrow hallway. She closed the front door to behind her. The carpet beneath her feet was threadbare and stained, the walls on either side scuffed and dirty. She looked into the kitchen to her left, and saw a Staffordshire Bull Terrier cowering under a table, shivering violently as it looked up at her. Next to it a puddle of piss was soaking through a thick pile of newspapers. The dog wagged its tail for a moment, then when McKittrick failed to respond, turned away and settled on a blanket in the corner of the room. Opposite the kitchen was a flight of uncarpeted stairs, the bare wood dirtied by footprints.

McKittrick pulled back her shoulders and reminded herself not to draw any conclusions from the state of the flat. It wasn't that different from the dozens of other council properties she'd seen. She headed for the door at the far end of the hall and peered into the room beyond through the three-inch gap between door and frame. A doughy ghost-faced woman sat on a leather sofa in the middle of the room fiercely hugging a small girl. Another woman, roughly the same age as the first, but stick thin, was sitting at a dining table pushed into the far corner, just next to a double-glazed door that led out onto some kind of narrow balcony. The woman was folding A4 sheets of paper, from the bright lettering and colour photograph, McKittrick supposed the sheets were 'missing' flyers. A boy with the woman's identical nose and mouth, who could have been no more than ten or eleven, sat at the table with her, leaning backwards on his chair, balancing precariously on the back legs.

'If you break your bloody neck, don't expect me to take you to the hospital,' the woman said without taking her eyes from her task. 'Sit properly or get up.'

'I want to take Tyson for a walk,' McKittrick heard the boy complain.

'I'm not letting you out of my sight.'

'He needs to go for a run.'

'I'm not arguing with you.'

A television flickered in the opposite corner. The woman on the sofa was staring blankly at it. The armchair next to the couch was occupied by a frowning teenage girl, already turning to fat.

McKittrick had seen enough to work out who was who and did her best not to make judgements about any of them. She pushed open the door and pulled out her warrant card. 'Ms Collins?' she said and waved her ID at the pale woman on the sofa.

The woman looked up at her and nodded. 'Have you found her?' She started to get to her feet.

'Hello, Ms Collins, I'm Detective Inspector Natasha McKittrick. Please, don't get up.' McKittrick moved swiftly into the room, holding out her hand. The little girl on Collins' lap reached up for it.

'Tell me you've found her,' Collins said.

'I'm sorry – I don't have any news for you.' McKittrick stared into the woman's bloodshot eyes.

'Then why are you here?' the thin woman said. She abandoned her task and marched into the middle of the room, arms tightly folded across her chest.

McKittrick ignored her and crouched down close to Collins. 'I'm working on the case, as part of a special task force,' she said, deciding not to tell her the name of the command unit. No need to raise alarm this early in the investigation by mentioning the word 'homicide'. 'I need to ask you some questions.'

'I've already told the policemen who were here before everything I know.' Collins sniffed noisily.

'That was the risk assessment team. I'm from another… department.'

'I don't understand. Don't you talk to one another?' The little girl on Collins' lap started to whine.

'Give her to me.' The thin woman held out her arms for the girl.

Collins squeezed the toddler tighter, making her whine even louder. 'Leave it, Lorraine. Lola's staying right where she is.' She looked up at McKittrick again.

'It's all part of normal procedure,' McKittrick explained. 'A family liaison officer will be here shortly to help support you during the investigation. In the meantime I have to follow up on the earlier interview.'

'Why? What do you think has happened to Casey?' Collins said.

'Oh it's far too early to form any kind of opinion.' McKittrick wished that were true. After the first twenty-four hours, the chances of finding a child unharmed reduced dramatically with each hour that passed.

'But you are looking for her?' Collins sniffed again.

'Absolutely. We've got teams of officers—' McKittrick was interrupted by a loud cough behind her. She stood up awkwardly and turned towards the man standing in the doorway. She gestured towards him. 'This is Detective Chief Inspector Barrow – my boss.'

The DCI nodded at Collins, then glanced around the room, studying each occupant in turn, much as McKittrick had a few minutes before. Except he was completely brazen about it. McKittrick felt obliged to fill the silence. 'What DCI Barrow and I will do now is go over the statement you gave to the risk assessment officer, point by point.'

'Again? You should be out there looking for Casey. Not wasting time going over the same ground with me.'

'As I said, we are looking for her. We've got sixty officers out there right now. But we're covering such a big area. We need to make sure we concentrate our efforts in the right places. That's why we need to talk to you.'

As Collins nodded her understanding, heavy tears fell from her eyes. 'Get up, Chelsea,' she snapped at the girl slouching in the armchair. 'Let the man sit down.'

The podgy teenager looked up at her mother but didn't budge.

Barrow held up a hand. 'No need to disturb yourself, miss.' He grabbed a dining chair from the other side of the room and placed it directly in front of Collins. McKittrick sat next to Collins on the sofa.

'Let's just start at the beginning, shall we, Ms Collins?' Barrow said, crossing his arms. He set his mouth in a thin line and stared at her unapologetically.

McKittrick slipped a notebook from her pocket and sat with pen poised.

Collins wrapped her arms tighter around the little girl on her lap and the child let out another whine. 'Casey's never gone off on her own before. Never. She wouldn't want to worry me. She's not like other kids her age. She's shy. She doesn't take to people easily. If she's in trouble she'll be too scared to ask for help. You've got to find her.'

'Why didn't you call us as soon as you realised your daughter was missing?' Barrow said, his tone unmistakably accusatory.

'What?' Collins looked up at him, a bewildered expression on her face.

McKittrick stared at her DCI, wondering what he thought he was doing, starting so aggressively, but he refused to acknowledge her. Instead he glanced down at a notebook.

'Your daughter was due home at three-thirty yesterday afternoon,' he said, his gaze now firmly fixed on Collins' face. 'Yet you didn't call us until six this morning. How do you account for the delay?'

More heavy tears fell from Collins' eyes. She shook her head, her confusion at Barrow's line of questioning deepening.

'We tried to find Casey ourselves,' the thin woman interrupted. 'We searched the whole estate.'

'And who are you?' Barrow shifted in his seat to face the woman who was sitting on the arm of Collins' teenage daughter's chair.

'Lorraine O'Donnell – Trisha's best friend.'

'You thought you would do a better job than trained officers?'

'I'm not being funny, but your lot aren't exactly welcome round here.'

'We're talking about the safety of a nine-year-old child,' Barrow said. 'Don't you think any antagonism towards the police might have been overlooked in the circumstances?'

'Christ almighty! We only did what we thought was best.'

Collins was bouncing her daughter on her knee and had managed to placate the child and stop her crying. When she eventually spoke again she did so quietly. 'We got in touch with all of Casey's friends, all the people we could think of.

We thought we should do that first. Before we... made it official.'

'And what about Casey's father?' Barrow asked. 'Where is he now? Still out there searching?'

O'Donnell snorted a laugh down her nose. 'That useless streak of piss?'

McKittrick rested a hand gently on Collins' arm. 'We will need to speak to Casey's dad too,' she said gently.

'I don't have anything to do with him.' Collins smoothed down a stray curl on her daughter's head.

'Are you saying you haven't told him about his daughter's disappearance?' The DCI practically spat out the words.

'I don't even know where he's living at the moment.'

'Is it possible Casey is with him?' McKittrick asked.

'How's she going to know where he is if I don't?'

'He has no contact with his daughter?' Barrow asked.

'If you met him you'd understand,' O'Donnell interjected. 'The kids are better off without him.'

'She's right,' Collins said. 'He's not exactly a good influence.'

The DCI shifted in his seat and shook his head, his disapproval of the Collins family's domestic arrangements evident. McKittrick glanced at Collins. Thankfully, either she hadn't noticed or she had chosen to ignore it.

'Let's move on, shall we?' Barrow leaned forward. 'How has your relationship with Casey been lately?'

'What are you trying to say?' Collins' face crumpled.

'Have there been any... misunderstandings?' McKittrick said.

'No! I told you – she's a good girl. She's never given me any trouble.' At that moment Collins glared at her teenage daughter.

'You'd be surprised how the smallest little thing can get blown out of proportion in the mind of a nine-year-old,' McKittrick said.

'You've got kids, have you?' O'Donnell asked McKittrick.

'No.' McKittrick held O'Donnell's gaze.

'So you wouldn't really know anything about it then, would you?'

'Perhaps Casey argued with one of her siblings?' Barrow turned to look directly at Chelsea.

The girl picked up a cushion and hugged it to her chest.

'How have you been getting on with your little sister lately?' Barrow asked her, his face set in a grim frown.

Chelsea didn't answer. She looked to her mother for guidance.

'Casey loves her brothers and sisters,' Collins said, her words faltering as she started to sob. 'And everyone loves Casey.' The girl on her lap started crying again too. 'Why would anyone want to hurt my baby?'

McKittrick stood up. 'We'll give you a few moments.' She hurried to the door and waited for Barrow to join her.

Reluctantly, the DCI followed her out of the flat and onto the exterior landing. As soon as he had pulled the front door to behind them, he leaned in close to McKittrick. She could feel his hot breath on her face. 'What was that? What did you think you were doing in there?'

'Sir?'

'Undermining me at every turn. You have to be firm with these people or they'll take advantage.'

'Her daughter's disappeared. What kind of advantage—'

He pushed open the door. 'Leave the rest of the interview to me. They have to be clear exactly who's in charge.'

FOUR

The distraught pharmacist was sitting on a chair next to the smashed glass display cabinet, sipping a mug of extra strong, heavily sugared tea. Detective Constable Ralph Mills had made it for her himself.

'Haven't you got hold of the owner yet?' the pharmacist asked him and laced her fingers around the hot mug. Her voice had a strong Antipodean twang to it. Mills couldn't decide if she was from Australia or New Zealand, so decided not to mention it, just in case he caused offence.

He and his colleague, Detective Constable Cath Murray, had been questioning the woman for nearly two hours. She'd refused to decamp to the station, adamant she should wait for the owner to make an appearance. But so far Mr Aktah had failed to materialise.

'Our crime scene examiners can secure the premises as soon as they've finished, they're pretty much packing up now,' Mills told her. 'There's really no need for you to hang around.' He stared into her face. Her plump cheeks had lost all their colour, her lips too. Mills worried she might be in shock. 'Perhaps we should drop you off at the hospital? They could take a look at you. Make sure everything's OK.'

'I'm fine. Really.' She shivered suddenly, despite the thick blanket draped over her shoulders. 'Look at this place.' She shook her head and surveyed the damage. 'Why'd they have to smash everything up like this?'

'You're certain the list of missing items you've given us is complete?' Murray asked.

The pharmacist nodded. 'As far as I can tell.'

'The CCTV footage should help with that.' Murray turned to Mills. 'It's all on video. We'll need to get it converted to digital. Might take a while.'

'We use the same VHS over and over,' the pharmacist explained. 'I can't vouch for the quality. The cassette must be years old.'

'Better than nothing.' Mills smiled at her. 'You'd be surprised what those geeky technical guys can do. Miracle workers.'

Murray's mobile rang, she took one look at the screen and picked her way carefully over the debris littering the floor to take the call outside. Mills peered through the shattered glass in the window and watched as a gang of four boys on BMXs circled her. If they weren't careful, Murray would lose her temper and nick the lot of them for obstruction.

The last of the CSEs left and Mills wrapped up the interview. 'If there's nothing else you can think of that might be relevant, I suppose that's us done.' He was reluctant to leave her there on her own. He handed her his business card. 'Anything else you remember, just call me. Or if there are any questions you'd like to ask.' He stared into her colourless face. 'Or even if you just need to talk about it.' He realised he was starting to sound like a trauma counsellor, but couldn't help himself. He had to say something reassuring.

'Thanks.' She smiled at him for the first time and slipped the card into a pocket.

Outside Mills spotted a car pulling into the kerb. A neat man in a smart suit got out.

'Thank goodness,' the pharmacist said and got up, carefully putting her mug on the chair behind her. 'It's Mr Aktah.'

'Right then – we can talk to him and you can get off. Remember – take it easy.'

The pharmacist handed him the blanket and nodded to Murray who was on her way back in.

'Boss wants us back at the station, ASAP,' Murray said. 'Sounded pissed off. Says he's sending Baker and Johnson to finish up here. We're off the case.'

'What?'

Murray shrugged at him.

'Did he say why?'

'He hung up on me before I could ask.'

Mills followed Murray to the door, and stopped to explain to the owner that two other detectives would be with him shortly.

'Another fan, I see,' Murray said when they were safely in the car and on their way back to the station.

'What?'

'That Kiwi – she took a shine to you. Disappointed she had to say goodbye, by the looks of things.'

'Rubbish.' Mills gripped the steering wheel tighter.

'Must be your big brown puppy dog eyes.' Murray slapped the back of her hand against his thigh and made him jump. 'I suppose I should be relieved you haven't managed to turn me.'

'Piss off.'

Mills snaffled the last parking space opposite the Camberwell Green police station, the car park at the rear uncharacteristically full. As he yanked on the handbrake he watched four vans full of uniformed officers he didn't recognise speed away from the front of the station.

'Christ – what's happening here?' Murray said as she climbed out of the car. 'A tenner it's a riot.'

The vans disappeared onto the main road. In quick succession five unmarked police cars emerged from the side street leading to the car park. In the eight months he'd been at the Camberwell station Mills had witnessed nothing like it. Even during the 2011 riots he'd not seen this much manpower.

He joined Murray who was already jogging across the road. 'I didn't see any riot shields in the vans,' he said when he caught up with her. 'Something else must be going on.' He stopped Murray at the steps leading up to the station entrance. 'Taylor said nothing to you about what this is about?'

'He just told me to get a move on.' She ran up the steps and held open the door. 'So I suggest we do that.' She impatiently gestured at him to hurry. 'My money's still on a riot.'

'It's February – riots only happen in the summer.'

When they got to Taylor's office the door was open and Detective Constable Manisha Kapoor was sitting in front of the DCI's desk looking decidedly uncomfortable. She gave them a weak smile.

'Where's the boss?' Murray said. 'I thought it was meant to be urgent. What's going on, Nisha?'

Before Kapoor had a chance to answer, Taylor arrived, red-faced and out of breath.

'Bloody hell,' he said. 'What a bloody shambles.'

'Sir?' Kapoor got to her feet.

'Sit down,' Taylor ordered. 'All of you.' He shuffled behind his desk and sank onto the chair, blowing out his cheeks, his fat lips vibrating.

'Boss?' It was the first time Mills had seen the DCI flustered.

'What's the emergency?' Murray chimed in.

'Kiddie's gone missing from the Shakespeare Estate.'

'What?' Murray leaned back in her seat, her shoulders slumped. 'Is that it? All this extra manpower for one kid?' She turned to Mills. 'You should've taken that bet after all.'

Mills frowned at her, silently pleading with his eyes for her to shut up. She couldn't have noticed the thunderous look Taylor was giving her. She carried on, oblivious.

'I mean, kids go missing from the Shakespeare day in day out. If we sent out a search party every time it happened, we'd never do anything else.' She turned back to the DCI and finally noticed the grave expression on his face. She ploughed on regardless. 'But they always turn up before teatime, not a scratch on them. I mean, boss… we are talking about the Shakespeare. I expect a majority of the mums living there haven't got a clue where their kids are from one minute to the next. Or what they're getting up to.'

Mills willed her to stop talking.

'Thank you for your in-depth analysis of the situation, constable. Now, if you've quite finished, perhaps I can furnish you with the actual details?'

'Just offering an opinion, boss.'

Taylor puffed out another breath. 'A *nine*-year-old girl has been missing since *yesterday afternoon*.'

Murray uncrossed her legs and sat up very straight. 'Oh.'

'Nine years old and missing for over eighteen hours. Overnight temperatures well below freezing.' Taylor stared directly at Murray. 'Any further insightful opinion to add?'

'Sorry, boss.' True to form, Murray recovered quickly. 'What do you want us to start on first? House to house? Or are the uniforms doing that? Is the misper unit coordinating?'

'No – HSCC. We've got half of MIT seven running the show.'

'They think she's dead? Already?' Murray said.

'Missing child – pretty much automatic,' Kapoor said, beating Taylor to it.

'Right,' Murray said. 'So you want us to liaise with the Murder Investigation Team?'

'No!' Taylor slammed a hand onto his desk. 'If you can button it for a second I'll tell you.'

Mills closed his eyes. For the last few minutes he had been trying to work out why the three of them seemed to have been singled out by the DCI for special attention. Now it dawned on him. He opened his eyes to see Kapoor's expression change from earnest attention to pure dread. She had worked it out too. They glanced at one another. Mills swallowed.

'You don't need me to tell you Missing Persons are stretched at the best of times. Especially now with Jenny on maternity leave, Brian's trying to cope on his own... so... well...'

Mills decided to put the DCI out of his misery. 'You need a Family Liaison Officer.'

A relieved expression spread over Taylor's face. 'Precisely.'

'And the three of us have had the most recent training,' Kapoor added.

'That's about the gist of it, yes. The MIT will be providing an FLO themselves, but only in a supporting capacity. They want someone with local knowledge to take on the bulk of the duties.'

'Christ. FLO – on the Shakespeare.' Murray looked first at Mills, then Kapoor, with a panicked look in her eyes.

'In theory I don't mind which of you volunteers,' Taylor said, obviously grateful to have passed on the unwelcome news. 'I'll leave you to decide amongst yourselves.'

'I'll do it,' Mills said quickly. Anything to wipe the stricken expressions off his colleagues' faces.

'Just to give you a little background on the family,' Taylor began, attempting a smile and failing. 'The mother's got another two girls and a boy living at home,' he said. 'The girls are fourteen and four years old, the boy's twelve.'

'No dad?' Mills asked.

'What do you think?' Murray interjected.

'Now, I'm going to visit the little boys' room,' Taylor said. 'By the time I get back, I want you to have made a final decision.' He left the room, shaking his head. He had the look of someone who'd just condemned a man to the gallows.

'I've already said I'll do it.' Mills opened his arms wide. 'End of discussion.'

'Yeah, then the boss told us about the mother and her *two* daughters. The *single* mother,' Murray said. 'It was obvious what he was getting at. Only he can't officially just ask Nisha and me.' She looked at Mills. 'You're here to make up the numbers, check some equal ops box. Jammy sod.' She shook her head. 'I was chatting to a community support officer about the Shakespeare the other day. It's pretty much a no-go zone for them. If they have to venture onto it they do it in teams of three or four. That's bad enough, but to actually be on your own inside one of the flats, practically *living* with a family…'

'I don't have a maternal bone in my body,' Kapoor said, staring into space, her eyes wide.

'And you think I do?' Murray said. 'Maybe the two of us should flip a coin.' She reached into a pocket. 'What do you reckon, Nisha? Who's got the best chance of surviving for more than twenty-four hours on the Shakespeare? A dyke?'

Kapoor looked up at her and said, 'Or a Paki?'

FIVE

After an excruciatingly prolonged conversation with Derek, the paper's hard of hearing seventy-year-old post 'boy', Angela Tate was no nearer discovering who had delivered the unmarked envelope to her desk than she had been before venturing into the murky depths of the subterranean post room.

But at least she was fully apprised of Derek's troubling in-growing toenail. And his gout.

He assured her he had never laid eyes on the manila packet. 'It's not been through the internal mail system – that much I can tell you. Have you checked on reception? Maybe it was delivered by hand.'

Tate had already discussed the possibility with Clive on the front desk. Nothing got past reception without him knowing about it. He hadn't seen the envelope before either.

Wearily, she trudged back to the second floor clutching the newspaper cuttings, throwing an occasional glance over her shoulder, wary of the new intern's stealth-like approaches. The girl had a habit of appearing from nowhere, at the least convenient moments. Right now Tate wasn't in the mood to parry the seemingly endless stream of banal questions the intern insisted on asking. She just wanted to burrow herself away, somewhere she wouldn't be disturbed.

When she returned to her desk, Tate discovered a handwritten note from Frank informing her she'd had another nuisance call while she was away. This time the caller had managed a faint grunt before hanging up. Tate glared at the phone, willing it to ring again. She'd prepared a long list of alliterative insults to shout at him the next time he called. Needless to say the phone remained stubbornly silent.

Keen to escape the main office, she decided to decamp to one of the conference rooms on the top floor. She chose the room furthest from the lift, hoping there would be less chance of being disturbed. She closed the door quietly behind her and exhaled slowly. She flicked on the large TV attached to the wall, muted the sound then flipped through the channels until she found *Sky News*.

Emptying the contents of the now dog-eared manila envelope onto the long conference table, she pulled a silver flask from her pocket, setting it to one side and promising herself a snifter only when she'd waded through a good proportion of the clippings. Her resolve lasted all of five seconds. She took a healthy slug, got up and deposited the flask at the other end of table. Then she kicked off her shoes and spread out the clippings, smoothing them flat as best she could. At first glance she recognised a handful of her own stories, filed in the days when she still used shorthand and typed all her copy on a Smith-Corona electric typewriter. She skimmed through a couple of articles and was mortified to discover just how clumsy her writing style had been. Where were the sub-editors? Why hadn't they tidied her awkward prose so that it at least made grammatical sense? At the time she'd thought everything she wrote was pure journalistic gold.

How arrogant must she have been?

Looking at it now she saw her copy plainly for what it was: bloated and self-indulgent. Which immediately made her think again of Ashley Montgomery, the intern. Perhaps she should attempt to be a little more generous when the girl asked for constructive criticism.

'Sod that.'

She eyed the distant silver flask and sighed, shoving the clippings she had just read back into the envelope. The stories all featured crimes of one sort or another, most of them committed in south London, the majority had some sexual element. Some clippings included the names of the publications printed at the top. Quite a few were from the freesheets delivered to households across south east London.

Now what? The call of the flask of brandy was too strong to ignore any longer. She hurried to fetch it. As she passed the TV, something on the screen caught her eye: an advert for a romantic weekend retreat in the Cotswolds, a special offer for Valentine's day.

Which reminded her of Frank's hapless attempt at asking her out. What did he think he was doing? Silly old sod. Why suggest something like that after all these years? Did she have the look of desperate woman? She peered at her reflection in the glass table top and ran a hand through her messy hair. She turned her head left then right, swallowing hard to reduce the beginnings of a double chin.

Desperate, moi?

'Don't answer that,' she told the slightly dishevelled woman looking back at her and wondered if it was time to give Botox injections another try. She sank a long mouthful of brandy, one eye still on the television as the ads finished and the early evening news programme started. The image quickly switched from the severe face of the newsreader to an outside broadcast. A line of police officers and a rag tag bunch of volunteers were moving slowly across a park. Then the scene changed to show another straggly line of people crossing an area of waste ground.

She snatched the remote from the table and turned up the sound.

A nine-year-old girl had gone missing from an estate in Camberwell, according to the voiceover. The police were appealing for witnesses to come forward. Then a close-up of a tear-streaked face filled the screen. Tate stared at the woman's features contorted with grief. It was a face that seemed somehow vaguely familiar. A name appeared at the bottom of the screen.

Trisha Collins?

As Collins continued her plea to camera for the safe return of her little girl, stopping every few words to fight back tears, Tate found it harder and harder to believe what she was watching.

What were the chances of it happening again?

The camera pulled back to reveal the façade of a dilapidated building Tate remembered all too well. The terrible events of 1979 played out in her mind. From the first report in the local paper, right up to her grisly discovery of the missing girl ten days later. A gruesome sight she'd wished for years afterwards she could have erased from her mind. But there it was, vivid in all its details. Still as clear today as it was then.

She squeezed her eyes tight shut and tried to will the awful vision away.

SIX

The incident room at Camberwell Green police station had been arranged so that the desks faced each other in pairs, with two long parallel rows stretching the length of the room. The Casey Collins investigation team crowded around the front eight desks.

Perched on the edge of a table behind DCI Barrow while he addressed the combined forces of MIT seven and most of the Camberwell Green CID detectives, Natasha McKittrick scrutinised the sea of faces before her, trying to pick out her colleagues from Lewisham homicide command. She had been based in the Lewisham station for less than two weeks and so far one face pretty much blurred into the next. The vast majority of detectives working in serious crime seemed to be white, male and aged between twenty-eight and forty-five. They always had names like Mick, Tony, Pete, Tom and Andy. Most of them favouring Marks and Spencer suits, or for the more casual look, leather jackets and chinos.

As she stared out into the crowd of generic Petes and Tonys she managed to identify a Colin, a Simon and a Mark. The Mark in question was DS Mark Black. He was charged with running the incident room. He saw her looking at him and nodded back. She forced a smile and looked away.

The DCI was currently in full flow, recapping the case for late arrivals to the team, explaining how murder investigation team detectives would be liaising with their colleagues in CID.

'I want this arrangement to be as seamless as possible,' he was saying. McKittrick tuned him out, staring at the side of his face as he stood in front of her. She still hadn't got the measure of him. Surprised at his attitude towards Trisha Collins, McKittrick had done some digging and discovered a possible cause for his prejudice.

In the past seven years Barrow had worked on two high profile missing person cases involving the disappearance of young girls. The first, in 2005, had happened in the London Borough of Sutton. The girl had gone missing from her grandmother's house and was later discovered in a wheelie bin just half a dozen streets away. Her grandmother's ex-boyfriend eventually confessed to the crime after the search team discovered the body during their third trawl of the area.

Then in 2008, the DCI had been seconded to assist an investigating team in Huddersfield. This time a ten-year-old girl had turned up safe and well after ten days, following a report from a concerned neighbour of strange noises from a nearby property. The property belonged to a friend of the girl's family. He was later convicted, together with the girl's mother, of kidnap and false imprisonment. The two had plotted the whole abduction together to claim the £50,000 reward put up by a national newspaper. The investigating team had been completely taken in by the mother's tears and emotional appeals to the media for the safe return of her daughter. Barrow had been one of the lead detectives, recruited because of his experience with the earlier case in Sutton. No wonder he had been so suspicious of Collins. He obviously didn't want to risk being duped again.

But it was no way to run an investigation. McKittrick decided she would handle as many of the interviews with the Collins family as she could herself. Let Barrow strategise from his office. It was the safest place for him.

At that moment Barrow raised his voice, prompting McKittrick to tune back in. No doubt exactly as he had intended. The DCI had moved on to discussing the overnight weather forecast.

'…four, maybe minus five degrees in exposed areas,' he said. 'If Casey Collins is outside overnight, we have to face the fact she is unlikely to survive until morning.' He paused then and let the information sink in. 'Her mother has told us that Casey suffers from asthma, so we know she has breathing difficulties. What we don't know is whether she has her inhaler with her. Her mother is sure she took it to school in her bag, but we can't assume she still has the bag with her.'

Barrow then outlined the allocation of duties for the next twenty-four hours.

'Neighbourhood searches will continue throughout the night, the night shift officers will liaise with their day shift counterparts before they go off duty tomorrow morning. All family members and close friends of the family should be formally interviewed as a priority.'

McKittrick shifted uncomfortably on the edge of the table. It sounded as if the DCI had already made up his mind someone close to Casey was responsible for her disappearance.

'I want the house-to-house interviews and property searches to continue tomorrow morning,' Barrow continued. 'We'll widen the search radius by another two miles.'

A detective sitting on one of the desks at the front of the room shoved his hand in the air. 'Has anyone been to Casey's school?'

'Not yet – it's on the list for tomorrow. Why?'

'I'd like to take it on if that's OK. I used to go there myself.'

'Fine – talk to DS Black about it. He'll amend the roster.'

Another hand was raised towards the back of the room.

'Yes?' Barrow was starting to sound irritated.

'The incident room number was only given to the press two hours ago. We've already had a few hoax sightings. Is there a strategy for dealing with time-wasters?'

'This level of publicity is bound to bring the nutters out of the woodwork. We'll look at each one on a case-by-case basis. If we have to make some arrests to set an example, we will.'

A general murmur of agreement rumbled through the room. McKittrick was sure she heard someone at the back helpfully suggest 'stringing them up by their bollocks'.

Barrow held up his hands. 'That said, we must treat every call as authentic until we're given sufficient reason to do otherwise. Leads can come from the most unexpected of places.'

McKittrick wondered if that was a veiled reference to the Huddersfield case.

'And what about the Shakespeare Estate itself?' A female detective at the front of the room asked without raising her hand.

'What about it?' Barrow suddenly looked very tired.

'How's all this police activity being taken? We're not exactly welcomed with open arms on the Shakespeare. Or any of the estates round there. What if the residents choose not to cooperate?'

'So far we've not encountered any problems. The residents' committee has organised shifts of volunteers to help with the search. We'll just treat everyone with respect, and hope, given the circumstances, they'll do the same for us.'

Respect? McKittrick wished Barrow had extended the courtesy to Casey's distraught mother.

'Right,' the DCI said, clasping his hands together. 'You don't need me bending your ears any longer than necessary. Just a couple of housekeeping matters and then we'll wrap up.'

McKittrick tuned out again as her boss went through the procedures for his new incident room. Her gaze wandered to the school photograph of Casey Collins the girl's mother had given them. A rosy-cheeked, blue-eyed little girl with a shy smile stared back at her. She had already been missing for nearly thirty hours. They were fighting against the clock. Once they passed the magic forty-eight hour mark the chance of finding her alive pretty much dropped to zero. McKittrick closed her eyes and sent up a silent prayer for the nine-year-old.

'Natasha?'

McKittrick snapped her eyes open and discovered the DCI was peering into her face expectantly. 'Sir?'

'Anything you'd care to add?'

She smiled sheepishly. 'I think you've pretty much covered all the bases.'

'Except for one thing, obviously.'

McKittrick was at a loss.

Barrow turned back to face the room. 'This is Detective Inspector Natasha McKittrick – my number two for this investigation.'

She nodded a brief hello to the room.

'Inspector McKittrick is new to Homicide Command. New to the Met in fact. So I want everyone to help her settle in wherever you can.' He managed a smile.

Suddenly McKittrick felt like the new kid in class, singled out by the well meaning, but misguided teacher, wishing desperately Barrow would just shut up.

'Can I have a volunteer to act as a general guide? Someone who knows the area well?' The DCI scanned the room.

The detective sitting at the front who had volunteered to go to Casey's school shoved his hand in the air again.

'DC Ralph Mills, ma'am.' He beamed at her. 'At your service.'

That prompted a sharp dig in the ribs from the female detective sitting next to him.

McKittrick forced a smile, wanting to scowl, wishing Barrow had let her know in advance what he had intended to do. She would have told him, respectfully, where he could shove the idea of a body man. She didn't need her hand holding.

Barrow asked if there were any final questions and sure enough, McKittrick's new minder stuck his hand in the air once again.

'Has anyone looked into the 1979 murders?' he asked.

Barrow said nothing. He stared at the detective blank-faced.

'Only the bloke responsible was released from prison two years ago.' He looked from the DCI to McKittrick. 'Just seems like too big a coincidence to ignore.'

'Go on,' Barrow ordered.

Mills levered himself off the desk and cleared his throat. 'Two girls disappeared from the two estates either side of the Shakespeare. One of the girls was nine years old, little blonde girl. Just like Casey Collins.'

SEVEN

Ashley Montgomery was tapping away on her iPad next to Angela Tate in the cab. Tate tried to ignore the irritating clicking sound. It was preferable to the intern's mindless chatter.

Tate had only agreed to let Ashley accompany her to the Shakespeare Estate because she needed someone to sit in the cab while she was talking to Trisha Collins. Tate didn't want to be left hanging around on the Shakespeare waiting for a minicab to arrive.

While Ashley was transfixed by something on her iPad, Tate took the opportunity to study the girl's face, which was bathed in the bluish glow of the ten-inch screen. Even in the unflattering light, her wrinkle-free mocha skin seemed flawless. Her features were classically proportioned, her eyes clear and bright. She even had an adorable dusting of cinnamon freckles across her nose. The girl couldn't have been more than twenty-one or two, yet had the confidence of a seasoned media professional. And the combined energy of a playgroup of hyperactive four-year-olds. Tate found herself hating both the girl's youth and her indefatigable enthusiasm.

Ashley looked up suddenly and caught Tate staring at her.

'Anything interesting?' Tate said, holding her gaze.

'Is Trisha short for Patricia?' the girl asked. 'What should I call her when we get there? Ms Collins? Or is that too formal?'

'Let's cross that bridge when we come to it, shall we?' Tate had no intention of letting Ashley get anywhere near the Collins family. 'What are you doing with that thing, anyway?'

'Setting up some "Find Casey" pages on the paper's social media platforms. I'll show you when I'm done.'

'Oh good.' Tate settled back in the seat and watched as the gentrified north Southwark streets just south of the Thames turned into the grimier thoroughfares of Newington and Elephant and Castle.

Fifteen minutes later they arrived at the Shakespeare and Tate jumped out of the cab shouting instructions over her shoulder to Ashley, ordering her to stay exactly where she was.

The estate looked just the way Tate remembered it. A central open square was flanked on three sides by identical five-storey blocks of flats, the architecture post-war, a mess of rendered concrete and frosted glass. Exterior walkways stretched out from central stairwells on either side, the individual front doors dotted along each walkway were painted the same colour, except for a bright white PVC one here and there: the result of Maggie Thatcher's *Right to Buy* scheme in the eighties. On the fourth side of the square was a small parade of shops. In 1979 there had been a newsagent's, launderette and betting shop. Now only the betting shop remained, the other two premises boarded up, the sheets of ply covering the doors and windows decorated with badly executed graffiti.

Tate quickly identified Montague House, the block directly opposite the shops, by the gathering of TV news crews and usual suspects from the tabloids and broadsheets. She headed for the entrance immediately beyond the heaving crowd, pushing her way through, getting jostled as she went. A uniformed policeman was standing sentry at the bottom of the stairs. Tate showed him her ID and he made a show of inspecting it carefully.

'When am I going to get my press credentials?' Ashley's voice was loud in her ear.

Tate spun round. 'I told you to stay in the cab.'

'And miss all the fun?'

Tate peered across the square and watched as the taxi sped away. 'Well you'll just have to stay out here with the rest of the rabble.'

'Oh plee-ease let me come with you. I promise I'll behave myself. I won't say a word. Unless you want me to.' She made a puppy-dog face.

Tate wanted to slap it. She might have, if a policeman hadn't been standing three feet away. 'I don't want a peep out of you. Is that clear?'

'Perfectly.'

The policeman finally handed back Tate's ID and the two women trudged up the stairs to the fourth floor, the final couple of flights taking their toll on Tate's tar-lined lungs. Another police officer greeted them at the top of the stairwell and once again Tate produced her ID. Finally they were admitted to the walkway leading to Trisha Collins' flat.

A woman was leaning over the balcony wall smoking a cigarette. She looked up at them as they approached and gestured towards the half-open front door.

She exhaled a long smoky breath and said, 'Trisha's in the front room, end of the passage.'

Tate nodded her thanks and smiled.

'You didn't waste any time getting here.'

'I'm sorry – do I know you?'

'Bloody typical.' The woman turned away. 'You're all the same. I expect you only remember Trish because it suits you.'

Tate dragged Ashley away before she could say anything and led her through the front door and down the hall, remembering the layout of the flats from the last time she'd stepped inside one. Her last visit had been to the Essex, an identical three-block estate just to the east of this one. The Marlowe, the third estate of the 1950s development, had been pulled down in the late nineties. Tate was surprised the other two had managed to avoid the bulldozers. They should have been condemned years ago.

As soon as Tate entered the cramped living room Trisha Collins jumped up to greet her. She flung her arms around Tate's neck and squeezed tight, not releasing her grip until Tate forcibly peeled away her arms and took a step back.

'You haven't changed a bit,' Trisha said.

'We both know that's not true.' Tate smiled at Trisha, taking a moment to study her face. She looked worse than she had on the *Sky News* report. Her skin greyer in the flesh, her eyes bloodshot and red-rimmed.

Ashley wedged herself between the two women and extended her hand towards Trisha. 'Hi, Trisha. My name's Ashley – I work with Angela at the *Evening News*.'

Slightly taken aback, Trisha took the offered hand in hers and looked enquiringly at Tate.

'Work experience,' Tate said and rolled her eyes.

'Don't stand on ceremony.' Trisha lowered herself onto the sofa and patted the adjacent seat cushion for Tate to join her. She scooped up a cuddly toy, a battered and grubby teddy bear, and hugged it to her chest.

The woman Tate had spoken to outside hovered in the doorway.

'Angela – you remember Lorraine? My best mate,' Trisha said.

Tate frowned at her. The woman frowned back. 'Lorraine… Benson?' Tate said after a long pause. 'Gary's sister?'

The woman nodded.

Tate saw the resemblance suddenly. She'd been thinking about Gary Benson in the cab. Over the years she had managed to forget about Benson and his part in what had happened in 1979. Since she'd seen Trisha on the news she could think of little else. 'Your brother not here, then?' she said, relieved not to have spotted him.

Lorraine ignored her.

'Do you want a drink, Ange?' Trisha tugged at Tate's arm and pulled her down onto the sofa. 'Lorraine, go and make us a cuppa will you?' She turned back to Tate. 'Unless you want something stronger? We might still have half a bottle of rum left over from Christmas somewhere.'

'Tea's fine – white no sugar.' As she watched Lorraine stomp out of the room, Tate wondered if she should have accepted the offer of alcohol. She could be in for a long and uncomfortable evening. A drink would have taken the edge off.

Too late now.

She glanced around the room and smiled at a dough-faced teenager slouching in an armchair. The girl was breathing through her mouth, a soggy tissue pressed against her nose.

'Hello,' Tate said. The girl said nothing.

'That's Chelsea,' Trisha told her. 'My oldest girl.'

'Trisha, can you— Oh, hello.'

Tate looked up to see a petite Asian woman dressed in a smart grey suit standing in the living room doorway. Trisha quickly introduced the woman as Manisha Kapoor – the family liaison officer the police had appointed to 'look after them.'

'I can't find anything to read to Lola,' the woman said. 'Where do you keep the picture books?'

Trisha smiled quizzically at the woman as if she'd just asked an unfathomable question. 'There's no books in the flat. I don't read to her.'

'Oh – I'm sorry, I just presumed…' The policewoman looked flustered and embarrassed.

'We tried her with books from the library. She just tore the pages out. Chelsea had to stick them back together again. Lola likes it better when I make the stories up as I go along,' Trisha explained, clearly trying to save the FLO any further discomfort. 'Not like Casey. She's always got her nose in a book. She's—' Trisha let out a sudden sob, unable to finish her sentence.

Tate put a hand on her arm and squeezed. She'd been wondering just how long Trisha was going to be able to keep up her cheerful front. Trisha lifted a hand to her mouth. She took a deep breath and swallowed, her body shaking as she tried to stifle another sob. 'I'm sorry.'

'It's all right, you let it out.' With the flat of her hand, Tate traced wide circles on Trisha's back. She offered a sympathetic smile and watched as Trisha gulped down further sobs and wiped away her tears with the back of a hand.

'I've got to hold it together,' Trisha managed after a few moments. She took a deep breath and exhaled slowly.

Lorraine arrived in the doorway just as the policewoman had turned to go back upstairs. 'Was I supposed to make her one too?' Trisha's friend looked down at the three mugs she was balancing in one hand. 'Only I think it's supposed to work the other way round. Isn't she supposed to be looking after us?'

'Manisha's been great.' Trisha gulped down another breath. 'She only came this afternoon and Lola's really taken to her. I couldn't let her out of my sight before Manisha arrived.' She dabbed her running nose with the cuff of her sweatshirt.

Lorraine dumped the mugs on the coffee table and perched on the arm of the sofa next to Trisha. Ashley crouched next to Chelsea's chair and pulled her iPad from her bag. She nudged the teenager's arm, handing the tablet to the girl.

'I'm setting up a Facebook page for Casey,' the intern said. 'Would you like to help me?'

Chelsea sat up and for the first time showed some interest in what was going on around her. She started swiping the iPad screen with a nail-bitten finger.

'Have you had a chance to think about what we discussed on the phone, Trisha?' Tate said, reaching for her tea.

Lorraine slipped a protective arm around her friend's shoulders. 'You don't have to do anything you don't want to, Trish. Don't let her bully you into something you're not happy about. She's no better than the rest of them. Like a lot of bloody vultures.' She glared at Tate. 'No offence.'

'I've heard worse.'

'Whatever you think will help get Casey back, I'll do it.' Trisha's voice cracked. She wriggled free of Lorraine's grip and squeezed the stuffed bear in her arms. 'Whatever it takes.'

'I'd like to run a series of features. Keep Casey right at the front of people's minds.'

Trisha nodded, the tears streaming down her face. 'Someone must have seen her.'

'We need to jog people's memories, nudge their consciences.'

'You don't think someone's taken her, do you?' Trisha sniffed.

Tate put a comforting hand on Trisha's knee, but couldn't muster an appropriate platitude. Nothing she could say would reassure her.

'She'd never go off on her own like this. She wouldn't want to worry me. She's such a good kid.'

'I'll make sure we feature Casey on the front page from now until we find her,' Tate lied. Her editor had agreed to nothing of the sort. If she couldn't come up with a sellable angle, she'd be lucky to get a three-inch column on page seven after the initial fevered interest had died down. 'I will need your help though, Trisha.'

'I'll do anything. I told you.'

'It'll mean photographs, of you, and the kids, pretty much unrestricted access.'

Trisha nodded.

'Exclusive access,' Tate added and glanced at Lorraine, bracing herself for a torrent of abuse.

Thankfully it didn't come.

Instead, Lorraine jumped to her feet. 'I need a fag,' she declared, grabbed a packet of cigarettes and lighter from the coffee table and marched out of the room.

Tate glanced at Ashley as Chelsea was nodding at something the intern had shown her on the iPad. Ashley seemed completely at ease in the unfamiliar surroundings. She had already adapted her accent to match Chelsea's, out were the Received Pronunciation consonants, in the sliding vowels and slang street phrases she could only have picked up from BBC3 documentaries. At that moment Chelsea looked up, met Tate's gaze and tugged on the intern's arm. She struggled to her feet and lumbered out of the room, dragging a compliant Ashley behind her.

'Don't touch any of Casey's things up there,' Trisha called after them. 'Do you hear me?' She turned back to Tate. 'Have you got any cigarettes? Lorraine's taken mine.'

Tate reached into her bag and retrieved an unopened pack.

'Not in here,' Trisha said and pointed to a double-glazed PVC door on the other side of the room that led out onto a small balcony. 'Manisha gets really funny about me smoking indoors.'

Outside, Trisha lit up and Tate told her to keep the packet. She drew deeply on the cigarette and exhaled a long lungful of smoke. A little of the tension seemed to leave her face. 'What's happened to her, Ange?'

'The police will find her. It's early days.'

'The police? They haven't got a clue. Do you know how many times they've asked me the exact same questions, over and over again?'

'It's what they do – in case you think of something new that might help.'

'Feels like they trying to catch me out. Like they don't trust what I'm telling them. They took the computer away this afternoon. I don't know what they think they're going to find. Casey doesn't even use it. Can they do that? Just take stuff away?'

'If they think it'll help, why shouldn't they?'

'I've spoken to Gary about it. He thinks I should have stopped them.'

'I can't believe you're still paying any attention to what Gary has to say.' Tate shivered suddenly as a blast of cold air whipped across the balcony. A vision of Gary Benson's hateful little face flashed into her mind. She hadn't laid eyes on him for over thirty years, but the image was crystal sharp.

'He's only looking out for me – just like he always has.'

Tate was about to suggest Gary Benson only ever had his own interests at heart, but managed to stop herself. Now wasn't the time.

'Gary said the *Evening News* should offer a reward. Papers do that, don't they? When something like this happens. That'd make people come forward, wouldn't it?'

Tate stared into Trisha's puffy bloodshot eyes and tried to read what was going on behind them. Why would she mention money at a time like this? 'It's not something we do,' she said. 'We're not that kind of paper.'

'But will you talk to somebody about it? Maybe they'll make an exception.' Trisha grabbed Tate's hand and squeezed it. 'Do that for me?'

Tate pulled her hand back and folded her arms. 'It's not as simple as that.' She eyed the packet of cigarettes in

Trisha's hand, wishing she'd taken one when she'd had the chance.

'Please, Ange.'

'I'll have a word with my editor.' Another lie.

Trisha nodded her thanks and took a long lug on her cigarette. She stared across the narrow access road to the line of garages behind the block of flats and towards the Essex Estate beyond, and gathered her cardigan closer to her. 'Christ it's cold.' She sniffed, then drew deeply on the cigarette. She stooped to grind the butt into the roots of a dead pot plant by her feet. 'Where is she?' She stared into Tate's eyes. 'Why is this happening to me?'

Tate saw the desperation in Trisha's expression and wondered how she was going to get through another night.

Trisha suddenly stuck out her hand and grabbed Tate's arm. She pulled her close, her grip stronger than Tate would have guessed. 'I can't help thinking I'm being punished because of what happened before,' Trisha said, her voice low and trembling.

'What do you mean?' Tate knew only too well what Trisha was referring to, but decided playing dumb might be more productive.

'Tell me I'm being stupid.'

'I'm sorry, Trish, I don't know what you're—'

'It's all right, forget it. I am being stupid.' She let go of Tate's arm. 'I just needed to say it out loud.'

EIGHT

Wednesday 8th February

Detective Constable Ralph Mills met DC Murray outside Burgess Park Primary School. It was barely eight a.m. and some mums, older siblings and the occasional dad were dropping off their children at the gates early.

'You look rough,' Murray said.

'Cheers.'

'Was it a late one?'

Mills watched the children as they skipped into the playground, all of them dressed in knock-off copies of designer kidswear their parents must have picked up cheap from East Street market.

'Bit different from when we went to school eh?' Mills pointed to a gaggle of perfectly turned-out little girls, in an attempt to change the subject. 'We were forced to wear regulation black trousers and grey pullovers when I came here.'

'I'll never forget the hideous powder blue polyester dress they made me wear. Used to itch under the arms.' Murray shuddered. 'I hated it.'

'You should be grateful it wasn't baby pink.'

'Now that I would have refused to wear.' Murray ducked out of the way of a running child, the hood of his anorak pulled low over his eyes. 'Where did you get to last night, anyway?' she asked. 'Didn't see anything of you after the new girl got her hooks in. When did the fragrant DI McKittrick finally release you?'

Mills felt his ears reddening. He hoped Murray hadn't noticed. So much for his attempt to deflect her initial question. 'I took the inspector on a quick tour of the neighbourhood.'

'Showing her the sights, eh? Must have taken all of ten minutes.'

'She wanted the rundown on the estates. My local knowledge. And she asked me about what happened in '79.'

'And?'

'And what?'

'I want to bloody well know too. You can't drop a bombshell at the end of a briefing like that and leave me dangling.'

'You could have just Googled it.'

'What – and miss out on your "local knowledge"?'

Mills picked up pace and hurried across the busy playground, kids screaming and shouting all around them.

'So?' Murray persisted.

'Paula Jeffries and Sandra Stockwell. Both went missing July 1979. Paula disappeared first – from the Marlowe Estate.'

'Don't know it.'

'It was demolished years ago.' He stopped as a little girl tugged on the bottom of his jacket. He looked down at her and she poked her tongue out and laughed. Mills gave her a hard stare and waited for her to run off before he continued. 'Sandra disappeared from the Essex Estate. Her body was found but not Paula's. The police at the time were convinced the same person was responsible for both murders, but there was only enough evidence to convict him of killing Sandra.'

'And he was released? I thought with child murderers they threw away the key.'

'He was sentenced to life with a minimum of twenty-five years. He'd served over thirty by the time they let him out.'

'Even so…' Murray watched a couple of chatting girls skip past them and shook her head. 'It's not right.'

'I know.'

'How comes you're such an expert anyway?'

'I've got a personal interest.'

Murray stopped in her tracks and grabbed his arm. 'Jesus Ralph – you didn't know one of the girls, did you?'

'How old do you think I am?'

Murray shrugged.

'The murders happened in the July, I was born the following September.'

'What kind of personal interest?'

Mills regretted having embarked on the subject. But he knew Cath Murray would keep at him like a terrier with a rat and not let go until she'd wrung out every last drop of information. He stopped and put a hand through his hair. No point in keeping it from her now. 'My dad,' he said and swallowed so noisily he could have sworn he heard the gulp echo around the playground. 'Detective Inspector Charlie Mills. He worked out of Camberwell Green at the time. Before he moved to New Scotland Yard. He was the lead officer on the investigation. Biggest case of his career.'

'Blimey. I never even knew he was one of us. You kept that close to your chest. Did he ever speak to you about it?'

'It was a rule of his. He never brought The Job home with him.'

'Yet you still followed in his footsteps?' Murray let go of his arm and they carried on towards the main building.

'Never wanted to be anything but a copper. I found out about his cases after he retired.'

'Chip off the old block?' She nudged him with an elbow.

'Hardly.'

'Why haven't you mentioned your old man to me before?'

Mills looked away. He couldn't tell her the real reason he didn't speak about his dad. If he did she'd never stop asking him questions. Charlie Mills' legacy wasn't something he felt able to discuss. 'It's never really come up.'

'So what's happening about this bloke? Has he been picked up? Who's questioning him? DI McKittrick?'

'He didn't move back here after he was released. He's living up north. Leeds. The local force are going to talk to him today. I'm due to have a chat with his probation officer this afternoon.'

'Leeds? So he's not a suspect then?'

'The DCI doesn't think so.' He shoved his hands into his pockets.

Murray stared closely at him. 'And you do?'

'No point in ruling him out this early on in the investigation.'

They'd reached the entrance of the red brick Victorian schoolhouse. A young apple-cheeked, frizzy-haired woman was waiting for them at the door. She introduced herself as Casey's form teacher and proceeded to lead them through a maze of dingy corridors, eventually arriving at a brightly decorated classroom. It was obvious from her puffy eyelids and the rawness of the skin around her nose that Miss Lancaster had taken Casey's disappearance particularly hard.

'She's such a bright little girl,' she said after they'd covered the preliminaries. 'Quiet, but really engaged and enthusiastic about every exercise and project she was involved in.' She smiled sadly at Mills. 'Sometimes the shy children can get a bit overlooked, you know – left out. But I always try to make sure Casey is included in everything.' She pulled at a corner of the tissue she was clutching. 'I shouldn't say it, I know – all the children have different qualities to bring – but Casey really is a bit of a star pupil. Well-behaved as well as gifted academically.'

'Really?' Murray hadn't bothered to disguise her surprise.

Miss Lancaster chose to ignore it. 'It's been two nights now. Poor little thing. What do you think has happened to her?'

'It's too early for us to form any kind of opinion, miss,' Mills said.

'But it can't be good, can it, being gone for so long?' She dabbed at her nose. 'I called her mum myself when Casey didn't show up for registration yesterday morning.'

'And how did Trisha seem to you?' Mills asked.

'Seem? She was distraught, of course.'

Murray scribbled some notes in her pad.

'Her mum always drops her off in the morning,' the teacher told them.

Murray wrote something else down.

'We'll need to speak to a few of Casey's classmates when they arrive,' Mills said.

'Is that strictly necessary? They'll be traumatised as it is, without having to talk to strangers. I can't have you scaring them.'

'We do have some experience, miss. We'll tread very carefully. You don't have to worry about that,' Mills assured her.

'Only I planned to get them to write down their feelings, draw a few pictures, just so they can explore their feelings in a safe environment.'

Murray shot Mills a look. He didn't respond.

'Do you know Trisha Collins well?' Mills asked.

'Not exactly, but she's always struck me as a very caring parent. Always takes an interest in Casey's progress. I get the impression she's really quite proud of her.' The teacher threw her tissue into the metal bin under her desk and retrieved another from her pocket. 'I don't like to judge, but some of the parents I meet are not much more than children themselves. They really struggle to cope. Not Trisha, though. She seems to have everything under control.'

'Did you teach any of Casey's brothers and sisters?'

'Ryan was in my class a couple of years ago. Not as bright as Casey, but a nice enough lad. Got himself into a little bit of trouble in year six.'

Mills raised his eyebrows.

'Oh nothing serious. Just a bit of truanting. We got Trisha in, the head had a word and we soon nipped it in the bud.'

'Are there any other teachers we should speak to? Any other classes Casey attends?'

'I pretty much teach my form the whole curriculum. Everything except music. The head takes the music lessons himself. Used to be in a band. Frustrated lead guitarist, I think. Casey's a member of the choir he runs. So you should definitely speak to Nigel.'

'Nigel…?'

'Cope.'

'Would he be in his office this early? Perhaps you could take us to him now?' Murray suggested.

'Normally he arrives around half seven. But he's not in today. Family emergency, apparently. Fareedah, the school secretary, can give you his contact details.'

Miss Lancaster deposited Mills and Murray at the headteacher's office, took a business card from Mills and hurried back to her classroom.

The school secretary quickly found the head's address and phone number on her computer and printed out the details. 'He's never had a day off sick in the eight years I've been here. Casey's disappearance must have really got to him. I know he thinks a lot of her.'

'I thought it was a family emergency,' Murray said as the secretary handed her the printout.

'Who told you that? No – he's really not well. I spoke to him myself. He sounded awful.'

Mills looked at Murray and retrieved his mobile from a pocket. Murray grabbed the phone on the secretary's desk and punched in the number from the printed sheet.

'No answer,' she said after a few moments. She tried the mobile number with the same result. 'Dead. Didn't even go to voicemail.'

Mills ran into the corridor and dialled McKittrick's number.

'We're at the school, boss,' he told her. 'We can't locate the headteacher. Some bloke named Cope.'

'You think it's significant?' McKittrick asked.

'We've spoken to two members of staff and they've given us conflicting information about the reason for his absence. He's quite close to Casey, by all accounts.'

'I want you and Cath to get down to his home address ASAP,' McKittrick said. 'Don't approach the house until back-up arrives.'

NINE

Despite claiming to have slept only three hours the previous night, Ashley Montgomery looked irritatingly fresh-faced and alert as she sat next to Angela Tate at the Camberwell North Community Centre. The largest room in the complex had been taken over by the police press conference for Casey Collins. The place was packed with reporters from every news outlet in the country, plus news crews from one or two international broadcasters. Frank Carter had pushed his way to the front and was busy chatting to the other photographers. Thankfully he hadn't brought up her rejection of his Valentine's Day plans.

Tate turned to her young companion. 'Are you ready to tell me what you were talking to Chelsea Collins about last night?' Ashley had been irritatingly coy about it the previous evening.

The intern handed her iPad to Tate. 'She seemed really interested in it.'

'What am I supposed to be looking at?' Tate peered at the screen.

Ashley leaned over and tapped it. Immediately a Twitter application opened. 'We got over thirty thousand new followers overnight. Isn't that amazing?' She tapped the screen again and the Twitter stream was replaced by a Facebook page. 'And nearly four hundred thousand likes.

Little Casey's disappearance has really struck a chord. I can show you the Pinterest boards too, if you give me a second.'

'It's OK – I'll take your word for it.' Tate looked closely at the girl's eager face. Was it possible she could have been this obnoxious at her age? Now that she had escaped the office and the tedious administrative duties that had been foisted on her, Ashley Montgomery had come into her own. Tate had started her own career as chief tea maker and fag fetcher. By rights, Ashley had another six months hard labour as general office dogsbody before she should get a sniff of any real journalism. She shouldn't really be here at all.

'Even my own blog has seen a spike in traffic. It's awesome.' Ashley tapped the screen and the browser refreshed. The banner across the top of the page displayed a bespectacled Ashley Montgomery with a pencil behind her ear pulling a serious face. 'But that's nothing compared to the *Evening News* Casey Collins page. Last time I counted there were a full ten pages of comments.'

'I'm pleased it's been so successful. Well done.' Tate managed to pinch her face into a smile, but wondered what all this effort and activity was actually achieving.

No one seemed any closer to finding Casey.

'It's just a shame the inevitable haters had to pitch in. But there's no avoiding them,' the intern said.

'Haters?'

'People saying really mean things about Trisha and the family. About…' Ashley lowered her voice. 'Chavs in general. I mean, what's it got to do with anyone how many partners Trisha's had? So what if her kids have different dads? Dads are totally overrated anyway.' She took back the tablet and her shoulders sagged a fraction.

Just as Tate was debating whether the girl had just invited her to ask about her low opinion of fathers in general, and possibly her own in particular, Ashley let out a long sigh and started tapping and swiping the iPad screen again. No doubt sharing minute-by-minute updates about the press conference. Even though nothing had actually happened yet.

Haters. Closely related to trolls, Tate supposed. It wasn't as if they were a new phenomenon. In the cab on the way to the community centre she had read a column in the *Telegraph* by a journalist who thought it perfectly acceptable to criticise Trisha Collins for her lifestyle choices. It simply hadn't occurred to him that choice was a luxury Trisha couldn't afford. She'd just made the best of whatever was on offer. Which, for the majority of her life, was bugger all.

Tate nudged Ashley's arm. 'Did Chelsea tell you anything interesting yesterday?'

'Interesting how?'

'What did she say about Casey?'

The girl opened her mouth and quickly closed it again. She frowned. 'I don't think she told me anything about her. She talked about herself most of the time. How her mum's really strict and won't let her stay out late. She really resents not being able to hang out with the cool kids.' Ashley sighed. 'Not that they'd want to hang out with her. She's a bit of a loser.'

'Do you think you should be making those sorts of judgments? In the circumstances?'

The intern shrugged and turned towards the sudden shouts of the photographers at the front of the room.

A slope-shouldered middle-aged man in a tired suit had appeared from a side door. He wearily made his way to the last seat at the end of a long row of tables. A woman cradling a laptop in her arms followed him out and took the seat next to his. Then the family liaison officer Tate had met the previous evening strode towards them with Trisha Collins bringing up the rear. The cameras at the front of the room started to flash and the shouting grew louder.

The woman with the laptop, which was now sitting open on the table in front of her, raised her hands for quiet then introduced the Senior Investigating Officer. DCI Graham Barrow thanked her and proceeded to go through the details surrounding Casey's disappearance that everyone already knew.

Tate stared at Trisha. Her face was blotchier than it had been the night before, her unwashed hair scraped severely off her face and tied in a ponytail. She looked as if she hadn't slept in a week. She was clutching Casey's teddy bear. When Tate had pressed her the previous evening to talk about what had happened in 1979, Trisha clammed up completely, refusing to answer any questions not directly related to Casey or her brothers and sisters. Tate watched as Trisha stared blank-eyed at the table in front of her, flinching now and then when a bright camera flash went off a few feet away.

Having revealed there were no new leads, to the general disappointment of those present, the senior investigating officer started wrapping up his statement. He reminded everyone that the police were gravely concerned for Casey's welfare, especially given her medical condition. Tate made a note to ask Trisha about the severity of Casey's asthma when she next spoke to her, just in case it was an angle worth pursuing.

DCI Barrow then slowly recited the number of the incident room and repeated his earlier appeal to the public to get in touch if they had any information regarding Casey's whereabouts. He paused then and looked at the woman sitting next to him. Immediately a dozen questions were shouted from the floor. He ignored them all. The woman pulled a mobile phone from her ear and nodded at him.

'And I would like to announce that a reward for any information that leads directly to the discovery of Casey has been generously donated by *The Herald* newspaper.' He picked up a note the woman next to him had pushed along the table. 'They are offering,' he peered down at the scrap of paper. 'Twenty-five thousand pounds.'

More excited questions from the floor. Even Ashley jumped to her feet and raised her hand. Tate grabbed her sleeve and pulled her back down. 'Wait until the end. We'll nab Barrow on the way out.' She kept her eyes trained on Trisha, who didn't react at all to the mention of the large reward.

The DCI held up his hands and begged for order. When a measure of calm had been restored he introduced DC Kapoor to the audience. In a quiet but steady voice she read a prepared statement on Trisha's behalf. When the detective described how much the Collins family were missing Casey, Trisha started to sob. Kapoor reached for Trisha's hand and, despite the explosion of camera flashes popping all round the room, managed to continue reading.

Until Trisha jumped to her feet.

'Please come home, Casey!' she said. 'I love you so much. Please, please, if you can hear this, wherever you are, just ask somebody for help.' She dragged a sleeve across her streaming eyes. 'And if anyone out there knows where she is, I beg you, please go to the police.' She took a deep breath, started to speak again but was interrupted by a loud voice coming from the back of the room. The audience turned as one to see who was responsible for the commotion.

A man wearing an ill-fitting black suit, an incongruous sweat shirt beneath the jacket, began pushing his way through the crowd, roughly barging past anyone in his path.

'You make me sick,' he shouted. 'Crying your eyes out like you give a shit!' He'd almost reached the line of tables when two uniformed officers grabbed him. He struggled against them. 'You two-faced bitch!' He wriggled and kicked and broke free of his captors. He ran towards Trisha.

Kapoor pushed Trisha behind her and squared up to him.

'She's not fit to look after a fucking dog.' He slammed both hands on the table, knocking one of the microphones to the floor. 'Maybe Casey's better off where she is.'

TEN

'Mrs Cope?' Murray said as the door of the suburban semi opened wide enough to reveal a middle-aged woman dressed in jogging pants and a sweatshirt.

The woman stared at the protective vest Murray was wearing beneath her jacket then frowned at Mills. She peered over Murray's shoulder to the two police cars parked in the street beyond her drive. 'Has something happened to Nigel?' she said in a whisper.

'Mr Cope not at home then?' Mills put a foot on the doorstep, just in case the woman decided to slam the door in his face.

'What's going on?' The woman's voice trembled. She leaned her weight against the doorframe.

Murray's walkie-talkie crackled suddenly, a static-filled message confirmed no one was attempting to leave the property at the rear.

'I don't understand,' the woman said. Her mouth dropped open.

'Can we come in, madam?' Mills showed her his warrant card. 'I'm Detective Constable Mills, this is my colleague, DC Murray. We need to have a word.' He opened his arms wide and leaned forward. 'We really would like to speak to you about your husband.'

'He's not here,' she said.

'Let's go inside, shall we? For a bit of privacy,' Murray said. 'No need to put on a show for the neighbours.'

The woman finally stepped back from the door and led Mills into the kitchen at the end of a wide hall. Murray followed them in, a couple of uniforms behind her.

'OK if the officers take a quick look around, Mrs Cope?' Mills said when he saw the woman glance over her shoulder at the two men trampling their dirty boots into her hall carpet.

'What for?'

'Your husband.'

'I already told you, he—'

'Just routine, madam. Something we have to say we've done. Is it OK?'

Mrs Cope nodded meekly.

'Is there anyone else in the property?' Murray asked.

'No – just me. Nigel's away. He's… What *is* going on?'

'Is that your husband's car parked in the drive – the red Volvo?'

'Yes. Why?'

'But he's not here?'

'I've already said.' Mrs Cope got as far as the kitchen table and turned, her expression more focused. 'What if I don't want you searching my home? Do you have a warrant?' She peered through the kitchen doorway. 'Why are they wearing rubber gloves? What are they really looking for?' She took a step forward and Murray held up her arms, barring the woman's path.

'If you could just stay in here and answer a few questions.'

'You can't do this.'

'Please sit down, Mrs Cope. It would be much easier if you agreed to the search. Get it over and done with now. Less inconvenience for you.'

'Why are you looking for Nigel?'

'Do we have your permission, madam?'

One of the PCs hovered in the doorway.

'Yes, all right. But I want you to know I'm not happy about it.'

Murray sent the uniforms upstairs.

'Where is Mr Cope, madam?' Mills said, removing his notebook from a pocket.

'He had to go away. His aunt's sick.'

'A family emergency?' He glanced quickly over at Murray who continued to stand sentry at the door. She raised her eyebrows.

'Yes – it was very sudden.'

'And where has he gone?'

'Northumberland.'

'Do you have the address?'

'Of course I do. But I'm not giving it to you until you tell me what's going on.'

'We need to talk to Mr Cope regarding an ongoing investigation.'

'Ongoing? What's he supposed to have done? Is this about the missing girl?'

'What makes you ask that?'

'He's been really cut up about it – she's in the school choir. Is that what this is all about?'

'We're interviewing everyone who knows Casey Collins. It's just routine.'

'Police surrounding my house, searching the place? Doesn't seem very routine to me.'

'We need to follow up every possible lead.'

'Is that what Nigel is? A lead?'

'Please, Mrs Cope – the sooner we locate your husband the quicker we'll eliminate him from our enquiries.' An impatient edge was creeping into Murray's voice. 'It'll be much better all round if you cooperate with us.' She hurried over to the table and pulled out a chair. 'Please, sit down. Just a few questions.'

'Surely you don't think Nigel knows anything about her disappearance?'

'Of course not,' Mills said, eager to try a less confrontational approach. 'The sooner we can account for your husband's movements, the faster we focus our efforts on other lines of enquiry. Really – this is not much more than a box ticking exercise.'

The woman ignored the proffered chair and snatched her mobile phone from the kitchen counter. She scrolled through it quickly then shoved it at Murray. 'I only have a landline number for her.' Murray took the phone and left the room.

'When was the last time you spoke to your husband?' Mills sat down, hoping to encourage Mrs Cope to do the same.

'Last night. He told me he'd arrived at Joan's safely.' She sank onto the chair opposite Mills.

'You haven't tried phoning him today?'

'I tried his mobile before I went to the gym. There was no answer.'

'We've been getting the same thing – since just after eight this morning. Does he often leave his phone switched off?'

'He obviously doesn't want to disturb Joan.'

Mills smiled at her. 'Of course not.' He shifted in his seat and sucked in a deep breath, preparing for his next question. 'Where was your husband on Monday afternoon, between three and five?'

'What?'

'Routine question – I have to ask it.'

'At school – where else would he be?'

'According to the school secretary he left early.'

'She must be mistaken. Why would he do that?'

'So you didn't see him at that time?'

'I was at work.'

'What time did you return home?'

'Six-thirty. Like I always do.'

'And Mr Cope was here then?'

She nodded.

'And how did he seem to you?'

'Fine.'

'Did he leave the house at any time during Monday night?'

'This is ridiculous.'

Murray returned to the kitchen and exchanged a glance with Mills.

'Well?' Mrs Cope glared at her. 'What did he say?'

'Are you sure about the number?' Murray said.

'Quite sure. If he didn't answer I expect he's just busy.'

Heavy footsteps sounded overhead. Mrs Cope looked up at the ceiling. 'What are they still doing up there? Do they expect to find Nigel hiding in the wardrobe? Or under the bed?'

'Can you let us have a key to the garage?' Murray asked.

'What for?'

'Just to complete the search.'

The woman pointed to a set of hooks next to the back door. 'It's the silver one on the far right.'

'Did your husband take the train to Northumberland?' Murray asked as she handed the key to one of the uniforms who had appeared at the door.

'He took my car – it's more comfortable for long journeys.'

'Make and registration?' Mills asked.

Mrs Cope gave them the details and Murray hastily scribbled them down. 'And the small room upstairs at the front of the house – what's that used for?' Murray said.

'It's my husband's study. Why?'

'Do you know anything about the computer?'

'You can't take it away – not without asking Nigel first.'

'There is no computer, Mrs Cope, just the empty cables under the desk and the monitor on top.'

'What?'

'Did Mr Cope take the PC with him when he left?'

'Why would he take it to his aunt's?'

'When was the last time you saw it?'

'I don't remember – I don't tend to go into that room – I told you, it's his study.'

Mills' phone started to buzz. He headed out of the back door to answer the call and saw two officers searching the bushes at the bottom of the garden. He started walking towards them.

'Hi Ralph, Mark Black here, office manager from the incid—'

'Hello, sarge,' Mills interrupted, wondering if Black felt the need to remind every member of Camberwell CID who he was when he spoke to them.

'We've just got the info you asked for on Nigel Cope. Took longer than I would have liked – the records hadn't been computerised.'

'He's got previous?'

'Way back in the seventies.'

Mills stopped dead in the middle of the garden, steeling himself for the worst.

'Conviction for aggravated assault and possession of a class A drug.'

Mills let out a breath. Not nearly as bad as he'd feared. But still – a headteacher with that kind of record? 'He managed to get a job in a primary school? What happened to the CRB check?'

'He started at the school in 2000 – before the checks were mandatory. Seems our Mr Cope has been decidedly economical with the truth.'

ELEVEN

Natasha McKittrick stood in the observation room staring at Lawrence Keating as he sat fidgeting at the table on the other side of the glass. She tried to spot a likeness to Casey Collins, but it was hard to reconcile this man's sharp nose and craggy features with the angelic image of the nine-year-old girl she'd become so familiar with. Perhaps Ryan looked more like his father.

After Keating had brought the press conference to an abrupt end and been escorted to the Camberwell Green station, McKittrick had run a preliminary check on him to discover, much to her surprise, that the man had no previous convictions. Not so much as a caution to his name. Yet the suit he was wearing looked like a cheap court appearance two-piece. McKittrick supposed he must have used it for funerals instead.

Keating looked towards the glass and stared directly at her. 'Come on then, shall we get on with this?' he said, his rasping voice coming through the loudspeaker on the desk beside her. 'I haven't got all bloody day.'

McKittrick was still waiting for DCI Barrow, who was speaking to the head of the southern area command unit. She hadn't yet had the pleasure of an audience with the Detective Chief Super, but it seemed the man believed in extended debriefings, judging by the amount of time Barrow had been on the phone.

Keating got up from his seat and strode towards the strengthened glass of the two-way mirror. He tidied his greasy shoulder-length hair and ran a pale pink tongue over his teeth. 'I know you're in there, watching me,' he said and tapped a finger against the glass. 'I'm a busy man. I can't be hanging round here for hours.' He ambled back to the table against the wall and straddled the chair, leaned his arms on the back, cupped his chin in a hand and blew a kiss towards her.

Wanker.

Ten minutes later, a drawn-faced Barrow finally made an appearance. He marched into the observation room, said 'Shall we?' and strode straight out again.

McKittrick entered the interview room first, introduced herself and Barrow, explained they would be recording the interview and sat down. She looked expectantly at the DCI, who had made it quite clear he would be leading the questioning.

'Can you tell me what you meant by "Casey is better off where she is"?' Barrow asked and leaned both forearms on the edge of the table.

Keating looked at McKittrick. 'Don't hang about does he?'

'Answer the question, Mr Keating.' McKittrick stared right back at him.

'Manchester is it, that accent?'

McKittrick had no intention of responding.

'I lived up there for a bit. All I remember is the freezing bloody rain. Pissed it down the whole time I was there.'

'"Better off where she is",' Barrow repeated. 'Do you know where your daughter is?'

'Course I don't know. You think I'd be wasting my time with you lot? I'd be out there rescuing her.'

'When was the last time you saw Casey?'

'Couple of weeks ago. I take Ryan and Casey to McDonald's for a burger and a shake once a month. Casey likes the McFlurry. It's her favourite.' His nostrils twitched.

McKittrick threw the DCI a sideways glance, but he didn't acknowledge her. Trisha Collins had been quite adamant Casey's father had no contact with the girl. McKittrick started to speak but Barrow cut her off.

'How long is your access visit?'

'Only a couple of hours. It's not official or nothing. Just something Trish and me sorted out between ourselves.'

'Do the children ever visit you at your home?' McKittrick asked quickly, before her boss could jump in and shut her down.

'They prefer McDonald's. Can't blame them, my place isn't what you'd call kid friendly.'

McKittrick checked her notebook. 'This is the hostel in New Cross?'

Keating nodded and sniffed.

'And do you pick up the children from Trisha's?'

'Mostly.'

'So you see Trisha most months?'

'Yeah – unluckily for me – selfish bitch.'

'Your break-up wasn't amicable?'

'You got to be joking.' Keating shook his head and folded his arms, the cheap material of his jacket straining around the seams. 'She's not fit to look after those kids. Just cos she's a woman, don't mean she's got what it takes, d'you know what I mean?'

'Can you account for your movements on Monday afternoon from three-thirty onwards?' Barrow let out an impatient breath and glared at McKittrick, making sure she knew who was in charge.

'What's that got to do with anything?'

'It's standard procedure, Mr Keating. We need to eliminate you from our enquiries,' McKittrick replied, undeterred by Barrow's warning look.

'I've heard that before – that's what they say on telly when they suspect someone of doing something.' He leaned forward and laid his hands on the table, spreading his fingers wide. 'I ain't done nothing. I'm the innocent party here.'

'The sooner you tell us where you were, the faster you can get out of here.'

'Maybe I don't want to go anywhere. Maybe I should stick around and register a complaint – I've been treated like a bloody criminal and all I want to do is look out for Ryan. He's still living in that nuthouse, poor little bastard. She's not fit to look after him.' He started chewing the inside of his mouth. 'Or Casey,' he added after he saw McKittrick raise her eyebrows. 'Christ – when she comes back home she shouldn't have to live there.' He stared hard into McKittrick's face. 'Did Trisha tell you that Casey wants to live with me?' He looked at Barrow, then down at his grimy hands. 'I bet she bloody didn't.'

McKittrick studied the rough, flaking skin on Keating's face, his flat hair parted high, almost in the middle of his scalp. She couldn't believe a nine-year-old girl would want to get anywhere near him. 'Casey told you this herself?' she said, thinking Lorraine O'Donnell's assessment of Keating as a streak of piss was positively generous.

'She didn't have to.' He raised a hand to his mouth and nibbled at a hard piece of skin on his little finger. 'Ryan told me.'

'When was this?'

'Couple of months ago.'

'Did you talk to Casey about it?'

'There was nothing I could do, was there? That cow's holding all the cards. I've got no rights.'

'And that makes you angry?' Barrow asked.

'I'm human ain't I?'

'Angry enough to take matters into your own hands?'

'What are you trying to say? I haven't done anything wrong.'

McKittrick glanced at the DCI. They were still trying to track down Casey's headteacher, but that fact hadn't dented Barrow's conviction that somehow the girl's family were behind her disappearance.

'Where were you on Monday afternoon?'

'At the dentist.' Keating smiled at McKittrick, showing her his grey teeth. 'You can check if you like. My appointment was at three. I had to have a tooth out, so they gave me an injection. You know, to knock me right out.'

'What time did you leave?'

'Listen, you're barking up the wrong tree if you think I've got anything to do with Casey going missing. It's Trisha should be locked in here answering your questions.'

'Why do you say that?' Barrow sat up a little straighter.

'You must have seen that flat of hers. What a shithole the Shakespeare is. It's no bloody wonder Casey wanted to get out. If it was me I'd want to run away too.'

'You think your daughter's run away?' The muscles in Barrow's neck tensed.

'Trisha don't look after her properly.'

'But why would you think she's run away?'

'She wouldn't keep doing it, if she was happy living there. Stands to reason.'

'Are you saying Casey has run away before?' McKittrick interrupted.

Keating nodded. 'Ask Trisha if you don't believe me.'

'You're quite sure?'

'Oh yeah. More than once. I'm not surprised if Trisha didn't mention it. Puts her in a bad light, don't it?'

TWELVE

When Angela Tate and Ashley Montogomery turned onto the final flight of stairs leading to the fourth floor of Montague House they found Lorraine O'Donnell leaning against the wall on the narrow landing between flights, a tall pile of white T-shirts in her arms.

'Here, let me help,' Tate said and grabbed the top third of the pile and shoved it straight onto Ashley. She peeled away a single T-shirt and studied it in the gloomy light of the stairwell. Emblazoned above a colour photograph of Casey Collins were the words 'Have you seen Casey?'. Beneath the picture was the missing persons hotline number and below that '£25,000 reward'. Tate spotted a spelling mistake on the final line of text, but decided to keep that fact to herself.

'How's Trisha been since the press conference?' Tate asked, trying to keep her voice light.

'Oh she's been laughing her head off non-stop. Never seen her so happy.'

'Please, Lorraine.'

'I'm not telling you anything. You're not putting me in one of your stories.'

Tate pulled her most sincere face and touched Lorraine lightly on the arm. 'I do care about Trisha, you know, what she's going through. We go back a long way. It's not all about the job.'

'Yeah... well... whatever.' Lorraine stared at the floor and let out a sigh so long Tate feared she might deflate completely.

'The T-shirts are a great idea,' Ashley said soothingly. 'Boost morale for everyone who's searching, won't they?'

Lorraine clucked her teeth.

'Has Trisha said anything to you about her ex turning up at the press conference?' Tate asked.

'Here we go – fake sympathy one minute, straight back to being a hard-faced cow the next.'

'What do *you* think of him?'

'What I think don't matter.'

'Seems to me Trisha's better off without him,' Tate said, hopeful she would still find a way to get Lorraine to open up.

'He's a waste of space. Always has been. He only turned up to get his face on telly.'

'Does Trisha have a boyfriend at the moment?' Ashley asked, shifting the pile of T-shirts from one arm to the other.

'What's that got to do with you?'

'Nothing!' Tate interjected and threw her young assistant a warning glare. 'Over-enthusiasm of youth, Lorraine. Take no notice of her.' She pushed past the intern and continued up the stairs.

The three women arrived at Trisha's flat to be greeted by the family liaison officer. Lorraine said something under her breath that Tate didn't catch and hurried inside. Tate and Ashley followed her into the living room.

Trisha was pacing up and down, an unlit cigarette in her mouth. She looked up, saw Tate and grabbed her by the hand.

'What was he doing?' she asked her. 'He had no right to ruin everything. Suddenly everyone wants to talk about him. They all forgot about Casey like that.' She snapped her fingers. 'Bastard.'

'Perhaps I should speak to him. You know, get a different perspective,' Tate suggested, wondering how she could spin an interview with the estranged father.

'You're going nowhere near him - he doesn't care about Casey. Never has.'

On the other side of the room Trisha's youngest started yelling. 'Casey! Look – it's Casey.' She pointed excitedly at the television.

Kapoor rushed across the room and scooped the child into her arms.

'Where's Casey?' the girl said. 'I want Casey.'

'She's gone away,' the FLO said.

'Where?'

'Not far – she'll be back really soon.'

'Promise?'

'Let's go upstairs and draw her a picture, shall we? For when she comes back?' Kapoor caught Tate's eye as she hurried little Lola from the room. The detective looked anything but hopeful.

'Christ, Trish,' Lorraine said, dumping the pile of T-shirts on the table in the corner of the room. 'That one's taking over. Next thing you know the kids'll be stinking of curry and turning Muslim.'

'What century do you live in?' Ashley dropped the T-shirts she was holding on the floor and marched over to Lorraine. 'Why don't you try thinking before you open your mouth?'

'And what's it got to do with you?' Lorraine yelled back at her. 'I don't remember Trish inviting you into her house!'

'For God's sake – shut up!' Trisha screamed.

Tate slipped an arm around Trisha's shoulders. 'We're all on edge. Sorry, Trish.' She squeezed tighter. 'I'm sure no one meant to upset you.' She glowered at Ashley, but the intern kept her eyes fixed on Lorraine.

Chelsea, who had remained silent throughout the exchange, lumbered out of her armchair and tugged on

Ashley's sleeve, pulling her away from Lorraine. She guided the intern towards the door.

'And what's going on there?' Lorraine turned to Trisha. 'You want to watch her. She might be a bit lezzie.'

Tate took a deep breath and attempted to count to ten. She made it to three before reaching for her bag and the packet of cigarettes within.

'Jesus – why are we all at each other's throats?' Trisha said. 'It's not going to help Casey, is it?' A loud bang on the front door made her jump.

Lorraine scurried into the hall, mumbling something about 'being an unpaid skivvy' as she went.

Trisha leaned in close to Tate and whispered, 'Every time I think of Casey I remember what happened to Paula… and Sandra, and I get this horrible feeling in the pit of my stomach. They've got to find her soon, Ange. I can't take much more of this.'

Tate grabbed Trisha's hand, looked into her face and waited for Trisha to make eye contact. 'Listen to me. What's happening now has nothing to do with what happened to Sandra and Paula. You've got to get that out of your mind. Casey is going to be all right.' Tate's words had a hollow ring to them.

Tears filled Trisha's puffy eyes. 'I want to believe that, Ange, I really do.' She banged a fist against her head. 'But I can't stop myself thinking—'

'You've got to. The police know what they're doing. They find kids all the time. It just doesn't always make the news.' It was a lie, but she felt obliged to make the right noises. Time was running out. They were about to hit the crucial forty-eight hour mark. 'If you want to talk about it, what happened before… not for the paper, just you and me, you know you can tell me anything.' Tate set her mouth in a sympathetic half-smile.

'Lorraine said you'd been sniffing about.'

Tate turned quickly to see a stocky, shaven-headed man standing in the doorway of the living room. It was a face she'd never forget and it was wearing the same cocky expression it had thirty-three years ago when she'd last seen it.

Gary Benson.

'You got a nerve coming round here,' Benson said, his upper lip curling. He looked her up and down.

'I was invited. By Trisha.' Tate lifted Trisha's hand in hers to prove just how close they both were.

'She's only here to help find Casey,' Trisha said. 'And we need all the help we can get.'

'Helping how? I don't see her paper offering a reward. You should be talking to *The Herald* – not wasting your time on her rag. How much is she paying you?'

'Nothing! Christ, Gary,' Trisha said. 'We've been through this already. It's not about money.'

'Get real. Everything's about money.' He strode quickly towards Tate, for a moment she thought he might walk straight into her. 'Isn't that right?' he said, his face only inches from hers.

She stared right back at him.

'You've outstayed your welcome,' Benson said. He reached for Tate's arm.

She pulled away quickly. 'I'm going nowhere.'

Suddenly the volume of the television ratcheted up. Lorraine stared at the screen, the remote in her hand. 'I knew I never liked the look of him. Thin-lipped.'

'What are you going on about?' Benson barked at her.

Lorraine held a silencing hand to her brother and immediately Trisha hurried to the television.

They watched in silence as a report about the headteacher from Casey's school played out.

'Did you hear that? Police want him to "help them with their enquiries".' Lorraine said when the item had finished. 'That means he's guilty of something.'

'Rule him out of their enquiries,' Trisha said. 'That's what I heard.'

'No smoke without fire,' Lorraine muttered. 'Must be some sort of paedo.'

Tate grabbed Lorraine by the elbow and started to walk her towards the door. 'How is that kind of talk going to help?'

'I don't understand why Manisha didn't mention anything to me about it,' Trisha said. 'Isn't she supposed to keep us up to date?'

'I told you not to trust her. You can't trust any of them.' Lorraine tried to wriggle free of Tate's grasp.

'Get your hands off her!' Gary caught up with them as Tate steered Lorraine into the hall. 'I can't believe you've turned up here, bold as brass, after what you tried to do.'

Tate loosened her grip on Lorraine's arm.

Benson prodded a finger into Tate's shoulder. 'I'll never forget it.'

Tate batted away his hand and he caught her wrist in his fist.

'I'll never forget it and I'll never forgive you either,' he said.

Tate tugged at her hand. Benson's grip held firm.

'Maybe now's the time for you to say sorry.' Benson squeezed harder.

'Don't hold your breath.' It wasn't Benson she needed to apologise to. 'Let go of my arm,' she said through gritted teeth.

'And what if I don't want to? What are you going to do about it?'

Tate levelled her gaze, staring directly into Benson's eyes. What was she going to do about it? Something she should have done thirty-three years ago.

'Leave it, Gary, come on. Let her go,' Trisha pleaded.

'Stay out of it, Trish. She's got it coming to her. Why don't you—'

A violent bang on the front door cut him short.

THIRTEEN

DC Kapoor flung open the door, her head half turned towards something inside Collins' flat that McKittrick couldn't see.

'Manisha?' McKittrick asked. 'What's going on?'

Kapoor opened her mouth, but had only managed to utter a single syllable when a stocky bald man pushed through the doorway, ignoring the FLO and both McKittrick and Mills as he forced a path through them. McKittrick watched him disappear onto the stairwell at the end of the walkway. 'Who's he?'

'Family friend,' Kapoor told her. 'Lorraine O'Donnell's brother, Gary Benson.' Trisha's youngest child appeared at Kapoor's side and clung onto her leg. She looked up saucer-eyed at McKittrick, then stared at Mills. Her mouth fell open.

'Hello, sweetie,' Mills said and smiled at her. 'What's your name?'

The girl hid behind Kapoor.

'Benson,' McKittrick repeated. 'Have we interviewed him yet?' she asked Mills.

'He's on the list. I remember seeing his name,' Mills said and pulled a packet of Smarties from a pocket. He crouched down and offered the cardboard tube to the little girl peeking at him between Kapoor's legs.

'Either of you come across him before?' McKittrick asked.

Kapoor glanced down at the child and lowered her voice. 'I did a bit of digging after I first met him. Got into trouble as a teenager, according to Trisha. Stolen cars, bit of vandalism, couple of fights. No convictions that I could find on the system though.'

McKittrick nodded, surprised at Kapoor's diligence, amazed the detective had the energy to do anything more than drag herself home to bed after a day with the Collins family. 'Thanks, Manisha. Well done.' McKittrick realised how patronising her words sounded only when they were out of her mouth and hanging awkwardly in the air.

'Thank you, ma'am.'

'God – don't call me that.'

McKittrick had already been through this with Mills. They'd managed to settle on a compromise of 'boss' after he'd explained he felt too awkward addressing a senior officer by her first name.

'Call me anything but "ma'am",' she said, peering into the hallway. 'Have we walked into the middle of something? Why did Benson leave in such a hurry?'

'I'm not sure, I was upstairs. Bit of a row, I think. Not sure who was doing the arguing.' Kapoor stepped out onto the walkway, holding a hand up to Lola for the girl to stay put. 'Can I have a quick word?'

'What is it?'

'I'm a bit confused about how formal my reports for DCI Barrow should be. And to be honest… I'm uncomfortable with the whole *reporting* thing anyway.'

'Reporting?'

'I thought I was here to support them, not spy on them. It's putting me in an tricky position.'

'DCI Barrow requested this?' McKittrick had heard nothing about it.

'He made a point of it. But I'm not sure if I'm supposed to put something in writing, or whether I should report verbally. And… well, how much should I be digging? What kind of dirt is he after?'

'If you talk to anyone, make sure it's me.'

'But the DCI wants a daily update.'

'You leave the DCI to me. Your role here is to support Trisha and her family. That's your priority. Is that clear?'

'Yes, boss.'

'Good.'

Kapoor stepped to one side and ushered McKittrick and Mills into the hall. A woman dressed in an elegantly cut black skirt suit was just coming out of the living room.

Kapoor did the introductions.

All we need, McKittrick thought, the press getting involved with the family. She scrutinised the journalist, taking in the heavy make-up, the wild blonde-grey curls and the supremely confident expression on the woman's face. She looked familiar somehow.

'Ralph Mills?' The journalist stuck out her hand and Mills offered her a smile and his firm handshake. 'I can't believe we've never met before.'

Mills suddenly seemed uncomfortable.

'Mutual friend,' Tate explained for McKittrick's benefit.

Mills flushed and he rocked back on his heels suddenly as if he'd been socked in the face. It was only at that moment McKittrick remembered where she'd seen Tate before. The journalist had been in the news herself a couple of years back. Tate looked different in the flesh. Older. Heavier. What was a celebrated journalist doing slumming it on a Camberwell council estate? McKittrick decided she'd have to grill Mills later about their 'mutual friend'.

'Is there news?' Trisha Collins appeared in the living room doorway and leaned against the frame. 'Just tell me she's all right.'

'No news as yet, Ms Collins,' Mills said.

'Why are you wasting your time here then?' Lorraine O'Donnell joined Trisha at the door. 'You should be out there looking for that paedo teacher.'

'Stop talking about him like that,' Collins snapped at her.

'Shall we sit down, Trisha?' McKittrick walked towards the two women, gesturing for them to return to the living room, aware the journalist was following close on her heels. She turned abruptly. 'We'll need to speak to Trisha privately,' she said. 'If you don't mind.'

'Nothing to do with how I feel about it,' Tate replied. 'Trisha – would you like me to sit in?'

Collins looked from McKittrick to the journalist, her gaze lingering for a moment, unable to decide. Eventually she answered, 'Come back later, Ange. I can't think straight at the minute.'

'You're sure?' Tate raised a severely plucked eyebrow.

Collins nodded once and quickly disappeared back into the living room.

'If you've got no news, what are you even doing here?' O'Donnell demanded as soon as Tate had been escorted by Kapoor to the front door.

McKittrick chose to ignore O'Donnell and spoke softly to Collins. 'Do you want Mrs O'Donnell to be present for the interview, Trisha?' She resisted the temptation to glare at the woman.

'Interview?'

'More of an informal chat, really.' McKittrick corrected herself.

'I'm going nowhere,' O'Donnell blustered. 'I'm like family.'

'Trisha?'

'Lorraine's fine where she is.'

'OK.' McKittrick perched on the dining chair Mills had fetched from the other side of the room. 'We've spoken to Lawrence Keating and we'd like to ask you some questions about what he's told us. Is that all right?'

Collins stared at both detectives in turn, her suspicion barely disguised.

O'Donnell answered for her. 'What's that bastard been saying? Whatever it is you can take it with a pinch of salt. He wouldn't know the truth if it smacked him in the face.'

'Why didn't you tell us that Casey had run away before, Trisha?' McKittrick said, ignoring O'Donnell completely.

'Is that what he told you?' Trisha seemed genuinely confused.

'When was the last time it happened?'

'She's never done it before.' Her eyes started to fill. 'Casey's a good girl.'

'I really need you to think carefully about this before you answer, OK?' McKittrick gave her a sympathetic smile.

Collins nodded slowly and pinched her bottom lip between finger and thumb.

'So, when was the last time Casey—'

'Oh this is bloody ridiculous,' O'Donnell blurted. 'You're prepared to take the word of that useless piece of shit over Trisha's? You wouldn't be treating her like this if that reporter was still here. I should get them back in here.' She started for the door just as Chelsea Collins appeared in the doorway. 'Go and fetch that reporter and your new little friend, go on.'

Chelsea looked at her mother.

'You stay where you are,' Trisha said. 'Sit down.' She sniffed loudly and blew her nose on a crumpled tissue. 'Make yourself useful, Lorraine. Put the kettle on.'

'What?'

'Please, Lor.'

Collins waited for O'Donnell to leave the room.

'She never ran away before,' Collins said. 'Not really.'

'Mr Keating told us—'

'For Christ's sake – you shouldn't listen to him. He doesn't care about Casey.'

'What do you mean "not really"?'

'She'd been pestering me to take her and Ryan to visit Lawrence's mum. Christine, Casey's nan, had been feeling a bit poorly. I told Casey I was too busy. I was juggling three jobs at the time. I had no time for anything. Anyone.' She blew her nose again. 'Should have just taken her. Christine isn't a bad sort. Don't know how she went so wrong with Lawrence.' Collins' attention seemed to drift, she stared towards the window.

'What happened?'

'Oh it really didn't amount to anything.'

'If you wouldn't mind telling us anyway?'

'Casey set off to see Christine on her own. Only it's three buses from here and she got confused about where she needed to change. She was too shy to ask the driver where to get off. First I knew about it some woman at the Crystal Palace garage was on the phone telling me she'd found Casey sobbing her heart out upstairs on the number three bus.'

'When was this?'

'Must be a couple of years ago now. Gary had to get over there and pick her up.'

'Gary?' McKittrick asked.

'Lorraine's brother. He's the only person I know with transport. I couldn't afford a cab.'

'And Casey was all right when you found her?'

'She was fine after a big cuddle and an ice cream.'

'And what about the other times?'

'There weren't any other times. The whole thing frightened Casey so much she promised never to do anything like it again. Soon as Christine was better we all went over to see her.'

'Why didn't you tell us about this before?'

'Why should I? There was no harm done. It's not like she actually ran away. I didn't think to mention it.'

'Is there anything else you have neglected to tell us?'

'You make it sound like I've been lying to you.' A sob hiccupped from her mouth. 'I haven't – why would I do that? I just want Casey back.'

'But why would Mr Keating tell us it's happened on a number of occasions?'

'Because he's stirring the shit.' O'Donnell was back, a mug of tea in each hand.

'Trisha? Are you sure you've told us everything?' McKittrick said.

'He's never forgiven me for getting custody.'

O'Donnell shoved a steaming mug at McKittrick. 'Milk no sugar.' The tea slopped over the edge of the mug, narrowly missing the leg of McKittrick's dry-clean-only trousers.

'Is there anything else you want to tell us? Something we might find out from someone else down the line?' McKittrick carefully set the mug down on the nearby coffee table.

'What are you getting at?' Collins refused the mug O'Donnell was shoving at her. 'I'm not keeping stuff from you, if that's what you mean.'

'When we spoke to you before you said you didn't know where your ex-partner was living.'

'I don't. If he says I do he's lying.'

'Why did you tell us Lawrence Keating has no contact with his children?'

'I never.'

McKittrick quickly referred to her notes. 'You suggested as much.'

Collins shrugged. 'You must have taken something I said the wrong way.'

McKittrick turned to a fresh page of her notebook. 'Talk me through Monday evening again.' She tried to keep her tone neutral, non-accusatory. The neighbours they'd interviewed so far hadn't mentioned seeing Collins on Monday evening.

'What about it?' Collins narrowed her eyes.

O'Donnell sat down heavily on the sofa next to her friend.

'Previously you told us you didn't realise Casey was missing until seven o'clock on Monday evening.'

'That's right.' Collins reached for Lorraine's hand.

'You didn't think anything was out of the ordinary before that time?'

'I erm…' Collins glanced at her teenage daughter, but Chelsea was busy studying her mobile phone. 'It might have been a bit earlier than that. I thought Casey was upstairs in her room.'

'You didn't check on her as soon as you got home from work?'

'I did.' She was playing with her bottom lip again.

'That's not what you said before.'

'Isn't it? I must have got confused. I came home, saw she wasn't here. Then phoned Chelsea to find out if she was with her.'

'Chelsea wasn't at home?' McKittrick made a point of flipping back through her notebook, even though she knew exactly what was written there.

'I can't remember. It's all a bit of a blur now.'

'You said Chelsea told you as soon as you got in that her sister was missing.' McKittrick looked up from the notebook and scrutinised Collins' face. The woman's cheeks were dimpled and she was gnawing her thumbnail.

'Don't blame me,' Chelsea blurted. 'It's not my fault. I haven't done anything wrong.' She stood up. 'Tell them, Lor.' She stared at O'Donnell. O'Donnell looked at Trisha.

'For Christ's sake, Trish.' O'Donnell let go of her friend's hand and, consciously or not, wriggled away from her towards the end of the sofa.

'What's the matter with you?' Trisha glared at her friend.

'You've got to tell them. They'll only find out some other way.' O'Donnell glanced towards Chelsea.

'Ms Collins?' McKittrick persisted.

Mills gave Collins a sympathetic smile, slumped his shoulders and leaned forward so that his head was at the same level as hers. 'It doesn't matter if you told the inspector something different before,' he said softly. 'It's more important that you—'

'All right!' Collins held a hand to her mouth and swallowed noisily as if she was about to throw up. Sudden tears streaked her face. 'I wasn't here Monday night.' She bit her lip. 'I didn't get home until just before six, Tuesday morning.'

1979

The seven-year-old girl pulled on Angela Tate's hand, five podgy fingers wrapped tight around hers. Angela looked into Trisha Collins' eyes and saw the little girl had been crying.

'What is it, Trish? What's happened?'

She wouldn't answer, she just tugged on her hand more firmly.

'Where are we going?'

'It's a secret.' The girl's face was set in a frown, eyebrows bunched towards her nose. She continued to lead the way, dragging the young journalist behind her as if she were steering a stubborn horse or donkey along the street that separated the Essex Estate from its neighbour.

Finally they reached the main road and Trisha stopped at the kerb, looked right, left, and right again.

'How much further, Trish? We can't be gone too long – your mum will worry.'

'Ssshhh! I'm listening for cars.' She checked up and down the street again, and, seemingly satisfied they were in no danger from speeding vehicles, yanked on Angela's arm and pulled her across the road. When they'd safely reached the opposite pavement, Angela congratulated the girl on her mastery of the Green Cross Code.

'We done it in school last week.'

'*Did* it,' Angela corrected.

'Did it what?'

'You *did* it at school last week.'

Trisha's face darkened. 'I just told you that!'

Angela smiled at her. 'And you're brilliant at it. You really are.'

For ten days, ever since news had first broken that a young girl had gone missing from the Marlowe Estate, Angela Tate had made a point of befriending all the children there and on the two neighbouring estates. It was her first really big assignment for the *South London Press* and she was keen to find an angle. She had used her age to her advantage and managed to win the children's trust. The endless supply of Mars bars and Maltesers hadn't done any harm either.

Trisha Collins had taken a particular shine to her and Angela surprised herself with just how patient she had managed to be as she gently coaxed information from her about the estates and the locals. Angela was more than happy to take on the role of big sister.

Especially if it meant an exclusive for the paper.

When a second little girl had disappeared, a general panic spread across the whole neighbourhood. It felt like a community under siege, lots of mothers insisting their sons and daughters play indoors, even though the mid-July heat was starting to build.

Trisha tugged on her hand. 'You're too slow. Come on!' She was quite breathless. A little sob escaping from her mouth every few steps.

They'd covered only half a mile since leaving the estate, passing the magistrates' court and the police station next door, finally turning up an unfamiliar side street. 'Where are we going?' she asked the child.

'I can't tell you. I'm not supposed to tell anyone.'

They turned again and Angela saw the black spiked railings of a park twenty or so yards away on the other side of the road. 'Are we going to the park? If you just wanted to play on the swings, we could have gone to the one next to the estate.'

'Come. On.' Trisha tugged on Angela's hand with all her might.

'Shouldn't we cross the road?' The journalist glanced at the rusted corrugated iron fence on their side of the street, barbed wire running along the top, *Keep Out* warning signs bolted to it at regular intervals.

'We're not going to the park.'

'Don't you want a go on the swings?'

'The swings are for babies.'

'Are they? I quite like the swings. Are you calling me a baby?'

Trisha slowed for a moment and her chest heaved.

'What is it?' Angela stopped and crouched down to properly look into the girl's face. Trisha turned her head away. 'Tell me, Trisha. Why are you so upset?'

Another sob escaped the girl's mouth. She ran her sleeve across her nose.

'You can tell me, you know. I can keep secrets.'

'We said a prayer today,' Trisha finally mumbled. 'In assembly. The whole school.'

'Did you?' Angela supposed they recited the Lord's Prayer every morning. Just like they had when she was at school.

'For Sandra.'

'Oh.' Angela dragged Trisha towards her and hugged the little girl. After a moment she pulled away and looked into her bloodshot eyes. 'And that made you sad?'

Trisha nodded and immediately her eyes filled with tears. She gulped down a breath. 'We're nearly there,' she said and pulled Angela further down the street.

They stopped where the run of corrugated iron did, at the start of an unpaved narrow lane, a chain-linked fence on one side, the back of an industrial estate on the other.

'Down here?' Angela asked. 'Are you sure?'

Trisha nodded and led her over the uneven rough track for fifty or so yards, stopping abruptly when they reached a small gap in the fence. She ducked down and started to crawl through. Angela grabbed the girl's T-shirt.

'Wait. You can't go in there.'

'You need to see.' She managed to wriggle free of Angela's grasp and slipped through the hole.

Angela called to her, 'Stay just there, by the fence. Don't wander off.' She stepped back and tried to gauge the dimensions of the gap. There was no way she'd squeeze through. She dropped to her knees and ducked her head through.

'Hurry up!' Trisha said.

'I really don't think…' Angela pushed further forward, snagging one shoulder against the jagged wire. Her jacket ripped. Her best jacket. She unhooked the material and tried to flatten herself against the dusty ground, crawling by inches, gradually managing to slither through until she was on the other side of the fence. Unsteadily, she heaved herself to her feet.

They were standing at the edge of an expanse of waste ground. Piles of broken bricks and rubble formed little hills across the landscape. It looked like a long-forgotten WWII bombsite. Determined weeds, thick and green, were growing in what was left of a row of demolished houses. Clumps of grass sprouted here and there, softening the hard edges of the mounds of masonry and shattered glass.

Trisha wrapped her warm little fingers around Angela's again.

'We can't go any further,' Angela said. 'There are guard dogs here, Trisha. It says so on the security signs. It's not safe.'

The girl's bottom lip pushed out. Again her eyes filled with tears. 'There ain't any dogs.'

'How do you know that?'

'Come on.'

They made their way slowly over the rubble. Every now and then Angela lost her footing, stumbling in her heels as Trisha pressed on, nimbly navigating the peaks and dips like a mountain goat.

After a minute or so, the girl stopped and let go of Angela's hand. She raised a trembling arm and pointed to a high mound thirty feet away.

'What's up there?' Angela asked her. 'Show me.'

Trisha shook her head emphatically. 'You need to see for yourself.'

Angela told the girl to stay exactly where she was and started to circumnavigate the uneven pile of bricks, broken concrete and glass, picking her way carefully over the rough ground, her high-heeled shoes slowing her progress. When she was half way round she lost sight of Trisha.

'Are you OK?' she hollered. Trisha didn't respond. 'Trisha?' Angela hurried back the way she'd come and found the little girl on her knees sobbing silently. 'What is it?' Angela reached down to her, but the girl shrugged her off and pointed again to the summit of the mound.

Angela grabbed Trisha's wrist, dragged her to her feet and tried to pull her towards the hill of rubble. 'Come with me. I can't leave you here on your own.'

Trisha let out a piercing wail.

'OK – I'll go but you have to promise me you'll answer when I call - OK?'

Trisha nodded, releasing another sob as she did.

'Stay right there.'

Angela continued alone, climbing up the mound, struggling to stay upright with each unsteady step. Halfway to the summit she glanced over her shoulder and saw Trisha still rooted to the spot, looking up at her. When she finally reached the top she discovered a thick sheet of blue plastic tethered to the ground by house bricks. One corner had escaped its mooring and was flapping in the breeze.

The wind changed direction suddenly, lifting the plastic higher.

Then the smell hit her. A smell that was rotten and sweet at the same time. It reached the back of her throat and she started to gag, the vomit coming so quickly she barely had time to bend forward.

When she was heaving nothing but saliva, Angela lifted an arm across her face in an attempt to shield her nose and mouth from the stench. She edged towards the loose corner of plastic, reaching it just as the wind picked up, throwing the sheet right back to reveal what was beneath.

Angela blinked, unsure what she'd seen as the plastic dropped back down again. It looked for all the world like a child's hand. She swallowed hard against another rising wave of nausea and reached for the plastic sheet. She lifted it from the ground.

Turned on one side, lying peacefully as though sleeping, was a child whose face Angela knew all too well. Sandra Stockwell's flesh was mottled in patches of ghostly white and bruised blue. She dropped the plastic and heaved again, turning her head to direct the vomit away from Sandra's body.

'What do you think you're doing!' a voice yelled in the distance. 'Get away from there, nosy fucking bitch.'

Angela dabbed her nose and mouth with the back of her hand, and stared blindly towards the shouting.

'Oi! Did you hear me?'

It was the voice of a child. A voice she recognised.

'Fuck off!' Louder now.

Angela raised a hand to her brow to shield her eyes from the glare of the sun and saw a boy running towards her, then two others behind him, struggling to keep up.

'Fucking bitch! Are you deaf?'

Gary Benson. The brother of Trisha's best friend.

Frantically, Angela scanned the waste ground beyond the approaching boys, searching for Trisha. The girl was exactly where she'd left her, her hands covering her face.

Gary Benson climbed quickly up the rubble, eyes on Angela all the way, without missing a step. 'Are you fucking deaf or fucking stupid?'

Angela couldn't help thinking he was using the F-word as if he'd learnt it that day and wanted to try it out as often as he could. She studied his snarling, thuggish face and reconsidered. Gary Benson had probably started swearing before he was out of nappies.

'I don't remember selling you a ticket,' he said, pointing an accusatory finger at her.

The two boys that had been trailing Benson finally caught up. They waved what looked like raffle tickets at her.

'Paying customers only,' Benson said, holding out a hand.

'What?'

'Two quid.'

'You ghoulish little bastard.' She made a lunge for him but he ducked out of reach.

'You can stay right where you are too!' he hollered.

Angela followed his gaze and saw Trisha on her feet, walking towards the mound of rubble.

'Don't come up here, Trisha,' Angela shouted. The girl slowed for a moment then continued walking towards them. 'What have you done?' Angela tried to grab Benson again, but he was too fast for her.

The boy screwed up his face and cleared his throat. He spat, a globule of saliva missing Angela's head by a few inches. She lunged again. Again she missed him, losing her balance. She started sliding down the slope, both shoes ripping from her feet as she went. She dropped onto her backside, managing to halt her descent, and scrambled onto her hands and knees. 'Tell me what you've done to Sandra,' she said and gulped down a breath.

'Who's Sandra?' Benson replied, his face a sudden picture of innocence. 'I don't know no Sandra.'

Trisha Collins was just a few yards away now and Angela struggled to her feet. 'Stay away,' she said, and held up her hands.

Trisha started to cry. 'Don't tell my mum,' she wailed between sobs. 'She loves Sandra.'

'Shut your fucking mouth, cry-baby.'

Trisha raised a fist to her mouth to muffle her sobs.

'It's all right. Don't listen to him.' Angela reached out to her. 'You don't have to be frightened. Just tell me what happened and I'll look after you. I promise.'

'You shouldn't make promises you can't keep,' Benson said.

'What did you think you were doing, bringing her here? Why show her this? Did you try to sell her a ticket too?'

'I don't know what you're talking about.' Gary Benson grinned at her.

'You've got nothing to smile about. Let's see if you're still smiling when the police get here.'

FOURTEEN

Thursday 9th February

'So she was at her boyfriend's flat the whole night?' Cath Murray clapped her gloved hands together then blew on her fingers.

Ralph Mills nodded at her, checked the address he'd written in his notebook and led the way along the exterior walkway of Devereux House on the Essex Estate. They were there to interview Lorraine O'Donnell's mother. The DCI had insisted all of Trisha Collins' friends and relatives – no matter how distant – were interviewed as a priority.

'Who was looking after the kids?'

'Chelsea, it seems. Though Collins says she'd arranged for her son… Kiefer, to babysit.'

'That's his name – Kiefer?'

He nodded but made no comment.

'And what happened to him?'

Mills shrugged. 'Didn't show. Chelsea phoned her mum to tell her, but Trisha didn't pick up.'

'So this Kiefer has confirmed his mum's story?'

Mills stopped at a door in the middle of the walkway. 'I expect he will. When we actually get to speak to him.'

'Where is he?'

He shrugged again. 'Not at home, not answering his phone.'

'And what about the boyfriend?'

'Same goes for him.'

'You haven't tracked either of them down?'

'Not so far.'

'Christ, it's all sounding a bit dodgy, isn't it? How is it I miss all the action? Why didn't you call me, let me know what was going on?'

'I'm telling you now, aren't I?'

'You get all the juicy work and I'm left on boring house-to-house enquiries. McKittrick must have really taken a shine to you.'

'What?'

'I've seen the way you look at her. The way your little face lights up when you talk about her.'

'Piss off.'

'What do you think? About Collins and her domestic arrangements?'

'I'm just doing what the DCI has asked me to do.'

'Come on, Ralph, spit it out.'

Mills wondered how frank he should be with Murray. Whatever he told her would be round the station in a matter of minutes. 'I don't understand why Barrow's taken against her quite as much as he has. Seems like an overreaction to me. That's just between you and me.'

'Of course – you know me, model of discretion.' She smiled at him. 'What happened with the bloke in Leeds? What's his name? You said you were following up.'

'His name's Raymond Dixon. I'm still waiting to hear back from his probation officer. They're short-staffed apparently.'

'Tell me who isn't.'

'Anyway, Barrow's made it quite clear chasing Dixon is not a priority.' Mills, nevertheless, had every intention of making it his. But there was no need to share that fact with Murray.

'Not when we've got old-aged pensioners to interrogate,' she said.

Mills rapped on the knocker. A dog started to yap inside the flat. A thick clunk sounded from the other side of the door as a heavy bolt was drawn across it. The door opened a crack, restrained by a safety chain. The muzzle of a Jack Russell appeared at the bottom of the gap moments before the suspicious face of a seventy-odd-year-old woman moved into view five feet above.

'Police is it?' The woman peered at both of them in turn. 'I've already spoken to your lot. I don't know anything. About anything.' The woman started to close the door and the dog's yapping grew louder.

'Mrs Benson, I'm DC Mills and this is my colleague DC Murray,' Mills said and waved his ID at the narrowing gap between door and frame. 'We're following up our colleagues' interview with you.'

'I've got nothing more to say.'

'Now that we've spoken to your daughter,' Murray said, 'we'd like to have another word with you.'

Mills glanced at Murray but she wouldn't look at him. She had never even met Lorraine O'Donnell.

'What's she been saying?'

'We just need to ask you a few questions about Trisha Collins and her family.'

The door closed to and quickly opened again, minus the safety chain. Mrs Benson stood in the doorway wearing a pink towelling dressing gown over a pair of jogging pants, purple suede moon boots on her feet. 'Well come in, if you're coming. No need to stand on ceremony. Brass monkeys out there.'

Mills followed Murray inside, trying to ignore the terrier snapping at his ankles.

'Don't mind Monty. He don't bite. Much.' The old woman laughed, the sound getting caught in her throat, triggering a hacking smoker's cough. She thumped a fist onto her chest and led them to a living room at the end of the hall, thick, cream shag pile carpet on the floor, an enormous maroon velvet three-piece suite taking up most of the space.

'You found that pervy teacher yet?' She pointed a remote and the wide-screen television fell silent. 'They've not said anything about it on the news. But then you wouldn't be here talking to me if you'd found him. And Casey.'

'We can't discuss the ongoing investigation, I'm afraid,' Murray said.

'Yes, but it's all right to harass people in their own homes, I suppose?'

'Mind if I take a look around?' Mills asked.

'What happens if I say no?'

'It's just routine. Whenever a child goes missing, we search every building in the neighbourhood.'

'Why didn't the first lot bother with that?'

'We've widened the search area.'

'All right then, but make it quick.'

Mills ran upstairs, quickly scanned the bedroom at the front of the flat, looking for anything that seemed out of place, then moved onto the bathroom and second bedroom. The final door off the upstairs landing was closed. He tried the handle. It was locked. He ran back down the stairs and found Mrs Benson standing in the doorway of the kitchen, apparently waiting for him. She waved a large silver key under his nose and slowly made her way up the stairs, the Jack Russell scampering past her.

Mills joined her on the landing as she threaded the key into the lock. She pushed open the door and stood back.

Around a dozen cardboard boxes were stacked under the small window opposite the door.

'What are these?' Mills crossed the room in three strides and inspected the box at the top of one stack. It was sealed with plastic parcel tape. 'Could you open this for me?'

'No. I've only just taped it up.' She stood next to him and placed a proprietary hand on the box.

'What's inside?'

'Nothing much. Books, CDs, DVDs. Odds and sods.'

'Having a clearout?'

'I do a bit of trading on eBay.' She folded her arms across her chest and shooed the dog away from the bottom box with the toe of her suede boot. 'No law against it.'

'Depends what you're buying and selling.'

'How's this helping you find Casey?' She walked out of the room and stood on the threshold, key in hand.

Mills traced a finger along the strip of parcel tape. The dog had started sniffing at the bottom box.

'Get out of there!' Mrs Benson shouted. For a moment Mills thought she was talking to him. The dog obediently trotted out of the room and down the stairs.

When they returned to the living room Murray looked at him expectantly. He shook his head as surreptitiously as he could.

'Don't know what you thought you were going to find,' Mrs Benson muttered. She scrutinised Murray. 'And don't think I don't know you've been poking around in here while I was upstairs.'

'As my colleague said, madam, it's just routine. We really appreciate your cooperation.'

'Don't give me all that flannel. I know what you think of us.'

'Madam?'

'Madam – that's a laugh. Your lot don't even think we're good enough to wipe the shit off your shoes.'

'I can assure you that—'

'Don't waste your breath.' Mrs Benson slumped into her armchair. 'Just ask me your questions and sling your hook.'

'When was the last time you saw Casey Collins?'

'Here we go – same questions the last lot asked. Haven't you got better things to do? I know I have.'

'It won't take long,' Mills said. 'When did you last see Casey?'

'Gawd knows. It's not something I keep a note of, is it?'

'But you see her regularly?'

'Trisha is Lorraine's friend, not mine. I don't see her kids from one month to the next. Why would I?'

'How long have you known the Collins family?'

'Why?'

Mills glanced out of the window. Through a gap between buildings he could clearly see the front of Montague House on the neighbouring estate. 'It's just a routine question, madam,' he said.

'Donkey's years. We moved onto the Marlowe the same time Tom and Maggie did – Trisha's mum and dad. Maggie was a childminder, so she knew lots of mums on the estates. Lorraine and Trisha were born the same year. They grew up together. Maggie minded Lorraine for a few years, when I was still working.'

'And yet you say you're not close to the Collins family now?' Murray asked.

'So?'

'And what about your son, Gary?' Mills turned back from the window.

'What about him?'

'He's close to the Collinses, isn't he?'

The woman shrugged and started to pick at bits of lint on the sleeve of her dressing gown. 'Not so much.'

'But surely he grew up with Trisha too?'

Mrs Benson narrowed her eyes until they were no more than slits behind her thick-lensed glasses. 'I expect you already know the answer to that.' She folded her arms.

'I really don't.'

'Gary and Trisha went out for a bit after Trisha left school. It didn't last. Thank God. My Gary was better off out of it.'

'What do you mean?' Murray said.

'Five kids, she's got. She couldn't keep her legs crossed if her life depended on it.'

'How long were they seeing one another?'

Mrs Benson looked up at Mills and studied his face. 'What's that got to do with anything?'

'Just trying to get some background.' Mills could feel his cheeks warming.

'What did you say your name was?' the woman asked after a long pause.

'Mills. Ralph Mills.'

'Bloody hell.' She clapped her hands together, triggering fresh yapping from the Jack Russell. 'I knew it. You've got his mouth. And his eyes, when you frown like that.'

Mills felt a pressure building in his chest. It was a reflex. He forcibly tried to control his breathing, preparing himself for whatever she was going to say next.

'Good bloke, your dad.'

Mills exhaled.

'He helped my Gary when no other bugger would.' She nodded to herself and her gaze slid away as she focused somewhere in the middle distance. 'Charlie Mills.' She shook her head slowly, smiling. Then quick as a flash, snapped out of it. 'You tell him I said hello.'

Mills twitched a half smile at her and said nothing. He wasn't keen to get into a conversation about his father.

'Shocking what happened to those little girls.' Mrs Benson tutted and scooped the dog onto her lap. 'You must be thinking something like that has happened to Casey.'

'We're not thinking anything just now,' Murray said.

'But the longer it goes on…' She held on firmly to the dog. 'You found Trisha's boyfriend yet?'

'We can't discuss—'

'All right – I know. Trisha kept that one quiet. Lorraine only found out about him Tuesday morning. What's so wrong with him she didn't tell anyone she had a new fella? That's what you've got to ask yourself.' She fished the remote from the side of the seat cushion and the television came back to life.

Mills looked at Murray who shrugged back at him. He thanked Mrs Benson for her time and insisted they could see themselves out.

'Make sure you shut the door properly behind you,' she said, then started to zap through channels as if the two detectives had already left.

Safely back outside on the walkway Murray let out a whistle. 'God – what do you make of all that? No love lost between that old witch and Collins.' Her phone started to buzz. 'Significant, do you reckon?' She answered the call and spoke in monosyllables for a few moments before hanging up.

'We've been summoned,' she said, pocketing the phone.

'Back to base? Is the boss asking for us?'

'No. Sorry to disappoint.'

'What's that supposed to mean?'

'I've seen the way you look at her when you think no one's watching.'

'Piss off.' He started towards the stairs. 'What is it then?'

'There's been another sighting of Casey.'

'Another one? How many hoaxes is that?'

'Might not be a hoax. Remember what the DCI said – we've got to judge every call on its merits. Might lead to something.' She overtook him and quickly reached the stairwell. 'Besides, this particular concerned member of the public is refusing to divulge the information to the uniforms with her.'

'Why?'

'Whatever she's got to say, she's only prepared to say it to CID.'

FIFTEEN

Judging by the look on her face, Ashley Montgomery was about to explode with excitement.

Angela Tate was sitting at her desk, on the phone, listening to the echoing rasp of her own breath. Another nuisance phone call. She'd promised herself she'd wait until the total went into double figures before she insisted the switchboard vet all incoming calls. This was call number ten.

As soon as she put down the phone Ashley grabbed her arm. 'Come with me,' she said. 'I've got someone I want you to talk to.'

'I don't have time for it, whatever it is.'

Ashley tugged a little harder. 'You are so going to thank me when you find out. I could have gone straight to Harriet with it. But I didn't.'

Harriet? What had possessed the lowly intern to refer to their esteemed editor by her first name?

'You've got five minutes,' Tate said. 'And that's your lot. Five minutes including travel time.'

'In that case, we'd better take the lift.'

Tate glowered at Ashley all the way from her desk to the lift. 'This had better be worth it,' she told the over-excited intern when the lift doors closed.

'Just you wait.'

For the last twenty-four hours Tate had been trying to devise a plan to permanently wipe the cocky smirk from Gary Benson's face. All she'd come up with so far were a series of increasingly frustrating dead-ends. She knew there was really only one person who could ensure Benson got what he deserved. And that person wasn't about to offer assistance.

The lift doors slid open and Ashley led Tate down the plushly carpeted corridor on the fifth floor. The intern ran ahead of her and stopped outside a glass and stainless steel walled conference room. She gestured for Tate to hurry.

'Does *Harriet* know you're using the board room?' Tate called after her.

'When I tell her why, I'm sure she won't mind at all.' Ashley grabbed the door handle as Tate drew near.

The journalist stared through the glass and was alarmed to discover a plump figure slumped in a leather and chrome chair, her head resting on a fat arm spread across the table, her other hand wrapped around a two-litre bottle of Coke. Chelsea Collins appeared to be asleep.

'What have you done?' Tate pulled Ashley from the door and marched her down the corridor.

'Wait till you hear what she has to say. It's dynamite!'

'I don't care what she's saying. The girl's fourteen years old. Her little sister has disappeared. Have you any idea how vulnerable she is right now? What's the matter with you?' Tate started back towards the lift. 'Take her home before I really lose my temper.'

'Five minutes you said.' Suddenly Ashley sounded like a petulant teenager herself.

'I doubt whatever Chelsea Collins can say to me will change my mind in the space of ninety seconds.'

'You won't know unless you listen to her story.' The intern ran past Tate and stopped in the middle of the corridor, blocking her exit.

'Does what she's told you help in finding Casey?' Tate asked.

'Not exactly.'

'Then stop wasting my time.'

'But it might. Somehow. Even if it doesn't, it's a great story. Honestly.'

Tate shook her head. 'One minute. Not a moment longer.'

Ashley ducked around her and opened the door. She barked something at Chelsea and much to Tate's surprise, the girl sat to attention. She wiped away the drool that had collected at the corner of her mouth and stared at Ashley as if waiting for her next instruction. Was it possible Chelsea Collins had something important to say about her missing sister? Up until now, the girl had displayed remarkably little concern.

Ashley sat next to the flushed-faced teenager. 'Tell Angela exactly what you told me,' she said.

Angela? Tate would have to have a word with her about that.

'There's no need to be nervous,' Ashley said.

Judging by the slackness of her expression, Chelsea appeared to be nerve-free. She turned her head towards her new best friend.

'Go on,' Ashley encouraged. 'She doesn't bite.'

Tate glared at the intern. The girl obviously had no understanding just how ferocious her bite could be. She might just have to find out the hard way. She turned to Chelsea and tried to soften her tone. 'Do you know something that might help find Casey?'

A flicker of confusion flashed across Chelsea's face. She looked again at Ashley, presumably seeking guidance. Or reassurance.

'I'm not pissing about with this.' Tate started towards the door. 'Take her home.'

'Wait!' Ashley said. And then more quietly, 'Don't let me down, Chelsea. Tell Angela what you told me. You promised me, remember?'

The teenager swallowed. Tate could hear the thick mucus in the back of the girl's throat.

'It's all right – go on. Tell her what happened on Monday.'

Chelsea took a breath and kept her eyes trained on Ashley. 'Mum left me to look after Casey. And Ryan and Lola. All on my own.' Her shoulders slumped in resignation, as if she'd just reluctantly revealed a much sought-after secret.

Tate blinked. 'Really?' She wheeled round to the intern. 'Is that seriously what you've dragged me in here for?'

Ashley dug an elbow into her young charge's fleshy ribs.

'All night, I mean. I'm only fourteen.'

Tate took a deep breath to control her rising irritation.

'It's not the first time, neither. She just leaves us. So she can be with her boyfriend. When she comes home she stinks of booze.'

Tate held Ashley's gaze. 'You think this is a story?' she said, speaking over Chelsea's head. 'In what sense of the word?'

'An exclusive. The real story behind the *suffering* mother. We can reveal what kind of woman Trisha Collins really is.'

'Outside. Now.'

Ashley reluctantly followed Tate back into the corridor.

'Do you have any idea how irresponsible this is?'

The intern started to speak, but Tate cut her off.

'Exactly how much of this genuinely came from her? And how much of it did you invent?'

'I haven't invented anything! It took a bit of coaxing to get her to open up. But as soon as she started to trust me, I couldn't shut her up. I'm like the big sister she never had.'

'Well then she's playing you.' Tate peered in at the teenager, who had resumed her previous slumped position, as if her skeleton could no longer support the weight of her body.

'Why would she lie about something like that?'

'That I haven't worked out. If she was going to make something up, you'd think she could have concocted a story a little more damaging than being forced to babysit her own brother and sisters. It's hardly child abuse.'

'It started a couple of years ago. She was only twelve at the time.'

'My God, you've lived a cosseted existence. I suppose the au pair was there for you twenty-four seven?'

'That's got nothing to do with it.'

'I expect she couldn't come up with anything more compelling due to a lack of imagination.'

'She also told me Casey was scared of her mother. That she'd tried to run away before.'

'And did Chelsea tell you why she hasn't mentioned that important fact to the police?'

'She's too frightened to.'

'Oh so now the whole family is living in fear?'

'You're too close to Trisha, you're not seeing anyone else's point of view.'

'I know when I'm being made a fool of.' Tate took another deep breath in an attempt to quell the anger rising up like bile from her chest and into her mouth. 'Have you even tried to corroborate anything she's told you?'

'How can I?'

'Dear God. Do you at least have specific dates and times?'

'I don't have an actual list as such.'

'Take her home before someone reports *her* missing.' Tate glanced into the room. Chelsea's chair was empty. The girl had wandered over to the floor-to-ceiling window and was looking out at the oblique view of the Thames.

'But it's wrong – a twelve-year-old child expected to look after her two-year-old sister all night. What if one of the kids had got ill?'

'It's not going to help get Casey back is it? Have you asked her how she feels about her missing sister? Has she volunteered any information about that?'

'Of course I've asked her. She clams right up. She's too upset to talk about it.'

Tate watched the teenager pressing her nose against the glass. 'Maybe you just haven't asked her the right way.'

'There's something else – something more serious. I wasn't sure how you'd react, so I told Chelsea not to mention it straightaway.'

Now Tate felt as if she was being played. 'This isn't a bloody game. There's a nine-year-old child out there, possibly terrified, probably dead. And yet somehow you think it's in the public interest to wreck the reputation of her distraught mother?'

'But it might just change your mind. About Trisha. About everything.' Ashley opened the door and joined Chelsea at the far end of the room. 'Great view isn't it?' she said, keeping her tone light.

The girl nodded without shifting her gaze from the window.

Against her better judgment, Tate stepped back into the room.

'Why don't you tell Angela what you told me? About the other stuff.'

'Why do I need to tell her? I thought you were going to write about me.'

'Just tell her.'

The teenager chewed on the inside of her cheek for a few moments. Finally she spoke. 'Mum gave us drugs,' she said quietly, keeping her face turned towards the window. 'So we wouldn't wake up while she was out.'

'What?' Tate stepped closer, tried to get a better angle on the girl's face, but Chelsea turned her head further away. 'What did you say?'

'I saw her once, crushing up pills and putting them into our drinks.'

'When was this?' Tate felt a knot of tension tightening in her stomach. Why wouldn't the girl look at her?

'She did it all the time,' Chelsea said.

'You're saying it's something she did every night?'

The girl nodded.

'Even when she wasn't going out?'

Chelsea looked at Ashley for support. Tate pushed them apart and forced herself between the teenager and the window. She stared squarely into Chelsea's face.

'And now? Are you saying she drugs you now?'

'Yeah. Especially Ryan. He never likes going to bed.'

'What pills?'

Chelsea shrugged. 'Sleeping pills, I suppose.'

'And this is something she does every single night, to all of you?'

'Not me, not anymore. Not since I saw her. I won't touch any drink she makes for me.'

'You do realise how serious this allegation is?' Tate asked her. 'You're sure it's true?'

Chelsea again glanced towards Ashley. 'I'm not making it up.'

Tate pulled her phone from a pocket. 'You have to tell the police.'

Chelsea stumbled away from her. 'No way.'

'If this is true, you have to make a statement. Then they'll talk to your mum about it. You have to be absolutely sure of what you're saying. Do you understand?'

'But Ashley said she was gonna write a story about me. She said you'd help her. I don't want to talk to the police.'

'I promised we'd protect her,' Ashley said. 'She's scared of the police.'

'Too bad.' Tate punched the first nine into her phone.

'Wait!' The intern held a hand over Tate's. 'Not like this. Let me talk to Chelsea first.' She squeezed the girl's thick arm.

Chelsea pulled away from her and hurried towards the door. 'I'm not speaking to them. You can't make me.'

Tate moved close to Ashley and lowered her voice. 'What did you think you were doing?'

'It's OK. Leave her to me. I can persuade her to talk. I can reassure her.'

They both turned and looked at Chelsea, who was snatching the two-litre bottle of Coke from the table and heading for the door.

'Do you really believe she's telling the truth?'

Ashley defiantly stuck her chin in the air. 'I'm not stupid. I can tell when someone's lying to me.'

'If this isn't true, and you do somehow persuade Chelsea to go to the police, have you any idea how much trouble she'll be in, wasting their time?'

'But it *is* true.'

'And have you thought about Trisha in all of this?'

'What about her?'

'Don't you think the woman's suffering enough already?'

SIXTEEN

In less than ten minutes DCs Mills and Murray had zigzagged their way off the Shakespeare Estate, headed south on Benhill Road and crossed over the A202.

And landed on another planet.

Camberwell Grove was a world away from the grubby brick and concrete low rises of the Essex Estate. The road was wide and lined with impressive hundred-year-old horse chestnuts. Mills pulled up outside a detached, double-fronted, red brick house. A squad car was parked on the paved drive next to a manicured rectangle of lawn.

Two uniformed officers were standing beside their vehicle, listening intently to a slim, immaculately dressed woman, her perfectly made-up face contorted with anger. She seemed to be giving the two constables a dressing down.

One of the officers raised his head for a moment, like a man coming up for air, and spotted Mills. Relief spread across his face.

'Brace yourself,' Mills said, more to himself than Murray.

Murray pulled down the passenger sun visor and checked her face in the mirror. 'Looks to me like she's making a complaint rather than providing information.' She produced a lipstick from a pocket and quickly applied it.

'What's with the war paint?' Mills asked.

'Just want her to take me seriously. My power suit's at the dry cleaners.'

One of the uniforms hurried over to their car. Murray buzzed down the window.

'Thank God you're here.'

'What's her beef?'

'She's demanding to speak to CID. Doesn't think we're up to the job.'

As they climbed out of the car Mills took a closer look up and down the street. On both sides of the road large detached houses had expensive cars parked outside, security alarms prominently displayed next to first floor windows, video cameras mounted above front doors. He was surprised the residents hadn't sought permission to erect giant iron gates at both ends of the street to keep out undesirables.

'We've followed up half a dozen false sightings already today,' the young PC said. 'And that's just us two.' He shook his head. 'What gets into people?'

'You think this is another one?' Murray asked.

'Can't tell – she won't say much to us. But she must have been convincing enough on the phone to the incident room, else we wouldn't be here at all.' He glanced towards his colleague, who was still getting his ear bent.

'Looks like she's got plenty to say,' Mills said.

'She's been complaining about the Neighbourhood Watch group.'

Suddenly the woman in the expensive suit turned towards them. 'Do you know how long I've been waiting for you to arrive?' she shouted.

'Madam.' Murray strode up the drive. 'We are rather stretched at the moment, as you can imagine, given the circumstances. We got here just as soon as we could.'

Instinctively, the woman took a step back and looked Murray up and down. 'Are you the officer in charge?'

'*Detective*, actually. Detective Constable Murray, madam.' She held out her hand.

'Fiona Wells,' the woman snapped, ignoring the outstretched hand. 'I'm expecting the estate agent in ten minutes.' She looked up and down the street. 'Seeing a police car in my drive isn't going to help me sell my house, is it?'

Mills ambled over to them, hands deep in his pockets.

'You called us, madam,' Murray said. 'The car's here at your request.'

'But that was over two hours ago.'

'Perhaps your prospective buyers could rearrange for another day?' Murray tipped her head to one side and set her mouth somewhere between a smile and a grimace.

The anxious homeowner turned back to the uniformed officer. 'Surely you can go now? Take your car off my drive?'

Mills was tempted to ask them to stay exactly where they were, just to spite the woman. But they had better things to do. There was no point in all four of them wasting their time.

'When did you see the girl, madam?' Murray retrieved her notebook from a pocket.

Mrs Wells watched the squad car reverse out of her drive, no doubt making sure her ornamental fence posts weren't in danger of getting clipped by a thoughtlessly positioned wing mirror. 'This morning,' she said eventually. 'After I dropped the children at school.'

'Time?'

'About eight-thirty.'

Murray scribbled a down a note. 'And you called the incident room straightaway?'

'More or less. I'm not sure.'

'It's OK – we can check the logs.'

'Can you describe the girl?' Mills asked.

'She looked exactly like the little girl in all the photos. I've already explained all this to the people I spoke to on the phone. Shortish, blonde hair tied back in a ponytail.'

'Was she with anyone?'

The woman frowned. '*With* anyone?'

'An adult? Another child?'

'No – she was all alone.'

'Can you show us where she was?'

Mrs Wells pointed across the street. 'Next to that tree over there.'

'And you saw her from inside your house, or out here on the drive?'

'What's that got to do with anything?'

'If you could just answer the question, madam?'

'Inside.' She nodded to herself. 'Naturally, if I'd been outside I would have crossed the street and spoken to her.'

'Naturally.' Murray smiled at her. 'And did you then leave your house? To try to speak to her?'

The woman paused to think. Mills wasn't sure if she was having trouble remembering what had actually happened or inventing the next part of her story. 'Yes – of course I did. But by the time I'd grabbed my keys and locked the door, she'd disappeared. That's when I called the police.'

'You don't know which direction she took?'

'No idea.'

'What was she wearing?'

'A yellow coat and green leggings. Little purple boots on her feet.'

Mills rocked back on his heels. He glanced at Murray, who shoved her notebook back into her pocket. Bloody time-wasters. He clenched his jaw, unable to trust what he might say if he spoke.

'What is it?' Mrs Wells said.

'Why did you call us out here today, madam?' Murray asked.

'What kind of question is that? I'm just doing my duty as a—'

'There was no girl, was there, Mrs Wells?' Murray blew out an exasperated sigh.

'I've told you. I saw—'

'The clothes you've described are the ones Casey Collins was wearing in the CCTV photograph taken three days before she disappeared – the photograph used on all the publicity material. The one you would have seen in the papers and on the news. On all the posters attached to lampposts and trees in the area. She was wearing something else entirely the day she went missing.'

Mrs Wells took a breath and for a moment Mills feared she would launch into another story to justify the mistake she had made in the first. Instead she exhaled and shook her head. 'Do you know how many burglaries we've had in this road, since the beginning of the year?' She didn't wait for a reply. 'Three.'

Mills clenched his fists.

'All this manpower suddenly appears for a few days and then what? You all melt away again as if you were never here. What happened to police visibility? A reassuring presence on every street in the borough? It's easy to make promises in glossy brochures. Quite another thing to follow through.'

'Are you suggesting we shouldn't bring in extra officers to search for a missing nine-year-old girl? What if it was one of your children?' Murray was doing a tremendous job of maintaining her cool.

'Of course not. I'm suggesting nothing of the sort.' She took another breath. 'I'm sorry – I must have been mistaken earlier. I did see a girl. But it was obviously a different one.'

Mills started to move away, unable to trust what he might say if he listened to this woman a moment longer.

'Please, don't go,' she said. 'I'd like you to look at something for me.'

'We really don't have time to—'

'It'll take less than a minute. Seeing as you're here anyway.' She marched down the drive and waited for them on the pavement.

Mills tilted his head and looked at Murray, who shrugged back at him and said quietly, 'Why don't we humour her?'

Once they joined her on the pavement, Mrs Wells led the two detectives five yards up the street to the neighbouring property. Peering through a gap in a dense evergreen hedge, Mills saw an ancient Ford Fiesta, its tyreless wheels balancing on four piles of house bricks. Three filthy double mattresses and half a dozen discarded white goods occupied the remaining space, weeds growing wild and thick between them. The windowpanes on all three floors of the house appeared to be plastered with old newspapers, the glass grey with a thick layer of London grime.

'It's a disgrace,' the woman exclaimed. 'Thank God for the hedge. At least that cuts out the worst of the eyesore. But it's still a monstrosity. I'm sure it must encourage vandalism. And burglaries too, I wouldn't be surprised. It's been empty all the years I've been here.' She was actually wringing her hands. 'And I know for a fact it's been putting my buyers off.'

'Oh we wouldn't want that to happen.' Mills wrapped his hands around the bars of an ornate metal gate straddling a gap in the hedge and shook it hard. The padlock held firm. 'Is this usually locked?'

Mrs Wells nodded.

He took a step back and looked up at the dirty windows.

'I've had environmental health round,' Mrs Wells said. 'But they won't do anything.'

'What is it you think we can do?' Murray asked.

'Make a report, get it condemned… something.'

'Don't you think we've got better things to do?' Mills checked the height of the gate from the ground. Barely three inches: not enough space for even a child to squeeze under. He looked again at the overgrown weeds beyond. They were completely undisturbed. No one had ventured inside for months. Maybe even years. 'Sorry, madam. Nothing we can do for you.'

'But as soon as people see it they refuse to even set foot in my house.'

'Having this "monstrosity" next door didn't put you off buying your property,' Mills said, his words clipped.

'My house was as dilapidated as this when we first moved in. I assumed someone would do this one up too.'

'Then you miscalculated, didn't you?' Mills could feel his throat tightening. 'Try knocking fifty grand off the asking price.'

'But I shouldn't have to do that.'

Mills took a deep breath, but before he started to tell this woman exactly what he thought she should do, Murray dragged him away.

'Bloody upperclass—' He stopped himself even though they were well out of earshot.

As they returned to the car a Land Rover Freelander pulled up to the kerb. Mills snatched his ID from a pocket, marched over to the vehicle and waved his warrant card at the driver as he tapped on the glass. The woman in the green quilted jacket opened her window, her face a perfect mask of Botox and thick make-up.

'Here to view the house?' Mills asked.

The woman, who, Mills was sure, would have looked concerned if she'd had some control over the muscles in her face, nodded back at him.

'I wouldn't bother,' he said. 'Notorious crack den just next door.'

SEVENTEEN

Angela Tate watched from reception as Ashley hooked her arm through Chelsea's and walked her out of the building. The intern waved down a black cab and heaved the door open. Chelsea Collins hesitated, looked over her shoulder at Tate then shuffled backwards on the pavement. Ashley threw her hands up in the air in frustration then bundled the teenager into the taxi.

Tate wearily made her way back upstairs to her desk and collapsed onto a chair. She hadn't really been sleeping since the Casey Collins story broke and when she did manage to drift off, her dreams were plagued with images of the Shakespeare Estate. Faces of people she hadn't seen for years loomed over her, all of them angry at her about something she couldn't understand. She leaned back in her chair and kicked her shoes off under the desk.

What had Ashley been thinking? The girl had supposedly studied journalism at university. Although, in Tate's opinion, anyone who seriously believed it was something that could be taught in a lecture hall or a classroom rather than on the job didn't understand the first thing about it. Ashley seemed bright and her ambition was as keen as her elbows were sharp. Yet still she had allowed herself to be taken in by a fourteen-year-old who would probably leave the local comprehensive with barely a GCSE to her name.

Tate lifted one leg over the other and started to massage the ball of her foot. She closed her eyes as she drove the tip of her thumb into the tender flesh and considered the possibility of Chelsea Collins managing to outwit a university graduate. Of course it was always possible that Ashley had engineered the whole thing herself, promising the suggestible and needy teenager with heaven only knew what in exchange for some dirt on her mother. Was that possible? Would an enterprising intern go to those lengths to haul herself up the career ladder?

'If you need a nap, maybe you should find somewhere less… exposed.'

Tate snapped open her eyes to discover Frank Carter sitting on the edge of the desk opposite hers. 'Jesus, Ange. You really do look done in.'

'You always could make a girl feel special.'

'It's a gift.' Frank smiled at her. 'Had any more dodgy phone calls?'

'Actually I was just about to sort that out.' She stared at his face, aware something didn't look right, but unable to identify what. 'Are you trying to grow a beard?'

'No "trying" about it. I'm going for the rugged look. Rugged and lived in.'

'I don't think you need any help with that. Who are you trying to impress, anyway?'

'Nobody.' He attempted a nonchalant shrug.

'Francis Carter, I do believe you've managed to get yourself a date. Found some poor cow to drag to that dreary musical on Valentine's, have you?'

'There's no need to mock.'

'So you do have a date. Do I know her?'

Frank ignored the question and pointed at the phone sitting on her desk. 'Has Mr Heavy-Breather actually spoken to you yet?'

'Not so far, but the breathing's definitely getting louder.'

'I don't want to be funny, Ange, but I could think of more appropriate material to wank over.'

'You mean the sound of my voice doesn't do it for you?' She reached under the desk for her shoes. 'It's not that kind of breathing, anyway.'

'Have the telecoms people tried to trace it?'

'It's a job for the police if I want to take it any further, apparently.'

'And do you?'

'I haven't decided yet. But I can't help thinking there's more to it, for it to be going on for this long.' Tate shoved her feet into her shoes and stood up.

'Where're you going?'

'I've got an editor to harass. Or I might just harangue her, depending on my mood by the time I reach her office.'

'I see you managed to shake off your limpid intern.'

'Ms Montgomery is busy learning some important lessons in journalism. The hard way.'

'You fixed up anything with the Collins woman for me to go round there again? I'd like to do more of a fly-on-the-wall series of photographs.'

'I'm not sure that's going to happen. Last time I spoke to her, Trisha was barely holding it together.'

Frank shook his head. 'I was looking through my picture archive last night. I've still got the negs from 1979. I found some group portraits of the kids from the three estates. I couldn't be certain, but I suppose Trisha Collins would have been in one or two of them.'

'Probably.' So would Gary Benson and his ghoulish little friends, Tate thought. She wondered if she should tell Frank about her confrontation with Benson the day before.

'Spooky it's happened again, all these years later. With little Casey looking so much like the girls who disappeared before.'

'Tragic is the word you're looking for, I think.'

'You don't suppose there's a connection, do you?' Frank started scratching at his new stubble.

The possibility hadn't escaped her, especially when Trisha had worried she was being punished because of what happened before.

'Do you?' he persisted.

'I'm keeping my mind open. First rule of journalism.'

'Tell that to your intern.'

Tate waved at Frank as she made her way to the exit. Trudging up the stairs to Harriet Fowler's office she thought again about Chelsea Collins' story. The more she considered the tale, the less she was convinced there was any truth to it. All that stuff about Trisha drugging her kids sounded far too similar to a case that had happened a few years back in Huddersfield. Chelsea was certainly old enough to remember the details. In fact, she would have been the same age as the girl who had been kidnapped. The story was all over the media at the time, it must have had quite an impact on an impressionable ten-year-old. But what would have possessed Chelsea to suggest her own mother was capable of something similar?

Tate reached her editor's office and banged on the door, opening it without waiting for a reply.

'Uncanny,' Fowler said. 'You must have read my mind. I was just about to call you.'

Tate's heart sank. 'Oh?'

'I need you to change tack for tomorrow's first edition. Our readers are bored with *a parent's worst nightmare* stories from Collins. The angle's been overworked by every rag out there.

'I'm not going to dish any dirt on Trisha, if that's what you're after. That's been just as done to death by the red-tops.'

'No – nothing like that. I want you to dig up as much as you can about…' She paused to look at a notebook sitting on her desk. 'Raymond Dixon.'

An instant pulse of adrenalin almost rocked Tate sideways. No one had mentioned his name to her in years. Over the last forty-eight hours she'd found herself thinking of him more and more. She sank onto the chair in front of Fowler's desk.

'Are you all right? What is it?'

'I'm fine.' Tate swallowed.

'I've been chatting to Rita – the librarian?'

'And?'

'She told me about the disappearances that happened in '79. Your name came up.'

'So?'

'It's not like you to be so monosyllabic. What *is* wrong with you? You really do look odd.' Fowler took off her glasses and tossed them on the desk. 'You were the paper's crime correspondent during the investigations, you've still got the best police contacts, I want you to write a feature comparing the historic cases with the Casey Collins one.'

'People don't want a rehash of something that happened that long ago.'

'Oh I think they do. I'm surprised the tabloids aren't all over it. It's only a matter of time before they dig it up. But right now we're ahead of the curve. So – I'd like something on my desk by close of play today. Starting with a profile of Dixon. Can you do that?'

'No.'

'What?'

'He's done his time. Why punish him all over again?'

'He was convicted of killing a six-year-old girl. Plenty of people think he should still be behind bars.'

'So we persecute him in print instead? This is the *Evening News*, Harriet. Let the tabloids do what they do. We're not in the business of stooping so low.'

'Believe it or not, we are in the newspaper business. Do I have to remind you what circulation has dropped to? You can use Ashley for support. Get her to do some of the legwork for you. Where is she, anyway? I haven't seen her at all today.'

'She had an appointment.'

'Work-related?'

'Oh yes.'

'And how are the two of you getting on?'

'That's why I came to see you.' She let out a sigh. 'We're not. I'm not the right… *mentor* for the girl.' Tate hated using the word. Especially about herself.

'Not feeling threatened by her youth and boundless enthusiasm are we?'

'I'm not sure we see eye to eye about… methodology.' Another management-speak word. Tate suddenly felt the urge to rinse out her mouth.

'That's precisely why she should work with you. Show her how to do things the right way.' She smiled.

'Why do you care? We have interns in and out of this place all the time. You've never taken an interest before.'

'Why *don't* you care is a better question.'

'I can write you a list if you want.'

'Give her another week and we'll reassess.'

Tate turned towards the door.

'So – this Dixon profile – end of play, yes?'

Tate let out a long breath before she answered. 'How does it help Casey Collins? Shouldn't she be our priority? Keep her on the front page. I've got photos from Trisha we haven't used yet. A big picture of an innocent, blue-eyed blonde girl – that'll shift some copies.'

'That's crap and you know it – what *has* got into you?'

'Get somebody else to do your hatchet job.'

Tate slammed the door on her way out.

She arrived back at her desk to discover an envelope sitting squarely on the desktop. For a moment she wondered if Frank had left her a ticket for another event on Valentine's Day. But her name was typed neatly on the address label and that wasn't Frank's style at all. Before she had a chance to open it, her landline started to ring. She picked up, hoping it was the heavy-breather, ready to give him an earful.

'Hello, Ange, is that you?' Trisha Collins' voice sounded thick and congested.

'Hi Trisha, how are you? Have you heard anything? Has there been any progress?' Tate wondered if she'd found out about Chelsea's visit, but couldn't risk mentioning it.

'No… nothing yet.' Trisha let out a long, hissing sigh. 'Listen, I'm really sorry… but I've been thinking about it and it's for the best.'

'What is?'

'I don't want to do any more interviews. I can't do it. My nerves won't take it.'

'We can ease back a bit, of course. But I really think you should—'

'I've made up my mind.'

'What's brought this on?'

'I've been speaking to Gary…'

Of course. Gary fucking Benson.

'And he thinks I should only speak to telly and radio people, that it'll do more good than a local paper.'

Local?

'But what do *you* think?'

'I just want my baby back. That's all I can think about.'

'Why don't I pop round now – we can talk it through.'

'No! Gary's here. I don't want any more trouble like yesterday. I can't cope with it. Sorry, Ange.'

She hung up.

Tate slammed the receiver back in its cradle and snatched the envelope from her desk. She ripped it open and yanked out a single sheet of paper. There were just a handful of lines printed on it. As she read them she felt a tingle creep up the back of her legs. She scanned the office then quickly made her way downstairs.

At reception Tate slid the envelope onto the high counter. 'Clive – when did this arrive?' She cast an eye around the large foyer. None of the handful of visitors milling about looked like couriers.

The uniformed receptionist plucked his glasses from the top of his head and studied the front of the envelope. 'Came about ten minutes ago.'

'Do you remember who brought it?'

'Just some messenger guy.'

'What did he look like?'

'I didn't see his face – he kept his motorcycle helmet on.' He lowered his voice. 'He wouldn't take it off when I asked him to.'

Tate ran outside. A bitter wind was howling up Blackfriars Road. She checked left and right and across the street, just in case the messenger had decided to hang around. There was no sign of him. After a few moments she slipped back inside, trembling slightly, unsure whether it was the cold or the shock making her shake. She looked down at the crisp white sheet of paper gripped tight in her hand and read the message again.

Why did you give up on me?
I needed your help then more than Collins does now
And I still need it. Help ME, not her. Before it's too late

Although there was no signature beneath the message, and no name on the envelope, Tate had absolutely no doubt who had sent it.

EIGHTEEN

The flat was colder than the early morning February street outside. Tate thumped the inert boiler attached to the bathroom wall with her fist. When the boiler didn't spontaneously spark back into life she padded back to the living room, cigarette in one hand, fortified mug of coffee in the other. She flipped on the television, wondering if sorting out her ailing central heating system might be a job she could safely delegate to the intern. She grabbed her mobile and selected Ashley's number from the long list of unanswered calls – Tate was determined not to add the intern's number to her phone's address book. For at least the tenth time in as many hours, Tate's call was diverted straight to Ashley's over-enthusiastic outgoing message imploring the caller to leave their details after the bleep.

She hadn't managed to speak to Ashley since the intern left the *Evening News* building with Chelsea Collins the day before. She suspected that as soon as the taxi pulled away into traffic on Blackfriars Road, Chelsea Collins would have confessed to inventing the allegations about her mother.

Thank God Ashley had come to her with the story first. Given her editor's attitude about the Raymond Dixon profile the day before, if Fowler had got her hands on Chelsea's fabrication, the story would have been all over the lunchtime edition.

Tate shoved the phone onto the dining table, right next to the note from the mysterious courier that had been sitting there since the night before. She gingerly picked it up by a corner and read the note again. There was no doubt in her mind that Raymond Dixon had written it. Who else would accuse her of giving up on them? Who else would mention Trisha Collins?

She re-read the last line: *Help ME, not her. Before it's too late.* Too late for what? Was that some kind of threat? She wondered if Dixon himself had been the helmeted courier and she'd missed seeing him by a matter of minutes. A shiver crept across her back and down her arms. She tried to shrug it off. If he really needed her help why hadn't he asked for it before? Why leave it until two years *after* his release.

When she'd returned to her desk the day before, after scouring the street for any sign of the courier, she'd wondered whether she should go straight to the police with the note, but decided instead to put in a call to one of her contacts in the Met, asking for any information he could dredge up about Dixon. Anything that she wouldn't be able to find herself via a Google search. She'd considered asking Rita for help, but given the librarian had already spoken to Harriet Fowler about Dixon, and as Tate had absolutely no intention of writing a profile of the man, she thought it better to leave anyone at the paper strictly out of the loop. Her Met contact had promised he would 'see what he could do'. She was still waiting to hear back from him.

She retrieved her current disposable mobile phone from her handbag and called the contact again, leaving a message asking him to get back to her urgently. Not that the word 'urgent' would prompt a faster response. Winkling information out of the Met seemed to be getting harder and harder with each day that passed.

Until recently, Tate had maintained a whole network of contacts in police forces right across the southeast. But since the Leveson Inquiry into press conduct, she could only rely on one or two high-ranking officers in New Scotland Yard to provide her with any information at all, and they got twitchy each time another high profile case came to court. At this rate she'd soon have no one left to help her at all.

She drained her mug and thought about making herself another coffee and brandy cocktail, more for its warming effect than alcohol content, when something on the television stopped her in her tracks. She scrabbled for the remote and turned up the volume, watching aghast as an ashen-faced Chelsea Collins was escorted from the Wapping headquarters of *The Herald* towards a waiting limousine. Tate scanned the faces surrounding the teenager, looking for Ashley Montgomery, wondering if the intern's ambition and impatience had got the better of her and she had taken Chelsea Collins' flimsy tale to a tabloid better known for celebrity scandals than in-depth reporting. Tate tried Ashley's number again and hung up as soon as the voicemail message kicked in.

The reporter on *BBC News* ran through the list of Chelsea's allegations about Trisha. On top of the things she'd told Tate the day before, Chelsea had added physical abuse to the crimes her mother had supposedly committed.

Where was the evidence of that? It seemed the girl possessed the facility of invention after all. Unless Ashley Montgomery had engineered the whole thing. If she had, her little plan had badly backfired. Chelsea Collins had jumped ship.

'You stupid, stupid girl,' Tate shouted at the television as she searched for Trisha's number in her contacts list. This call went straight to voicemail too. Tate left a sympathetic message and hurried to the bedroom. She flung open the wardrobe doors and was about to pull out a recently dry cleaned suit when the ringtone of her disposable phone trilled from the living room. She ran the length of her flat and managed to pick up on the last ring.

'You took your bloody time,' she said and padded back to the bedroom.

'You think I don't have better things to do?' her contact said, sounding remarkably pissed off so early in the morning.

'What did you manage to glean?'

'Not much.'

'I'll take whatever you've got. You can start by telling me Dixon's current address.'

The line went quiet.

'Paul? Are you still there?' She sat down on the bed.

'Look, I can't speak for long – do you know how risky this is getting?'

'I didn't hear you complaining the last time I handed you a thick envelope of used twenties.'

'I'm just… it's—'

'Address?'

'You're not going to see him.'

'Is that a question or an instruction?'

'He lives just outside Leeds. Has done since his release.'

'He didn't move back to London?'

'Would you if you'd killed a kid there?'

'The jury's still out on that one.' A fresh image of Gary Benson's tormenting nine-year-old face popped into her head.

'Not the one who convicted him in 1980. Besides… no – I'll get to that in a minute.'

'Give me his address.'

'I can't.'

'Can't or won't?'

'Christ – give me a break will you?'

'What will you tell me?'

'Dixon's on a life licence, seeing a probation officer every fortnight. Should be every week, but what with the cuts… anyway, he's been behaving himself since he got out. Doing a spot of voluntary work, gardening for old people who can't manage it themselves. He completed a course on landscape gardening while he was inside.'

'That's all deeply fascinating,' Tate said. 'But no use to me. Is he allowed to travel freely?'

'He can go wherever he likes in the UK, but he can't go abroad.'

'So in theory he could be in London as we speak?'

'In theory, but he's not likely to want to visit the old neighbourhood is he? Why are you asking about him, anyway? Is it connected to this missing kid?'

Tate didn't want to tell him she'd received a note from Dixon. Not until she'd worked out why he'd sent it. And why he'd chosen to send it now. She managed a non-committal, 'just wondering' and left it at that.

'It seems Dixon is a model ex-prisoner. Not put a foot wrong in nearly two years.'

'If he did do something,' Tate said, choosing not to be specific, 'what would it take for him to go back inside?'

'There's a long list of prohibited activities, but Dixon's been meeting all the conditions of his licence. If he committed an actual offence his feet wouldn't touch the ground. If he only broke a condition he'd get a warning. But three strikes and he's in.' He started laughing at his own joke. 'Come on, Ange – you've got to admit that was a bit funny. It is only eight o'clock in the morning. And I had a rough night.'

'What was it you were going to tell me before?'

'I don't remember. Look I've really got to go.'

'Something about his conviction?'

'Oh yeah – Dixon insisted he'd been wrongly convicted right up until 2004.'

'You're not telling me he actually admitted he was guilty?'

'Not as such, no.'

'Then what happened in 2004?'

'He got another knockback. He was refused parole for a third time. After that he agreed to take part in his first offending behaviour programme. It's not admitting guilt exactly, but it is effectively agreeing that he had behavioural issues he needed to address.'

'And what would that entail?'

'Oh you know the sort of thing… sitting round in a circle talking through his feelings, taking an anger management course, maybe. Agreeing to go on anti-depressants.'

'And suddenly a bit of therapy is the same as an admission of guilt?'

'It's the way some people see it. Anyway – it worked. Eventually. He got released, didn't he?'

'So are you telling me if he hadn't admitted he had problems he could still be banged up right now?'

'That's the thing with indeterminate sentences – long as a piece of string. Even though he pretty much kept his nose clean all the time he was inside.'

'Pretty much?'

'Look, I really do have to go.'

'Oh come on, Paul.'

He let out a noisy breath that sounded like a fierce wind blowing at the other end of the line. 'Because of his offence, Dixon was kept on a special wing of each prison he was held in, for his own protection. With the nonces and the ex-cops. Must have got to him eventually, keeping that sort of company, because during a stint in Wormwood Scrubs he hit a fellow inmate so hard the bloke spent three days in the prison hospital.'

NINETEEN

Ralph Mills still had his fist raised, ready to bang on the door again, when it opened.

Trisha Collins stood in the doorway. She took one look at McKittrick and Mills then rocked up onto her toes and peered down the landing towards the stairwell. 'Where is she?'

'If we could just come in, Trisha.' McKittrick said gently.

'Where's Chelsea? Why haven't you fetched her home?'

'Let's go inside shall we?' McKittrick took a step forward, forcing Collins to retreat into the hall.

Mills let out a breath he hadn't realised he'd been holding, preparing himself for whatever chaos would greet them inside. The living room was eerily quiet. Lorraine O'Donnell perched on an arm of the sofa and Kapoor was sitting on the rug trying to keep the youngest Collins child distracted.

'What's happening?' Trisha demanded. 'Chelsea's only fourteen – why haven't you brought her back to me?'

'Please sit down, Trisha.' McKittrick was quiet but firm. She guided Collins to the sofa. 'Social services are involved now. We're making arrangements to pick her up from *The Herald*'s headquarters.'

'Social services? Who called them? Jesus Christ. I'm not having Chelsea caught up with that lot.'

'At the moment, we have to believe it's for the best.' McKittrick paused and drew in a quick breath. 'Chelsea has made it clear she doesn't want to come home.'

'Why the bloody hell is anyone listening to her? Hard-faced bloody liar,' O'Donnell said. She opened a packet of cigarettes and shoved one in her mouth.

Collins grabbed her friend's hand and dragged O'Donnell towards her so hard the cigarette flew out of her mouth. 'If you say one more word about Chelsea, you're leaving. And don't expect to come back. Do you understand me?'

O'Donnell yanked her hand from Trisha's grasp and rubbed her wrist. 'Jesus, Trish, I was only saying—'

'Leave it!'

Hearing her mother shout, Lola started to wail.

'Come here, baby. It's all right, mummy's all right.' Collins held out her arms, but Lola buried her head into Kapoor's chest and flung her arms round her neck.

The FLO struggled to get to her feet with the four-year-old clinging on to her like a lab monkey. 'I'll take her to the park for half an hour, Trisha,' Kapoor called over her shoulder as she left the room. At the mention of the park Lola's whining stopped.

'I don't understand why she would make up stories about me. Why would she do that? What's got into her?' Collins stared blankly at the empty space on the carpet where Lola had been moments before. She shook her head. 'I just don't understand it,' she said again.

'I'm really sorry, Trisha,' Mills said, keeping his voice low. 'But we really need to go through all the claims Chelsea has made with you.' He glanced at McKittrick, who nodded at him to continue.

'You don't believe her?' Collins looked at McKittrick, then back at Mills. 'She's made it all up.'

'Course she has,' O'Donnell added.

'Why do you think she might do that?' Mills asked Collins, turning away from O'Donnell to try to discourage her from making any further comments.

'I really don't know. Why would she want to put me through this?'

'She doesn't care about anyone except herself,' O'Donnell said, glancing at Collins. 'I'm sorry, Trish, but you know it's true.'

'Maybe she's jealous of all the attention Casey's been getting,' Collins finally conceded after a long pause. 'But she loves her sister. Why would she think like that?' She shot a warning look at O'Donnell, who had been about to speak, but wisely stopped herself. Collins yanked an old tissue from a pocket and started to pull it apart.

'You have to admit at least part of what Chelsea has said is true. You did leave her to look after Ryan and her sisters on Monday night,' McKittrick said.

Mills was relieved she'd taken on the role of unsympathetic cop.

'I told you before – Kiefer was supposed to come round. I didn't expect to be out all night. I'm never out all night.' She tore the tissue in two. A sudden sob burst from her mouth. 'I'm sorry. Will you speak to Chelsea for me? Make her see sense. Make her tell you the truth. Tell her I love her just as much as Casey.'

O'Donnell grunted and reached down to retrieve her cigarette from the floor. 'You tracked down that paedo teacher yet? You should be out there looking for him, not putting Trisha through it.'

'Oh Christ, Lor,' Collins said. 'Don't bring that up again. I can't think about Mr Cope doing anything—' A strangled sob cut her sentence short.

'I know this is painful for you, Trisha, but we do have to ask you these questions.' Mills gave her a brief smile.

'Have you left the children overnight before? Is it something that happens regularly?' McKittrick asked.

'Of course not!' She turned to her friend. 'Tell them, Lorraine.'

'If I do that means I'm calling Chelsea a liar. You jumped down my throat last time I did that.'

'I don't leave them, honest. Lorraine has Lola with her most days until I get in from work.'

'Another claim Chelsea made about—'

'I've never laid a finger on any of them. Take a look at Lola now if you want. Christ – ask Manisha – she helped me give her a bath yesterday. Don't you think she would have noticed if Lola was covered in bruises?'

McKittrick held up her hands. 'I'm not making any judgments. But we do have to follow up all of Chelsea's accusations.'

'Ask her why she's doing this to me, will you? Ask her why she's wasting everybody's time when you should be looking for her sister.' She pulled in a uneven breath and wiped her nose with the disintegrating tissue.

'There remains the other matter that your daughter has alleged,' McKittrick said.

Collins' mouth fell slack, her eyes widened in disbelief. 'Surely you don't believe all that rubbish about drugging her?'

'Do you keep drugs in the flat, Trisha?'

'No!' She glanced at O'Donnell. 'Not how you mean.' She sighed. 'I don't even take them.'

'What do you have?'

'Just some sleeping pills. I can get a bit… wound up sometimes. I might take a pill now and then when I really can't get off to sleep. But I swear not one has passed my lips since Casey disappeared.'

'Where do you keep them?'

'In the bathroom.' She started to get up. 'I'll fetch them for you.'

Mills jumped to his feet. 'It's all right Ms Collins. I can do that.'

McKittrick stood up too. 'You stay here, Mills. I'll go.' She produced a pair of purple nitrile gloves from a pocket and proceeded to snap them on.

'You'll find the pills in the cabinet above the basin,' Collins called after her as she left the room. 'I really don't use them,' she said, turning back to Mills.

'Shouldn't she have a warrant for that?' O'Donnell said.

'Leave it, Lor.'

'You should put your foot down, Trish. Ask for a warrant.'

'We don't actually need one,' Mills said, still on his feet, aware he was looming over the two women.

'You would say that, wouldn't you?'

'Misuse of Drugs Act. 1971.' Mills attempted a neutral expression, but from the inside it felt more like an embarrassed grimace. His phone started to ring. 'I really should take this,' he said, grateful for the excuse to leave the room.

'It's me.' Cath Murray never referred to herself as anything but 'me' when she called him. 'I'm trying to get hold of the boss. She's not picking up.'

'Hang on,' Mills said. 'I'll go and get her.' He bounded up the stairs three at a time, stopping halfway when he spotted McKittrick through the open bathroom door slipping something into her pocket. He continued to watch as she reached up and collected a handful of packets from the top of a wooden mirror-fronted cabinet. She opened one slim box and withdrew a couple of blister packs. Mills still had the phone pressed to his ear. Murray was rambling on about something. He tuned her out, holding his breath as he saw McKittrick slip the foil-backed strips into her pocket.

Mills exhaled, slowly climbed the remaining stairs and knocked on the open door. McKittrick turned suddenly, a shocked expression on her face. She recovered after a beat.

'What is it?' she snapped.

He waved his mobile at her. 'It's Cath, boss – she said you weren't answering your phone. I just thought I should…' The words tumbled out of his mouth in an awkward rush.

'Tell her I'll call her back.' She narrowed her eyes. 'Is that it?'

'Did you find anything?' he said, unsure whether his boss had any idea what he'd just witnessed.

McKittrick pointed to a folded piece of paper sitting in the cabinet, wedged between a bottle of mouthwash and another of cough syrup.

'You could say that.' An unmistakable tremor had crept into her voice. She carefully placed the packets of pills that were still in her hand on the wide ledge beneath the bathroom window and withdrew the paper wrap from the cabinet, using her gloved middle and forefinger. Her hand was shaking. She laid the paper flat on one opened palm and slowly unwrapped it. Caught up in the central fold was a partially crushed pill sitting on a bed of pale blue powder.

'Perhaps Chelsea's story isn't so far-fetched after all.'

TWENTY

Natasha McKittrick paced the corridor outside the interview room, waiting for DC Murray to arrive. She had expected to continue interviewing Trisha Collins with Mills, but he'd excused himself as soon as they'd returned to the station, complaining of a sudden-onset stomach upset.

He had driven her back from the Shakespeare Estate in silence and McKittrick wondered what he'd seen in Collins' bathroom. The three strips of Temazepam were safely stashed inside her locker, but she wouldn't feel happy until she'd removed them from the station altogether. What if Mills had seen something? She hardly knew the man, it was impossible to assess the risk he might pose. As soon as the drugs were off the premises she'd feel much less vulnerable.

'Boss!' Cath Murray called from the other end of the corridor. 'Sorry I'm late, I was interviewing one of Trisha's boyfriend's neighbours.'

'And?'

'She said she doesn't really know White. Surprised to discover he had a girlfriend, as a matter of fact.'

'You didn't tell her your enquiries were connected to the Casey Collins investigation?'

'No, I didn't see any point in giving her too much information. We've had enough uncorroborated sightings of the headteacher to contend with, without adding Trisha's boyfriend to the mix.'

'We don't know if he is involved,' McKittrick said. 'Best to keep an open mind. Well done, Cath.'

The detective constable beamed at McKittrick and stood a little straighter. 'The neighbour did say her husband might be able to help. He's on nodding terms with White. I've asked her to get him to give me a call.'

'Good.'

'So, how are we playing it with Collins?' Murray glanced down at the folder McKittrick was holding. 'Do you want me to take the lead?'

'I don't think that'll be necessary.' McKittrick shoved the folder under her arm. 'Do you know anything about Ralph's mystery stomach bug?'

'Probably just a dodgy sausage sandwich for breakfast.'

'Have you spoken to him since we got back?' McKittrick was aware the question sounded more earnest than she'd meant.

'No – why? Don't think he's swinging the lead, boss. Mills isn't like that. Hardest working copper I know.' She smiled slyly. 'Apart from me, of course.'

'Let's get on with this, shall we?'

Inside the interview room Trisha Collins sat fidgeting at the table. 'Have you found her?'

McKittrick and Murray looked at one another before they sat down.

'Tell me you've found Casey.'

'I'm sorry, Trisha,' McKittrick said. 'We don't have any news for you about Casey.'

'You've got to let me get back home. I can't have my kids taken into care. I've seen what happens. Jesus, it's not like I'm a junkie or anything. There's a couple of smackheads in our block still looking after their babies. Please – just sit Chelsea down and have a proper talk with her. She'll tell you how she's made it all up. I've got to get out of here.'

McKittrick watched as Collins finally paused for breath and took her chance to interject. 'We just need to ask you a few more questions, Trisha.'

'Christ, haven't you asked enough already? It's not me you should be speaking to. Have you even seen Chelsea yet?'

'I can't discuss that with you.'

'What are you talking about? She's my daughter for Christ's sakes.'

'Please, Trisha. We need you to calm down now.'

'Lola watches her mum being dragged off by the police and you want me to calm down?'

'I need to speak to you about the drugs we found in your flat.'

'What do mean, "found"? Like I was hiding them or something. I'm the one who told you where to find them.'

McKittrick nodded to Murray and she set up the digital recorder, stating date, time and persons present. 'Ms Trisha Collins has declined her right to a solicitor,' she said.

McKittrick produced a photograph from the folder on her lap and pushed it across the table to Collins. 'Exhibit COL158(a). Have you seen this before Trisha?'

Collins squinted down at the colour photo, an enlarged shot of the paper wrap McKittrick had discovered in her bathroom. She looked up at McKittrick and narrowed her eyes.

'Have you seen it before?' McKittrick repeated.

'Of course I have – it's from the cabinet in the bathroom.'

'Can you explain what it was doing there?'

'I divide my pills in two. A whole one zonks me right out. I don't like feeling that out of it with the kids and everything. You know, I might have to get up in the night for them. Lot of good I'd be doped up to the eyeballs.'

'This would appear to be a crushed pill, not half of one.'

'They don't cut easy. You just end up with one big chunk and a load of dust. It's why I don't like taking them. They're more trouble than they're worth.'

'Why don't you ask your GP for a lower dose?'

'This is the lowest dose.'

Murray scribbled something in her notebook.

'Look, I know what you're getting at – Chelsea says I'm drugging the kids and you find a crushed-up pill. I realise it doesn't look good, but it doesn't mean I'm guilty of anything. As if I'd do something like that to my own kids.' She leaned her elbows on the table and buried her face in her hands. 'How could she lie like that about me?' She let out a low moan. After a few moments she re-emerged, energised suddenly. 'Have you spoken to that reporter girl – the one Angela brought with her?' She looked from McKittrick to Murray. 'I bet she's been filling my Chelsea's head with all sorts. Chelsea wouldn't make this stuff up on her own. She's had somebody poisoning her mind. Turning her against me. I should have listened to Lorraine – she said Chelsea had been spending too much time with her.' She leaned her arms on the table. 'Have you spoken to her?'

'We can't discuss that with you, Trisha.' McKittrick slipped the photograph back into its folder. Angela Tate's assistant was next on her list of interviewees. If she could ever track the woman down. 'Let's go through your movements on Monday night, shall we?' McKittrick could hear Barrow's voice in her head.

Collins blinked at McKittrick, her mouth fell open. 'You don't think… are you trying to say…? Jesus Christ. Is that what this is about? You think I've done something to Casey?' She let out a sudden sob. 'I don't believe it.'

'We have to pursue all possible lines of enquiry. We have to be thorough.'

'If you was being thorough you would have found her by now.' Another sob escaped from Collins' mouth.

'Is Casey particularly close to Terence White?' McKittrick sounded just like Barrow. She hated herself for it.

'Close to him? What are you getting at?'

'How many times has Casey been alone with him?'

'That's it! I'm not taking any more of this.' Collins stood up suddenly, sending her chair clattering to the floor. 'You lot, you're all the same. You think we're scum, don't you? Lorraine's right. Just because we live on a council estate you think we're the lowest of the low. Well you can fuck off with your fucking questions. I'm not answering any more of them. Get out there and find Casey.'

'Sit down, Trisha. Please.' McKittrick nodded to Murray who had dashed round to Collins' side of the table.

'I want to go home,' she said. 'I have to get back for the kids.'

'I'm sorry, Trisha, that's just not going to happen.'

Murray grabbed the overturned chair from the floor and gently encouraged Collins to sit back down.

'I'm not saying another word until I've got a lawyer.'

There was a sharp knock on the door and a uniformed officer that McKittrick didn't recognise appeared in the doorway.

'Ma'am – have you got a minute?'

McKittrick left Murray to formally record the end of the interview and stepped outside.

'Essex Police have just been in touch.' The officer looked down at a scribbled note on a Post-it. 'At 14.38 this afternoon they found Nigel Cope's car in a wooded area just outside Chelmsford.'

'Any sign of Cope?'

'Yes, ma'am. I was just getting to that.'

McKittrick blinked slowly at him but said nothing.

'Officers on the scene found a man meeting Mr Cope's description in the car. Dead. Looks like carbon monoxide poisoning.'

'Anything else?'

He nodded gravely. 'He'd written the word "sorry" in the condensation on the inside of the driver's window.'

TWENTY-ONE

Angela Tate got to Camberwell Green police station to find the entrance of the building overrun with news crews and reporters. She decided to avoid the melee at the front of the building and hurried to the car park at the rear, planning to slip inside through the back door just as soon as someone exited. She was sure once inside she'd have a better chance of getting to see Trisha.

She spotted DC Mills pacing up and down a narrow channel between a brick wall and the first line of parked police cars. She hurried towards him while he had his back to her, and was only a few feet away when he started to turn.

'Detective!' she said brightly.

Mills started and quickly pulled his hands from his pockets. 'How did you get in here?' He glanced around the car park.

'I need to speak to Trisha.'

'Not possible.' Mills scanned the car park again. 'You need to leave. Wait for the press statement with the rest of your colleagues.'

'They're no colleagues of mine, believe me. Backstabbing bunch of bastards.' She ventured a smile. 'It wouldn't take long – just a quick chat with her. As a friend, you understand, not a journalist.'

'Unless you've just taken your articles and qualified as a solicitor overnight, there's no way you're getting in to see her.'

'At least tell me how she's bearing up – you can do that for me, can't you? You can't lump me in with the rest of the pack. You and I do have a mutual friend after all.'

Mills shook his head and shoved his hands back in his pockets. 'Incredible,' he said. 'Why can't you just take no for an answer?'

'Wouldn't be doing my job if I did.'

'Your job? I thought you just said this was personal?' He glared at her, his mouth pursed into a tight 'o'.

In that moment Tate realised who Mills reminded her of. It hadn't occurred to her when she'd first met him at Trisha's, she was too busy making a different connection. Now she couldn't believe she'd been so slow. Mills. The name alone should have sparked the memory – she'd had enough run-ins with Detective Inspector Mills over the years.

'Charlie Mills?' she said. 'You have to be related to him. Am I right?'

Mills blinked slowly and looked away for a moment. Not the reaction she was expecting at all. When he turned back to her his face had adopted a flat, blank expression. 'My dad,' he eventually confirmed.

Tate tried to remember the last time she'd spoken to his father. She'd most likely argued with the belligerent bastard. She studied Mills' face. The resemblance she'd seen so clearly just moments before had disappeared completely. From what their mutual friend Caroline Barber had told her about him, Detective Mills the younger was nothing like his old man. Chalk and cheese. 'How is the old sod?' she said.

'Dead.'

'Oh… I'm… sorry.' She forced out the word. One less sadistic bastard in the world could only make it a better place.

'Look – I've got to get back to work,' Mills said, clearly unwilling to talk about his father.

'Can you at least tell Trisha I tried to see her? I don't want her thinking I don't care.'

'Care about her or your next headline?'

'Ouch – that's a bit harsh. I have a job to do, just like you.'

He shook his head again and Charlie Mills returned for a split second. 'Difference is,' he said, 'I can sleep at night.'

'Nice to know the stuff you see every day doesn't give you nightmares.' She didn't want to get into a fight with him, but the memory of his dad had triggered a reflexive response.

Mills turned quickly and strode towards the rear entrance of the building.

She couldn't let him slip away that easily. 'Level with me,' she called after him. 'You don't really think Trisha has anything to do with Casey's disappearance, do you?'

He looked back at her. 'We're investigating all possible lines of enquiry.'

'Oh come on. Really? Don't you think the accusations Chelsea's made – the drugging... and the neglect – are alarmingly similar to the 2008 Huddersfield case? Think about it. Chelsea is the same age as that girl. It must have had a big impact on her. And now this happens to her sister... Chelsea's getting someone else's story mixed up with her own.'

'That's not for me to comment on.'

'You've seen Trisha with her kids. Does she strike you as a feckless mother? Criminally negligent?'

'What I think isn't important. It's my job to concentrate on the facts and the evidence.' He started to push through the door.

'What evidence? The word of a vindictive teenager?' Tate caught up with him. The door had almost closed behind him. 'What about Dixon?' Up until that moment she hadn't decided whether or not to mention him. Now there was no going back.

Mills froze. 'What about him?' He turned on his heels to face her. 'Do you know something?'

'Have you spoken to him? It would make sense, given the family connection. Not one of your dad's finest moments.'

Mills snatched a breath, his face flushing.

'Do you think there's a connection between Dixon and current events?' she asked. 'Or are you just trying to cover your dad's arse?'

The muscles in Mills' clenched jaw bulged alarmingly.

'I know all about DI Mills' interrogation methods. I would think you do too, given the expression on your face. Did you also know he sent an innocent man to prison?'

'If you're referring to Ray Dixon, you know as well as I do, he was not innocent.'

'He didn't kill Sandra Stockwell.'

'He killed both girls, Paula and Sandra. We just didn't have enough evidence to convict him of Paula's death. You know that. You reported on the cases at the time.'

'Did Charlie tell you all about it, growing up? Book at bedtime, was it?'

He narrowed his eyes. 'I know you found Sandra Stockwell's body.'

'And that's how I know Dixon didn't kill her.'

'If you thought he was innocent thirty-three years ago, why even bring up his name now?'

Given DC Mills' heritage, Tate wondered if she should mention the note. He might read more into it than was actually there. 'At least tell me you've ruled him out of your enquiries.'

'I can't tell you anything.'

'Off the record?'

'In my experience, when a reporter says that it's anything but.'

Tate rested a hand over her heart. 'You have my word. Caroline Barber trusted me. I think you should too.'

Mills started to speak then checked himself.

'Just tell me what *you* think.'

'Off the record?'

'I swear.'

'I don't believe in coincidences,' he said after a long pause. 'Trisha Collins was a big part of the Sandra Stockwell investigation. And now her own child goes missing from the estate next door? With Dixon out on licence? There has to be a connection.' He rubbed a hand across his face. 'You can't tell me it hasn't crossed your mind.'

Tate didn't want to believe Dixon had anything to do with Casey's disappearance, but if not telling the police about the note he'd sent her in anyway delayed Casey's discovery, she wouldn't be able to forgive herself.

She reached out and touched his arm. 'I think we should go inside. There's something I need to tell you.'

1979

'When are you going to release Raymond Dixon?' Angela Tate stood with a pen poised over her reporter's pad.

'Who let you in here?' Detective Inspector Charlie Mills glanced around the inner compound of Camberwell Green police station, a half-smoked cigarette dangling from his lips. 'It's a restricted area,' he said and grabbed her arm.

'Get your hands off me!' Angela wriggled free and waved her pad in the detective's face. 'You can't hold him any longer. Not without charging him. It's not legal.'

Mills drew deeply on his cigarette then plucked it from his mouth. 'You're telling me what's legal? That's bloody rich. What do you know?'

'I'll get him a solicitor. A proper one – not one of yours.'

'Really?'

'My paper will.'

'The *South London Press* got money to burn has it?'

'I'm at the *Evening News* now,' she said, almost under her breath.

'Ah – promotion was it? Well done you. Nothing like using the death of a little girl to advance your career.'

She took a step closer to him. 'Charge Dixon or release him – it's a simple choice.'

'Is that so? Well here's an exclusive for you.' He dropped the cigarette and ground it under his shoe. 'We have charged him.'

'With what?'

'Why don't you run along back to your office and write next week's horoscopes like a good girl?'

'What have you charged him with?'

'You'll find out soon enough – with the rest of your hack friends.' He pointed towards the exit. 'Now piss off.'

'You mean *your* hack friends. I know all about the little arrangements you've got with the tabloid reporters.'

'You want to be careful what you insinuate. That sort of thing can get you in a lot of trouble. With the law. With your employers.'

'Threaten me all you like – makes no difference to me.'

He shoved his hands in his pockets and let out an impatient sigh. 'If you do intend to stay in this game – and frankly I can't see you lasting the course – you need to find out the way things work around here. There are proper channels. You can't come here flashing your legs and expect me to divulge confidential information. That kind of privilege needs to be earned.' He grinned at her and winked. 'If you know what I mean.'

'What have you charged Raymond Dixon with?' He could shove his privilege up his arse.

'Jesus, you just don't give up, do you?' He shook his head. 'Like I say – it won't be long before we make an official statement.'

'He's innocent. You know he is.'

'Do I?' He looked her up and down, letting his gaze linger on the ten inches of bare leg between the top of her boots and the hem of her skirt.

If this was his idea of intimidation, he needed to go back to cadet school for a refresher course. In the last two years Angela had slapped down enough lecherous advances to get listed in the *Guinness Book of World Records*. She stood up straighter, planted her hands on her hips and thrust out her chest.

Intimidate that.

'What makes you so bloody sure Dixon didn't do it?' Mills said, once he'd torn his gaze away from her breasts. 'I'm asking out of professional curiosity, you understand.'

'Speak to Trisha Collins. She took me to Sandra Stockwell's body. She was terrified. She still is. She knows what happened to Sandra.'

'What has she told you?'

'Not much, not yet. She's too upset.'

'Then how do you know Dixon isn't involved?'

'Because I know Gary Benson is.'

'Who?'

'Do you know what he was doing before Trisha took me to Sandra?'

'Do I look like I care?'

'He was selling tickets to his little friends to look at her dead body. Selling tickets! He's the one you should be interrogating.'

'How old is this lad?'

'Nine, ten… maybe eleven.'

'You're seriously suggesting I arrest a nine-year-old boy?'

'Trisha's terrified of him – that's why she won't speak out.'

'I can't believe I'm listening to this.'

'Gary Benson is a nasty little bully.'

'So? Doesn't make him a murderer, does it?'

Angela shoved her notebook into her bag and started walking towards the rear entrance of the building. 'If you won't tell me what you've charged Dixon with, I'll find someone who will.'

'You can't go in there.'

'Watch me!'

Mills caught up with her and blocked her path. 'If I tell you, will you promise to leave, like a good little girl?'

'Fuck off.'

'Charming language from a young lady.'

'Are you going to tell me or what?'

'The abduction and murder of Sandra Stockwell.'

Angela froze. 'You can't – there's no evidence.'

'I've no idea what makes you think that, but even if there wasn't, it wouldn't make a scrap of difference.' His thin-lipped mouth broke into a smile. 'Not when the suspect has made a full confession.'

'I don't believe you.'

'Stick around for the press conference then.'

'But he's only seventeen.' Angela closed her eyes for a moment and immediately her mind was full of images of Raymond Dixon being threatened by Mills and his thuggish colleagues until he gave in and confessed. 'I want to see him.'

'Tough.'

'What did you do to him?'

'Shouldn't you be asking a different question? Like what did *he* do to those poor young girls?'

'I need to see for myself that he's all right. Take me to his cell. At least let me look at him.'

Mills laughed. 'It's not a petting zoo.' He ran a hand through his lank Brylcreemed hair. 'He's not here, anyway. We've already transferred him to the cells at the magistrates' court. It's more secure in there.'

'You really think he'll try to escape?'

'No – but I think the locals round here might want to beat the shit out of him.'

'He's just a boy.' The last word snagged in her throat.

Mills laid a meaty hand on her shoulder. 'All getting a bit much is it, love?'

Angela flung up her arm and batted his hand away. 'How do you sleep at night?'

'More soundly than you, I reckon. At least I know I'm doing my bit to lock the sick bastards away.'

'He's seventeen.'

'So you keep reminding me. I don't know why you think that puts him above suspicion.' Mills sucked up a deep breath through his nose. 'Do you know why we picked him up in the first place?'

Angela blinked. Since Dixon had been arrested she'd heard plenty of rumours circulating the estates, each one more lurid than the last.

'Just over a year ago we caught the little pervert flashing to a group of schoolgirls on the upper deck of a number twelve bus.'

'I don't believe you. He'd have a record if that was true.'

'I'm not making it up. Maybe you should do your research more thoroughly. He was cautioned for it. Soon as Paula Jeffries disappeared we started to haul in all the dirty old men in their filthy raincoats.'

'He's not a dirty old—'

'That's why it took us a bit longer to bring him in. We went for the convicted perverts first.'

'And when you got nowhere with them you arrest schoolboys and bully them until they tell you whatever you want to hear?'

'You have no idea what it's really like, do you? You wait – few years on the crime desk and you'll lose your faith in the goodness of human nature.'

'I'm not naive.'

'I think we're finished here.' Mills was staring at her legs again. 'I can escort you to the street through the building or the car park – it's up to you. But believe me – you are leaving.'

'My paper won't let you get away with this.'

'I'd go steady on talking for your paper. Let's wait until they make you editor, shall we?'

Mills grabbed her by the arm led her into the building and through a warren of corridors until they eventually reached the main entrance.

'Confessions can be withdrawn,' Angela said as he opened the heavy door. 'Especially ones obtained under duress.'

'You're absolutely right,' Mills said, a vague smile playing across his mouth. 'Fortunately, we don't have to rely solely on Dixon's confession.'

'What?'

'This is off the record. If you try to put this in your newspaper, I swear to God your life won't be worth living.' He tightened his grip on her arm and dragged her down the stone steps and onto the pavement. 'The forensics people have found blood on Sandra's shoes. It isn't hers.'

'How do you know that?'

'The girl didn't have any open wounds.' Finally let go of her. 'Dixon, however, has a rather nasty cut on his arm.' The sickly, thin-lipped smile was back. 'It'll take a while for the blokes in the white coats to do their stuff, but that's OK. I'm a patient man.'

'You're lying.'

'Oh no, sweetheart – this is all the God's honest.' He smiled again, one hand pressed to his chest. 'Once we match the blood type to Dixon's, he's as good as convicted.'

TWENTY-TWO

'How long have you been sitting there?' Manisha Kapoor quietly closed the door to DCI Barrow's temporary office on the first floor and sat next to Mills on the window ledge. 'Have you been waiting for me?'

'Not really. Just happened to be passing.' Mills twitched a smile at her. It was the most he could manage after his exchange with Tate. What did she know about his dad anyway? He looked towards the DCI's door and considered for a moment whether he should tell him about Dixon's note. Given Barrow's attitude towards Ray Dixon's possible involvement in the Casey Collins case, he quickly decided to wait until Tate had brought the note in. Better to be armed with the physical proof. 'Can I buy you a coffee?' he eventually asked Kapoor.

'Is something wrong?'

'It's not that unusual is it? Can't a bloke buy a mate a drink?' He wasn't ready yet to tell her why he'd been waiting for her to finish with the DCI for the last twenty minutes.

'All right.'

Mills led her to the end of the corridor and down the stairs. 'How was Barrow in the debrief?'

'His usual cheerful self. Can't quite make him out. Always looks like there's somewhere else he'd rather be. Do you know he chewed his way through half a dozen indigestion tablets while I was in with him. Must have an ulcer the size of a dinner plate.'

Mills didn't respond.

'You all right?'

He hated the fact that Tate had managed to get him so rattled. Why had he risen to the bait? Kapoor was staring at him expectantly. Had she just said something he'd missed?

'I think all he was interested in was any dirt I could dig up about Trisha and her family.' Kapoor said.

'How did it go with Lorraine after we left?'

'She was a complete nightmare.'

They arrived at the deserted canteen in the basement, quickly ordered their drinks and took them to the table furthest from the counter, and both sat facing the door. A habit they'd adopted after Cath Murray was overheard slagging off a senior officer when the superintendent was only a couple of feet behind her.

'Lorraine's got herself all worked up,' Kapoor said after taking a sip of cappuccino. 'She wanted to come to the station to be with Trisha. But I told her she'd be better off staying with the kids.'

'Is she looking after them tonight?'

'Kiefer is due to relieve her when he finishes work.'

'Work? I didn't think he had a job.'

'Why wouldn't he?'

Mills shrugged. He hadn't given it much thought.

'It's not like you to make assumptions.' She nudged him with her elbow. 'I think the Collinses are what the government likes to call the "deserving poor".'

'What happens if we keep her in custody overnight? Will he still want to be taking care of them tomorrow? And the next day?'

'Trisha was desperate to keep social services out of it. She's seen what happens to kids that get caught up in the system.'

Mills blew on the surface of his tea too hard. Ripples slopped over the other side of the mug and hot tea dribbled over his hand. 'Shit!'

'What is wrong with you?'

'I'm fine. Are you going back to the Shakespeare later?'

'I'm finished for the day. Lisa, the FLO from Lewisham MIT, relieved me. I don't envy her job. She's got to get the kids down to the doctor's surgery so urine and hair samples can be taken.'

'Shouldn't they come here for that? See the police surgeon?'

'They're kids, Ralph. Lola was practically hysterical by the time I left.'

'She's taken a shine to you – not bad for a woman with no maternal instinct.'

'Oh I still don't have any. But she's a sweet little thing. She doesn't say much, but she's really good-natured. Poor love. She doesn't know what's happening.'

Mills pushed his mug away. He hadn't really wanted tea anyway. 'What do you think? About Trisha? Do you reckon she has been drugging her kids?'

'We'll find out soon enough. They're analysing the sample from Casey's hairbrush too. The results will either condemn Trisha or exonerate her.'

'But you know her better than any of us. What kind of mother do you reckon she is?'

Kapoor shook her head and let out a long sigh. 'All the time I've been there she hasn't stopped talking about Casey. I get the impression she's Trisha's favourite. Though she'd never admit it. I think she's amazed how well Casey's doing at school. Trisha's always quick to put herself down, saying how stupid she is before anyone else can. But I think that's just what people have told her over the years and she ended up believing them.'

'You think she's all right then?'

'I've been wrong about people before. But, yes… I think Trisha Collins is basically a good sort.'

'I hope you're right.'

'Why aren't you with McKittrick, interviewing her?'

'Bad gut – had to excuse myself.'

'See – I knew there was something wrong. Maybe you should have gone home.'

'It passed off – I'm all right now.'

'So you say.'

'We should be getting back upstairs.'

Kapoor decanted her coffee into a cardboard cup and they left the canteen. Halfway up the first flight of stairs, Mills stopped and turned to her. 'I haven't had a chance to ask you,' he said, trying to sound casual, worrying he was coming across as anything but. 'What do you make of McKittrick?'

'I don't really know her? Why?'

Mills thought about the pills he'd seen McKittrick slipping into her pocket, wondering now what he had actually seen. He should have confronted McKittrick about it straightaway in the car on the way back to the station. But it hadn't seemed appropriate somehow. Now he was worried the longer he left it, the more impossible it would be to bring the subject up. But he couldn't go to a senior officer about it, not before he'd spoken to McKittrick. He needed to be one hundred per cent certain about his facts.

'Ralph? Are you sure you're OK?

'How does she strike you?'

'You've seen more of her than any of us. What do you think?'

'I've been chatting to a couple of the DCs from Lewisham MIT. Apparently she's a fast track appointment.'

'We could have guessed that. How old is she? Thirty-three, four maybe? Pretty impressive to have made inspector that young.'

'She's thirty-five. She made inspector at thirty-two. So she's not exactly hurtling through the ranks.' Mills started walking again, realising he was sounding too interested in the DI, hoping forward motion would make the conversation seem less intense.

'Maybe she likes being an inspector – that way she gets to be more hands-on. Getting stuck in on the front line.'

Yes and getting the opportunity to steal prescription drugs at the same time, Mills thought.

'So, what else do you know about her?'

'She went to Warwick Uni – degree in criminology. A first, apparently.'

'Blimey – puts my Desmond to shame.' Kapoor smiled.

They reached the landing between the flights of stairs and she stopped and sipped her coffee. 'She doesn't have a Midlands accent though. Where's she from originally?'

'Manchester, though she started her training in the Nottinghamshire force. Don't you think that's a bit strange? Why not join the GMP?'

'Makes sense to me – you wouldn't want to be a copper on your own doorstep. Might end up arresting your old schoolmates.'

'It's never happened to me – I'm Camberwell born and bred.'

'Maybe she went to a rougher school than you.'

Mills shrugged and hurried up the stairs to the exit leading onto the second floor. He held open the door.

'What's brought all this on anyway?' Kapoor said. 'Have you had a falling out with her?'

'No – nothing like that.' Mills felt his face warming.

'You're being weird – whatever upset your stomach has addled your brain.'

*

Mills put down the phone and sank back into his seat. He looked over at Kapoor who had chosen that moment to finally tear her gaze away from her computer and the CCTV footage collected from shops within a two-mile radius of Casey's school that she'd been studying for the last two hours. A task she'd actually volunteered for.

'What's up?' she said.

'The techies have completed their preliminary examination of the headteacher's computer.'

'I didn't even know it had been recovered. Where was it – in the car with him?'

'Didn't Barrow tell you in the debrief?'

'He was too busy interrogating me about Trisha. What did they find in his car?'

'So far nothing to link him to Casey's disappearance. But then we're not really expecting to now.'

'What's happened?'

'Barrow really hasn't told you anything about Cope?'

'I was going to ask him, but like I said, he was more interested in Trisha. What I thought she was capable of.'

'He's already made up his mind about her.' Mills got up to stretch his legs. Too long sitting at a desk always made him feel as if he was incrementally turning to stone.

'Tell me about Cope – where was his PC?'

'In a local repair shop – the disk drive had stopped working and Cope took it in Monday afternoon to get it fixed.'

'That's why he left school early?'

'Yeah – seems that way.' Mills scratched at his sideburn. 'He had a long chat about it with the guy who runs the shop. Then they moved on to the subject of gaming. Apparently Cope was quite an expert. He didn't leave the place until after five. We've got CCTV of him going from the repair shop to the swimming baths. Then home.'

'So he's got an alibi for the whole of Monday afternoon and evening?'

Mills let out a sigh and nodded.

'And what have the techies found on the hard drive?'

'Oh… nothing. Nothing dodgy.'

Kapoor stared into space, processing the information Mills had just given her. 'Why did Cope kill himself, if he had nothing to do with Casey's disappearance? Surely not just because he hadn't told the school about his previous conviction?'

'He'd lied about his qualifications too.'

'But that's no reason at all.'

'He'd based his whole career on a series of lies, maybe he couldn't bear the shame of being found out.'

'If he hadn't run away like that, we might never have looked into his background that closely. And the school would have been none the wiser. For a man to take his own life...'

'It's a bloody tragedy. Even if he had lost his job, so what? Jesus, in the scheme of things… It's such a terrible waste.' Mills sucked in a deep breath, and clenched his fists. He hoped Kapoor hadn't noticed the sudden tremor in his voice.

'Ralph, are you OK?'

'I'm fine.' He needed to change the subject. 'Did you spot anything on the CCTV?'

'No. It was a long shot. None of the shopkeepers remembered Casey anyway.'

'I don't know how you can stare at that stuff for so long. Puts me to sleep.'

'Makes a nice change after being at Trisha's all week.' She smiled and was about to say something else when the door at the far end of the incident room burst open.

Cath Murray came marching in, her face red, her chest heaving.

'What's happened?' Mills said.

'We're going to search Terence White's flat. McKittrick said I should take you with me.'

'White's back?' Mills asked.

'No – his neighbour phoned me a little while ago with some new information. Said he didn't think anything of it at the time. It was only talking to his missus that made him see it in a new light. She put two and two together and worked out we wanted to speak to White about Casey's disappearance. It's all kicked off from there.'

'Can you slow down? You're not making any sense.'

'Oh – sorry.' She took a breath. 'Bloke who lives next door to Trisha's boyfriend said he saw him leaving his flat on Monday night carrying a big bundle in his arms. Shoved it on the back seat of his car. At the time he assumed it was a rucksack or duffle bag.'

'So White's definitely gone away for a while then?'

'That's not what he was getting at. He said the way White was struggling with it, the bundle was much too heavy to be a bag of clothes.'

TWENTY-THREE

Saturday 11th February

'Yes thank you, I am well aware it's the weekend.' Natasha McKittrick pushed her thumbnail into a loose splinter of wood in the doorframe of the incident room. She stared in at the near-deserted office. Only a handful of civilians were manning the phones. 'The world doesn't stop turning just because it's Saturday,' she said, trying her best not to shout. 'As soon as you get any of the results back, call me.' She hung up, cursed the lab technician under her breath and headed for the DCI's office.

A simple urine toxicology screen would have been processed much faster in the Avon and Somerset force, she was certain. She pulled a Biro from her pocket and wrote *Met tox* on the back of her hand and wondered how easy it would be to find out in advance about spot tests in the Met. Ideally she'd like three or four days' notice. She'd cut it very close at times when she was in Bristol, she didn't want to risk it here. She hadn't yet sourced a reliable supply of clean urine.

She arrived at Barrow's office to find it empty. Frustrated, she phoned him on his mobile, impatiently waited for his voicemail instructions to finish, left a curt message and returned to the incident room.

After Trisha Collins had spoken to her solicitor she had refused to answer any further questions. McKittrick still wasn't sure what to make of her. Lying about being at home the evening Casey disappeared was her first error of judgement. Then all that business about Casey not having run away before. Plus the drugs in the bathroom cabinet. There had been too many inconsistencies in her story to ignore. But what did they amount to? Could Collins be responsible for her own daughter's disappearance? If she was, then the woman should get an Oscar. The tears had seemed genuine enough. But this 'no comment' silent routine? That smacked of a woman who thought she was about to be found out. Still, all they really had at the moment was circumstantial evidence. They'd have to let her go if they didn't uncover something else in the next twenty-four hours. There was no way a magistrate would agree to extend the custody period without hard evidence. The toxicology results would decide Collins' fate one way or the other.

McKittrick returned to her desk in the incident room just as her landline started to ring. She picked up the phone but stayed on her feet, too on edge to sit down. 'McKittrick,' she snapped.

'Ma'am, this is Sergeant Warner… on the front desk? We've got a man here insisting on speaking to DCI Barrow.'

'He's not here.'

'I know that ma'am. But he says he wants to see the SIO – quite adamant about it.'

'Who is he?'

'Keating, ma'am. Casey Collins' father.'

'Tell him he'll have to make do with me. Give it ten minutes then have someone bring him to the interview suite, would you?'

Lawrence Keating was ushered into the brightly lit, cheerfully decorated room used to interview witnesses and victims in the Camberwell station. McKittrick gestured for him to take a seat on one of the leather sofas.

'This is a bit different to the room you had me in before.' He ran a hand over the upholstery. 'How much did this cost?' He whistled. 'Very nice. No wonder they're cutting the number of bobbies on the beat.'

'What new information do you have for us, Mr Keating?' Keating's inane chatter had already started to grate.

'It's very important. That's why I need to speak to the top bloke. No offence. Where is he? Fucked off for the weekend?'

'Any information relating to the Casey Collins investigation has to go through me.'

Keating pursed his lips and pulled his head back, as if McKittrick had just made an unsavoury suggestion. 'Not sure about that.'

'You really want to delay any action that may help us find Casey?'

'Now – I didn't say that.'

'So, what is it?'

Keating ran his tongue over his crooked and stained teeth. 'Suppose you're as good as anyone else.' He relaxed back onto the sofa and folded one leg over the other, ankle resting on knee. 'About a week ago Trisha phoned me to ask a favour.'

'She has your phone number?'

'Course she does – how else would she get in touch? About visits and that?'

McKittrick could have sworn Collins had told her otherwise. 'Carry on.'

'She asked me if I wanted to go on a little trip.' He spread his arms along the back of the sofa, making himself even more at home. 'I can see her face now – right sly, if you know what I mean. She always used to get that face when she wanted something.'

'I thought you said she phoned you.'

'What? Yeah – she did. Figure of speech. I mean I could *picture* her face when she was talking to me. She had that wheedling tone in her voice, you know? Used to do my head in when we were together. Reminded me just how much she wound me up.' He smacked his lips together noisily. 'Any chance I could get a cup of tea? I'm dying of thirst here.'

Why was he stringing it out like this? McKittrick wondered if he just wanted somewhere warm to sit on a cold Saturday afternoon and thought about suggesting the library on Peckham Road. 'Perhaps later,' she said instead. 'Tell me about this trip.'

'She wanted me to take Casey away. I've got cousins living up in Norfolk. She thought I could take Casey there with me. Stay for a couple of weeks.'

'Did she say why she wanted you to do that?'

He shrugged. 'I said I couldn't go nowhere without some cash. And she said she didn't have any. But she would soon. Which I thought straightaway sounded a bit iffy. I asked her how soon and she got well cagey. Then she changed her mind altogether – told me to forget the whole thing. I said forget what? You haven't even said anything.'

'Then what happened?'

'She hung up.'

'And you're telling me this now because…?'

'It's obvious. I wouldn't go along with her little plan so she got some other bugger to. Bet you anything Casey's holed up with some bloke Trisha knows. Few more days down the line, lo and behold, Casey turns up right as rain and Trisha's boyfriend claims the reward. Like those people up north did a few years back. Well and truly backfired on them didn't it?'

The similarity to the Huddersfield case of 2008, the one Barrow had worked on, had already occurred to McKittrick.

'Why didn't you tell us about this when we interviewed you before?'

'I didn't think nothing of it at the time. Hadn't put two and two together, had I? Now you've banged her up, it's all fell into place.'

'You're quite sure she asked you to go away with Casey? There can be no mistaking her intentions?' She studied his face. He looked straight back at her with a blank expression. She couldn't read it.

'Quite sure.' He puffed out his cheeks. 'She showed her true colours. Devious. Always has been. Just like the way she hoodwinked that judge in the family court.' He leaned forward. 'While I'm here, can you help me with social services?'

'I'm sorry?'

'I've got to get Ryan away from that lot. No point him being looked after by a bunch of strangers when his own dad is willing and able to take him in. I'm staying at my mum's at the minute. Moved out of the hostel. Proper stable home for him – it's gotta be a good thing.'

'I think you might be getting a bit ahead of yourself, Mr Keating. You shouldn't get your hopes up.' Especially if I have anything to do with it, she thought.

'But you'll have a word with them for me?' He smiled at her. 'After all – blood's thicker than water, isn't it?'

McKittrick didn't answer. The text alert on her mobile sounded. 'Excuse me.' She walked to the other side of the room and opened the message. She read it once and stared over at Keating. He nodded and smiled back at her.

'Not bad news, I hope?'

It struck McKittrick that Keating hadn't asked her once how the investigation into Casey's disappearance was continuing. She read the message from the lab again and was forced to reassess Keating's statement.

Blood sample results for benzodiazepines:

Chelsea Collins: -ve
Lola Collins: -ve
Ryan Collins: +ve (Temazepam)

TWENTY-FOUR

Mills and Murray took the final turn in the stairs leading to Mrs Benson's landing, when her son, Gary, came trundling down the steps, straining under the weight of one of his mother's large cardboard boxes. He pulled up short when he saw them.

'Got you helping out, has she?' Mills said and pointed to the box.

'Don't know what you're talking about.' Benson attempted to push past them. Mills blocked his path.

'Helping your mum with her eBay stuff, are you?'

'None of your fucking business.' Benson put his head down and forcibly made a space between the two detectives.

'You want to watch yourself,' Murray warned him.

Benson hurried down the stairs muttering. Mills thought he picked out the words 'fucking' and 'dyke'.

'Debonnaire and charming sort, isn't he?' Murray said, not giving Mills a chance to comment. She smiled at him and gestured up the stairs to the landing above.

'Maybe we should get after Benson - we still need to interview him,' Mills said.

'O'Donnell's our priority for the moment – McKittrick's made it quite clear. Let's just get on with it, shall we?'

Lorraine O'Donnell answered the door herself. 'What's happened?' she said. 'Have you found Casey?'

'I'm afraid not,' Mills said.

'Mum's not up to speaking to you. She's feeling a bit out of sorts.'

'That's OK. We're here to see you. This is Detective Constable Murray.' Mills smiled at her. 'Your husband told us we'd find you here.'

O'Donnell left the door open and hurried down the hall towards the living room. By the time the two detectives had reached the over-heated room, O'Donnell was standing by the window, mobile phone to her ear. 'Christ, Mick – you might have warned me they were coming.' She hung up as soon as they entered the room.

'No Monty today?' Mills said, relieved the terrier wasn't sniffing around his shoes, snapping at his ankles.

'He's upstairs with Mum.'

'Shall we sit down, Lorraine?' Murray lowered herself onto one of the armchairs.

'What's this all about? Shouldn't you be searching that pervert's car?'

The discovery of Nigel Cope's car had been leaked to the press the night before, presumably by someone on the Essex force. What hadn't yet been disclosed was the fact that Cope had been eliminated from their enquiries.

'It means Casey's dead, doesn't it? Have you told Trisha you found the filthy bastard?'

'We really can't—'

'I bloody hope you haven't. She'll be going off her head. And she's the one who thought he was a good bloke.' She paced across the room, wrapped her cardigan more tightly around her and paced back again. 'So why are you here? What do you expect me to be able to tell you?'

'We just need to ask you a few questions.' Mills managed to crank his mouth into a smile. 'It's nothing to worry about.'

'Who said I was worrying?' O'Donnell retrieved a packet of cigarettes from the overly ornate mantelpiece that topped her mother's gas fire and lit up. She stared at them narrow-eyed through a cloud of smoke, then, folding her thin legs beneath her, sank onto the plump sofa. 'I don't know much about the headmaster – my Alfie's always kept out of his way. But I've never liked the look of him. Got a face you can't take to.' She drew on the cigarette. 'When are you letting Trisha out?'

'I'm afraid that's something else we can't discuss,' Murray said.

'Bloody Chelsea – getting her mum carted off like that. I could swing for that girl. There's a streak of evil in her, I've always said. Can't mention it to Trish, of course. According to her, all her kids are angels.'

'You still maintain Chelsea Collins made up her allegations regarding her mother?' Murray batted away the smoke that was drifting in her direction.

O'Donnell nodded and picked a speck of ash from her bottom lip. 'Evil. Must get it from her dad, whoever the hell he is.'

'You don't know?'

'How can I? If Trisha don't know who he is herself?'

Mills saw Murray raise her eyebrows and prayed she wouldn't say anything inappropriate. He leaned forward in his seat, gripping his knees, and lowered his voice to what he hoped was a conspiratorial level. 'That's actually partly why we've come to see you.'

'Chelsea's dad?'

'Not exactly.' Mills tried another smile. 'We want you to tell us what you know about Trisha's current boyfriend, Terence White.'

O'Donnell took a long drag on her cigarette and blew it out above her head before she answered. 'Never met him.'

'What has Trisha told you about him?' Mills continued the gentle approach, soft tones and what he hoped was an open, encouraging expression. No point in bullying her. After the search of White's flat produced no evidence of

Casey ever being there, and with Trisha sticking resolutely to her vow of silence, they needed to keep O'Donnell on side. At the moment she was the only possible source of information about the man.

'She's told me eff all. Probably didn't want to give me the chance to slag him off. She has shit taste in men. Almost makes me grateful I found Mick.'

'But she did tell you that's where she'd been all of Monday night?' Mills asked.

'Well she couldn't keep him a secret after what happened while she was over at his place, could she?'

'Didn't you ask her about him? Weren't you curious?'

'What? You think I was going to sit her down for cosy chit-chat about him, with Casey God knows where?'

'Let's go over the events of Monday night and Tuesday morning again, shall we?'

'Haven't you made enough notes yet?'

'If you wouldn't mind?'

She blew out another long smoky breath. 'First I heard about it, Chelsea was banging on my door ten o'clock Monday night, face all blotchy, shivering from head to toe. She told me Casey hadn't come home and she didn't know what to do.'

'When did she realise her sister was missing?'

'When she didn't come home from school.'

'You're sure about that?'

O'Donnell shrugged. 'That's what she told me. Maybe you should ask her. You have spoken to her, I suppose?'

Mills drew in a breath.

'Oh don't tell me you haven't.'

'Why do you think it took Chelsea so long to come to you?'

O'Donnell ground her cigarette into a nearby ashtray and jumped up to fetch another from the packet on the mantelpiece. 'Look – I only know what she told me. I'm not getting myself all caught up in this.' She lit the second cigarette and remained standing. 'She said that before she came to see me, she'd called all Casey's friends and even knocked on a few doors on the estate. I don't know why she didn't come to me straightaway.'

'And then what did you do?' Mills asked, referring to his notes.

'What are you looking at in that little black book of yours? Are you trying to catch me out?'

'That's not how it works.' Mills studiously avoided making eye contact with Murray. She knew as well as him probing for inconsistencies was standard practice. 'So, after Chelsea arrived, what did you do?'

'I called Gar—' She stopped herself.

Mills looked up to see O'Donnell staring down at his notebook. 'You called who, Lorraine?'

She screwed up her face so tight it looked as if someone was pinching her. She didn't take her eyes off the notebook. 'I called Gary.'

'So you didn't organise the search of the estate off your own bat?' Mills closed the notebook. 'That's what you told us before.'

O'Donnell swallowed. 'I called Gary and asked him what I should do.'

'You called Gary instead of calling 999?'

'I thought about it – but you know what it's like round here. Your lot turn up and it's any excuse for a riot. So I asked Gary what to do.' She stared at the cigarette burning between her fingers.

'And what was Gary's advice?'

'He told me to sit tight. Until he arrived.'

'And you thought that was good advice?'

'He knows what to do about most things. He told me not to call the police.'

'Did he explain why?'

'Said you were all either bent… or useless.' She looked up at Mills and stared him straight in the eye. 'Or both.'

TWENTY-FIVE

Monday 13th February

Her handbag safely stored in an HMP Holloway locker that reeked of vomit, Angela Tate was forced to endure the indignity of a full body pat down by a prison warder with the worst case of halitosis she'd ever come across.

'I'm not sure what you're expecting to find,' she said, prompting a non-committal grunt from the guard.

The weekend had been long and cold. Tate still hadn't found a plumber to fix her ailing boiler and had been forced to decamp to a hotel on Saturday night. She spent most of Sunday evening in a hot bath, wrinkling steadily, wondering at the wisdom of telling DC Mills about the note from Dixon. What if Dixon had genuinely been reaching out to her for help? Wasn't going to the police tantamount to slapping him across the face? She wrestled with her own thoughts about his possible involvement in Casey Collins' disappearance for hours and still hadn't come to any conclusions. Right now, all she could do was wait for Dixon to make his next move. Assuming, of course, that he planned to make one. Why had he chosen such a strange way to contact her in the first place? Why be so cryptic? One thing Tate knew for sure: Raymond Dixon was not responsible for Sandra Stockwell's death.

Trisha Collins was one of the few people who knew what had happened to Sandra thirty-three years ago. Tate had to at least try to persuade her to start talking.

The halitoxic, monosyllabic guard finally completed her search and escorted Tate down a featureless, disinfectant-sluiced corridor.

After less than fifteen minutes inside the women's prison just off the Holloway Road, Tate could feel the walls and low ceilings closing in on her. She wouldn't last more than a day in a place like this. She dreaded to think about what mental state Trisha would be in when she saw her.

The corridor finally opened up to a wide reception area, a metal gate clanged shut behind her, and Tate was directed towards another corridor by a second guard. This guard reeked of peppermints and anti-bacterial hand gel.

They reached the door to the prison hospital and Tate was introduced to the nurse on duty, who quickly directed her to a bed located at the very end of the brightly lit ward. Tate found Trisha reclining on the bed, her upper body propped up on a collection of pillows stuffed into greying pillowcases that were fraying at the edges. Trisha had her eyes closed and Tate took a moment to study her bruised jaw, broken nose and split lip before announcing her arrival.

'Trish,' she said gently.

Trisha opened her eyes, started to smile, then winced as she stretched the stitches in her top lip. Tate smiled back. 'I didn't know what you might want, so I plumped for a couple of magazines. They wouldn't let me bring them in with me. You should get them later.'

'Have they found Casey?'

'Not yet, Trish.'

'They don't tell me anything in here. Do you know what's happened to the kids? Are they all together? Lola needs her brother and sister. Why can't they just let Kiefer look after them?'

Tate shrugged. She wasn't about to tell Trisha that her son was too busy helping the police with their enquiries to be available for babysitting duties. 'I've contacted a couple of solicitors for you, like I said I would. One of them should make contact later today.'

'Thanks, Ange. I knew you wouldn't let me down.'

After their phone conversation that morning had been interrupted by Trisha getting her face smashed in, Tate thought it was the least she could do.

'How long before he can get me out of here, do you think?'

'I'm not sure you should pin any hopes on getting bail. One of the reasons you were refused it in the first place was for your own protection. Feelings are running high on the estate.'

'My own protection? What's this then?' Trisha pointed to her face. 'It's not like I'm any safer in here.' A single tear appeared beneath the swollen lid of her left eye. 'I've got to get out. I need to get my kids back.'

'Terence is bound to turn up soon – hopefully what he says will help your case.'

'Hopefully?'

'His face has been all over the media for the last day or so. And yet he still hasn't come forward. That's led some people to speculate he has something to hide.'

'I expect he's got plenty to hide. He's not exactly an angel.'

'Do you think he's capable of doing anything to Casey?'

'Of course he isn't. He might be a bit light-fingered, but he wouldn't do anything like that.'

'How well do you know him?'

'What are you saying?'

'How long have you been seeing him?'

'Long enough to know what kind of bloke he is. It's funny – I actually thought Terry was different from the rest of them. For a while, he seemed to really care about me, you know? But now the bastard's just buggered off. Right when I need him.'

'Have you got any idea where he might have gone?'

'Don't you think I would have told the police if I did?'

'Do you know why he would have disappeared?'

Trisha looked down at her hands. 'We had a row. I'd been drinking… Then he stormed off. Cried myself to sleep after that. Like a soppy bloody teenager. Christ, I want my head examined. Should have known he was just the same as all the other bastards. That's me off blokes for good now.' She drew in a deep breath and pain flashed across her face.

'What is it?'

'Bruised ribs.' Trisha reached out and grabbed Tate's hand. 'I've got to get the kids back, Ange. Will you find out where they are for me? Maybe get a message to them? Tell them their mum still loves them?' Tears were flowing freely now down both cheeks. 'Can you go with Kiefer to social services? He's not good with all that official stuff. If you're with him you can make sure he says the right thing.' She squeezed Tate's hand tighter. 'Promise me you'll do that.'

'I'll do what I can. But I can't make any promises, Trish.' The way things were panning out, Kiefer might not be in a position to look after anyone.

'Has Chelsea said anything else about me? Someone needs to sit down and have a proper talk with her. How long can she keep this up?'

Tate swallowed. 'There's still the matter of the traces of drugs they found in Ryan's urine sample.'

'That's just a mistake, plain and simple. They need to do the test again. You don't believe I'd drug my own kids, do you?'

Tate hesitated for just a moment too long.

'For God's sake, Ange!' Trisha had raised her voice, another spasm of pain contorted her features. The guard at the other end of the ward looked up at her and frowned.

'You of all people have to believe me. We go back too far. You can't give up on me.'

'I'm doing nothing of the sort.'

'You mustn't. I'm relying on you. Please, Ange.'

'I'll do my best.' Tate reached over to a high cabinet next to the bed and handed Trisha a plastic bottle of water with a straw sticking out the top. 'Have a drop of this.'

'I've got to get out of here,' Trisha said again. 'I feel so bloody helpless. It's like everyone's forgotten about Casey. The police are still looking for her, aren't they? They haven't stopped because I'm in here?'

'Of course they're still searching.' Tate couldn't tell her they'd narrowed the search to the properties of her friends and family.

'I've got to get out.'

'You will. You just need to find a way to get through it until then.' Tate smiled at her, waited for Trisha to finish with the water then put the bottle back on the cabinet, making her movements slow and deliberate while she worked out how best to raise the subject she'd come here to discuss.

'I want to feel like I'm doing something useful,' Trisha said.

It was now or never.

'Actually, you could help me. I need some information.'

'About Casey? I swear to God I've told the police everything I can think of.'

Tate waited a beat then waded in. 'Not about Casey. Not exactly.'

'I don't understand.'

'Do you remember what you said to me last week, how you've been thinking a lot about Paula and Sandra?'

'You don't think the same thing has happened to Casey?'

'No! I'm not saying that.' Casey had been gone a week now. Everyone suspected she was dead. But no one was saying it out loud. 'Don't you think it's time you told me what happened to Sandra?'

Trisha's battered mouth fell open. 'What?'

'I understand why you've never said anything before. You were scared. Rightly so. I don't blame you, really I don't.' She reached out and gently patted the blanket covering Trisha's legs.

'Is that why you're here? To rake over all that?'

'I came to see you – see how you're coping.'

'Well you've seen – I'm not.' Trisha started weeping again.

'I'm sure if you told me you'd feel better in yourself.'

'Only one thing will make me feel better.' Trisha drew the blanket up over her shoulders. She shivered. 'And that's my Casey coming back home.'

'There's no need to be scared now,' Tate said and smiled reassuringly at her. 'Gary can't hurt you anymore.'

'Gary looks out for me – why would I be scared of him?'

'I know what he's like.'

'I'm tired. I think you should go now.'

'Please, Trisha.'

'You're wasting your time. I don't know anything.'

'But Gary took you to see Sandra's body. Did he tell you how she died?'

Trisha stared down at her lap.

'Gary was only nine years old at the time,' Tate continued. 'You wouldn't be getting him into trouble. He was too young to be punished then. He won't be punished now.'

Trisha said nothing.

'Just tell me what happened.'

'I don't know. Sandra was already dead when they found her.'

'Who found her?'

'Christ – I can't be going over all this now. I've got more important things to worry about.'

'You said something to me the other day – that you thought you were being punished. What did you mean?'

'Did I say that? I don't remember. I didn't know what I was saying. I've been going out of my mind.' She interlocked her fingers and squeezed her hands tightly together.

'Who do you think is punishing you?'

'I don't remember saying it.' She turned her face away.

'Do you think you're being punished for not coming forward with information about Sandra? Do you think Raymond Dixon is punishing you?'

'No!' She had raised her voice again. 'I don't know.' She let out a loud sob. 'What if he is? What if he's done something to Casey?'

'Tell me about Sandra.'

'No! Shut up!'

Tate glanced at the guard sitting at other end of the ward. The woman looked right at her, held her gaze and stood up. She started ambling towards them.

'I don't know anything about it.' Trisha lowered her voice. 'I can't tell you what I don't know.'

Tate let out a breath. The guard was almost upon them. She had no choice but to drop the subject.

'Just help get me out, Ange. Please. I don't know what might happen if I have to stay in here much longer.'

'Come on, Trisha. You've got to hold it together.'

'I'm not asking for myself. I've got someone else to think about now.' Trisha laid a protective hand on her stomach. 'I'm pregnant.'

TWENTY-SIX

The car swerved towards the pavement at the last minute and the front passenger wheel mounted the kerb. Natasha McKittrick opened her door before the vehicle stopped. She and Cath Murray ran towards the entrance of the ITV building on the South Bank, followed by two more detectives and a dozen uniformed officers. Flashing her warrant card at the two receptionists at the crescent-shaped desk on her right, McKittrick headed for the security turnstiles immediately opposite the main doors. The security guard was already releasing the glass barriers when she reached him.

'Where's the green room for *This Morning*?' McKittrick yelled at him.

'It's complicated, there isn't a direct route,' the guard replied. He nodded to a colleague. 'Keep an eye on the barrier, will you?' He turned back to McKittrick. 'I'll take you.'

McKittrick ordered six of the uniformed officers to stay in reception. A voice crackled through her walkie-talkie confirming a further half dozen men were in position in the car back at the building's rear exit.

After three lift journeys and a dash along what seemed like a mile of identical corridors, McKittrick, Murray and the two remaining uniforms arrived at the green room door. 'Ready?' McKittrick asked and when everyone nodded back at her she pushed through the door, her warrant card held high in her fist, shouting a warning as she went.

Terence White turned quickly, in one hand a fat sandwich oozing its filling, in the other a glass of sparkling wine. 'Oh shit.' He took a bite of the sandwich, shoved what was left on the table next to him and downed the wine in one. He wiped a sleeve across his mouth and swallowed. 'You arrived quicker than I expected.' He looked at each officer in turn. 'I think the stab vests and Tasers are a bit over the top, don't you?' His gaze finally came to rest on McKittrick. 'Well? What are you waiting for?'

'Terence White, I am arresting you on suspicion of perverting the course of justice.' McKittrick took a breath. 'You have the right—'

'Yeah, yeah... whatever. I'd like you to meet my publicist – Alex. You'll be meeting my solicitor later.'

Half an hour earlier McKittrick had been in the station canteen, standing in the queue, unconsciously gazing at the television on the opposite wall to the counter, when she saw Terence White introduced as the next guest on a daytime TV chat show. He was sitting on the sofa next to a minor soap star, smiling confidently at the camera. Dressed in a cheap suit, a pair of gleaming white trainers on his feet, he looked for all the world like a low-rent comedian flogging his latest DVD.

Cocky little bastard. Even now he still had the same self-satisfied smirk on his face.

She finished reciting his rights, then watched as the uniforms bundled him out of the room.

When they arrived back at the station, the DCI was waiting for her in the incident room.

'Good work, Natasha.'

It was the first time he'd uttered anything approaching a compliment and it caught her off-guard. She thanked him awkwardly and wriggled out of her jacket and protective vest.

'I assume you'd like to sit in?' the DCI said.

Twenty minutes later, sitting at the table in interview room four, the one, McKittrick had discovered, that smelled permanently of vomit, Barrow kicked off the interview.

'Where were you on the afternoon of Monday 6th February at three-thirty p.m.?'

'Straight to the point – I like that.' White smiled. The gaps between his teeth were plugged with morsels of chicken and avocado.

'Please answer the question, Mr White.' Barrow sat perfectly still, his face blank.

White made a point of leaning away from the table, raising a hand to his mouth and whispering something to his smartly dressed solicitor. An expensive lawyer hired by White's newly appointed publicist, McKittrick supposed. 'I'm a busy man, officer,' White answered, eventually. 'I may have to consult my diary. Unfortunately you have confiscated my phone. So I'm afraid I can't help you.'

Remarkably, Barrow's face remained expressionless. McKittrick, meanwhile, was pressing a fingernail into the fleshy pad of her thumb. The pain took the edge off her need to wring White's neck.

'As you've been away, Mr White, I can only assume you are not aware of the seriousness of the situation. A vulnerable nine-year-old girl had been missing for seven days. Surely, under the circumstances, you'll want to cooperate fully.'

'Nothing to do with me – I've never even laid eyes on her.'

'How long have you been in relationship with Ms Collins?'

More whispered conferring with his solicitor.

'I'm not.'

'How long *were* you in a relationship with her?'

'See that's where you've got me all wrong – I wasn't *ever* in a relationship with Trisha. She might have thought I was, but then birds can get weird ideas about stuff like that.' He glanced in McKittrick's direction, a sneer on his face. 'Know what I mean?'

McKittrick pressed the fingernail further into her flesh. She tried very hard to mimic her boss's impassive expression, and could only hope she was managing to pull it off. Right now she wanted to slap the smirk of White's ugly pockmarked face.

'Allow me to rephrase the question,' Barrow said. 'How long have you been acquainted with Ms Collins?'

'Been seeing her on and off since last summer.'

'And yet you never met her daughter, Casey, in all that time?'

'Never saw the point – why would I be interested in her kids?'

'Where were you on Monday afternoon?'

'Oh – we're back to that one are we?' He leaned back and ran a hand through his dirty blonde hair. He glanced at his solicitor, who nodded back at him. 'Sorry to disappoint you, but from lunchtime on Monday right up until I met Trisha, I was at the snooker hall on Coldharbour Lane.'

'Can anyone confirm your presence there?'

'There was a few faces down there I recognised. Ask them nicely, I'm sure they'll tell you.'

'And you left the snooker hall when?'

'Bit before eight. I picked up Trisha from the betting shop a little while after that.'

'Why didn't you come forward straightaway? As soon as we put out our appeal?'

'Scared, wasn't I? I've heard what can happen to people in these situations.'

'What situation would that be?'

'Anything to do with little kids. Don't matter if you're innocent, like me – people don't bother to find that out.

Before you know it you've got a mob after you. I had to protect myself. Get proper representation.' He waved a hand at his solicitor. 'Wouldn't have him here looking after my interests if I hadn't gone to *The Sun* first.'

McKittrick pulled in a silent breath. First Collins and the *Evening News*, then Chelsea with *The Herald*, and now this.

'And yet even with legal representation, it seems your first port of call after the newspaper was a television studio rather than a police station.' Barrow hadn't taken his eyes from White's face.

'You were next on my list, I swear.'

'Monday evening, then.'

'What about it?'

'You picked up Ms Collins. Was she alone?'

'Of course she was – don't think Trisha'd be up for anything kinky.' He winked at McKittrick. She ignored him.

'So you picked her up and did what?'

'Got a kebab and a few beers then went back to mine.'

'Directly?'

'Golden Grill, off-licence, mine.'

'How did Ms Collins seem to you at the time? Did you notice anything different about her?'

'Yes I bloody did. I've never seen her so—' He checked himself, quickly glancing at his lawyer again to seek his approval. 'She was really stressed, you know? Edgy. Couldn't sit down, smoking one fag after another. Would have drunk all my beer if I'd let her.'

'Did she indicate why she was behaving in that way?'

'Christ you've got a complicated way of saying things. Yes she did. We had a stand up row about it.'

'About what?' Barrow leaned forward in his seat. It seemed to McKittrick as if he was holding his breath.

'She told me I'd got her up the duff.'

Barrow exhaled, clearly disappointed.

'I called her a liar,' White continued. 'Then she shouted at me. I mean – you can understand me not believing her, can't you? I thought she was too old to get pregnant. She said she'd done one of those tests from the chemist's. She had the bloody thing in her handbag. Got it out and started waving it around. Jesus! I mean – she'd pissed on the bloody thing!' He pushed his chair back from the table and threw his hands in the air. 'Disgusting. I asked her how she knew it was mine. Then she shouted at me even louder. Started thumping me. With her fists, like. It bloody hurt.' He rubbed a hand across his chest. 'Still got the bruises to prove it.'

'So you argued. Then what?'

'She calmed down a bit. Drank a bit more beer. Meanwhile I'm panicking. I don't want to be saddled with a kid. I seen it happen to too many of my mates. Christ, I'm only twenty-eight.'

McKittrick's mouth dropped open. She stared more closely at White's haggard face. He looked nearer forty than thirty. How desperate could Trisha Collins have been to think this man was a good option? And to be carrying his baby? McKittrick felt an unexpected pang of sympathy for Collins.

'Look, can we finish up here? I'd like to get going. I've got a lot of appointments lined up for this afternoon.'

'I'm afraid we've barely started, Mr White.' A faint smile tweaked the corners of Barrow's mouth upwards. 'You'll be with us for quite a while yet. I expect your highly efficient publicist will cancel all your engagements on your behalf.'

White turned to his lawyer. 'How long can they keep me here?' His cocky attitude seemed finally to be waning.

'I think it might be time for a comfort break,' the solicitor said. The first words he'd uttered since McKittrick and Barrow had been introduced to him.

'Just a few more questions before the end of this session,' Barrow said, the earlier suggestion of a smile now becoming more firmly established. 'When did Ms Collins first bring up the notion of abducting her daughter?'

'What? Christ – where did that come from?'

McKittrick watched White's face carefully. His shock seemed genuine enough.

'You've got to be kidding me.'

'What was in the bundle you carried to your car at just after midnight on Monday night?'

'Don't know what you're talking about.'

'You were seen leaving your flat struggling with a heavy load.'

'Don't know who told you that. They must be mistaken.'

'Did you leave your property at that time?'

White pinched his top lip between his teeth. His solicitor mumbled 'no comment' at him.

'Mr White? Yes or no?'

White said nothing.

'What was in the bundle?'

'Look – there was no bundle, OK? Trisha fell asleep on the settee. Too much beer I expect. She was spark out. I took my chance when I could. I couldn't even bear being around her. She'd got all clingy. I couldn't face waking up the next morning and having to talk about, you know, the baby and everything. It's not my problem.'

Barrow looked at McKittrick. She didn't react.

'So you left your flat carrying…'

'Clothes, just some clothes in a bin liner, I swear. I had to get away.'

'You left the area and didn't return?'

'Would you?'

'So you have no idea when Ms Collins left your property? Or what she did after you went?'

'No! How could I?'

Barrow stood up suddenly and noisily scraped back his chair. 'I think it may be time for that comfort break.'

'You mean I've got to stay here?'

'We'll come back later. You can walk us through your movements from Monday night right up until this morning. I should imagine it'll take some time.'

When McKittrick joined Barrow in the corridor outside the interview room, his smile had disappeared to be replaced by a clenched jaw. 'No alibi for Collins for the rest of the night. Have we looked at all the CCTV footage from the streets around White's flat yet?'

'We're working through it.'

'Let me know when it's done. In the meantime I want to bring in any of Collins' friends and acquaintances we haven't yet interviewed. Anyone with any connection to the woman at all. And I want their properties searched thoroughly. This is our absolute priority.'

'But we've interviewed pretty much everyone.'

'Well you'll just have to start from the beginning and do it again.'

'You're really that convinced Collins is behind Casey's disappearance?'

'If White's alibi can be corroborated, we have to assume someone else helped her. All we need to do is find out who.'

TWENTY-SEVEN

Angela Tate asked the cab driver to drop her off on the street that ran between the Shakespeare and Essex Estates. No need to attract attention from the handful of journalists still hanging around Montague House.

She ducked behind Trisha's block and headed for Devereux House on the Essex Estate. Her mobile trilled from her handbag and, after checking no hooded youths were circling the vicinity on their BMXs, scooped out her mobile and peered at the screen. It wasn't a number she recognised. She answered anyway and was rewarded with an echoing silence at the other end of the line.

'Raymond? Is that you?' she whispered.

Still nothing.

'It's OK – you can speak to me.'

A definite inhalation of breath, then, 'Angela?'

A woman's voice. It took Tate a moment to place it.

'You've got a nerve,' Tate said. 'Radio silence for three days and only now you decide to call? What the hell happened with Chelsea?'

Ashley Montogomery said nothing.

'Well?' Tate said, 'Why are you phoning me now?'

'I'm sorry.'

'That's it?'

'That's why I'm phoning. To apologise. I've been too embarrassed to get in touch before. You were right about

Chelsea. She must have been playing me. As soon as we got into the cab outside the office she told me she'd changed her mind. She didn't want to go to the police. She begged me to take her home.'

'And you took her straight to *The Herald* instead?'

'What kind of person do you think I am?'

Tate hadn't analysed Ashley Montogomery's character beyond *annoying* and *ambitious*.

'I would never go to a rival paper. Never.' She sounded positively indignant.

Tate had almost reached the entrance to Devereux House. 'So, what happened?'

'I dropped her off at the Shakespeare and left. She must have gone straight to the nearest reporter and offered them the story.'

'So what have you been doing since Friday? Lying low, licking your wounds?'

'I was stupid to think I was ready to take on something like that on my own.'

Humility? Really? Tate wondered just how sincere Ashley's apology actually was. It sounded more like a well-rehearsed performance.

'When you answered just now, you said "Raymond". Who did you think I was?'

'Doesn't matter. Forget it.'

'I've been doing some research. I know all about Raymond Dixon. What made you think he was calling you?'

Tate didn't respond.

'Do you think he's connected to Casey's disappearance?'

'Look I don't have time to get into all of that now. Are you calling from the office?'

'No. I can't face Harriet. I was hoping you could put in a good word for me first.'

So that was her real reason for calling.

'I feel so stupid. I wouldn't be able to bear the humiliation.'

Tate felt an unexpected and quite unwelcome pang of pity for the girl. God only knew why. 'I didn't tell her about the Chelsea Collins… debacle,' she said. 'As far as Harriet's concerned you simply went AWOL on Thursday afternoon. That's the only thing you have to explain. I'd suggest you blame your absence on a bad case of the norovirus.'

'Thanks, Angela – I really appreciate it. Where are you now? Can I buy you lun—'

Tate hung up, put the phone on silent and shoved it in her bag. She plodded up the stairs to the first floor of Devereux House and rehearsed the speech she'd been planning in the cab on the way over. She hadn't spoken to Sandra Stockwell's parents for over thirty years. Setting the appropriate tone was crucial if she was going to get what she needed from them.

She reached the Stockwells' door and took a deep breath, pressing a finger against the doorbell. A distant buzz sounded inside. She straightened her coat and pulled her face into what she hoped was a sympathetic expression.

After more than a minute, a fragmented figure appeared behind the rippled glass panels in the door, moving slowly towards her. The door opened and Tate fought hard not to seem surprised. She'd expected to see a marked change in Joyce Stockwell's appearance, it was over three decades since she'd last set eyes on the woman, but there had been such a dramatic change that Tate was struggling to control her reaction.

Joyce Stockwell's hair had turned completely white, deep lines were etched around her eyes and mouth, the skin hung loosely from her jaw and cheekbones. There wasn't an ounce of spare flesh on her.

'You?' Stockwell said, after scrutinising Tate's face as closely as Tate had hers.

Tate rocked back on her heels. She scrambled for the right words, a perfect phrase to convey her sympathy, but her brain remained stubbornly blank. So much for rehearsing a speech.

Stockwell filled the silence for her.

'Where the bloody hell have you been?'

Tate wasn't sure how to respond.

'I had your lot crawling round here end of last week. I told them all where they could go. What's taken you so long to turn up?'

'I… erm… Can I come in?'

Stockwell stood aside and pulled Tate in by the arm. 'Kettle's just boiled. I expect you'll be wanting a cup?'

'That'd be lovely.' Tate followed the direction of Stockwell's pointing hand and made her way to the living room. The layout of the flat was an exact replica of Trisha's.

Every flat on the Essex and Shakespeare Estates was pretty much identical to the next, all laid out according to a post-war architect's vision of modern urban living. After the blitz had cleared half the slums from London in the forties, the London County Council replaced them in the fifties and sixties with high-rise blocks and low-rise complexes. They were all reaching the end of their functional lives.

Tate reached the living room and was surprised to find Joyce's husband sitting in a wheelchair parked in front of a large television.

'Hello, Jimmy,' Tate said and planted herself between Mr Stockwell and the TV. 'Joyce didn't tell me you were here. How are you?'

The frail old man didn't react.

'Don't mind him. He can't hear you.' Joyce Stockwell came into the room, a brightly coloured mug of tea in each hand. 'Stroke,' she said bluntly, by way of explanation. 'I haven't sugared it.' She put the mugs down on a low table sitting between the sofa and single armchair. 'I know what you lot are like – always on a diet.'

'My lot?' Tate smiled at Jimmy before stepping around him.

'You know – telly people, reporters, presenters.'

'Thank you for talking to me.'

'Nothing to thank me for. I've only invited you in out of respect for my Sandra. I shan't be giving you a story, if that's what you were after.'

Tate was about to explain exactly why she had come when Stockwell cut her off.

'I've never forgotten the lovely things you wrote about Sandra. Meant a lot to me, that did. And Jimmy.' She glanced towards her inanimate husband.

'She was a lovely girl.'

Stockwell let out a long sigh. 'It's brought it all back, that little one going off. Poor Trish.' She lowered herself into the armchair, her eyes still on Tate. 'Not that it ever went away.' She tapped the arm of the sofa. 'Sit down if you're stopping.'

'How are you? It's been a while.' Tate perched on the edge of the sofa and picked up the steaming mug of tea.

'As well as can be expected. Wendy lives up Woolwich way now, but she visits regular, brings the kids when she can.'

'She must be, what… forty-three now?'

'Forty-four in May.'

Tate nodded absently, distracted by the subject she'd come to discuss. Still unsure quite how to bring it up. She took a sip of inky tea.

Stockwell was staring at a spot on the carpet, her mouth working as if she was having a silent conversation with someone.

'Do you see much of Trisha?' Tate finally asked.

'Not as much as I used to, when Maggie and Tom were still alive.'

'I know Trisha's mum and dad were both devastated about what happened.'

Stockwell bobbed her head in agreement. 'Maggie blamed herself, she told me as much. But it wasn't her fault. What could she have done any different?' She clutched the mug in her lap. 'She had her hands full. Four kids she was minding at the time, five if you count her Trisha. She didn't have eyes in the back of her head. Kids go wandering off all the time.'

It sounded as if Joyce Stockwell was still trying to convince herself all these years later, saying the words without any real conviction.

'Did Trisha or any of the other children ever tell you who was playing in the park with them when Sandra disappeared?'

Stockwell eyed Tate suspiciously. 'You sure you're not writing a story about it? Not like those others who were round here? Not after all this time?'

'Absolutely not – you have my word.'

'Not sure that means very much, in your line of work.'

Tate chose to ignore the dig and press on. 'I always got the impression Trisha knew more than she let on.'

'What makes you say that?'

'She seemed scared of something. Someone, perhaps.'

'Scared of that pervert. Why wouldn't she be? They should never have let the bastard out. Life sentence he got. It's a joke. Life should mean life. I haven't slept properly for days now – ever since I found out he was back on the streets.'

'Who told you?'

'One of your reporter friends. He wanted to know what I thought about it. I told him where he could go.'

'You only just found out?'

Stockwell nodded, her eyes trained on the back of her husband's head.

'No one got in touch with you at the time he was released?'

'Why would they? Everyone had forgotten about Sandra by then. You included. Weren't interested in talking to me then, were you?'

Tate didn't answer.

'Why'd you want to know about what happened in the park now?'

'I've been spending a lot of time with Trisha. She brought it up.' It was a weak justification for her questions, but she hadn't managed to come up with anything better. 'I've spoken to Lorraine about it too. And her brother.' Another lie.

'Gary Benson?'

'You know Gary?' The mere mention of his name raised Tate's blood pressure.

'Now there's a nice bloke.'

Tate jerked in her seat so violently, she was grateful she wasn't still clutching a mug of hot tea.

'Do you know him then?' Joyce Stockwell was smiling for the first time since Tate's arrival.

'Not really.' More than I want to, she thought.

'He was only a little kiddie himself when it happened, of course, but do you know, every year, on Sandra's birthday, he brings me a bunch of flowers. Regular as clockwork.'

Tate struggled to conceal her surprise. What was that about? Gary Benson soothing a guilty conscience? Tate was amazed to discover Benson had any conscience at all. But if he did, a bunch of flowers once a year was a small price to pay.

'He's taken me to the cemetery a couple of times too.'

Tate guessed the only reason Benson visited Sandra's grave was to get some kind of sick thrill from witnessing the suffering of her mother up close. The sadistic bastard.

'Was Gary there at the time? In the park?' Tate asked.

'He's never mentioned it. Why?'

'Just trying to build a picture in my mind. I'm sure if I knew more of the details, it might encourage Trisha to talk. Might help her somehow. I know it preys on her mind.'

'Have you seen Trisha since they put her away, then?'

Tate nodded. She pictured Trisha in tears, sitting on her hospital bed. Trisha's revelation hit her again. Pregnant? Didn't she have enough on her plate already?

'How's she coping?' Stockwell asked.

'Oh – you know.' What could she say?

'The police are clutching at straws locking her up.'

'You don't think she's done anything to Casey?'

'Gawd no – I know it happens – you hear such terrible stories. But not Trish. She loves those kids. I think she had so many because she's an only child herself. She wouldn't harm a single hair.' She let out a long sigh. 'Surely you don't think she could do anything like that? I don't know what Chelsea's playing at, accusing her mother of all sorts.'

Tate remembered Trisha's battered face and her desperate pleas for help. 'No – no I don't think Trisha could.'

'It makes you wonder what's happened to Casey, doesn't it, her being missing this long?'

Tate looked away.

'I mean, that pervert's out of prison and another girl goes missing. How much of a coincidence is that?'

Tate looked into Stockwell's face, the woman's expression twisted with disgust.

'I was talking to Gary about it the other day. He agreed with me,' Stockwell said.

I bet he did, Tate thought. 'Do you see much of Pamela Jeffries?' she said, eager to change the subject.

Much to her surprise, the look of disgust on Stockwell's face hardened at the mention of Jeffries' name.

'Don't talk about that woman in my home.' She puffed out an angry breath. 'Calls herself a Christian? There are some things that should never be forgiven.'

'I'm not following.' Tate had assumed the two grieving mothers would have found some comfort in one another over the years. A shared loss, an understanding that most people would never even get close to.

'Do you know Pamela Jeffries goes to church with that monster's mother?'

'Beryl Dixon? But I thought she'd moved out of the area years ago.' Raymond Dixon's mother had left the neighbourhood shortly after her son's conviction, but not soon enough to prevent her windows being smashed. Tate had been trying to get hold of Mrs Dixon's address ever since she'd received the note from her son.

'They could have transferred her to the other side of the world and it still wouldn't be far enough away.'

'Which church does she attend?'

'Why do you want to know? Sniffing out another story for yourself?'

'Of course not.'

'I don't know which one. I don't want to know. All those years she swore blind he never did it. I'm surprised she has the nerve to even set foot inside a church.'

'You can't blame Beryl for anything.'

'She raised him, didn't she?'

Tate thought about trying to steer the conversation back to the park and what she knew about it. But she could see it was already a lost cause. She was running out of people to speak to. Pamela Jeffries was next on her list. She got to her feet, sensing she'd outstayed her welcome.

'There's something I…' Joyce Stockwell clamped her bottom lip between her teeth. She shook her head.

'What is it?'

'When it came I promised myself I wouldn't tell a soul.'

'What came?'

She shook her head again and levered herself awkwardly out of the armchair. 'I'll see you out.'

Tate hesitated by the living room door. 'If there's something you want to tell me, it can stay between us. I promise you – I'm not writing a story.'

Stockwell folded her arms tight across her chest and hunched up her shoulders. 'I haven't even told my Wendy. I wanted to keep it to myself.' She slowly crossed the room and opened a drawer in a dark wood shelving unit that ran the length of the wall opposite the window. Carefully she pulled a small object wrapped in tissue paper from the drawer. 'It's brought back so many memories.' She unwrapped the tissue tenderly, taking her time with each fold. When she'd finished, she set it on a shelf and stepped away. She motioned for Tate to take a closer look.

A small silver bracelet sat on the bed of crumpled tissue.

'Sandra was wearing it the day she died.'

Tate reached a hand towards the bracelet. Stockwell quickly slapped her arm.

'I didn't say you could touch it.'

Tate peered at the inscription that ran around the whole inside circumference of the little bangle. *With much love from Mummy and Daddy*. She glanced over at Jimmy Stockwell. He was completely oblivious.

'Whenever I asked about it at the time, the police told me they couldn't help. They never found it. Not on Sandra. Or at Beryl Dixon's. They said he must have taken it from her and dumped it somewhere.'

'How did you get it?' Tate's mind was racing – she didn't remember the bracelet being on Sandra's wrist when she saw her body. Who had taken it from her? Benson? 'How long have you had it?'

'It came through the door last Friday night.'

'You must take it to the police.'

'I've only just got it back, I'm not losing it again.'

'But it could be used as evidence. There might be traces of—' Tate stopped after she saw the darkening expression on Joyce Stockwell's face.

'Evidence to prove what? They're not going to lock him up again, are they?' She bit her lip. 'I hate to think of him hiding it somewhere, tormenting me all these years.'

'Who?'

'Dixon – who else?'

'I'm sure the police would take good care of it. If they could just have it for a little while.'

'Wouldn't be any point them having it.'

'What if they found traces of someone else's DNA on it?'

'Whose? What are you saying?'

'If Raymond Dixon wasn't the one who took it.' Tate could picture Gary Benson snatching it from Sandra's wrist, keeping it as a trophy.

'Of course he took it.'

'I just…' Tate wanted to shove the bracelet in a pocket and run.

Stockwell lifted it carefully from the shelf before Tate had the chance. 'The police wouldn't find anything on it anyway,' she said as she rewrapped the tissue paper. 'I scrubbed it clean as soon as I got it.'

TWNETY-EIGHT

Tuesday 14th February

The hold music was something poppy from the eighties, distorting nastily through Ralph Mills' mobile. He wandered from the incident room all the way to Manisha Kapoor's desk before a distant voice thanked him for holding. He nudged Kapoor on the shoulder. Yet again she was engrossed in CCTV footage, watching it at triple speed.

'I'm beginning to think it's some kind of weird perversion with you,' he said. 'Like you get a kick out of staring at that stuff.'

She hit the pause button and turned round to face him. 'What are you doing up here? Haven't you got a distant relative of Trisha Collins to arrest?'

The hold music paused. Mills held up a finger. Then the music started up again. 'I just found out you've been taken off the case – for what it's worth I think it's really shitty. I'd put in a good word for you, but I'm not sure my word means very much to the HSCC lot. I just wanted to come and tell you… you know. I can imagine how pissed off you feel.'

Kapoor shrugged. 'The DCI asked me for my honest opinion of Trisha. Now he says he can't rely on my objectivity. Says I'm "too personally involved". I wasn't going to start lying to him, just to stay on the case. I didn't dig up any dirt on her. That was the mistake I made.'

'We'll just have to sit tight and wait for Barrow to be proved wrong.' Mills pulled the mobile from his ear to check he was still connected.

'Meanwhile Casey's still missing,' Kapoor said. 'And we're wasting valuable time.'

'I'm not sure there's much hope now of finding her alive.'

Kapoor let out a shuddering sigh. 'Trisha must be going out of her mind.'

'Hello?' Mills thought he heard someone on the other end of the line. But the music continued as before.

'Who are you trying to speak to, anyway?'

'Ray Dixon's probation officer.'

'Is it a new lead?'

'Not exactly.' Mills hadn't cleared his pursuit of Dixon with McKittrick or Barrow. His enquiries were strictly unofficial, and because he couldn't go throwing his weight around with the upper echelons of the probation service in Leeds, he'd been kept on hold for the last fifteen minutes.

'You think Dixon is responsible?'

'Let's just say if I manage to rule him out I'll sleep a lot easier.'

'But I thought he'd already been eliminated from the investigation. Didn't the local force interview him days ago?'

'They were supposed to. I only found out this morning that no one had actually got around to it.'

'Crossed wires?'

'Something like that.' He decided it was wise to change the subject. He peered at the frozen image on Kapoor's monitor. 'That's the chemist on Camberwell New Road.'

'Very observant. I've inherited the pharmacy break-in case.'

'Getting anywhere?'

'Only just started.'

Finally a voice on the phone crackled in his ear. Mills quickly confirmed his identity and reason for calling.

'I meant to call you yesterday,' the woman at the other end told him. 'Only we've been snowed under, I haven't had a moment.' She went on to tell him why she'd wanted to speak to him and Mills snatched a Post-it from Kapoor's desk, his pulse quickening as he rapidly scribbled down the details.

When the probation officer had finished, Mills shoved his phone into a pocket and ran towards the exit, waving a cursory goodbye to Kapoor as he barged through the door.

He found DI McKittrick chatting to Mark Black, the incident room manager. 'Sorry to interrupt, boss,' Mills said. 'But it's kind of urgent.'

'Well?' McKittrick said when DS Black had walked away.

'I've just been speaking to Ray Dixon's probation officer.'

'Why? He's been eliminated from our enquiries.'

Mills took a deep breath. He had no choice but to admit he'd been following up on the Dixon angle. 'Things have moved on a bit since then. That was before I had a long conversation with Angela Tate.'

'The journalist?'

Mills nodded.

'What's she got to do with it?'

Mills told McKittrick about the note Tate had received, allegedly from Dixon.

'Do you have it?'

'It's with forensics - they're checking for fingerprints.'

'Why didn't you mention any of this to me before?'

'Everything was kicking off with Collins when I spoke to Tate – I assumed you wouldn't take it seriously.'

'You don't want to assume anything about me, constable.' She looked into his eyes, holding his gaze for a long moment.

Mills wondered if he was meant to pick up on some underlying subtext.

'Personally I like to keep an open mind before I jump to conclusions,' she said, not taking her eyes off him.

Mills started to feel so uncomfortable he was forced to look away. *Keep an open mind*? She had to be referring to the pills she'd taken from Collins' bathroom. What was she trying to do? Provoke a reaction? Was she testing him? He decided not to rise to the bait.

'And you consider the note to be threatening?' McKittrick asked.

'Tate wasn't taking it that way… but if you read between the lines…'

'What did you ask the probation officer?'

'Just whether it sounded like something Dixon might have sent.'

'And what did she say?'

'She wouldn't commit to an opinion, one way or the other.'

McKittrick pushed up her sleeves. 'Is that it? You said you wanted to tell me something urgently.'

'I was just getting to that.' He shoved his hands in his pockets, uneasy at the way McKittrick's gaze was still boring into him. 'According to Linda, the probation officer, Dixon was set to catch the seven-thirty from Leeds to Kings Cross this morning.'

'He's in London?'

Mills checked his watch. 'He should be by now.'

'And did Linda tell you why Dixon has come down here?'

'It's a bit awkward, actually.' Mills pulled his hands from his pockets and shoved them under his arms. 'I was hoping to have a quiet word with him – if it was OK with you, of course.'

'So what's the problem?'

'He's in London to bury his mother.'

Mills and McKittrick reached the municipal cemetery in Honor Oak in under twenty minutes. Mills nosed the car slowly through the gates and parked behind a long line of dark saloons. He scanned the sprawling graveyard and spotted the cortege a hundred or so yards away. A second, smaller group was heading towards the first, a few people waving what looked like placards above their heads. The sound of raised voices carried towards him on the wind.

Mills jumped out of the car started sprinting towards them, lengthening his stride and pumping his arms as the shouting grew louder.

Still thirty yards away from the open grave, Mills glimpsed a man he recognised leading the second group. Gary Benson. Benson shoved two fists into the chest of a tall, straggly-haired man who had broken away from the cortege. He was wearing a shabby grey suit, the legs of the trousers ending a good three inches above his shoes. As he drew closer, Mills saw the tall man was Raymond Dixon. Benson shoved him again. Dixon did nothing to defend himself.

'OK – you can stop that,' Mills hollered.

Benson shoved again.

'What's the matter, Benson?' Mills heard Dixon say. 'Feeling threatened? You should be. I know all about you. What you've been up to.'

Benson shoved a fourth time and Dixon stumbled backwards.

'Worried your little business enterprise is about to go under?' Dixon said as he threw out his arms in an attempt to stay upright. 'You should be.'

'That's enough!' Mills stepped between them and held up his hands. He glanced up to see McKittrick running towards them, mobile phone glued to her ear.

She pocketed her phone as she approached. 'Raymond Dixon?'

The tall man in the badly fitting suit turned his torso towards her and nodded, his gaze still trained on Benson.

'I'd like to have a few words, sir,' McKittrick said. 'If that's OK? Down at the station.'

'It's not me you should be arresting.' He glared at Benson. After a few moments he finally looked at McKittrick. 'I'm not going to the station or anywhere else,' he said emphatically. 'Not until I've buried my mother.'

TWENTY-NINE

Ray Dixon had refused to be interviewed with Ralph Mills present, so McKittrick grabbed Cath Murray just as she was returning to the incident room from the canteen, a polystyrene box in her hands.

'I need you in the interview suite. I'm afraid you'll have to forget lunch,' McKittrick told her. 'Will it keep?'

'Slice of pizza and chips? Not really.' Murray dumped the box, plastic fork and paper napkin in the nearest bin.

'Sorry.'

'Wasn't that hungry anyway. I'll grab a salad later.'

McKittrick explained the situation on the way.

'Did Dixon say why he'd taken such a dislike to Ralph?' Cath asked when she'd heard the full account.

'He refused to elaborate. Mills spooked him for some reason.'

'Not really something you associate with Ralph. Not exactly threatening is he?'

McKittrick didn't answer. She hadn't yet assessed how much of a threat Mills might prove to be. That would mostly depend on how much he'd seen in Trisha Collins' bathroom.

They reached the interview suite and McKittrick turned to Murray. 'Ready?'

Murray nodded enthusiastically. 'For anything.'

Inside they found Ray Dixon sitting with his arms wrapped around his ribs, hugging himself tightly.

'Apologies for the delay.' McKittrick strode to the seat opposite Dixon's, but remained on her feet. She waited for him to look up at her. 'This is Detective Constable Murray, she'll be sitting in during our conversation.'

'Conversation? Is that what you call it now?'

'You're not under arrest, sir.'

'I don't understand why I'm here – I haven't done anything.'

McKittrick sat down and indicated to Murray to do the same.

'We do appreciate your coming in to talk to us, especially at such a difficult time.'

Dixon sniffed loudly, his gaze fell to the floor.

'We just have a few questions we'd like to ask you and then you can be on your way.'

Dixon jerked his head up and glanced around the room. 'Bit different to the last time I was questioned in this place. Still smells the same though.' He looked at Murray for the first time. 'Doesn't it get to you, that stench?'

The detective constable shifted in her seat a fraction, and stared back at Dixon, her face blanker than the beige wall behind his head. McKittrick was beginning to warm to DC Murray.

'Must get into your clothes.' He lifted a sleeve to his nose and sniffed. 'It does. That's disgusting. How am I going to get rid of it?'

McKittrick opened the cardboard folder in her lap and pulled out a sheet of paper, print side down.

'What's this?' Dixon eyed first the paper then McKittrick's face.

'Where were you last Thursday, Mr Dixon?'

'I don't remember.'

McKittrick turned over the sheet and handed it to him. He stared down at the three lines printed on it, his eyes tracing along the words. For a moment there was the faintest spark of recognition. It quickly faded. 'What's all that about?'

'This is a copy of the note received by Angela Tate at the *Evening News* offices. The note you delivered to her by hand on Thursday of last week.'

He shook his head, handed the sheet back.

'Still not ringing any bells? You took it to the building on Blackfriars Road.'

'I don't even know where that is.'

'What did you want the journalist to help you with, Mr Dixon?'

'It's nothing to do with me.' He sniffed his sleeve again and mumbled 'disgusting' into the crook of his arm. Then his left leg started to jiggle, the heel bouncing up and down.

'You deny contacting Angela Tate?'

'Last time I spoke to her was in prison. Thirty-three years ago. Why would I get in touch with her after all this time?'

McKittrick stared at him, maintaining eye contact until he looked away. They'd received the fingerprint analysis back from forensics. The only prints they found belonged to Tate. Whoever sent it had made sure they would remain anonymous. She slipped the sheet back into its folder. 'Where were you on Monday of last week?'

'Can't remember.'

McKittrick wondered if that would be his knee-jerk response to every question.

'Leeds or London?'

'Why would I be in London?'

'Visiting your mother, perhaps?'

'Nope. Didn't visit her.'

'When was the last time you did?'

'Haven't been back down here until today.'

McKittrick stared hard into his eyes. He looked away. 'Not once since your release?' she said.

He shook his head, his mouth trembling slightly.

'Can I ask why?'

'Nothing for me here.'

'But you must have visited your mother, before she passed away?'

'Nope.' His leg bounced more vigorously. 'I didn't like the people she was associating with. Churchy types. They wanted to save my soul.' He stopped fidgeting for a moment and leaned forward. He looked up at McKittrick, widening his eyes, the bloodshot whites showing above and below the irises. 'Only my soul doesn't need saving. My conscience is clear. I've done nothing wrong. She knew that – they just tried to poison her mind.'

'You've not visited London in the past two years?'

'One year, eight months, two weeks, three days.' He slumped back, his thin frame sinking into the soft upholstery.

'Not once, in all that time?'

'I don't have many fond memories of the place. You saw what happened today at the cemetery.' He looked up at the clock on the opposite wall. 'How much longer are you going to keep me here? I've got to get to the station soon.'

'You're going back today?'

'I can't miss that train – I can't afford to buy another ticket.'

'What about when your mother fell ill? Didn't you visit her in hospital?'

'She wasn't in hospital – she had a heart attack.' Dixon wrapped his long arms around his ribs again. 'I really can't miss the train,' he repeated.

McKittrick decided to change tack. 'At the cemetery earlier you spoke to Gary Benson – what did you mean when you said…' She referred to her notebook. "I know all about you, what you've been up to"? What has Benson been up to?'

'Dunno.'

'You don't know what you meant by it?'

'Don't remember saying it.'

'My constable heard you.'

'He must be mistaken.'

'What did you mean?'

'No point in asking me about something I didn't say. You should be asking "your constable" why he's making stuff up.' He mumbled something McKittrick couldn't make out.

'What was that?'

'Nothing.'

'I could just bring Mills in here and you could ask him yourself.'

'No way.'

'Why not?'

'Not having him anywhere near me.' He shuddered. 'Look – I came here because you asked me to. I'm not under arrest. You can't make me stay.'

McKittrick scrutinised Dixon's face. A muscle in his cheek, just below his right eye, had started to twitch.

'I've got to get my train.'

'I'll make sure an officer takes you to Kings Cross. We won't let you miss it.'

'I don't need you to do that – I can catch the bus. I just want to get out of here.' He raked his long fingernails though his thinning hair. 'What did you do with Benson? Is he here in the station? Did you arrest him?'

'You don't have to worry about Gary Benson. He's in custody.'

'Who said I was worried about him?' His leg was jiggling again. 'Benson can't hurt me. Not anymore.' He stood up. 'I'd like to go now.'

'Please, Mr Dixon, just a few more minutes.'

Dixon slumped back down.

'I'd like you to have a good think before you answer this question.'

The twitch under his eye was more noticeable. What was he hiding?

'What question?'

'Where were you on February 6th, after about three in the afternoon?'

Dixon opened his mouth to speak, but McKittrick held up a hand. 'Just have a think. Please. Last Monday afternoon. I'd like you to account for your movements.'

'Why?'

'I need to eliminate you from a current investigation.'

Dixon stood up. 'No way. I want to leave. Now.'

'Just a quick rundown of where you were, what you were doing, who you were with.'

'I had nothing to do with that little girl going missing.'

'Which little girl, Mr Dixon?'

'Don't try to get clever with me. I had nothing to do with *any* of them.' He walked around the sofa. Murray jumped to her feet.

'Surely you want us to officially eliminate you from our enquiries?' Murray said. 'Why not tell us what you were doing?'

'I haven't got time for this.' Dixon moved towards the exit. Before he reached it, the door swung open.

DCI Barrow marched in. 'Inspector. A word. Now.'

McKittrick followed Barrow out of the room and along the corridor.

'What possessed you?' he hissed at her, a fine spray of saliva issuing from his mouth. 'Dixon has *nothing* to do with this investigation. Why is he even here?'

McKittrick quickly explained about the note Angela Tate had received, half running to keep up with Barrow's long strides.

'Irrelevant. In case it has escaped your mind, there's a nine-year-old girl out there somewhere, possibly being held captive by a friend of Collins, if we're lucky, possibly already dead if we're not. Interviewing Collins' acquaintances is our number one priority. You know that.'

'But, sir… I was just making sure—'

'Enough!' Barrow raised his hand. 'Picking up an ex-convict at his mother's *funeral*, for God's sake, is not going to help us find Casey.' Finally he came to a halt and McKittrick almost ran into him. He turned to her. 'Stop wasting your time with Dixon. I want him out of this station and on a train back to Leeds.'

THIRTY

The incident room was eerily quiet. Ralph Mills paced up and down the long aisle between two rows of desks and wondered what was happening downstairs with Ray Dixon. What if McKittrick asked him the wrong questions? No one was as qualified as Mills to interview him. He'd made it his business to find out as much about the man as he could. Frustrated at being excluded from the interview, Mills had requested permission to interview Gary Benson, but McKittrick had insisted he leave Benson to her. He was starting to feel like a spare part.

A phone rang on an unoccupied desk at the other end of the office, Mills started towards it, eager to do something useful, but as he approached, the ringing stopped. A nearby uniformed officer smiled and gave him the thumbs up, a phone cradled between her neck and shoulder. She'd beaten him to it, diverting the call to her own desk. He was about to suggest he relieve her from her duties so she could take a ten-minute breather when his mobile started buzzing in his pocket. He glanced at the screen: a mobile number he didn't recognise.

'Mills.'

'Hi. You told me I should ring if I had any information.' It took Mills a moment to place the voice. Where had he heard that accent recently? It came to him suddenly – the pharmacist from the chemist's on Camberwell New Road.

'I'm afraid I'm not working on the case now, Miss er…'

'It's Rachel.' She sounded disappointed he'd forgotten her name. 'I don't have anything new to tell you about what happened… I was just checking in, really. To find out if you needed anything from me. Before I leave.'

'You've got another job?'

'Not exactly. I'm going back to New Zealand.'

'You never mentioned you were planning—'

'I only decided last week. The break-in was the last straw. It's my second since I started working in London. I don't need the stress.'

Mills left the incident room and started heading upstairs to find Kapoor. 'I'm not sure where the case is at the moment,' he said. 'You should talk to my colleague.'

'Oh – OK.' Again the disappointed tone.

Mills pushed through the door into the main CID office and saw Kapoor staring at her monitor, exactly the position she'd been in when he'd left her the day before. 'I'm with my colleague now. Hang on a sec.' Mills handed the phone to Kapoor, quickly explaining the situation.

She pressed the phone to her ear and said hello, pulling it away after a couple of seconds. 'She hung up.'

'Really?' Mills snatched back the phone.

'Is this the Kiwi that Cath thinks fancies you?'

'Cath's got an overactive imagination.'

'Well the woman clearly wasn't interested in speaking to me.'

Mills was about to select the call back option when Kapoor held a hand over his.

'Before you do that,' she said, 'I'd like you to take a look at something for me.' She rewound the CCTV footage on her screen. 'It's here somewhere.'

After a few seconds the video started to play in real time. 'What am I looking at?' Mills asked.

'Turns out the chemist's was burgled twice. This is what happened just after one-thirty a.m. on Tuesday 7th.'

Mills watched as two slight figures dressed in black, balaclavas over their heads, walked into camera shot. The shorter of the two started gesticulating at the other, who then made straight for a shelf behind the main pharmacy counter, scooped up a handful of boxes, shoved them in a supermarket carrier bag and quickly rejoined his companion. The two figures then exited without taking anything else.

Kapoor hit the pause option.

'But that makes no sense,' Mills said. 'The place was wrecked. These two barely disturbed the dust.

'I told you – the place was robbed twice. Look.' She advanced the video at triple speed until four hooded and masked figures rushed into view. Two of them kicked down the door leading to the rear storeroom and disappeared inside. Meanwhile their accomplices set about smashing up anything breakable in the shop itself. The two storeroom thieves remerged, arms full of boxes and all four left.

'It was burgled twice and the alarm didn't go off once?' Mills said when Kapoor paused the footage again.

'The owner couldn't explain it, according to his statement. Though I suspect if I do a bit more digging I might discover the big yellow alarm attached to the wall on the outside of the shop is just a dummy box with a flashing LED.'

'But the thieves wouldn't have known that.'

'Maybe they got lucky.'

'Why did the first two only nick one thing?'

'Seems they were quite specific about what they wanted. But the video quality isn't good enough to make out exactly what that is.'

Mills dialled the pharmacist's number. She answered after a single ring and quickly apologised for getting cut off.

'That's OK,' Mills said and switched the call to speakerphone. 'I've just been looking at the security video from the chemist's on Camberwell New Road. Can you tell me what you kept on the shelf immediately behind the counter? Second up from the floor, far left.'

The pharmacist said nothing for a few moments and Mills wondered if she was about to hang up on him again.

'Second from the bottom?' she said eventually.

'Looks like small boxes, about four inches by two,' he said.

'That'll be Ventolin – inhalers for asthma.'

Kapoor frowned at Mills. 'You're sure about that?' she said.

'Who's this?' The pharmacist sounded alarmed.

'That's my colleague, DC Kapoor – she's taken over the case.'

'Oh, OK. I'm sorry – what was the question?'

Kapoor didn't say anything, she was just staring into space, her frown deepening.

Mills answered for her. 'You're sure the boxes contained Ventolin inhalers?'

'Why?'

Mills shrugged and looked at Kapoor who was scrabbling for something on her desk. She retrieved a pen and notepad and quickly wrote the words *Casey suffers from asthma.*

'We... er... we just need to be sure of the facts. It was definitely Ventolin?'

'Blue and white boxes?'

'Hard to tell, could be.'

'Is is significant?'

Given the woman was about to travel to the other side of the world, Mills saw no harm in telling her about the CCTV footage. He quickly described what happened during the initial robbery.

'They took just the Ventolin, nothing else?' the pharmacist said when he'd finished.

'That's the way it seems.'

'Well that's plain weird.'

'That's just what we were thinking. Presumably you stocked tranquillisers and methadone? Surely they would have helped themselves to a lot more?'

'No – I don't mean the fact that they only stole one thing,' the pharmacist said. 'Though that is peculiar. It's weird because it's happened to me before.'

'I don't understand.' Mills looked at Kapoor who shrugged back at him.

'The first break-in – at the pharmacy I worked at last year. Only one thing was taken there too.'

'When was this?'

'Last October. I'm not sure of the exact date. But I suppose you have a record of it?'

Kapoor shook her head.

'Where was this chemist's?'

'Just up the road from the other one. Kennington.'

'Was the same thing taken?'

'No. Not Ventolin that time. They cleared out our entire stock of Femodene.'

Mills was none the wiser. 'Can you tell me what that is?'

'A contraceptive pill,' Kapoor and the pharmacist said at the same time.

1979

'Thank you for agreeing to see me, Raymond. Can I call you Raymond?' Angela Tate didn't wait for a reply from the pale, greasy-faced adolescent sitting on the other side of the dirty Formica-topped table. 'Good. Raymond it is then.'

'I'm only talking to you because Mum told me to. She said you want to put me in your paper.' He folded his arms. 'I don't want any photographs.' He spoke quietly, his eyes darting around the room, never settling on anything for more than a fraction of a second.

'I don't want you to think I'm here only in a professional capacity. I want to help you.' Angela tried to hold his a gaze for a moment, to prove her sincerity, but he refused to make eye contact. 'You do know that, don't you, Raymond?' She leaned in. 'You know you can trust me. Don't you?'

A passing prison guard rapped his knuckles on the table and glared at her until she moved away from Dixon.

'How are they treating you in here?' She couldn't help but stare at the yellowing bruise above his left eye and the thick line of scabbed skin running from his top lip to his nose. There were deep scratches on his forearms too, some fresh, some less so, criss-crossing an existing network of faint pink scars. The remnants of earlier injuries, Angela supposed. She resisted the urge to ask him how he got them. That particular line of questioning could wait for another visit. First she had to gain his trust.

'I keep myself to myself. It's the best way,' he said, after a long pause.

Angela cleared her throat and scraped her chair a little further under the table. 'I spoke to your mum this morning, actually.'

Immediately Dixon's face darkened. 'Is she all right? I haven't spoken to her for days. I can't call her – we don't have a phone at home.'

'That must be really hard for you. Feeling so isolated in here.'

'Is Mum all right?'

'Your mum misses you. I won't pretend she isn't worrying about you. But she's keeping well. She knows she's got to stay strong for you.'

'Next time you see her, will you tell her I'm OK?'

Angela nodded, and quickly glanced up at the clock. She only had fifteen minutes to get what she needed. 'What I came to speak to you about… I mean, what your mum asked me to…' She gave up and started again. 'Since you withdrew your confession, your mum thought it would be a good idea to get you a new solicitor.'

'She can't afford anything like that. I'll stick with the old one.'

'It's OK – you don't have to worry. Your mum's not paying for it. My paper is.' Angela swallowed, uneasy with the deception. She didn't want to start her relationship with Dixon with a lie, but she wasn't sure an admission that the new lawyer was being held on retainer courtesy of her own dwindling Post Office savings would do much to encourage him to put his faith in her. It wasn't exactly an orthodox approach. 'I've arranged for the solicitor to come and speak to you tomorrow,' she said and flashed him a brief smile.

'Why would your paper pay for my solicitor?'

It was a good question. One she hadn't prepared for.

'Because they believe in you – just like I do.' Another lie. She was yet to convince anyone at the *Evening News* that Dixon was a cause worth fighting for. But if she was going to stake her fledgling career on proving Raymond Dixon had nothing to do with Sandra Stockwell's murder, she had to make sure he had someone more qualified than her in his corner. He needed all the help she could get him.

'Will he get me out of here?'

'That's his job.'

'I haven't done anything wrong,' he said, almost to himself.

'And he'll help you prove that.' Angela reached a hand across the table, saw the guard approaching again, and quickly withdrew it.

'Nobody can help me. The police have made up their minds. They don't like me. They think I'm disgusting. That's what they said.'

'Because of what you did before? I mean, the thing on the bus—'

'That was ages ago. I was just a kid. I never hurt anyone. I never would.'

'They don't think you're disgusting – they just want to solve a crime – you weren't the only person they questioned. Did you know that?'

'What?'

'They picked up anyone who had a previous conviction for…' She lowered her voice. 'A sexual offence.'

'I didn't have sex! I never touched anyone.'

'I know that – it's just what they call it.'

'He called me filthy.' Dixon was fidgeting and glancing around the room again. 'The policeman – the one in charge.'

'Inspector Mills?'

Dixon nodded, but still refused to look at her. 'He's been in here to question me too. Keeps asking where Paula Jeffries is, what I've done with her. I haven't done anything

– how would I know where she is?' He glanced at Angela for a moment then quickly looked away again.

The police investigation into the disappearance of Paula Jeffries had stalled completely. Angela was surprised they hadn't tried to include her murder in Dixon's original coerced confession. But with her body yet to be found, presumably that tactic was just too risky.

'Mills says if I tell him where Paula's body is, then the judge will give me a shorter sentence. But I don't know where she is. How can I tell him when I don't know?' He was getting louder, talking faster, breathing more rapidly. He looked as if he might jump from his seat at any moment.

'You mustn't listen to Mills. You can't trust anything he says.' Angela tried to keep her tone level and calm, not wanting to alarm Dixon any more than he was already. 'Mills was relying on your confession – he doesn't have any actual proof. Now you've withdrawn your statement, he's back to square one. There's no real case against you.' She shifted in her chair to try to make Dixon look at her. 'He brought in lots of people and questioned them all, pushing and pushing until one of them cracked. That person was you, unfortunately. If someone else had confessed first, you'd be at home right now with your mum.'

Dixon started scratching at one of the scabs on his arm. He broke the skin and bright red blood bloomed along the jagged brown line.

'Who did that to you? Who cut your arms like that?'

Dixon shoved his hands behind his back. 'No one.' He sucked in a long trembling breath and stared down at the chipped tabletop. 'It's true,' he said quietly. 'I am disgusting.'

'Don't talk like that. I know it's hard, but you can't let Mills get to you.'

'It's not just him. It's the guards as well. And the other prisoners. They all hate me. It's just like the estate. They hate me there as well.'

'That's not true. What about your friends? I'm sure they don't hate you.'

'Don't have any.'

'Of course you do. What about all your friends at school?'

He shook his head. Angela could see he was scratching his arms behind his back. 'They're pleased I'm in here.'

'I don't believe that!' Angela was struggling to stay upbeat.

'The kids on the estate bully me. They're younger than me, so I can't fight back, they know that and it makes them even worse.'

'What do they do?'

'Call me names. Throw stones and stuff at me whenever I have to walk past them. When I was arrested before, for… for doing… on the bus… they shoved dog mess through the letterbox.'

'Did you tell the police?'

'They don't care.'

Angela threw back her head, gulped down a breath then slowly exhaled. This was proving to be harder than she'd imagined. 'Listen carefully to me, Raymond. What's happened in the past isn't important now. We need to concentrate on getting you out of here. Speak to the solicitor when he comes tomorrow. Answer all the questions he asks you as best you can. That way he has a better chance of helping you. Can you do that?'

He wouldn't answer.

'Do it for your mum so she won't worry. Promise me you'll do that.'

'I'll try,' he said after another long pause.

'Good.'

A loud bell, shrill as a fire alarm, sounded from the loudspeakers mounted high on each wall of the visiting room.

'We're going to get you out of here. You have my word.' Angela wasn't at all sure that meant anything to him. 'You just have to keep it together until we do. OK?'

He nodded and looked away, his eyes brimming with tears.

As she filed out of the room with the other visitors and joined the slow-moving line snaking along the corridor leading to the exit, Angela spotted DI Mills chatting with a prison guard. He said something that made the guard throw his head back and snort an explosive laugh through his nose.

'I don't know what you've got to joke about,' she said when she drew level with them. 'Most people take miscarriages of justice more seriously.'

'If it's not my favourite cub reporter,' Mills said and winked at the guard. 'You've got to be able to see the funny side in this game. You'll learn. You can't walk around like you've got a stick up your arse. Not if you're going to last more than five minutes.'

'You make me sick.'

'And there was me thinking we were getting on famously.' He stepped back and inspected her, his eyes roving over every inch. 'Very sombre outfit. Been talking to the condemned man?'

'Get lost.'

'I suppose I've got you to thank for Dixon withdrawing his confession?'

'I don't know what you're talking about.'

'Not that it matters.'

'Did you get a kick out of beating up a seventeen-year-old boy?'

'What?'

'He didn't give himself a black eye.'

'Very unfortunate, him walking into a door like that. He really needs to watch where he's going.'

Angela stepped to one side, eager to reach the exit. She didn't want to breathe the same air as Charlie Mills. He shuffled sideways to block her path.

'You don't intimidate me,' she said.

'Oh I wouldn't dream of doing anything of the sort. I just don't want us to part on bad terms. I thought we could have a little chat. I might be able to help you out.'

'I'll pass on that.'

'But you haven't even heard what it is yet.'

She tried to move around him, but he blocked her again.

'So you're not interested in an exclusive for the *Evening News*? I thought you'd be keen to make a good impression in your new job.'

Angela wanted to ignore him, but couldn't resist the bait. 'What is it?'

'A witness has come forward.'

'A witness to what?'

'A witness who saw Dixon leading Sandra Stockwell away from the park on the day she disappeared.'

'They can't have. They must be lying. Raymond was nowhere near the park when Sandra went missing. His mother told me.'

'I wouldn't trust anything Mrs Dixon tells you. She's only got Raymond's word for it. And he's a devious bastard, take it from me.'

'Save your breath – I'm not listening to any more of your crap.'

'Don't be so quick to judge. Our witness happens to be very reliable. Gone into the minutest of detail in his statement. I'd go so far as to say it's watertight. Put that in your paper.'

'If he's so credible, why didn't he come forward straightaway?'

'He was scared. It's got to be frightening, hasn't it? Coming down to the police station, talking to a lot of strangers for hours on end. It's traumatic enough for anyone. Must be terrifying…' He paused and smiled at her. 'For a nine-year-old boy.'

THIRTY-ONE

'You're a hard man to track down, Mr Benson,' DCI Barrow said as he sat down beside Ralph Mills, opposite a stony-faced Gary Benson and his equally inanimate solicitor. 'We've been wanting to speak to you all weekend. How lucky that my detectives bumped into you at the cemetery today.'

Benson arched his back and jutted his chin out.

Mills watched Barrow's face. There was no flicker of a reaction.

Mills had been fully expecting to interview Benson with DI McKittrick, but the DCI had insisted Mills lead the interview himself, sidelining McKittrick completely. According to Cath Murray, the DCI was seriously pissed off with his second in command.

Before the interview Mills had managed to do a quick bit of research on Benson's criminal history and reported back to Barrow. From what he had managed to glean so far, it seemed Benson had been arrested a handful of times, mostly for petty offences committed when he was still a juvenile: taking and driving away, driving under the influence, disorderly conduct. But he was never actually charged with anything. In fact, he had been picked up so many times with no more than a caution to his name, Mills presumed that the teenage Gary Benson must have had connections inside the force. A friendly copper willing to turn a blind eye, bend the odd rule here and there. There was nothing on file to suggest Benson had been a police informant, but it was the most logical explanation to account for the special treatment he'd received. Mills wondered whether his dad might have been behind the leniency, especially given Mrs Benson had sung the old man's praises so enthusiastically when Mills had spoken to her. He didn't share his theory with the DCI.

'Constable?' Barrow had turned to him. 'Would you like to make a start?'

Mills cleared his throat. 'Can you tell me why you went to the cemetery today?'

Benson folded his arms and let his head loll to one side. 'I'm sure you can work it out.'

'For the record, sir?'

'Just doing my civic duty.'

'By disrupting the funeral of a seventy-year-old woman?'

'Dixon needs to know he's not welcome round here.'

'So you decided to make it clear by physically assaulting him?'

Benson quickly glanced sideways at his silent solicitor. 'No comment,' he said after his lawyer blinked slowly at him.

'We have plenty of eye witnesses.'

'No comment.'

'What did Mr Dixon mean when he said he knew what you've been getting up to?'

'What?'

Mills consulted his notebook. '"I know all about you. What you've been up to." That's what he said.'

'How should I know what he meant? I can't account for the shit that comes out of that pervert's mouth.'

The lawyer pointedly cleared his throat.

'You need to ask Dixon what he meant,' Benson continued. 'I'm not a fucking mind reader.'

'You did hear him say it, then?'

The solicitor coughed again.

'No comment.'

Mills saw Barrow close his eyes and wondered if that meant he should hurry up or change tack.

'Have you locked him up?' Benson said. 'Got him back behind bars where he belongs?'

Mills wished they had. Instead, he'd seen Dixon climb into a patrol car that sped him away to Kings Cross station.

'You should bang him up and throw away the key. You know – for his own protection.'

Barrow snapped his eyes open. 'Is that a threat, Mr Benson?'

'As if I'd threaten anyone? Can't speak for what other people might do though. You should shut him away before he gets properly hurt.'

Mills was about to ask another question when the DCI held up a hand.

'Where were you on Monday 6th February from three-thirty onwards?' Barrow stared into Benson's face.

'Where did that come from? Jesus! Did you ask him that? He's the fucking child killer. Christ almighty.' Benson slumped back on his chair and shoved his fists under his armpits. 'How they ever let him out in the first place is a mystery to me. They're sick in the head people like him. Don't deserve to be walking around like the rest of us. Inside or out. They don't change, not deep down – he's just fooled the lot of you. The prison authorities, the arse-wipe trick-cyclists, the judges, all too blind to see what's right in front of your eyes.'

Mills had to stop himself from nodding his agreement.

'You're an expert on the rehabilitation of offenders, are you?' Barrow said.

'Doesn't take a university degree to add two and two together. They can't be rehabilitated. It's just not possible.'

'Thank you for your insight. Now, if we can get back to my question: where were you on last Monday afternoon and evening?'

'No comment.'

'How well do you know Trisha Collins?'

'This is getting insulting now. You've got a fucking nerve.'

'According to your mother, you had a relationship with Ms Collins.'

'That was years back. It wasn't a relationship. There's no way Mum would have called it that either. That's you putting words into her mouth. But it's what you lot do, isn't it?'

'What would you call it, if not a relationship?'

'We were not much more than school kids. I'd call it a bit of a fumble behind the bike sheds.'

'How long did it last?'

'The fumble?' He sneered a smile at Barrow. 'I got well shot. Dumped her long before she started to go to fat. They all do, eventually.'

Mills glanced across the table at Benson's stomach, solid fat forming a rigid shelf below his chest.

'But you're still close to the Collins family now?' Barrow continued.

Again the solicitor cleared his throat.

'Not really. Put it this way – I'd have to think twice about pissing on them if they were on fire.'

'But you would agree that Ms Collins is your sister's best friend?'

'Nothing to do with me who Lorraine chooses to knock about with. You'd have to ask her.'

'So… where were you on Monday afternoon and evening?'

'Christ – Casey going missing has nothing to do with me. Can't you get that into your bloody plod head?'

'Let's take it slowly, shall we? Where were you between three-thirty and five o'clock?'

Benson let his chin drop to his chest. He puffed out his cheeks. 'No comment.'

'We've got all day. In your own time.' Barrow sat back, rested his hands one over the other on the edge of the table and waited.

'Is he getting this treatment?'

'I'm sorry?'

'That fucking pervert. You treat me like a criminal, what are you doing with him?'

'That really isn't any concern of yours.'

'Of course it is. Every decent human being should be concerned about filthy bastards like him. Go and ask him what he's done with Casey.' He folded his thick arms across his chest and glared at his lawyer.

'What time did your sister call you on Monday evening?'

'No comment.'

'We've already spoken to Mrs O'Donnell, we know that Chelsea Collins contacted her when she couldn't find her sister.'

'You'd have to ask Lorraine about that.'

'We have.'

'Then why are you bothering to ask me?'

'What we don't know is why you drove nearly ten miles from your home in Beckenham to organise a search party when it would have been infinitely easier to pick up the phone and report the disappearance to the police.' Barrow smiled thinly. 'We have specially trained search teams, Mr Benson.'

'Haven't had a lot of success so far, have they?' Benson planted his hands on the table and leaned his weight on it so that the metal legs creaked. 'You know what I think?'

'Enlighten me.' The DCI blinked at him.

'I think you should stop arsing around asking me pointless bloody questions and concentrate on interrogating Dixon. Search his place. See what your specially trained team finds then.'

THIRTY-TWO

As Angela Tate picked her way across the litter-strewn square of the Essex Estate, she noticed a couple of discarded and ripped 'Find Casey' T-shirts. Most of the missing posters that had been prominently displayed on street lamps and post boxes in the area had been torn down. It seemed the residents on the Essex had already decided Trisha Collins was guilty.

Tate approached York House, on the northern edge of the estate, and spotted a familiar figure loitering near the entrance.

'Who told you I was coming here?' Tate hollered.

Ashley Montgomery tugged at the bottom of her thin jacket and hurried towards her. 'Frank – don't blame him – I wheedled the information out of him.'

'That a speciality of yours, is it, wheedling?'

The girl shrugged, almost apologetically. But not quite. 'Please Angela – I know I've let you down. But you've got to give me the chance to put things right.'

'Does Harriet know you're here?'

'It was her idea for me to come.'

'You've spoken to her?'

Ashley nodded enthusiastically. 'She thinks I should shadow you.'

Tate could only assume Fowler was punishing her for not agreeing to write the Raymond Dixon profile. With the media spotlight firmly pointing towards Trisha and her extended family, Tate was relieved when Fowler gave up pursuing the Dixon angle.

'If I called Harriet right now she'd confirm what you're telling me?' Tate reached into her bag for her phone.

'I'm sure she would.' She sounded anything but sure.

'You really want to put things right?'

'I'm so sorry about what happened with Chelsea – you know that. I'll do anything to make it up to you. If we could just start up where we left off... I promise not to let you down. You have my word.'

Tate was sure Ashley Montgomery's word was worth as little as any other hack's. But she had to admire the girl's determination. 'OK – if you really want to help...' She dipped her hand into her bag and retrieved her house keys. She gave Ashley her address and watched the girl's face crinkle in confusion.

'Why are we going there?'

'Not we – you. You can source a plumber on your way. I want you to stay at the flat until a fully qualified, Corgi registered heating engineer fixes my broken boiler.'

'But I'm supposed to be shadowing you.'

'Tough – after the stunt you pulled with Chelsea you have to earn back my trust. Bit by bit. This is the first step.'

The intern reluctantly took the keys and shoved them in a pocket.

'Don't let the plumber go until every radiator is piping hot. Got that?'

Ashley blinked at her rather than answering.

'Do this right and I'll think about letting you tag along next time.' Tate dismissed her with a wave of her hand and watched as the girl angrily marched off towards the main road. 'Walk up to Camberwell Green – I'm sure there must be a bus that'll take you all the way to Kennington,' she shouted after her.

Tate's gaze lingered for a moment on the back of the block of flats she'd visited the day before. The recent reappearance of Sandra Stockwell's bracelet had been troubling her from the moment Joyce Stockwell had shown it to her. Tate still suspected Gary Benson had kept it for years as some kind of grisly trophy, but why deliver it to Joyce Stockwell now if he'd hung onto it for so long? Unless, now that Casey Collins was missing, Benson wanted to raise suspicion about Dixon all over again. Thankfully Joyce Stockwell had resolutely refused to even tell the police about it, so if Benson did have a plan it had failed.

Tate shook the image of a nine-year-old gloating Benson, silver bangle wrapped in his grubby fist, from her head and made her way to the ground floor walkway of York House.

She pressed the bell of flat seven and was rewarded with a digital rendition of *Greensleeves*. The woman who opened the door moments later was dressed entirely in black, from patent leather court shoes to the veiled hat sitting slightly askew on her head.

'Mrs Jeffries?' Tate offered Paula Jeffries' mother a tentative smile. 'I'm Angela Tate. I don't know if you remember me. I work at—'

'I know very well who you are. And where you work. You didn't waste much time. She's barely cold in the ground.'

'I can see I've called at a bad time. But I do really need to speak to you. I'd come back another day, only it's urgent.'

'I've only just got in. How did you find out about it? I'm sure no one in the congregation would have contacted the papers. Who told you? The same person who told the rabble that turned up I suppose.'

'I'm not sure what you're… Look, can I come in? It's really important.'

Pamela Jeffries peered around Tate across the square towards the road. 'Actually I'm expecting someone. It's not convenient. What do you want?'

'Just a few moments of your time. I promise I won't keep you.'

The woman let out a pitiful sigh and gestured for Tate to follow her inside. 'Ten minutes, but don't think I'm going to tell you anything about what happened today at the funeral. I suppose we should be grateful the police turned up when they did.'

Tate was dying to ask Jeffries what she was talking about, but conscious she only had ten minutes with the woman, couldn't allow herself to veer off track.

Jeffries led her into the small kitchen to the left of the hall. Tate sat down and marvelled at the neatness of the room. The work surface was lined with matching blue and white striped ceramic containers of various sizes, each bearing a label describing what was inside. Mrs Jeffries opened the pot nearest the kettle and threw three teabags into a waiting teapot. She added a fourth. 'I can't abide helpless tea.' She poured steaming water from the kettle and gave the liquid a vigorous stir. She lifted off the lid of a circular tin and eased a perfect Dundee cake onto a plate. 'This is for the vicar, but I'm sure he wouldn't begrudge you a slice.'

Once the tea and cake had been arranged neatly on the table, Pamela Jeffries finally asked Tate what she wanted to speak to her about.

'A friend of yours. She doesn't live on the estate and I wondered if you could let me have her contact details. I need to track down her son.'

'Oh yes – who's that?'

'Beryl Dixon.'

Mrs Jeffries put down the cup she had just lifted to her lips with a clatter, the tea slopping over the rim and onto the saucer. 'But I assumed you were here because of the…' She shook her head. 'You're too late.'

'I don't underst—'

'We buried Beryl Dixon this morning.'

The slice of almond and cherry-topped cake dropped from Tate's hand. 'What? When did she… pass away?'

'Just four days ago.'

'Had she been ill?'

'Not at all. She suffered a massive heart attack. She'd been complaining of indigestion for a while, but… I had no idea… The doctors say it would have been quick. So that's a blessing. It meant her son never got the chance to say goodbye, mind.'

'Was he at the funeral?'

'Why wouldn't he be?'

'He's here in London right now?'

'I think he was planning to go straight back up north later today. Unfortunately, what with the police and everything, he didn't even manage to get to the wake.'

'The police?'

Jeffries blew lightly across the surface of her tea and took a sip. 'A mob turned up to shout abuse at him. Placards and everything. At his own mother's funeral.' She tutted. 'No respect.'

'How did they even know about it?'

'I've been trying to work that out myself. I told no one.' She broke off a corner of cake and popped it carefully into her mouth. She chewed slowly and when she'd finished said, 'The police carted Raymond off as if he'd caused the disturbance. At least they arrested the ring leader too. I've never liked Maureen Benson's boy. He's always been a troublemaker.'

'Gary Benson was at the funeral?'

'Orchestrated the whole demonstration, as far as I could see.'

It sounded like something Benson would do. Still tormenting Dixon after all these years. 'Where did the police take Raymond, do you know?'

'Camberwell Green police station. Why?'

'Oh no reason. Just curious.' Tate glanced at her watch. It was just possible she could get to the station before Dixon left. She needed to wrap things up here as quickly as possible. 'You say Mrs Dixon died four days ago?'

Pamela Jeffries nodded.

'Why was the funeral arranged so quickly?'

'Raymond wanted it that way. He's a sensitive soul. I don't think he liked the idea of his mother lying at the undertaker's for too long. I helped him arrange it.'

Tate sat back in her chair and took a moment to study Pamela Jeffries' face. There wasn't a trace of bitterness in the woman's expression. In her career Tate had witnessed true forgiveness only a handful of times. Now she had another example to add to the list. Even though he was never charged with Paula's murder, most people suspected Dixon was responsible for her death. Yet here was her mother, describing him as a 'sensitive soul'.

'When was Raymond last in London, do you know?' Tate said after a long silence.

'I'm not sure – he came down whenever he could. Beryl used to send him the coach fare.'

A chill crept up the back of Tate's legs. Was it possible he'd been in London the day Casey disappeared?

'Beryl had told me how different he is now. Even compared to the way he was when she used to visit him in prison. I saw it for myself this morning. I—' She raised a hand to her mouth. 'I shouldn't say any more.'

'I'm not here to write a story about him. Honestly.' Tate sipped her tea. 'Different in what way?'

Pamela Jeffries eyed her suspiciously.

'I swear.'

'He looked old before his time. Weary. You can only guess what he would have gone through in prison.'

'You never saw him yourself on his previous visits to London?'

'Beryl only told me he'd been down once he'd gone back up north again. He didn't want to see anyone, you know, from before. You can't really blame him.'

'I'd really like to speak to Raymond,' Tate said. 'Could you give me his contact details?'

'Of course not. You must think I was born yesterday.'

'It's not for a story, I promise you. I think he may be in trouble and need help. I might be able to help him.'

Jeffries looked her up and down. 'I'm sure he's getting all the help he needs. I told him the whole congregation is praying for him. He found that a great comfort.'

'I'm sure he did. Even so, if I could at least get a message to him, I might be able—'

'I promised Beryl I wouldn't tell a soul. Nothing you can say will change my mind.'

'I completely understand. But in the circumstances… I only want to help him. Surely Beryl would have wanted that?'

'I gave her my word.'

'What about passing on a message to Raymond for me? Could you do that?'

'A promise is a promise.'

Tate took a sip of tea and weighed her options. There wasn't really much point in hanging around now, Jeffries seemed adamant. She should get down to the station. It was her best hope of speaking to Dixon. She pushed back her chair. 'I should be going – your vicar will be turning up soon.' Tate stood up. 'I really admire your faith. It almost makes me wish I hadn't lapsed.'

'You lost your faith?'

Tate nodded solemnly. 'A long time ago. I was raised a Catholic.'

'It's never too late to rediscover it.'

Tate raised her eyebrows. The four horseman of the apocalypse themselves wouldn't be able to drag her back to the church. 'I'm glad you've found such comfort in yours, over the years.'

'I think it was the only thing that kept Beryl going.'

Tate grabbed her handbag from the table, hesitating for a moment before heading for the door.

'Was there something else?' Jeffries asked her.

'I have to be honest, I'm surprised you've been such a close friend of Beryl Dixon's… in the circumstances.'

'You would say that. I'm sure you don't come across a lot of compassion in your line of work.' Pamela Jeffries stacked her cup and saucer on top of her plate. 'Beryl lost her child too. We had a lot in common, after all.'

Jeffries' capacity for forgiveness was apparently limitless.

'Even so.' Tate smiled at her.

Jeffries stood up. 'I'll show you out.'

Tate followed her out of the kitchen. Something in the room across the hall snagged her gaze. Through the half-open door she saw a large teddy bear nestled between half a dozen cushions ranged beneath the headboard of a single bed. Jeffries noticed her looking.

'Go in if you want.'

Tate pushed open the door and stepped into the small bedroom. It was decorated in pinks and pale purples. A dressing table under the window was laden with hair products and make-up, a jewellery case taking pride of place at its centre.

'I've always kept up with the latest fashions.' Jeffries flung open the doors of a double wardrobe to reveal two rails of clothes, all covered in dry cleaning plastic. 'It all has to be just right.' She reached in and pulled out a two-piece skirt suit and held it against her. 'What do you think? Smart isn't it?'

Tate nodded and scanned the remainder of the room. A flat screen television sat on a storage unit, a hi-fi complete with iPod docking station on a shelf beneath.

'No point in keeping all the old things.' Jeffries beamed at Tate. 'I want everything to be just so.' She carefully returned the suit to the wardrobe and closed the doors. 'For when my Paula comes home.'

THIRTY-THREE

Natasha McKittrick was about to enter the interview suite when Kapoor called to her from the other end of the corridor. The detective constable started running towards her.

'Have you got a minute, boss?'

McKittrick sighed and looked at her watch. The DCI had made it quite clear he wanted Chelsea Collins processed as quickly as possible. 'A box-ticking exercise' was the way he'd described it to her, once he'd finished giving her a bollocking over the Dixon interview. She was still smarting from his tirade. 'Make it quick.'

They withdrew to a small room next to the interview suite. 'What is it?'

Kapoor described in detail a burglary that had recently taken place at a local pharmacy.

'What does this have to do with me?'

'They stole *Ventolin*,' the detective constable explained, her face bright with enthusiasm.

'And?' McKittrick really didn't have the time or the patience for this. She thought about the Temazepam pill burning a hole in her trouser pocket. The sooner she dispatched Chelsea Collins, the faster she could have a much needed quiet moment to herself. She ran her fingertips lightly over the outside of her pocket.

'Casey suffers from asthma,' Kapoor continued. 'What if she *has* been abducted by someone? What if she didn't have any Ventolin on her when she was snatched and needed it urgently? Whoever's taken her wouldn't be able to just pick some up over the counter. And they couldn't exactly pop down to their local GP and ask for some.'

'You really think that's relevant?'

'We can't ignore it, surely?'

'When was the Ventolin stolen?'

'Early hours of Tuesday morning.'

'So you're saying someone snatched Casey off the street some time Monday afternoon, discovered she needed medicine, then calmly set about getting her some, just a few hours later?'

Kapoor's enthusiastic expression faded. 'It's not impossible.'

'And what's this person's connection to Trisha Collins?'

'There isn't a connection. That's my point. If there was a connection they would have got more Ventolin from Trisha. I'm presuming this is a complete stranger.'

McKittrick sighed again, more impatiently this time. 'I know you've built a relationship with Trisha over the last week, and I can understand how you don't want to believe the worst of her—'

Kapoor started to speak, but McKittrick silenced her with a raised hand.

'If you want me to take an alternative scenario seriously, it has to be at least plausible. This pharmacy burglary is just a coincidence.'

'Do *you* think Trisha's guilty of doing anything to hurt Casey?' Kapoor asked her.

'What I think doesn't matter,' she managed after a beat. 'We've got to deal with the evidence in front of us.'

'Does that mean you're not personally convinced she's guilty?'

'Get back to work, Manisha.'

McKittrick ushered Kapoor into the corridor and returned to the interview suite. Chelsea Collins, Marjorie, the appropriate adult social services had appointed to attend the interview, and Cath Murray were all waiting for her inside.

Chelsea Collins was gazing at her mobile phone and didn't bother to look up as McKittrick sat down. 'How are you, Chelsea?'

The teenager finally tore her eyes from the phone. 'Thirsty. Can I have a Coke?'

Murray jumped up and collected a can of Coke from a small fridge on the other side of the room. She opened it and handed it to Chelsea, who snatched it from her without a word of thanks.

'So – you know why you're here?' McKittrick leaned forward in an attempt to encourage the girl to make eye contact. She failed. 'We need to go through all the things you said about your mum in the paper. Is that OK?'

Chelsea shrugged, then proceeded to drink half the Coke in one. She belched when she was finished.

McKittrick quickly explained the interview would be recorded on video. Chelsea immediately flicked her long hair forward so that the chewed ends sat in front of her shoulders, framing her podgy face. She looked around the room. 'Where's the camera?'

'It's nothing to worry about,' McKittrick told her and pointed to a small digital camera attached to the ceiling.

Chelsea adjusted her pose and looked up, a faint smile on her lips. She suppressed another belch and finally looked McKittrick squarely in the face. 'Do I have to stay in that crappy place again tonight?'

'I believe social services are trying to find an alternative so you can all be together. You'd like to be with Lola and Ryan, wouldn't you?'

Chelsea shrugged. McKittrick pulled in a deep breath. At this rate the 'box-ticking exercise' was likely to take all day.

For the next two hours, McKittrick laboriously went through all of the accusations Chelsea had made about her mother, insisting the girl was specific about each instance of abuse, providing times, dates and details. On more than one occasion the teenager contradicted herself. McKittrick hoped they wouldn't have to rely on her testimony in court. Any defence barrister worth her salt would tie Chelsea up in knots within minutes.

'I'm tired now. I want to go,' Chelsea said after failing to answer a straightforward question about when her mother had last physically abused Lola.

'Just answer this and we can take a break,' McKittrick said.

'She…' The girl looked at the appropriate adult as if she might be able to answer for her. 'She hurts Lola all the time. Always pinching her, or slapping her legs and that.'

'We know that can't be true.'

'I'm not lying!'

'The doctor has examined Lola – she isn't showing any signs of injury.'

Chelsea looked again at Marjorie. 'Please, tell them I need to stop.'

'Just answer the question, Chelsea,' McKittrick said gently.

'She must have stopped when the policewoman came. She couldn't hurt Lola with her there, could she?'

'Are you sure about that?'

The girl looked away.

'Chelsea. Do you understand how serious the allegations you've made about your mum are?'

Chelsea nodded slowly as her eyes filled with tears. 'I don't want to go back to that house tonight. The other kids were really horrible to me yesterday. Can't I stay with Lorraine?'

'That won't be possible.' Lorraine O'Donnell had made it quite clear she didn't want anything to do with the girl.

'Then I want to go home.'

'Chelsea, listen to me.' McKittrick reached out and put her hand over Chelsea's. 'Are you absolutely sure about everything you've told me today? Do you want to think again about all the things you've said about your mum?'

The teenager said nothing.

'Before we make this official – now's your chance to think again.'

'Will I be able to go home if I do?'

'All we need from you is the truth. That's the most important thing here. For you, for Ryan and Lola. Most of all for Casey.'

At the mention of her sister's name, Chelsea flinched.

'You haven't asked about Casey all the time you've been here,' McKittrick said. 'Yet you must be really worried about her.'

Chelsea pushed out her bottom lip. 'Can we have a break now?'

'Are you worried, Chelsea?'

'Why are you even asking me that?' A single tear dribbled down her cheek. 'I haven't done anything wrong!' She started to get up.

'I'm not saying you have – it's OK.' McKittrick raised both her hands and the teenager slumped back onto the couch and mumbled something.

'What was that?' McKittrick wriggled forward on her seat, she looked at Murray who shrugged back at her.

'Nothing,' Chelsea said.

'You know you can speak freely to us.'

The teenager glanced up at the camera in the ceiling. 'I said, everyone's worried about Casey. Only Ashley cares about me. When can I see her? I've been asking all the time.'

'Ashley Montgomery, the reporter?'

'She's my friend. I should be allowed to see her.'

'If she's your friend, why did you go to another newspaper with your story?'

Chelsea started gnawing her top lip.

'Chelsea?'

'I'm tired.'

'I promise this is the last question before we take a break. Why didn't you tell Ashley all about what your mum had been doing? Why did you speak to another journalist?'

'I did tell Ashley. And the other lady… Angela? She told me I had to come here and tell you.'

'She did?'

The girl nodded slowly. 'I just wanted someone to…' She sniffed. 'No one was listening to me. What would happen to me if…' Chelsea grabbed a cushion from the sofa and hugged it tightly. 'Would I get in trouble if I wanted to change what I've told you?'

THIRTY-FOUR

When the vicar arrived at Pamela Jeffries' flat, Tate managed to have a quiet word with him. He confirmed that she regularly spoke of Paula's return and emptied her daughter's wardrobe every year or so to make way for newer clothes. Although he was always grateful for the addition of so many items to church jumble sales, he nevertheless never missed the opportunity to gently suggest perhaps it was time for her to accept what had happened to Paula.

'I'm afraid my words fell on deaf ears,' he told Tate. 'She clings to the idea of Paula's return rather like a drowning man clinging to a raft. Who am I to take that away from her?'

Tate left the estate and returned to the office via Camberwell Green police station, hopeful Raymond Dixon would still be inside, helping them with their enquiries. But by the time she arrived he had already been dispatched to Kings Cross by patrol car.

Back at her desk, she willed her phone to ring, desperate for another nuisance call. She was now convinced Dixon was her mysterious caller. If he would just make contact again, she was certain she could find something to say that would persuade him she was ready and willing to help, if he would just tell her how. Helping him now might not put right the wrong she'd done him three decades ago, but it might go some way to salving her bad conscience.

She spent the next few hours struggling with an uninspiring feature exploring the reasons Southwark Council's plans to demolish the Shakespeare and Essex Estates had stalled after the Marlowe had been razed to the ground. She found herself forcing out each sentence, wringing out every word, and eventually submitted the story to the sub's desk just before seven. Her landline didn't ring once in all that time.

Perhaps Dixon had given up on her.

On her way out of the building she asked reception to set up a call divert to her mobile and headed home.

The cab driver dropped her off at her closest off-licence, where she bought a large bottle of Three Barrels and a twenty pack of Marlboro Lights. She wearily dragged herself the hundred yards between the shop and her front gate, trying to convince herself with each step that tomorrow would be a more productive day. She realised something wasn't right before she'd even closed the gate behind her. She eased down the stone steps leading to her basement flat slowly and deliberately, conscious her knees might buckle at any moment. At the bottom she caught her breath and tried to make sense of the painted message dripping down the glass of her front door:

You'll never find her
Bitch
RD

She reached out a hand to test the wetness of the paint and noticed with a fright that the message was on the *inside* of the glass. The door was open a crack. A sound came from within the flat. The bang of a slamming door.

Without hesitating, Tate snatched the brandy bottle from her bag and smashed it against the bottom step. She pushed open the door, her trembling arm outstretched, the fingers of her right hand wrapped around the neck of the broken bottle. She heard another bang from the other end of the hall. She tiptoed towards the noise, holding her breath. Another door slammed. Behind her. Tate wheeled around and ran towards a tall figure pressed flat against the wall. As she lunged for him he ducked sideways and Tate swiped nothing but air, throwing her off balance. She fell heavily against the wall.

A scream came from the other end of the hall. Tate struggled to stay upright and managed to turn her head towards the kitchen. Ashley Montgomery was running at her, both arms waving frantically.

'Stop!' the girl shrieked. 'It's just the plumber!'

Tate spun back towards the door, the broken bottle held tight in her fist. The tall man raised both his arms and shielded his face.

'For God's sake keep her away from me!' he whimpered.

Tate gawped at the cowering man in blue overalls. She tried to speak but managed no more than a croak. She tried again. 'I'm sorry.'

'Jesus – what was all that about?' The plumber finally lowered his arms.

'I thought you were a burglar.' Tate pointed to the daubed message. 'I thought you were responsible for this.'

The plumber stared at her open-mouthed.

'How long has this been here?' Tate turned back to Ashley. 'It wasn't there when you arrived?'

The intern shook her head.

'It wasn't there when I went out to the van. About ten minutes ago.'

'What?' No wonder the paint looked wet. 'Did you see anyone hanging around while you were outside?'

He shrugged his shoulders.

Tate pushed past him, flung open the door and scrambled up the steps to the pavement. She scanned the street, left and right. Not a soul on either side of the road. She took a breath.

Ashley hurried up to her. 'Are you OK?'

'What do you think?' Tate looked down at the sticky trail of brandy covering her hand. She dropped the broken bottle into the gutter.

'Who's RD?' Ashley pointed towards the message and lowered her voice. 'Do you think it's Raymond Dixon?' There was an unmistakable thrill in her voice. 'Should we call the police?' She waved her ever-present iPhone at Tate. 'It's OK – I'll do it,' she said when Tate didn't respond.

Tate put a hand over the phone. 'Leave it. I'll decide whether or not to call the police.' She wandered back down the steps and studied the message again.

'Are you sure you don't want me to call 999?' The intern skipped down the steps to join her, almost wriggling with excitement. 'They need to get here fast don't they? In case he's still in the area.' She stared down at her phone, her thumb hovering over the touch screen.

'I said leave it.' Why would Dixon leave a message like that?

'That's me done. All fixed up,' the plumber announced. He was standing just inside the hall. 'When was the last time you had that boiler serviced?' A large metal toolbox sat at his feet. He produced a handwritten invoice and handed it to Tate. 'Shouldn't really accept cheques, but given it's late and I need to push off, I'll make an exception.'

Tate glanced down at the total scribbled at the bottom of a long list of seemingly random numbers. 'What did you do? Replace the old boiler with a gold-plated one?'

'Very funny. I've only charged the going rate. You should get a new boiler though – a condenser model – save you money in the long run.' He pulled a phone from the breast pocket of his overalls and stared at the screen. 'Christ – it's later than I thought. I really do need to be pushing off.

Just make the cheque payable to JL Wayne,' he said, then proceeded to spell out the letters for her.

Tate blinked. This man's name was Wayne? Was he serious? She didn't ask what the 'J' stood for. 'Oh don't worry,' she said, 'you can "push off" right now. Send me a proper itemised invoice and I might consider paying you.'

'But I can't just leave—'

'It's not as if you don't know where I live.'

The plumber huffed out a breath and scooped up his heavy toolbox. He took a long look at the message on the door. 'Yeah – and it looks like I'm not the only one.'

1979

Angela Tate knocked on the frosted glass panel of her editor's door and waited to be summoned inside.

And waited.

The man who had been running the *Evening News* as if it was his own private empire for the last decade had a reputation for keeping people waiting. Everyone from prime ministers to minor royals had to accept a supporting role in Ronald Wesley's universe. After five minutes of hanging about in the corridor she wondered whether it would be wiser to walk away or risk knocking again.

'Oooh – look at you, outside the headmaster's office. Have you been a naughty girl?'

Angela turned to see a man she vaguely recognised sauntering towards her. He was wearing a leather jacket that seemed a few years out of date and a tight pair of Farahs. Too tight, she thought, leaving nothing to the imagination. She looked away and felt her cheeks flushing.

'Don't tell me you're in his bad books already?' As he approached, Angela noticed a cigarette shoved behind his ear. 'And so soon after joining us.' He shook his head and held out a hand. 'Frank Carter, or as the critics like to call me, "the new David Bailey".'

'Who's he?' Angela shook his hand but wasn't about to let him think she was impressed. She glanced towards the editor's door.

'Good luck in there, sweetheart,' he said and promptly banged twice on the wooden frame surrounding the glass.

'I'm not your sweet—'

A bellowing voice on the other side of the door cut her off. 'For fuck's sake, come if you're coming! I haven't got all day.'

Angela waved two fingers at the retreating photographer and gently eased open the door. She seemed unable to move beyond the doorway: she'd never heard anyone with such an upper class accent use the F-word before. It threw her momentarily. Wesley had a phone receiver wedged between his shoulder and ear and a cigarette dangling from his mouth. She watched as a half inch of ash dropped onto his desk. Impatiently he waved her in and pointed to the single wooden chair sitting in the middle of his office. It had thin arms and a straight back. She imagined Ronald Wesley strapping wayward reporters into it and torturing them until they came round to his way of thinking. Trying to push the image from her mind, she lowered herself onto the seat and gripped the arms.

'Well fuck off then!' Wesley shouted and slammed the receiver onto its cradle. 'Bloody amateurs!' He stared at the phone for a moment, as if he was expecting it to ring again. When it didn't he finally turned his attention back to Angela.

'Tate?' He stubbed out the cigarette in a silver ashtray.

'Yes, Mr Wesley?'

'Just checking I've got the right person sitting in front of me.' He gazed for an extended moment at her bare knees. 'Haven't had the chance to welcome you into the fold. How long have you been here?'

'Just over a week.'

'Well – not too remiss of me, I suppose.' He spread his arms wide, almost knocking over a bottle of whiskey sitting on his desk. 'Welcome.'

'Thank you – it's always been my ambition to work—'

'You can cut the crap. *Always* your ambition? How old are you exactly?'

'Twenty-two.' Her voice let her down. From the inside she sounded more like a twelve-year-old. She coughed. 'The *Evening News* is the paper I want to work for, more than any other.'

He raised a single eyebrow and looked, for a split second, the image of Roger Moore. Then he pulled open a drawer and retrieved two cut glass tumblers. He poured a generous measure of whiskey into each and pushed one to the far side of his desk towards her.

'Oh – no thanks,' she said. 'It's a bit early in the day for me.'

'You watched me pour it – I'm not wasting ten-year-old malt because the sun's not over the fucking yard arm.'

Reluctantly Angela got up and collected the glass from the desk. She took a tentative sip. It burned her throat on the way down. In much the same way cheap booze always did.

'For God's sake,' Wesley barked. 'Knock it back.'

Angela did as she was told and was amazed her eyes didn't start watering. Her boss held the bottle aloft and Angela quickly held a hand over the top of her glass. 'Not for me – I wouldn't want you to waste any more of it.'

Wesley waited for her to sit down before he spoke again. 'Congratulations on the Sandra Stockwell story. Best piece of writing I've seen in that rag for a bloody long time. Ever, probably.' He smiled at her. 'But I suppose you know that already – given you've allowed yourself to be headhunted.'

'I don't want you to think I won't be loyal to the *Evening News* – as I said, it's the job—'

'Yes, yes – you have said. Loyalty is all well and good for most of the population – but you'll get nowhere in this business with too many lofty principles.'

Angela was about to argue that once a journalist loses their principles they may as well hang up their notepad, but something about the expression on her editor's face convinced her to hold her tongue.

'Which is why, in a roundabout sort of way, I wanted to see you.' He poured himself another shot of whiskey.

Angela gripped the arms of the chair again. Perhaps the bigheaded photographer she'd just met in the corridor was right: she had done something wrong. This wasn't a welcome chat at all, but the precursor to her premature sacking. After only a week. She squeezed the arms of the chair tighter until the wood pressed painfully into the fleshy part of her palms. She took a deep breath to try and stop her mind racing any faster.

'This young chap they've arrested.' Wesley drained his glass and shoved both tumblers back in the drawer. 'He has withdrawn his confession, I believe.'

'I helped persuade him to.' Angela felt she was on firmer ground now. Even the great Ronald Wesley couldn't object to upholding the principle of *innocent until proven guilty.*

'You did what?'

'Raymond Dixon didn't kill Sandra Stockwell. When I found out he'd confessed… well… I could hardly just sit back and do nothing.'

Wesley rubbed a hand across his eyes and let out a moan. Angela's certainty she was about to be dismissed returned in an instant.

'So I suppose you planned to present me with an exclusive interview with the unfortunate victim of a major miscarriage of justice?'

'Dixon hasn't signed anything, but he's as good as told me he won't speak to anyone else when the time comes.'

'And you were going to tell the newsdesk editor about your scoop when, exactly?'

'When I had more material. While Dixon's still in custody it's tricky getting to speak to him.' She let go of the arms of the chair and flexed her aching fingers.

'I've had the chief superintendent on the phone. He told me about your visit to the Young Offenders' Institution, and about the solicitor you recommended. The solicitor that apparently this paper is paying for.'

'I've made my own arrangements with the law firm regarding the solicitor's fees.'

'If that's the case they were obviously paying you far too much at the *South London Press*.'

'This is important to me – more important than having some stupid nest egg.' She stood up, saw her boss's face darken and quickly sat down again.

'And why, pray, are you so convinced of this man's innocence?'

'I'm practically one hundred per cent certain someone else is responsible.'

'Based on what evidence?'

'Not evidence exactly. The girl who led me to the body is terrified of a gang of little ten-year-old thugs on her estate. I'm sure one of them killed Sandra Stockwell. I know I'll get her to tell me what happened soon. Then I can take her to speak to the police – I'm working on it at the moment. She trusts me. She just needs to trust them. I have to make her understand they can protect her.'

'You're telling me you have nothing more than the word of some little council estate guttersnipe?'

'I grew up on a council estate,' she said, almost under her breath.

'And it seems you're finding it difficult to leave that inauspicious start behind you. There's no need to wear your social class on your sleeve as if it were a badge of honour.'

Angela held her tongue.

'So your whole case hinges on what one child may or may not decide to tell you? If indeed she knows anything at all.'

'I know she does.'

'Nothing you've said has convinced me the police don't have the right man.'

'He's still a child. Raymond Dixon is only seventeen.'

'Yet you seem intent to blame children even younger.'

'Because they're guilty. I've tried speaking to some of the parents, but they're closing ranks. No one will tell me anything.'

Wesley rolled his eyes. 'Perhaps I was wrong in taking you on. Perhaps your former position at the *South London Press* is still vacant?'

'No! I can't go back there.'

The editor raised an eyebrow.

'I mean… I want to stay here.'

'The chief superintendent isn't happy. And neither am I. The *Evening News* always does its best to support the Met – we're certainly not here to take potshots at them. We work *with* the police. Not against them.'

'The police have no proof that Dixon killed Sandra Stockwell.'

Wesley wrenched himself from his leather chair and walked slowly round the desk. He sat down heavily on its edge. 'I'm not sure you understand the significance of this little chat of ours.'

Angela held her breath and waited.

'I'm not asking you to drop your "campaign" to free Raymond Dixon.' He folded his arms. 'I'm telling you.'

'But it's a miscarriage of justice.'

'The only person speaking in those terms appears to be you. Think for a moment, would you, about your career. You told me only moments ago that working at this paper has been your greatest ambition.'

'You're saying if I don't drop it, you'll sack me?'

'That's the idea. I knew you'd catch on eventually. You have a simple choice to make – your career or this… doomed campaign.'

Angela let out an angry breath. 'It's not doomed – I can't believe that.'

Wesley wearily shook his head. 'The chief superintendent told me something this morning in the strictest confidence, but I see now I won't be able to convince you to walk away from this… foolish endeavour, without some solid evidence pointing to Dixon's guilt.' He exhaled an exasperated breath. 'After I tell you, I'll hear no more about this case from you – is that clear?'

Angela pressed her lips tightly together.

'Is it clear?'

'There is no evidence.'

'The blood that was found on the victim's shoes matches Dixon's. According to the superintendent it's a rare type – only seven per cent of the population have it.'

'Blood-type matching is only useful in ruling people out. Not proving guilt.'

Wesley pushed his glasses onto his forehead and pinched the bridge of his nose between forefinger and thumb. 'But together with the witness statement—'

'The witness is lying – Gary Benson is one of the thugs I was telling you about. He's just covering his own back by pointing the finger at Dixon.'

'Well the decision is yours. Do you wish to continue working here?'

What kind of a choice was he giving her? How could she abandon Dixon's cause when she'd promised his mother she was working hard to help secure his release?

'You've got twenty-four hours to make your decision. I sincerely hope it's the right one.'

THIRTY-FIVE

Wednesday 15th February

'And the boss wasn't interested in your theory?' Mills lowered himself onto the edge of Manisha Kapoor's desk, balancing on one thigh.

'Pretty much dismissed it as coincidence.'

'You told her the Ventolin was stolen the same day Casey disappeared?'

'Yep. That's the part she *really* didn't buy.'

'Have you checked the CCTV from the burglary back in October?'

'It's the same two perpetrators.'

'You're sure?'

'It's not like they took off their balaclavas and waved at the camera, but they were dressed the same and had the same MO – I mean, how many burglars have you come across who only steal one item then leave? As far as I can tell it's the same two men.'

'Had any thoughts as to why they stole the contraceptives?'

'However you look at it, it makes no sense. Why not go to the GP for something like that?'

'Maybe they can't – maybe they don't want anyone to know. For… I don't know – religious reasons or something.' Mills suddenly felt uncomfortable. He wasn't sure where Kapoor stood on that sort of thing. Assuming she had an opinion at all. He didn't want to embarrass her.

'Then they'd go to the local sexual health clinic. Bypass the GP completely. It's easily enough done.'

Mills decided he should change the subject before he embarrassed himself.

'I just thought,' Kapoor continued before he got a chance to say anything, 'if there was a connection between the robbers and Casey, that would mean… it sounds ridiculous saying it out loud… I just thought it'd mean that someone was looking after her – if they cared enough to steal medicine for her. It would mean that on some level she was all right. Alive at least.'

Mills blew out a breath. 'We're really no further forward, are we? Chelsea Collins is on the brink of withdrawing her statement. All we have against Trisha at the moment is Keating's story about her asking him to take Casey away… and Ryan's positive urine test.'

'That's enough as far as Barrow is concerned.'

Mills' mobile started to vibrate in his pocket.

He turned away from Kapoor to take the call. 'Mills.'

'Hello, detective. This is Linda Kerridge – we spoke yesterday. I'm Raymond Dixon's probat—'

'Has something happened?' Mills jumped to his feet.

'It's nothing significant, I'm sure.' The woman paused. Mills listened to her breathing. 'He didn't turn up for his session with me this morning. He's usually here every fortnight, regular as clockwork. I suppose he decided to stay on in London.'

'He can't have. One of our officers personally escorted him to Kings Cross yesterday afternoon.'

'I suppose he could be holed up at home. He has just lost his mum. I'm sure it's nothing to worry about.'

Mills wondered what she wasn't telling him. If it was nothing to worry about, why call him at all?

'Only I've tried phoning Raymond, you see, but there's no reply,' she said. 'It's not like him. He would have phoned to cancel. At least left me a message. I can't help thinking something's happened to him. Perhaps he's been involved in an accident?'

'Have you contacted the local force?' Mills mouthed the word 'Dixon' to Kapoor who was staring at him.

'I'm sure there's no need to bring the police in.'

'You're calling me.'

'In an unofficial capacity. I fully expected you to inform me he was down south, dealing with his mother's affairs.'

'If he does get in touch, will you call me back? Urgently?'

'I'm sorry – I shouldn't have phoned. Just forget about it.' She sighed. 'Sorry to have bothered you.'

As soon as Mills hung up Kapoor handed him a scrap of paper with a telephone number scrawled across it. 'It's the number for West Yorkshire Police,' she explained.

Mills quickly got through to the right team and explained the situation as he hurried back to the incident room. The local duty sergeant agreed to arrange for a couple of community support officers to visit Dixon's property.

When Mills reached the incident room he found McKittrick staring at the detailed map of Southwark attached to the white board.

'We've interviewed every single contact of Collins, did you know that?' she asked him, not taking her eyes off the map. 'Some of them twice. And we've searched their properties. I'm not sure there's anything more we can do. Or anywhere left to look.'

'I think I might have something,' Mills said. He repeated his conversation with the probation officer and requested permission to visit Dixon's mother's flat.

'You think he's still in London?'

'I think it's worth checking out. What harm could it do?'

McKittrick took a moment to consider then grabbed her jacket from the back of a chair. 'Do you mind driving?' she said as they hurried out of the room.

They arrived at the fifteen-storey block in Rotherhithe in just over ten minutes. It would have been even quicker if McKittrick hadn't insisted Mills refrained from using the blues and twos. 'No need to draw attention to ourselves,' she'd said as they cleared the station car park.

They took the urine-stained lift to the twelfth floor, and, after checking the numbers of the flats listed on a plaque next to the lift, McKittrick led the way down an interior walkway that ran at right angles off a small lobby area. They quickly reached the flat and Mills thumped the door with a fist, then leaned in to listen for movement on the other side. He banged again. Listened again.

'Did you hear that?' McKittrick said after a few moments.

'Boss?'

'Sounded like a cry for help.'

Mills had heard nothing of the sort. What was she talking about?

'There it goes again. We can't ignore it.'

'I can't hear anything.'

'Come on, Mills, for God's sake,' she said. 'Play along.' She glanced back down the dingy corridor. A door had opened halfway down. 'It's all right,' McKittrick hollered. 'We're coming to help you!' She looked at Mills expectantly. 'Well go on then, what are you waiting for?'

'You want me to…' He checked up and down the corridor and lowered his voice. 'Break down the door?'

'That's it. We can't waste a moment – it sounds like someone's in trouble in there.'

An image of McKittrick pocketing the pills in Trisha Collins' bathroom popped into his head. What was she on now? He hesitated.

'That's an order, constable.'

Mills took a step back and lifted his foot high, powering it forward towards the lock. The wood creaked, but the door held fast.

'It's OK – police.' McKittrick waved her warrant card towards the head that had poked from the doorway down the corridor. The head ducked back inside and the door slammed shut.

Mills tried again. This time the wood around the lock in the doorframe splintered. One more kick and he was through.

'Mr Dixon?' McKittrick pushed past him. 'Hello? Mr Dixon, are you here?' Slowly, she levered down the handle of the first door on the left. As the door opened bright light poured into the hall.

Standing behind her, Mills peered into the room. A kitchen. Two wooden chairs balanced seat down on a small table in the corner furthest from the door, the linoleum tiles beneath spotlessly clean. A fridge stood in the opposite corner. Its door was open a crack, the plug flung over the top. 'Getting ready for the house clearance company?' he suggested.

McKittrick ducked around him and checked the room directly opposite the kitchen. The bathroom. It was equally clean, the smell of bleach and disinfectant even stronger.

'It's as if the industrial cleaners have been in,' Mills said.

McKittrick opened the next door to reveal a sparsely furnished bedroom, a single bed pushed up against the wall under the window, bedding stacked neatly at one end. Bright winter sun filtered through the unlined curtains drawn across the south-facing window. Mills ventured into the room and, pulling his sleeve over his hand opened the double doors of a pine wardrobe. The hanging rail was empty, sitting on the floor were two bulging black bin liners. A musty, charity shop smell wafted upwards. He turned back to McKittrick who had pushed up her sleeves and was snapping on a pair of disposable nitrile gloves.

Mills supposed she must always carry a supply with her. She lifted the lid of a highly polished wooden chest at the foot of the bed. On one side was a large stack of yellowing comics, science fiction paperbacks sat in a pile beside them. Balanced on top were a cheap plastic telescope and a worn cricket bat, still reeking of linseed oil.

'She kept his stuff,' Mills said and immediately regretted stating the obvious. 'It all looks so ordinary. So normal.'

'What were you expecting?' McKittrick enquired.

'I don't know… some indication of his… state of mind?'

'We'll leave that to the psychologists to ponder, shall we?' She turned away and left the room, quickly making her way to the final closed door. She flung it open. Large undressed windows took up most of one wall, the February sunshine flooding the room.

'Do you smell that?' McKittrick stepped into the room, stopping short of a three-seater settee.

Mills sniffed in a deep breath and wished he hadn't. The pungent odour of stale sweat filled his nostrils.

The DI looked down at the floor beside the settee. A long rectangular patch of carpet had been flattened by something.

'Impression of a sleeping bag? Or a bedroll maybe?' Mills said. 'You think Dixon's been staying here?'

'It's a fair bet.' McKittrick lifted the seat cushion from the threadbare armchair next to the settee and ran her hand along the edges where the seat met the rear and sides, then she moved on to check the settee and repeated the procedure. Mills wasn't sure what she was looking for. He considered asking if she had a spare pair of gloves so he could help out. He felt useless, just watching. 'Should I make a request for a CSE team to attend, boss?' Mills reached for his phone.

McKittrick removed the final cushion from the settee and peered more closely at the narrow gap between the base and the arm. She carefully pincered something between first and middle fingers and slowly withdrew it from the gap. She angled what looked like a ticket stub towards the window. 'Can you make out the date?' She held the ticket closer to Mills' face.

He squinted at it. 'It's a coach ticket.'

'Thank you, Ralph. That much I'd already managed to work out.'

Mills stared harder at the faded print, shifting his position to get a better look. He swallowed. 'Sixth of Feb,' he said and risked stating the obvious again. 'The day Casey disappeared.'

THIRTY-SIX

After suffering a restless night's sleep, Angela Tate wasn't at all prepared for a full shift at the paper. She couldn't muster any enthusiasm for the story she was writing, and on more than one occasion considered giving up on the day entirely and retiring to the pub.

She tried all her police contacts, in the Met and further afield, but not one of them was prepared to divulge Ray Dixon's contact details. She needed to speak to him now more than ever. She was pretty much convinced he wasn't responsible for the message on her front door: why implicate himself in Casey's disappearance? But then if Dixon hadn't written it, who had? And more to the point, why?

Just after one o'clock Trisha called her from prison. She was petrified of being released from the hospital wing, even though the deputy governor herself had told her she wasn't going back into the general prison population. They had arranged a place for her in a specially secured unit.

'Where they shove the baby killers and kiddie fiddlers,' Trisha complained. 'Christ, Ange, I don't know how much more I can take. I still can't get anybody to tell me how the kids are. Did you manage to find out if they've been kept together?'

Tate took a deep breath. 'Lola and Ryan are together. Chelsea's with another foster family.'

'They should all be at home with Kiefer. It isn't right for them to be split up. Can't you help him convince the social?'

Tate was unsure how to answer. The police still hadn't ruled Kiefer out as an accomplice. There was no need to tell Trisha that yet. She'd find out soon enough. 'I'm doing everything I can.'

'That lawyer you sent is no better than the last one. She keeps telling me to be patient. How can I be when the kids have been farmed out God knows where? I'd like to see her being patient in my position.' Finally she paused to draw breath. Then carried on before Tate had a chance to interject. 'I just don't know what to do, Ange.'

'I'm sorry, Trish, I really am. I know you don't want to hear me say, "hang in there" but it's all you can do. It's temporary. Hold on to that. You've been through tough times before.'

'Not without my kids I haven't.' She said something away from the mouthpiece that Tate couldn't hear. 'Look, I've got to go. I'm getting aggro. You still believe in me, don't you, Ange?'

'Absolutely.' She hoped she sounded sufficiently convincing.

Unable to concentrate, Tate left the office early and stopped by the off-licence on the way home. Fresh bottle of Three Barrels in hand, she tentatively descended the steps to her front door and was relieved to discover it remained securely locked. Ashley had insisted on scraping off the paint before she left the night before and there was only the odd fleck of white gloss on the glass. Tate hurried inside and stepped into a sodden hall. A slow dribble of water oozed from one end of the radiator. Judging by the state of the rug it must have been leaking for hours. She squelched down the hall to the kitchen to retrieve the plumber's business card, relieved she hadn't settled the bill the day before. The cowboy heating engineer had lived up to his namesake.

She quickly located the card, called his number and left as calm a message as she could manage. No point in winding him up if she wanted him to come out after hours. She poured herself a generous glass of brandy and rooted around in a kitchen drawer for a radiator key, almost certain she'd once been bought one by a very practical and remarkably unromantic boyfriend. As she sifted half-heartedly through detritus she had amassed over many years, her thoughts wandered back to her conversation with Trisha. She was sounding more desperate each time Tate spoke to her. Hopefully she would be able to hold things together until the flimsy case against her collapsed. Tate let out a long sigh, drained her glass and slammed the drawer shut. She squelched back down the hall to the bathroom, grabbed a couple of bath towels and wedged them between the leaking radiator and the skirting board. As she started to roll up the long sodden rug there was a bang on the front door. She levered herself up and hurried to the door, ready to let rip at the hapless cowboy plumber.

She wrenched open the door to discover someone else standing on her doorstep.

'Don't tell me,' she said, looking him up and down. 'Let me guess. You're Mr Wayne's deputy and you're name's… Gary Cooper? No wait – it's Clint Eastwood, isn't it?' She peered into the sunken-cheeked face. 'Where's your poncho?'

'Hello, Angela,' the thin man said. 'It's been a while.' He pulled something from his pocket and waved it close to her face.

Tate shoved the door at him, but he was too quick and too strong, his shoulder and foot stopping the door halfway.

'Is that any way to treat an old friend?'

Ray Dixon jabbed the knife at her again and pushed hard against the door.

Tate stumbled backwards.

THIRTY-SEVEN

Natasha McKittrick looked down at the carpet beneath her feet, sure she must have worn it bare with her pacing. She was outside Barrow's office back at the Lewisham station. She'd been trying to see him since returning from Dixon's mother's flat with Mills.

As soon as they'd found the coach ticket she had called the DCI to inform him of their discovery. Once again he quickly dismissed the notion that Ray Dixon was involved in Casey Collins' disappearance. In fact, he was actually angry with McKittrick for wasting his overstretched resources visiting Dixon's mother's flat in the first place.

She leaned close to Barrow's door and listened as he droned on about excess overtime requests. After a few moments the droning stopped and whoever was with him didn't reply immediately. McKittrick took her chance. She rapped briskly on the door, levering down the handle at the same time. The uniformed man sitting opposite Barrow turned awkwardly in his seat. It was the borough commander. A man she'd met just once since joining the murder investigation team based in his borough.

'Sorry, sir. I had no idea DCI Barrow was in a meeting.'

'What is it?' Barrow scowled at her. 'Have you got something new to report?'

'I need to speak to you urgently.'

The borough commander smiled at her. 'Hope you're settling in all right, Natasha.'

'Yes, sir. Thank you.'

'I'm sure I'll be finished with the chief inspector shortly. Will it wait fifteen minutes?'

'Of course, sir – sorry for interrupting.' She closed the door quietly, avoiding Barrow's glare as she withdrew.

Deciding against lurking in the corridor to wait for the DCI's meeting to finish, she took the stairs down to the next floor, collected a bottle of Coke from the vending machine, and slipped into the ladies. She chose the cubicle furthest from the door and blew out a long steadying breath once she was safely locked inside. She lowered the toilet seat and sat down. Then pulled her warrant card from a jacket pocket, opened it and laid it flat on her lap. She retrieved a blister pack of pills from another pocket and pressed a small blue tablet through the foil back. Wriggling her grandmother's signet ring from the little finger of her right hand she proceeded to grind the tablet into the plastic cover of her ID until it had been reduced to a fine powder. She tapped the powder into the fold of the cardholder and tipped it straight into her mouth. The bottle of Coke opened with a noisy fizz and she chased the crushed Temazepam down with a mouthful of cola. She'd convinced herself over the years that crushing pills made them work faster. She wasn't sure whether that was actually true, or whether she had become addicted to the ritual. She took another swig to make sure no trace of the drug had got caught between her teeth or under her tongue and wiped her ID clean with a sheet of toilet paper. She was just easing the signet ring back onto her finger when her mobile buzzed to inform her she had a text message.

Finally Barrow was ready to see her.

The DCI's door was open when she returned to the third floor. Barrow was standing behind his desk facing the window.

'Take a seat, inspector,' he said without turning round.

McKittrick presumed the rumours she'd heard about Barrow having eyes in the back of his head were all true and sat on the chair recently vacated by the wide arse of the borough commander. The seat was still warm.

'You said it was urgent,' Barrow began, still gazing out of the window. 'I hope you don't intend wasting my time on more impossible resource requests.'

'Ray Dixon lied to us about his movements when we interviewed him.'

'Yes – you told me as much this morning. Has anything changed?'

'His probation officer has confirmed he's been visiting his mother in Rotherhithe regularly since his release. Dixon told us he hadn't been back down south at all in the past two years.'

'And this amounts to what exactly?'

'Why would he lie?'

'What does it prove?'

'That he has something to hide. Surely it's worth pursuing? We can set up three eight-hour shifts, one officer per shift. How much of a drain on manpower can that be?'

'You don't even know that Dixon is still in London.' Finally Barrow turned to face her. He remained on his feet.

'The local boys in Leeds have confirmed there's no response from Dixon's place up there. He told us he was eager to get back home. We even escorted him to the station. Why didn't he go?'

'The man has just buried his mother. Perhaps he's taken a break somewhere.'

'Without reporting it to his probation officer? He's on licence. Why would he jeopardise his freedom for the sake of a simple phone call?'

Barrow snatched a box of Rennies from his desk and pushed two chalky tablets into his mouth. McKittrick watched as he chewed silently for a few moments. Could he really be so set against investigating this lead because it might be seen as admitting he had been wrong about Collins?

'I'm interviewing Chelsea Collins again this afternoon,' she said.

Barrow swallowed and pulled a face.

'She's set to withdraw her previous statement about her mother.'

The DCI made no comment.

A moment later McKittrick felt the pill she'd taken in the ladies kick in. Nothing spectacular, just a levelling off of the tension she'd been carrying around all day. A pleasant loosening of the muscles in her arms and legs. 'The case against Collins is disintegrating,' she continued. 'All we really have now is Ryan's positive drug test and the word of a disgruntled ex-partner.'

Barrow washed down the remainder of his Rennies with what looked like a cold cup of coffee.

'Talking of which, I'd like to get Lawrence Keating in again as soon as possible,' McKittrick said. 'See if his story holds up. I've just heard from social services that he's been making noises about getting custody of Ryan. According to them, they're still assessing his suitability. But they'll be bending over backwards to approve him. You know what they're like. They'd rather Ryan is placed with his father than continue in foster care. I want to bring Keating in before that happens. It's more and more obvious to me he invented that conversation with Collins to make it look bad for her. He's wanted custody of his son for years. He probably had no idea his statement would result in Collins' arrest and imprisonment.' She exhaled a breath and felt the tension in her neck and shoulders ease.

Barrow rubbed a fist against his chest and belched quietly. 'There was a critical mass of evidence against Collins. You know that as well as I do.'

'But there isn't now.'

'I think we're finished here, inspector.'

'What happened with the family in Huddersfield doesn't set a precedent. Not all single mums living on council estates can be tarred with the same brush,' McKittrick said as she stood up.

'What?'

'I realise it was a difficult investigation, I'm not saying you—'

'I'd think very carefully before you say anything more at all.'

McKittrick was about to defend herself when there was a knock on the door.

'Come in!' Barrow hadn't taken his eyes from her face.

A PC marched into the office and handed a sheet of paper to Barrow and another to McKittrick. McKittrick skimmed the two short paragraphs.

'Thank you.' Barrow watched the constable leave the room.

'No trace of benzodiazepines in Lola's hair sample,' McKittrick said once they were alone. 'Or Chelsea's.'

'According to Chelsea's statement, we weren't expecting to detect any in her hair,' Barrow shot back.

'But more importantly, there's no trace in Casey's hair either.'

Barrow breathed out a long exasperated sigh and closed his eyes. When he opened them again he looked more exhausted than he had at any other time during the investigation. 'OK – bring Keating back in. I'll interview the man myself.'

'And Dixon?' McKittrick finally felt as if she was getting somewhere. Her optimism was short-lived.

'Leave the poor man alone to grieve.'

THIRTY-EIGHT

'What's happened here?' Ray Dixon looked from the damp floorboards to Tate, a half smile playing across his lips.

Tate pressed herself flat against the wall and, when Dixon glanced back towards the leaking radiator, started to edge sideways, inch-by-inch. Dixon shot out a hand and grabbed her arm.

'Where do you think you're going?' He waved the knife under her nose.

'I have a key for the radiator somewhere in the kitchen,' Tate said as Dixon squeezed her arm tighter. 'Why don't I just go and see if I can find it?'

'Stay where you are!' He shouted with so much force she flinched and stumbled slightly. He pushed the blade back into its casing. It was part of a multi-purpose tool. With one hand still on Tate, Dixon selected a pair of long-nose pliers from the tool and moved closer to the radiator. 'They make these with slotted heads now,' he said as he tried to turn the stubborn nut. 'Means you can use a screwdriver to do the job.' He let go of her arm and tapped the top of the radiator with his knuckles. 'Quite old, is it?'

'I'm not sure.' Tate waited for him to turn back to his work and slid slowly along the wall, towards the front door.

'I can see you, you know. I wouldn't try anything if I were you.' He gave the nut a final twist and snapped the pliers back into their casing. 'There,' he said, straightening up. 'All fixed.' He smiled at her, stained, uneven teeth appearing between his thin lips. She nodded back her thanks, for the moment unable to speak. 'Now,' he said, 'I think you and me need to have a long talk.'

Tate swallowed. 'I've been expecting you,' she managed in a croak. She swallowed again. 'Shall we go through to the living room? It's dry in there.'

Dixon followed her into the room and sat down only after she had. He balanced on the edge of the sofa cushion, ready to pounce if he had to.

Tate stood up again. 'There's a bottle of—'

Dixon jumped to his feet. 'Sit down!'

Tate lowered herself slowly back into the armchair. 'What do you need from me, Raymond?'

'Let's not get ahead of ourselves. I thought we might start with you explaining why you abandoned me thirty-three years ago. Do you know how many letters I sent to you at your paper? Mum sent plenty too. What happened?'

Tate blinked slowly. What could she tell him? Though he'd slipped the knife back into his pocket, it wouldn't take him a moment to pull it out. 'It's not something I'm proud of, believe, me.' She clasped her hands together. 'I was very young then. Just starting out. I was too easily influenced by other people.'

'You just dumped me. No word of explanation. No apology. Nothing. First I knew about it was the solicitor telling me he was no longer representing me.' He leaned towards her. 'Don't you think you at least owed me an explanation?'

'I'm so sorry. If I could turn the clock back…' Tate's heart was beating so hard and so fast she was finding it hard to breathe.

'What? Are you telling me you'd do anything different?'

Tate saw Dixon's hand move towards his pocket.

'I was naive. Desperate to impress my new boss. I wasn't brave enough to make a stand. Like I say – I was very young.'

'You had a good five years on me. Seventeen I was, when they arrested me. Seventeen.'

'I'm sorry.' Tate looked down at her hands. The knuckles were white she was clasping them so tightly.

'Not enough is it? Being sorry now?'

'What do you want from me?'

Dixon blew a long breath through his nose. Muscles rippled in his cheeks as he clenched his jaw. Tate glanced at the door. Dixon had closed it behind them. Could she get through it, down the hall and out the front door before he caught her?

'There's something I need to know,' Dixon said after a long pause. 'You have to be honest with me. It's important you're honest – OK?'

Tate nodded rapidly.

'Did you think I killed that girl?'

She wasn't sure how to respond. If she said no, and reaffirmed her betrayal, she risked Dixon getting even angrier. But how could she say yes when she was still so sure someone else was responsible? 'After all these years, what does it matter to you what I think?' It was a weak reply. The best she could come up with. She closed her eyes, dreading his response.

'When I was arrested only you and Mum believed I was innocent. Just the two of you against the world.'

Tate opened her eyes to see Dixon had slumped back on the sofa, his gaze turned away from her. She glanced towards the door, wondered again if she could make it as far as the street. She edged forward. His eyes locked back onto hers.

She'd missed her chance.

'Then you abandoned us,' he said, his hand hovering over his pocket again. 'And I only had Mum sticking up for me. Now Mum's gone.' He drew in a shaky breath. 'I need to know there's still one person on this planet who doesn't think I'm a murderer.'

Tate glanced at the door again.

'Tell me!' he yelled.

Tate jumped, clutching her chest. 'I don't believe you killed Sandra Stockwell.'

Dixon sagged, as if his anger had been the only thing holding him upright. 'Thank you,' he said quietly. 'Thank you.'

Tate stared into his watery eyes, searched his face for some trace of the seventeen-year-old she'd given up on over three decades ago. Nothing of that boy remained. She noticed a pale pink ragged scar on his left temple. 'What happened to your head?' She tapped a finger against her own temple.

'General prison wear and tear. Nonces get special treatment.' He traced along the uneven skin with his fingertips.

Tate started to apologise again, but checked herself. The words seemed to sound more hollow with each repetition.

'What about the other girl?' Dixon said. 'Paula Jeffries. You don't think I had anything to do with her death?'

Was he testing her? Over the years she'd managed to convince herself there was a chance Dixon was responsible for Paula's disappearance, mainly to temper her guilt for giving up on him. After her conversation with Paula's mother, she wasn't sure what she believed.

'Well?' He jumped out of his seat and grabbed the arms of her chair, pressing his face close to hers. Expecting a blast of sour breath, she turned her head away, but the only thing she could smell was a faint aroma of menthol.

Her mouth had gone dry. She tried to moisten her lips with her tongue.

'It's a simple enough question!' he shouted into her face.

'No!' She snatched a breath. 'I knew you weren't capable of anything like that.' She looked at his snarling mouth, spittle collecting at the corners. After thirty-odd years in prison she was decidedly less sure what he might be capable of now.

He pushed away from the chair and started pacing a small circle in the middle of the room.

Now was her chance. She leapt up and threw herself towards the door. She'd barely wrapped her fingers around the handle when he was on her, clawing at her hand.

'What do you think you're doing?' he said, pushing himself between her and the door. He shoved her backwards. 'I thought we were having a perfectly civilised conversation.'

'I just wanted…' Tate looked down at her hands. They were trembling. She coughed and started again. 'I just wanted a drink – and a cigarette. That's all. They're in the kitchen.'

Dixon stuck his hands under his armpits and squeezed his arms tight across his chest. 'I'm sorry. I didn't mean to hurt you. I thought you were running out on me.'

'I would never do that to you,' she lied.

THIRTY-NINE

Tate snatched her handbag from the kitchen counter and retrieved a fresh pack of Marlboro Lights. 'I'm supposed to be giving these up,' she said and forced a smile. She offered the pack to Dixon. He took it and slipped the cigarettes into a pocket.

'I meant have a smoke – not the whole lot.'

Dixon pulled the pack from his pocket. 'I didn't think… old habits. I could trade twenty cigarettes for a month's supply of toilet paper. Or soap. Or…' He let out a long sigh. 'Currency,' he explained, shaking the pack at her.

'Can I have one?' Tate asked.

'Actually, I'd prefer it if you didn't.'

She looked longingly at the unopened pack as Dixon threw it onto the counter.

He glanced around the small galley-style kitchen. 'When I pictured you in your home I imagined something a bit posher than this,' he said.

'Really?' Tate followed his gaze. What was wrong with her flat?

'I mean – you must have made a few bob on that book you wrote.'

Tate frowned at him.

'With that civil servant woman. You must have sold a ton of copies.'

'How do you know about that?'

'I've been keeping tabs on you.'

A tingling chill ran up the back of her legs as she tried to calculate how quickly she could reach the cutlery drawer and retrieve a knife. The thought of him watching her turned her stomach.

'Quite the heroine, weren't you?'

Tate spied the knife block at the other end of the counter. It was just a few feet away. 'I only wrote the story. Nothing heroic about that.' She glanced at her handbag. If he looked away for a moment, she might have enough time to retrieve her mobile phone and slip it into a pocket.

'Let's go back to the living room,' he said after a beat. 'Too many sharp objects in here. They're make me twitchy.'

He must have read her mind.

Tate led the way and returned to her seat. Dixon stayed on his feet. He stared at her, working the muscles in his jaw but saying nothing.

'I will help you,' Tate said, needing to break the silence. 'If I can.'

Finally he spoke. 'I requested a DNA test in 1992.'

'You did?' Why didn't her Met contact tell her about that?

Dixon nodded, his gaze suddenly distant. 'Of the blood they found on Sandra Stockwell's shoes. I knew it wasn't mine.' He started shaking his head. 'My request took months to go through all the right channels. Mum helped as much as she could, but she wasn't great filling in forms and dealing with the authorities.' He puffed out his cheeks. 'At the beginning of '93 they finally got back to me.'

'I don't understand – if they analysed the DNA, why didn't that automatically trigger an appeal?'

'They didn't.' He shook his head. 'Analyse it. The evidence had been lost. They lost her shoes. Along with everything else they'd recovered at the scene. They said it was regrettable, but sometimes mistakes happen.'

'What do you mean "lost"?'

'Destroyed. All evidence is meant to be kept for thirty years. Just in case there's an appeal request. But it was destroyed some time in the twelve years after my conviction. No one could tell me when exactly.'

Tate couldn't help thinking that kind of 'mistake' might have been orchestrated by Charlie Mills, eager to scupper any chance of an appeal.

'It had to have been mixed up with evidence from an earlier, unrelated case, they said.'

'I'm so sorry.' Tate could imagine DI Mills' self-satisfied grin.

'At the time I thought about getting in touch with you. But after you'd ignored all my previous letters, I didn't really see the point.'

Tate closed her eyes for a moment. How much guiltier did he need her to feel?

'You can make amends by helping me now,' he said.

'But if the evidence has gone, what can I do?'

'Speak to the investigating officers. See what they know. They're all retired now. They might be more inclined to speak.'

'Charlie Mills is dead.'

'I know.' A grimace flashed across his face. 'But Mills wasn't the only one working the case. I can give you a list.'

'What makes you think they'd talk to me?'

'Maybe some of them have developed a guilty conscience.' He finally sat down, sinking onto the sofa.

'Why didn't you just ask me for help straight out? The silent phone calls – that was you, wasn't it?'

'I couldn't put into words what I wanted to say – I thought you'd just hang up once you knew it was me.'

'Yet you continued to call?'

Dixon shrugged. 'I didn't have anyone else to turn to. Each time I phoned I hoped I'd be able to get over my nerves. But I never managed it.'

'You're nerves didn't stop you today. You managed to force your way in here.'

He dropped his gaze to the floor. 'I'm sorry about that, the knife and everything. I had to be sure you'd listen to me.'

Tate remembered what her contact had told her about Dixon attacking a fellow inmate. Hospitalising him. Her stomach lurched. 'The note asking me for help – that was you, wasn't it?'

He nodded, almost meekly.

'If you wanted my help, why not include a contact number? Some way I could actually get in touch with you?'

'I couldn't have you just ringing me up out of the blue. I can't… think on my feet.'

'And the newspaper clippings? They were from you too?'

'I wanted to make you curious, get you interested.'

'How did you even know they'd get to me? The envelope wasn't marked.'

'I handed it to a woman going into your building. Told her it was an early Valentine's present. I asked her to put the envelope on your desk for me and not say anything.'

'You could have just spoken to me.'

Dixon shrugged. 'It's hard.'

'How did you get hold of the clippings? I can't imagine you were allowed to collect them in prison.'

'I asked Mum to save them for me. Every time someone new joined my wing in prison I found out their name, what they were in for and where they were from. All the ones from London I got Mum to keep an eye out for. If ever their names were mentioned in the paper, she'd tear out the page, keep it in a shoebox. She looked for their names in the phonebook too, made a note of their numbers and addresses.'

'Every new inmate? Why?'

'Every inmate on the nonce wing. A lot of them already knew one another. Like some sort of members club. I made myself chat to them, especially if they came from London. I thought one of them might know something about Sandra Stockwell.' He rubbed a hand across his eyes. 'Some of the things they told me… they were disgusting. They brag about what they've done. What they've seen.' He sat very still for a moment. 'I asked them about Paula Jeffries too. The police thought the two killings were connected. Maybe they were right. I thought if I could find out what happened to Paula, that might lead to information about Sandra. But no one seemed to know anything about either of them. I got Mum to keep a track of them all the same. She kept all the sexual offence stories too. I wanted to collect as much information as I could. Someone had to know something.'

Tate wondered if Dixon had any idea just how unhinged he was sounding. 'And you wanted me to look into the cases from the newspapers too? You really should have just asked.'

'I know.' He slumped further into the sofa.

Tate glanced at the door again. She inched forward on her chair.

Dixon tensed. 'You are going to help me?'

Tate just wanted him out of the flat. Right now she'd say anything to get rid of him. 'Why did you leave it so long to get in touch?'

He stared at her but said nothing.

'You were released in 2010. Why wait until now?'

'I've been doing my own research. Talking to some of the men I met inside.'

Tate wasn't sure she believed him. 'But you've already said they didn't know anything about Sandra or Paula.'

'I had to do something.'

'So you came to me when you hit a dead end?'

'I haven't hit a dead end.'

'What?'

'When I spoke to them one name kept cropping up.'

'Who?'

'You promise you're going to help me – speak to the other officers who worked on the case?'

'I'll do what I can. There's no guarantee any of them are still alive.'

'But you'll try?'

'Tell me the name, Raymond.'

He blinked at her.

'Please.'

'I can't tell you. I still need to be sure. I think he's in contact with someone I met inside. Someone I haven't been able to find.' He rubbed his hands over his stringy hair. 'Someone who knows something about Paula Jeffries.'

'How do you know that?'

'I got talking to this bloke once, chatting the way I did with all of them, forcing myself to listen to his stories. As soon as I mentioned Paula Jeffries' name to him he just got up and walked away. Wouldn't speak to me at all after that. No matter how much I tried to persuade him.'

'Who is he?'

'I'm getting closer to tracking him down, I'm sure of it.'

'Then why not go to the police?'

'If they had any idea I'd been in touch with convicted paedophiles my feet wouldn't touch the ground. It's a breach of my licence. They'd send me straight back to prison. I can't go back there.'

'Tell me his name. Maybe I can help find him.'

'No – I can't tell you. Not yet. You start with the retired policemen. When I know I can trust you, then I'll give you his name.'

'The police could find him faster than either of us.'

'No police – I don't want them getting involved until I'm sure.'

'Sure about what?'

'Where he's buried Paula Jeffries.'

FORTY

Thursday 16th February

Eine Kleine Nacht Musik was about to loop around for the fifth time when Angela Tate slammed the phone down. She had been transferred three times before the hold music kicked in. It was proving to be more difficult getting hold of an actual human being at the Met's evidence storage facility than an out-of-hours plumber in south London. Her attempts to speak to her various police contacts had also come to nothing. It seemed no one was prepared to take her calls.

Tate stared at the inert phone and willed it to ring. Anything to drown out the irritating conversation taking place four feet away. Ashley Montogomery had installed herself at the vacant desk next to Tate's and Frank Carter was busy regaling the girl with war stories from his photographic past. The intern was rapt, and despite her annoyance, Tate didn't have the heart to tell the girl the closest Frank had been to an actual war zone was photographing Kate Adie at a *Women of the Year* awards ceremony.

Finally, Tate's landline rang and she snatched up the receiver to discover she had a voicemail message from Clive at reception. He must have called while she was on hold. She listened carefully to the message, gathered dictaphone, cigarettes and lighter from her desk drawer and headed for the door.

'Where are we going?' Ashley called after her.

'*We* are going nowhere. Why don't you continue to stroke Frank's ego. I've got work to do.'

'I'm supposed to be shadowing you.'

'Well you don't need to follow me to the ladies. And that's where I'm going right now.'

Tate arrived at reception after a five-minute detour to the car park and a much needed cigarette. She spotted the people waiting for her without any prompting from Clive. A woman in her mid-thirties was busy studying her mobile phone, thumbs working hard over the onscreen keyboard, completely ignoring the young blonde girl sitting next to her. The girl was staring into space, biting at a fingernail.

'Mrs Shaw?' Tate said as she approached. She stuck out a hand and plastered on a smile. 'Have you been waiting long?'

The woman looked her up and down. 'You're nothing like your picture in the paper. Taken a while ago, was it?'

Tate forced another smile. She had only agreed to see the woman to escape the ever-present Ashley. She presumed that if Mrs Shaw had something to say about the Casey Collins case, which was what she'd told Clive, and that information was in any way pertinent, she would be sitting in a police station right now, not the reception area of the *Evening News*. Tate had decided the woman was a time-waster before she'd laid eyes on her.

'You have something to tell me about Casey Collins?'

'You don't expect us to speak to you out here? All these people milling about.' The woman nudged her daughter with an elbow. 'I thought we could go somewhere private.'

'Your daughter wants to speak to me too?' Tate stared at the girl, who looked away, clearly embarrassed. 'About Casey Collins?' She crouched down to look directly into the girl's face. 'Are you a friend of Casey's?'

'Of course she isn't!'

'Then I don't understand—'

'There must be a room you can use to interview her.' The woman got to her feet and dragged the girl up by the arm. 'I could just take her to another paper.'

'If she has information to help the police inquiry, she should be speaking to them. Not me.'

'You saying you're not interested?'

'Not without more details. What information do you have?'

'Enough to get that Collins woman out of jail.'

Tate glanced at the girl who was now staring down at her shoes. 'What is it you know?' she asked her.

'Don't say anything, Courtney. Not yet. Not till I tell you to.' She clamped a hand on her daughter's shoulder. 'So – are we going to this room or what?'

Tate escorted them to a tiny meeting room just behind reception. Four high-backed chairs were arranged around a small rectangular table in the centre of the room. Tate sat down first, switched on her dictaphone and slipped it onto the table.

'I haven't agreed to that,' Mrs Shaw said, nodding at the digital recorder.

Tate snatched it up again. 'Fine, I'll show you back out to reception. And there was I thinking you wanted me to take you seriously.' Tate made it as far as the door before the woman called her back in.

'I'm just looking out for Courtney.'

'Of course you are – you're her mother – it's only natural.' Tate sat back down and encouraged Mrs Shaw and her daughter to do the same. She slipped the dictaphone into her pocket, but didn't switch it off. 'So – what information do you have?'

'We need to agree on terms first.'

'Terms?'

'How much is it worth to you? I've not brought her here for my health. I need to know I'm going to be properly… compensated.'

Tate let out a long sigh. 'I'm afraid that's not how it works.'

'Papers pay for stories all the time.'

'Not this one. Why did you choose to come to me?'

'You've been sticking up for the girl's mum – the only reporter who has, seems to me.'

'I'm not sure I see how that's relevant.' Tate looked at the girl. She was chewing her fingernail again.

'You'll find out when she tells you. But I need to know how much the story's worth.'

'As I just explained, the *Evening News* doesn't stoop to chequebook journalism. It's a newspaper, not a gossip rag.' Tate got to her feet again. 'I'm sorry to have wasted my time.'

'What?'

'Either you have something to report that will impact on the police investigation, or you don't. I can't force you to tell me, or the police, but I'm certainly not paying for the privilege.'

'It's not a story!' the girl blurted. 'I haven't made it up. It's true.' Sudden tears filled her eyes.

'Then why don't you tell me all about it?' Tate said gently. She sat back down and smiled encouragingly at the young girl. 'In your own time.'

'Wait a minute – Courtney! Don't you dare breathe a word—'

'What happened to that girl... it happened to me.' Courtney said and ducked away from her mother's outstretched hand. 'Someone tried to grab me in the park.'

Tate flashed a look at the girl's mother. Her face was rigid with fury. 'Who was it? What did they look like?' Tate said.

'I didn't see his face. He crept up behind me.'

'When did this happen?'

'Three days before Casey Collins went missing,' Mrs Shaw interjected.

'And it's taken you this long to tell anyone about it?'

The girl buried her face in her hands.

'Courtney?' Tate said. 'It's OK – I'm not blaming you. Just tell me exactly what happened, in your own words.' She held up a hand to Mrs Shaw. The woman had interrupted enough.

The girl looked at Tate, her teary eyes red-rimmed. 'I've told you everything already. I was in the park, someone came up behind me, grabbed me round the throat and started dragging me backwards.'

'Grabbed you how? With his hand? His arm?'

'His arm, right across my neck.'

'Bare arm?'

'No.'

'What was he wearing?'

'His sleeve was thick and soft – like a sweatshirt or something.'

'What colour was it?'

The girl shrugged. 'Dark, black or dark blue maybe.'

'Then what happened?'

'I kicked him in the leg, then rammed my elbow back into his stomach. He let go then and I ran.'

'Did he say anything? Yell? Holler, when you hit him?'

'No – but I heard him breathe in, like I'd hurt him.'

'Did he run after you?'

'Don't know – I didn't look back.'

'What happened after that?'

'I ran to where there were lots of people – the bus stop near the front gates of the park.'

Tate dragged her chair around the table so that she was sitting next to the girl. 'You're not in any trouble. But you must tell me why you've been keeping this to yourself all this time.'

The girl's nose twitched, she shot a quick glance at her mother. 'I'm not supposed to go to the park. Mum told me not to.'

'She hangs about with the wrong types. Getting up to all sorts,' Mrs Shaw explained.

'How old are you, Courtney?'

'Thirteen.'

'She's still twelve – her birthday's not for another three weeks.'

The girl was small for her age, Tate would have guessed ten or eleven. 'So you didn't tell your mum what happened because you thought she would be cross with you?'

'I was right. She was.'

'Only because she's worried about you. What made you tell her, in the end?'

'We had the police round,' her mother replied. 'Just routine, they said. We were on their list to interview, like everyone else in the area.'

'You didn't mention what happened to the police officer?'

Courtney shook her head, her eyes trained on her mother's face. 'I was too scared. I didn't want to go to the police station.'

'She told me yesterday evening. Been bottling it up ever since the police came round.'

'You must tell the police everything you've told me. All of it.'

'What about some compensation – for the inconvenience at least?' Mrs Shaw said. 'Out of pocket expenses or something?'

'I can pay for a cab to take you to Camberwell Green police station. And another to take you home. That's the best I can do.' Tate turned back to Courtney. 'You've been very brave. You're doing the right thing, going to the police.' She smiled at her. 'Now, is there anything else you remember about the man who tried to snatch you?'

The girl thought for a moment.

'Anything on his sleeve? Or his arm? A watch, maybe? Or a tattoo?'

'Nothing like that, but there was something weird about him.'

'You never told me!' Her mother glared at her.

Tate raised her hand again at Mrs Shaw. 'What was it, Courtney?'

'He smelled of cough medicine.'

FORTY-ONE

When Natasha McKittrick arrived in reception she discovered Lorraine O'Donnell standing over someone sitting on one of the plastic seats attached to the wall, jabbing a vicious finger at them.

'Don't you use language like that with me – you little bastard,' McKittrick heard her say. 'Just you wait till I tell your mum what's been going on. She'll string you up if she's got any sense.'

McKittrick closed her eyes for a moment, bracing herself for another difficult conversation, Collins' best friend no doubt continuing to be as obstructive as possible. McKittrick had only just finished her first session interviewing Lawrence Keating with Barrow. Collins' ex-boyfriend had obviously been drinking, his inebriated state adding to his confusion about what he'd told them before. The interview had been suspended after Keating had tied himself in so many knots he refused to answer any more of their questions without a solicitor present. He'd pretty much managed to contradict his previous statement every time he opened his mouth. So much so that even McKittrick had lost track of what was fact and what was fiction.

Questioning Lorraine O'Donnell again was another brilliant idea of the DCI's. Anything to bolster the crumbling case against Collins. This interview he'd palmed off onto McKittrick, making up some excuse about having to speak to the chief super.

She cleared her throat.

'Lorraine,' she said, once O'Donnell had stopped haranguing the seated figure. 'Thanks for coming in. It shouldn't take long.'

'You're wasting your time. I can't tell you any more than I have already. When are you going to let Trisha go? It's getting bloody ridiculous now.'

She stepped back to reveal Ryan Collins slumped in the plastic seat, the hood of his top pulled low over his head, his hands buried deep in his pockets. Next to him sat O'Donnell's son, Alfie.

'I'm sorry, Lorraine – I need to speak to you in private. We don't have the facilities here to look after—'

'Where's that whasisname? The long streak of piss in the brown suit? I thought I was supposed to be talking to him. He was the one that phoned me.'

'Detective Constable Mills is otherwise engaged. I am heading the operation locally. It's me you need to speak to.' McKittrick looked at the two boys sitting next to one another. O'Donnell's son seemed oddly subdued. 'I'll have a word with the desk sergeant – we might be able to get one of the PCSOs to keep an eye on them for you.'

'Oh you'll need to keep more than an eye on him.' She nudged Ryan's leg with the tip of her boot. 'Deceitful little bastard.' She kicked him again.

'Ow!'

'That's enough, Lorraine.' McKittrick stepped forward.

'If I hadn't gone to pick Alfie up early from school because I was coming here, I might never have found out what this one's been up to. Look at the state of him.'

'I don't understand…' McKittrick looked more closely at O'Donnell's son. His eyes were swimming, his head lolling to one side. 'What's wrong with him? Does he need to see a doctor?'

'I've got an emergency appointment with the GP after I'm finished here – I can't stay long.' She put a hand against Alfie's forehead. 'He feels all clammy. Get someone to sit with him for a bit, but I'm not going to leave him for more than a few minutes.'

'Let's continue this conversation in private, shall we?' McKittrick hurried to the door leading from the reception to the corridor beyond.

O'Donnell yanked Ryan from his seat and marched him to the door. 'You stay where you are, Alfie. I won't be a minute.'

McKittrick watched as O'Donnell shoved Ryan towards the door. 'I meant just you and me, Lorraine.'

'It's not me you need to speak to. Wait till you find out what he's been up to.'

After agreeing with the desk sergeant that he'd keep an eye on Alfie, McKittrick led O'Donnell and the Collins boy down several corridors until she found a vacant interview room. They settled themselves around a table pushed up against one wall, O'Donnell surveying the room. 'Take a good look round, Ryan,' she said. 'This is the sort of place you'll need to be getting used to.'

'What's the problem, Lorraine?' McKittrick did little to disguise her irritation.

'This one's the bloody problem. Go on – tell her.' She prodded a finger into the boy's arm.

Ryan sucked in a breath. 'I didn't mean nothing, yeah?'

'Just tell her for Christ's sakes.' O'Donnell dragged the hood from his head.

'What's happened?' McKittrick gazed into the boy's smooth-cheeked face.

He stared down at his lap.

'Tell her!'

'Perhaps, if Ryan has something he wants to speak to me about, he'd feel more comfortable with another adult present? We can arrange that – it may take a while to organise.'

'He wouldn't be here at all if I hadn't frogmarched him all the way from school.' She pinched his arm hard. 'Tell her about your mum's pills.'

A nerve twitched in McKittrick's leg. She disguised the sudden jerking movement by shifting in her seat.

'I just wanted to try them out, innit?' Ryan said quietly.

'What pills, Ryan?'

'Trisha's bloody sleeping pills,' O'Donnell answered for him. 'Those tests you did came back positive because the cheeky little sod's been helping himself to his mum's tablets.'

'Is this true, Ryan?'

'You're not gonna arrest me though? Are you? I only did it for a laugh.'

'Do you realise how dangerous it is to take someone else's medicine?' McKittrick asked him.

'Dangerous? You don't know the half of it,' O'Donnell said, standing up. She loomed over the boy and wagged a finger at him. 'Are you going to tell her the whole story? Or is that up to me as well?'

He shrugged. O'Donnell swiped a hand towards him, but stopped just short of his head. She sat back down looking defeated. 'I don't know how Trish got it so wrong. Chelsea lying her head off and this one selling his mum's pills to little kids.'

'Selling?'

'Staggering around in the playground, my Alfie was when I went to pick him up. I thought he was pissed at first, but I couldn't smell anything. Then I spotted this one lurking.'

'Is this true, Ryan?'

'You won't arrest me, though? I promise I won't do nothing like it again. Honest – swear to God, innit?'

'Do you have any idea how much trouble you've caused not saying anything about this earlier?' McKittrick said. 'What effect this has had on your whole family?'

The boy shrugged. 'I didn't mean to.'

'Say you're sorry,' Lorraine told him. 'Go on.'

Ryan mumbled a half-hearted apology.

'It's not really me you need to apologise to.' McKittrick closed her eyes for a moment and took a deep breath. 'We'll have to take a formal statement.' She spoke directly to O'Donnell, successfully keeping the anger from her voice. 'Are you OK to stay a while longer?'

'I need to check on my Alfie. The doctor's appointment is at three o'clock.'

There was a loud rap on the door. Without waiting, Mills stuck his head into the room.

'Inspector – do you have a moment?'

McKittrick looked at Ryan. 'Do you know how much damage you've done?' She shook her head and followed Mills outside.

'What's she want?' Mills asked. 'Was that Trisha's boy with her?'

'It's like a bloody soap opera. It'd take too long to explain.' She wasn't about to raise the subject of Collins' sleeping pills with Mills. 'What is it?'

Mills ran a hand through his hair, flustered for the moment, whatever vital piece of information he needed to impart momentarily escaping him.

Why was he still so uncomfortable around her? If he had seen something in Collins' bathroom, why hadn't he said something by now?

'I haven't got all day, Mills.'

'Sorry, boss. I've just got off the phone with that journalist, Angela Tate?' He shifted his weight from one foot to the other, as if he was reluctant to break bad news. 'She's been talking to a girl who says someone tried to snatch her from the park three days before Casey Collins disappeared.'

'Another hoaxer?'

'Really doesn't sound like it. I'd trust Tate's instinct on something like that. She says the girl seems genuine. Really shaken up apparently.'

'If it's true, why is she talking to a journalist and not us? And why is she only just coming forward now?'

'Tate says the girl's been terrified to mention it to her mother. Bit of a monster, by all accounts.'

'Where's the girl now?'

'*Evening News* offices.'

'Get down there. Take Murray with you.'

'You don't want to speak to her?'

'Just bring the girl and her mother here. I'll get the DCI to interview her himself. He needs to hear her account personally.' She checked her watch. It was already two-thirty.

'If this girl's statement pans out, that's Trisha Collins pretty much in the clear, isn't it, boss?'

'If the DCI doesn't decide what to do about Collins soon she'll end up spending another night in prison.'

Mills started towards the door, McKittrick called him back. 'Did Tate say whether the *Evening News* is planning to run a story about it?'

'It wasn't really that sort of conversation.'

'Get back to her before you leave – tell her to keep the girl and her mother there until we arrive. Politely request she doesn't make the story public for the time being.'

'I'll do my best.'

'Did the girl see the abductor's face?'

'Doesn't seem that way.' Mills hesitated for a moment. 'I don't suppose… I mean… without Collins in the frame, do you think the DCI might take the possible Dixon lead a bit more seriously?'

'Once step at a time, Mills.'

*

DCI Barrow emerged from the interview suite on the third floor wiping his brow with a limp handkerchief. Natasha McKittrick was waiting for him in the corridor.

'What do you think of the girl's account, sir?'

'Have you been waiting for me?'

'Only a couple of minutes. I've just finished writing up my notes on Ryan Collins' first foray into drug dealing.'

'What a family.' Barrow carefully folded the hanky in fours then slipped it into a trouser pocket.

'Do I have your permission to start the process of getting Trisha Collins released?'

'Not quite yet.'

'But the girl's account of the attempted abduction was credible?'

'Credible, yes.'

'Then that exonerates Collins, surely?'

'It may be a coincidence. Casey's disappearance might not be connected to what happened to this girl.'

Oh please just admit you were wrong.

'Before we do anything about Collins I want to discuss the matter with the chief super.'

'But you have to agree the case against her has pretty much collapsed? Surely it's a matter of when rather than if the charges are dropped? Can we at least ramp back up the search for Casey in the meantime?'

'I'll call you once I've seen the chief super. Don't do anything until you've heard from me. Is that clear?'

'Crystal.'

'Good.'

'And what about Raymond Dixon?' McKittrick felt she had to press the point. Dixon was out there somewhere, a potential threat to public safety, and they were doing nothing to track him down.

'What about him?' Barrow's irritation was mounting.

'Will you reconsider a watch on his mother's flat. Just in case he turns up there? We have to talk to him again.'

'We have nothing on the man.'

'He lied to us about his whereabouts.'

'So you pointed out to me before. If that's all you have—'

'It's all we have *for now.*'

'I don't have the resources for wild goose chases.'

'I'll even take the first shift myself.'

'Don't be ridiculous.' Barrow turned again and dismissed McKittrick with a wave of his hand.

As soon as he was out of earshot, McKittrick pulled her phone out of a pocket and dialled Mark Black's number.

The incident room manager picked up after only one ring. 'Boss?'

'Get as many officers as you can back on search duties.'

FORTY-TWO

Friday 17th February

The cab was forced to drop Angela Tate on the main road just north of the Shakespeare Estate, the access road blocked with double-parked cars and television news vans. A crowd had gathered at the entrance of Montague House, with more residents leaning over the balconies from the first floor to the fifth waving at the television cameras below. Hanging from the fourth floor walkway was a homemade banner, black painted letters scrawled across an old bed sheet: *WELLCOME HOME TRISH.* Trisha's front door was open, a thickset man dressed in black standing in the doorway interrogating each visitor as they arrived.

Tate pushed through the crowds of reporters and rubberneckers and wondered how Trisha Collins' release from prison would be reported in tomorrow's papers by the hacks who were universally condemning her not twenty-four hours ago.

'Hypocritical bastards,' she muttered, jabbing with an elbow any careless reporter who strayed into her path. She finally made it to the stairwell of Trisha's block and paused for a moment to get her breath back.

The morning had been a frustrating one. She had spent too many hours trying to find a decent private investigator local to the Met's evidence storage facility. In the end she'd plumped for the first firm with a receptionist who sounded halfway competent. She'd arranged for a PI to sift through the records of any case investigated in the Camberwell area from the early eighties onwards. It was a long shot, but she hoped they might uncover something to explain why the evidence from the Sandra Stockwell case had been destroyed.

It was no more than a straw to clutch at.

Which was exactly what this visit to Trisha Collins felt like.

She took a deep breath and started up the stairs, wondering how she was going to get Trisha on her own for long enough to have a proper conversation with her. She reached the flat and gave her name to the bouncer guarding the front door. He looked up after a brief scan of his clipboard and shook his head. 'Sorry, darling – can't let you in.'

Tate stared into his wide, blank face and wondered if he could actually read. 'Just tell Trisha I'm here. She's expecting me.'

'She can't be – you're not on the list.'

Please God save me from gorillas in Emporio Armani.

A shout came from inside the flat. Tate stretched up on tiptoes to peer over the bouncer's shoulder. A scuffle had broken out in the hall. A moment later a bright light appeared at the living room door. Dazzled for a moment, Tate held up a hand to shield her eyes from the glare and saw the light was mounted on top of a large hand-held video camera.

'What are they doing here?' she asked the bouncer.

'Documentary, Channel Five.' He straightened his tie and smiled at the camera.

'Trisha agreed to that?'

The brawling guests lurched towards them. The bouncer quickly stepped between the two drunken men, unable to resist glancing into the camera lens a second time as it moved closer. Tate took her chance and slipped through the door. She squeezed past the growing crowd of onlookers and hurried into the living room.

Lorraine O'Donnell was holding court on the sofa in the middle of the room, surrounded by neighbours from the estate who had decided to don their 'Find Casey' T-shirts specially for the occasion. Tate surveyed the room. No sign of Trisha. She pushed past the mob in the hall and glanced into the kitchen. It was full of men drinking cans of lager. Tate grabbed the man closest to her by the arm.

'Where's Trish?' she said.

'Who?' The man narrowed his eyes and looked her up and down.

'Shame none of you were here for her when she needed you.'

The man tugged back his arm and turned to his friends. 'Mad cow.'

Tate ignored him, navigated around the bouncer, who was still preoccupied breaking up the fight for the benefit of Channel Five, and made her way upstairs. She tapped on the only closed door. Hearing nothing from within, she quickly pushed down the handle and opened the door.

Trisha Collins sat on her bed hugging Lola, the little girl trying hard to wriggle from her mother's arms. The family liaison officer was sitting next to her.

Trisha's face was still badly bruised, the scab on her top lip red and angry as if she'd been picking it.

'Ange!' Trisha struggled to get to her feet but couldn't quite manage it. 'Thank God you're here.'

'Were you expecting all of this?' Tate pointed towards the door.

'Lorraine said she'd get a few people round to welcome me back. I had no idea she'd planned anything like this.' She squeezed Lola closer and kissed the top of her head. She lowered her voice. 'It's like everyone's forgotten about

Casey. They might be wearing the T-shirts, but none of them really care.'

Manisha Kapoor grabbed her hand. 'We're still doing everything we can, you know that, don't you?'

Trisha looked down at the hand covering hers. 'It's not good enough though, is it? All this time I've been kidding myself Casey was all right, you know? Just so I could get through another day. But it's been so long now.' She dragged a sleeve across her nose. 'I want her back, Ange. I just want her back.' Trisha dropped her voice to no more than a whisper and held on to Tate's arm. 'I've been punished enough, haven't I?'

'You've got to stop thinking like that.' Tate glanced at the FLO who was getting to her feet.

'Why don't I take Lola into her room, Trish? Give you a chance to speak to Ms Tate on your own?' She held Tate's gaze for a moment, then scooped a pliable Lola into her arms and left the room.

'What's happened to Casey? Where's my baby?'

'I'm sure the police really are doing everything they can.' Tate sat down heavily on the bed, unable to extricate her arm from Trisha's grip.

'But they've been wasting all this time thinking I'd done something.' She shook her head. 'They should have been looking for her.' She squeezed Tate's arm tighter. 'That girl who came forward. Someone tried to snatch her. And now the police reckon the same thing must have happened to Casey. But I can't bear to think about it. What if somebody's taken my baby?'

'You've got to stay positive, Trish. For the sake of the kids.' Tate wondered where the prodigal son and daughter were holed up. Trisha had welcomed them both home, despite what they'd put her through.

'I know, Ange. But it's so hard.' She started crying, full-throated sobs erupting from her mouth. 'What if he's come back, the one who killed Sandra? What if he's done this to punish me?'

Tate pictured Dixon's drawn features, his desperate appeal for her help.

'Maybe he wants to get his own back,' Trisha said.

Tate forcibly peeled Trisha's fingers from her arm and looked her square in the eyes. 'Tell me why he would want to punish you.'

Trisha looked away.

'What really happened to Sandra? If you're feeling guilty about Dixon, maybe it's time to unburden yourself.'

'I never said that I was feeling guilty.'

'Then why keep talking about being punished?'

'I don't know anything about Sandra.'

'You took me to her body. You must know something.'

Trisha started sobbing again.

'Tell me what Gary did to her.'

'What?' Trisha pulled away just as the door burst open. Lorraine stood in the doorway, the camera crew standing behind her on the landing.

'They want you to come downstairs, Trish. Why don't you, eh? Just for ten minutes. Everybody wants to see you.'

Trisha jumped to her feet and shoved Lorraine out of the room, pushing her into the cameraman. 'For fuck's sake!' she screamed. 'What do you think you're doing? Get them out of here.' She dropped her head and continued to push against Lorraine until she'd forced her and the cameraman to the top of the stairs. 'Get them out of my sight and don't let them back in.'

After a few moments she returned to the bedroom, her chest heaving, tears and snot running down her face. Tate grabbed a box of tissues from the nightstand and handed them to her. She put a comforting arm around Trisha's shoulders, guided her back to the bed and waited until her breathing returned to normal.

'Tell me what Gary did,' Tate said quietly. 'It doesn't have to go any further than these four walls.'

Trisha grabbed a handful of tissues and blotted her damp face.

'It's time to stand up to him. You're not that seven-year-old frightened little girl anymore, Trish. Just tell me what happened.'

Trisha took a long, stuttering breath, staring straight ahead, wringing the handful of tissues she was clutching. 'She was dead when he found her. Just like he told the police.'

'You don't have to go on protecting him.'

'Who says I am?'

'I know about Sandra's bracelet. I know it was Gary who posted it through Joyce Stockwell's letterbox last week.'

Trisha tensed, then wriggled her shoulders free of Tate's arm. 'You don't know what you're talking about.'

'Sandra was wearing a silver bangle when she disappeared. She wore it all the time, according to her mum. You must remember it?'

Trisha shook her head and refused to shift her gaze from the wall opposite.

'Sandra didn't have it on when you took me to her. So Gary must have taken it.' Tate shuddered as a sudden chill swept over her. 'Just tell me what he did – isn't it time?'

'It's not going to bring Sandra back, is it?' She let out a wild sob. 'What if that bastard has dumped my Casey somewhere?'

'Come on, Trisha, please. If you really think Dixon has done something to get back at you, at least tell me what really happened.'

Trisha shook her head, fat tears rolling down her cheeks.

'You don't owe Gary Benson anything. What is he to you, really? Your best friend's brother. From what I can see, even Lorraine doesn't think that much of him. You wouldn't be betraying her.'

Trisha snatched a breath. 'You can't breathe a word of this to Lorraine – do you hear me?'

'I've told you – this is just between you and me.'

And Raymond Dixon.

'Just tell me.' Tate leaned in close and held her breath.

Trisha dabbed her nose and eyes and finally turned to face her. 'I've never told a soul. Nobody knows about this. You've got to swear this goes no further.'

'You have my word.' Tate put a hand on her chest to emphasise the point.

'I would never grass up Gary. No matter what he did.'

Tate pulled back her head, saw the steely glint in Trisha's eyes. 'I thought you were going to tell—'

'There's no way I'd ever say anything that'd get him in trouble. How could I?' She held Tate's gaze. 'Gary is Chelsea's dad.'

FORTY-THREE

Saturday 18th February

Ralph Mills was exhausted. For the second night in a row he had stayed up until the early hours watching Dixon's mother's flat, waiting for Dixon to return. On Thursday night he had discovered the door of the flat had been repaired, but he hadn't managed to find out if that was the work of the council or if Dixon had been there himself to fix it. He yawned. Two nights with hardly any sleep and still no sign of Dixon. As he approached the steps leading to the station entrance he heard someone call his name from across the road.

'I need to speak to you – it's urgent!'

Mills turned to see the woman from Camberwell Grove, the time-waster, rushing across the street towards him.

'Another urgent environmental health issue, is it?' he said as she approached. He shoved his hands in his pockets. 'Try the council.'

'I've been trying to call you. All morning.'

Mills glanced at his watch. It was two minutes to eight. This woman was about to make him late for his shift. 'Go inside and take a seat. Someone'll be with you shortly.'

'But I want to talk to you – or your colleague.'

'Detective Murray?' Mills quickly scanned the street in both directions, with the forlorn hope that Cath Murray might be running late so he could foist this woman onto her. 'I'm sorry, Mrs Wells. I have a meeting.'

'But it's about the missing girl – you're still working on the case, aren't you? Especially now the mother's been released? Back to square one for you, I suppose.'

Mills bit his lip, fighting hard to keep his anger in check.

'I saw someone,' she said, shuffling towards him and lowering her voice, as if she was concerned about being overheard.

'Another mysterious little blonde girl, was it?'

A shrill wolf whistle sounded from the other side of the street. Mills let out a breath and waved at Murray as she crossed the road.

'Who's the new woman in your life?' Murray ran across the pavement and punched him on the arm, her smile quickly disappearing when she saw who he was talking to.

'Mrs Wells wants to speak to you,' he said.

'Actually, I'd like to talk to you both.'

Mills rocked back on his heels. He couldn't shake the woman off.

'You've got to believe me – I was mortified when you left before. I couldn't believe I'd been so stupid and selfish.' She reached out and lightly touched his arm. 'But you simply *must* take me seriously this time.'

'Really?' Mills decided he'd already wasted too much time listening to her. He started turning towards the entrance of the police station. 'Like I say – if you have information, the duty officer will arrange for someone to speak to you.'

'But I've seen him!'

'Who?' Murray snapped.

'Well, the abductor, I presume.' Mrs Wells waved a small black and silver camera at them. 'I have photographic evidence.'

Mills shook his head. 'Un-bloody-believable,' he said under his breath.

'Please, officer. Just let me explain.' Wells slipped the camera back into her pocket. Murray threw Mills a glance, one eyebrow raised.

'I was at the front of the house – in the hall, with the front door open.' She took a breath and looked from Mills to Murray. 'That's when I saw him. Just standing there, across the road. Standing and staring right at me.' Her eyes widened. 'He had to have seen me looking at him, but he didn't move, not even a twitch or a turn of the head. Still as a statue. I grabbed the camera from the pocket of my raincoat – I always carry it with me when I'm walking – it's so much better than the one on my phone… anyhow, I took a few pictures of him, as fast as I could – before he could get away.'

'What makes you think this man has anything to do with the Casey Collins case?' Murray asked when Mills said nothing. He wasn't about to encourage the woman.

'I have two young children – Becca's the same age as the girl who went missing. He must have been watching her. Waiting for an opportunity.' She shivered. 'When I think what that poor woman must be going through…'

'Did he see you were taking photos?' Murray asked.

'Not at first – it seemed to take him a while to work out what I was doing. As soon as he did, he ran across the road towards me. I slammed the door and called you straightaway.' She looked directly at Mills. 'I got your voicemail.' She brought out the small camera again. 'I'm afraid the photographs aren't as clear as I would have liked. I think my hand must have been shaking when I took them.' She switched on the camera, scrolled to the appropriate shot and handed it to Mills. 'I'm not sure you can actually see his face in any of them.'

'You're sure it's a man?' Mills asked, squinting down at the small images.

'Quite sure. I saw his face.'

Murray took the camera from Mills and scrolled backwards, using the zoom function to enlarge the image on the small screen. 'Can you describe him?'

'He was in his fifties, mid to late, I would guess. His hair was shoulder-length, lank and grey. He was quite tall and very thin. I noticed his trousers didn't fit him properly. They were too short in the leg. Flapping around his ankles.

Mills stared into her face. 'Do you think you'd recognise him again?'

'Absolutely.'

'We need to hold on to the camera – is that OK?' Mills asked.

'Of course. Of course it is – anything I can do to help.'

'We'll need to hold on to you too, Mrs Wells. Get you to look at a few mugshots.' Mills led the woman up the steps and into the station.

Once they'd found a spare computer, Mills logged into the main database and ran a search for men listed locally on the sex offenders' register. He skimmed through the faces quickly.

'Can you slow down?' Mrs Wells asked. 'You're not giving me a chance to take a proper look.'

Mills apologised and handed her the mouse. 'Take as long as you need.' He did his best not to fidget or look at his watch as she slowly clicked through each image. After ten minutes of listening to Mrs Wells hum and haw, watching her reject each face that appeared on the screen, Mills switched to another database. At the third face Mrs Wells sat bolt upright and pointed a finger at the screen.

'That's him.' She peered more closely at the features. 'The man I saw has greyer, longer hair. Is this a recent photo?'

Mills check the details on the screen. 'It's five years old.'

'But you think this is the man you saw?' Murray asked.

'Yes… yes, I'm positive.'

'Thank you, Mrs Wells. Detective Murray will take a full statement and see you out.' Mills threw Murray an apologetic look and ran from the room.

Natasha McKittrick shifted her weight from one buttock to the other. Her left foot was going numb. She tried to wiggle her toes to get some life back into them. She stared at DCI Barrow, only half listening to his speech about the lessons learned from the 'mis-step' they'd made in the Casey Collins investigation. He made the incarceration of an innocent woman sound like an administrative oversight.

'I'll need a full review from you covering all the events leading up to Ms Collins' arrest and the subsequent investigations,' Barrow told her. 'We simply cannot allow this sort of thing to happen again.'

McKittrick continued to stare at her boss, her mouth gaping. Barrow was rewriting history. Conveniently forgetting that *he* was the driving force behind Collins' imprisonment. She started to object, saw the DCI raise an accusatory eyebrow, and decided to let it pass. Choose your battles, she thought. This one wasn't worth the aggravation. She was too new to the job to get a reputation as a troublemaker. What was it her old chief inspector used to call her? She pictured his fat whiskered face and red nose. A firebrand. That was it. Silly old sod. Though she'd take him any day over her current DCI.

'Preliminary report on my desk first thing Monday morning,' Barrow said.

McKittrick blinked.

'Do you have a problem with that?'

Again, she kept her opinion to herself.

'We have to be able to defend our actions,' Barrow droned on. 'The press have already started to question our methods. I won't have it. Not on my watch. We can only hope Ms Collins doesn't decide to make a formal complaint.'

Perhaps you should have listened to your team and taken Kapoor's opinion of Collins more seriously, McKittrick thought. How could he be talking about learning lessons when the investigation was still open? Casey Collins was still missing for God's sake. Why wasn't Barrow busy working on a new strategy to try to find her, rather than wasting time with all this bureaucratic crap?

There was a bang on the door. Then another. Mills burst in, his face flushed and shiny. His chest heaving.

'Boss,' he said looking at McKittrick. 'Sir.' He glanced at Barrow. 'We have a witness who's seen a man acting suspiciously in her street. Not ten minutes from the Shakespeare.' Mills gulped down a breath, as if he'd run all the way there and forgotten to breathe on the way.

'Suspiciously how?' McKittrick asked.

'Loitering, then running away as soon as he clocked the witness taking photos of him.'

'Are there officers on the scene?' Barrow barked.

'Murray's taking a statement from the witness. The man is long gone. The point is, she's ID'd him from our records.'

'And?'

'It's Ray Dixon.'

McKittrick stood up. 'We need to get to his mother's place. It's just possible he's gone back there.'

'That's all you have?' Barrow asked Mills. 'A man vaguely fitting Dixon's description "loitering" in the street?'

'The witness, she's got a nine-year-old daughter. Little blonde girl.'

'And?'

'She believes this man, Dixon, was there targeting his next victim.'

'Based on what?'

'We should at least question Dixon,' McKittrick said. 'Let me organise half a dozen uniforms from the local station in Rotherhithe and get down to his mother's place,'

McKittrick said and moved towards the door. 'Can we pick up this meeting again on Monday?'

'No we bloody well can't. Sit down.'

'But, sir…' Mills said, glancing at McKittrick.

'When we're finished here you can take a couple of officers from the investigation team down to the mother's flat. If Dixon's there, bring him in for an interview. Ask him nicely. After the fiasco with Collins, I don't want any more balls-ups. Got that?'

Mills nodded and backed out of the room. McKittrick heard him mutter something under his breath on the other side of the door.

'Now, Natasha…' Barrow gave her a begrudging smile. 'Where were we?'

FORTY-FOUR

The noisy metal doors closed behind Angela Tate and she heard the lift slowly descending back down the twelve floors to the scruffy entrance of Beryl Dixon's council block in Rotherhithe.

Bright white light flooded through the grubby windows that ran along the whole length of the corridor stretching out in front of her, the February sky cloudy with the odd patch of blue showing here and there. She suddenly felt stranded and vulnerable.

When she had agreed to meet Dixon at his mother's flat she hadn't thought twice about it. She needed him to believe she was on his side. She was here, in part, to prove it. But now she was standing all alone on the twelfth floor landing, it seemed a foolish thing to have done. Why hadn't she insisted they meet somewhere neutral? Public? No one even knew she was here. She ferreted in her handbag for her phone and found Ashley's number. She tapped out a brief text message giving the intern the address and asking her to phone the police if she hadn't heard from her again in thirty minutes. She could only hope the girl would be conscious this early on a Saturday morning. Tate checked the time: nine thirty-five. Only a few minutes late. She set off down the corridor, scrutinising door numbers as she went, aware of radios playing and people clattering about inside their flats, preparing breakfast, probably making plans for the weekend. She wondered what Dixon had lined up for the next forty-eight hours and supposed that might depend on what she had to tell him.

The private investigator sifting through the Met storage facility had been in touch to inform her he had discovered several exhibits in the store from the late seventies and early eighties that had been mislabelled. He warned her not to get her hopes up, but there was just the outside chance he would find some evidence relating to the Sandra Stockwell case amongst the collection. It wasn't much to share with Dixon, but at least she wasn't coming to him completely empty-handed. Her attempts to speak to the detectives who had investigated the case had so far yielded no results. Two of them had retired to Spain and were proving impossible to track down. A third was living in a care home, suffering from Alzheimer's.

She reached the end of the corridor. As she approached Dixon's door, she noticed it was ajar, wood splintered from the frame near the lock. She pushed against it gently and tentatively called inside.

'Raymond? Are you there? Is it OK if I come in?' She listened carefully, waiting for his reply. 'Raymond?' Pushing the door wider, she hesitated on the threshold. She glanced at the splintered wood and considered for a moment whether she should call the police. Perhaps there had been a break-in. She reached into her bag for her phone. Then remembered how insistent Dixon had been about not getting the police involved. She had to respect his wishes. He'd never start trusting her otherwise. Squeezing her handbag tight under her arm, she stepped inside the flat, called his name again and stood waiting in the hallway for some sign of life.

'It's Angela,' she called. 'Is everything OK in here?' She took a step forward while all her instincts were telling her to turn around and run away as fast as she could. She called his name again and noticed for the first time that all the doors leading off the hall were closed. She had no idea what might be lurking behind any of them. She swallowed hard and reached for the handle of the first door on her left. Her hand was trembling. She pushed down the handle slowly and opened the door. Inch by inch she poked her head into the gap. An empty kitchen. She exhaled. She was about to open the next door when a faint moan sounded from the other end of the hall. She froze. Listened. The moan came again, louder this time. She ran towards it and flung open the door, pulling up sharply when she saw Dixon lying in the middle of the room, his hands clutching his stomach, blood oozing between his fingers. His eyes were wide open, his face ghostly. He moaned again and blood dribbled from his mouth.

Her heart thudded loud in her ears. She stared at him, unable to move.

He moaned again.

'It's OK – don't try to speak.' Tate kneeled on the floor beside him, quickly unwrapped the scarf from her neck and scrunched the length of silk into a ball. She pressed it against his wound.

He let out another groan.

'I'm sorry.' She managed to stuff the material under his hands and retrieved her phone from her bag – the smooth plastic slippery in her blood-soaked fingers. She got as far as the second nine when Dixon moaned again, this time the sound forming into a distinct word.

'Girl,' he managed. More blood trickled down his cheek from the corner of his mouth.

'It's OK – we need to get you an ambulance – you can tell me later.' She punched in the third nine and waited to be connected, doing her best to apply pressure to the sodden scarf with her free hand. She shouted Dixon's address at the dispatcher and asked for an ambulance. The woman she was transferred to calmly asked about the nature of the emergency.

'He's bleeding from a stomach wound. There's a lot of blood.'

'Is he conscious?'

Tate leaned close to Dixon's face. His breathing was coming fast and shallow. His eyes were closed. 'I'm not sure.'

'Apply pressure to the wound.'

'I am.'

'The ambulance will be with you shortly.'

Tate hung up. 'It's OK, Raymond. Everything's going to be all right.'

'Paul—a,' he breathed.

She pushed the matted hair from his forehead. 'Do you know where Paula is?' she said softly.

Another low moan.

'Have you found her?'

He moaned again, but it was impossible to work out if he was saying yes or no.

'Where is she buried, Raymond?'

Dixon's head started to turn slowly towards her.

'Don't move. It's OK.'

Her scarf was drenched now, the blood oozing around it as she continued to apply pressure, not entirely sure it was the right thing to do, even though the ambulance dispatcher had told her it was.

'Paula… I just—' Dixon said, the sentence stalling in his throat.

'Where, Raymond? Where is she?'

He moaned again.

'Raymond! Please!'

Dixon's head fell away. She moved closer to his mouth, held her own breath and listened again for his.

He was still breathing.

'Who did this to you?' It suddenly struck her that whoever had attacked him could still be in the flat. She glanced around the room, her heart thudding even harder.

A loud bang sounded from the hall. Tate started.

Dixon let out a low groan.

'Hello?' a man's voice called.

Was it possible the paramedics had arrived this quickly? She hadn't heard sirens.

'We're in here,' she hollered over a shoulder. 'For God's sake hurry.' She turned back to Dixon. 'Where's Paula, Raymond?' She leaned close to his face. 'Tell me where she is.'

'Get away from him!' A woman's voice this time. Tate twisted round, expecting to see a paramedic, but instead discovered the detective inspector she'd met at Trisha's standing in the living room doorway. 'Nice and slowly,' the detective ordered. 'Both hands where I can see them.'

'Where's the fucking ambulance?' Tate shouted.

'Move away from him now,' McKittrick repeated.

'For God's sake – I can't – I have to keep the pressure applied until the ambulance gets here.'

Ralph Mills appeared behind the inspector and walked slowly towards Tate, hands held aloft. 'Let's take it easy, shall we?' He crouched down next to her, careful to avoid the pool of blood expanding beneath her knees. 'Why don't you let me do that.' He spoke softly. Tate stared at his hands moving over hers. He was wearing a pair of disposable rubber gloves. 'Here,' he said and stuck his hands beneath hers, pressing firmly against the wound. 'Please move away from Mr Dixon now.'

'No – I should do this while you do CPR – you must know how to – you've had training, haven't you?'

'Please – I've got this under control. Move away now.'

'What? Why? What do you think I'm going to do?'

Mills glanced at his boss.

'Please, Ms Tate,' McKittrick said. 'Step away from him.' Her face was set in a hard frown. She reached for something attached to the thick vest she was wearing under her jacket.

'Dear God – you can't think… you don't believe I've got anything to do with… oh come on.' Tate looked at Dixon's face, then down at his chest. It wasn't moving.

The wail of a siren sounded in the distance.

'Thank God,' Tate said. 'You should go down to meet the paramedics, show them the way,' she said. 'We're running out of time.' She looked towards the door and the hallway beyond and saw two uniformed officers she hadn't spotted before. 'What is this? What are you doing here anyway?'

'Step away from the body, Ms Tate,' the inspector repeated, as if it was the only thing she knew how to say.

'The body? For Christ's sake, he's not dead!' She looked back at Dixon. Mills had removed the blood-soaked scarf and was sitting back on his haunches.

'Don't just sit there,' Tate said. 'We have to give him mouth to mouth. 'At least until the paramedics get here.' She started to move towards Dixon's head. Mills put up his arm to block her.

McKittrick crossed the room swiftly, a pair of cuffs in her hand. She cleared her throat and said, 'Angela Tate, I am arresting you on suspicion of murder.'

FORTY-FIVE

Tate looked down to see traces of Ray Dixon's blood still under her fingernails. There were dark brown stains in the creases of her knuckles too. A fresh wave of nausea rose up from her stomach and she had to swallow it back down.

After the forensics people had taken swabs of her hands, she'd been allowed to wash them in the ladies. But even though she'd soaked them in a basin of hot water, it had been impossible to scrub them completely clean.

Shortly after Tate had arrived at Camberwell police station, McKittrick confirmed that Ray Dixon had died before he reached the hospital – though the paramedics had managed to revive him temporarily, his organs had already begun to shut down.

'He'd lost too much blood,' the DI had told her, not a trace of regret in her voice.

Tate wasn't surprised by the detective's attitude. She got the impression Dixon was just where the police wanted him – tucked up in a refrigerated drawer in the mortuary, awaiting the pathologist's examination. A convicted child killer off the streets for good. The world a safer place without him in it.

She fidgeted on the cold plastic chair trying to get comfortable. The paper babygrow they had given her to wear after taking her clothes away for analysis creaked and rustled every time she moved. She was waiting for her solicitor to arrive. It was over three hours since she'd been arrested and still the 'best criminal lawyer in London', promised by her editor, had failed to materialise. If he took much longer about it, Tate could see herself spending a night in the cells. It wouldn't be the first time she'd stayed in a police station overnight, but it hadn't happened for more than a decade. Certainly not since she'd become accustomed to a luxury pocket-sprung superking-sized bed. She wasn't sure her joints could take an overnight stay on a hard bench softened only by a half-inch foam mattress.

She checked the clock on the wall: one-thirty. In her experience, top lawyers of any variety tended not to work on the weekend. The chances of one turning up any time before Monday morning were slim to none. Being held in custody for over forty hours was not something she was prepared to contemplate. She glanced down at her hands again, started rubbing at a line of dried blood embedded in a crease between her fingers, while her mind worked through the options. She only really had one.

But it went against her better judgment.

After another fifteen minutes of clock-watching, she finally cracked and informed DI McKittrick she was ready to give up her right to silence. Ten minutes after that Mills and McKittrick joined her at the narrow table in the brightly lit interview room. Fresh CDs were fed into the slots of the digital recorder. Tate looked at the red light on the machine and wondered again if perhaps she was making a huge mistake.

'Ms Tate,' McKittrick began. 'Can you tell us what time you arrived at Mrs Dixon's flat?'

Tate held up a hand and shook her head. 'Listen, you and I both know I had nothing to do with Raymond's death. Can we just accept that now and move on?'

'Please answer the question, Ms Tate.'

Tate let out a long sigh. If they insisted on asking her ridiculous questions, maybe silence would be the best option after all.

'Shouldn't you be asking me *why* I was there?'

'What time did you arrive?' McKittrick grabbed a plastic beaker of water from the table and downed it in one. When she looked at Tate again, her eyes seemed to swim for a moment, as if she was having trouble focusing.

'Are you all right?' Tate stared at her, watching as the detective blinked rapidly, the lines deepening at the corners of her eyes.

'Perfectly. Now, if you could just answer the question.'

For half an hour Tate answered a series of increasingly banal questions with as much patience as she could muster. Finally the detective inspector moved on to the reason for her visit to Rotherhithe.

'I was helping Raymond. I had some information for him.'

'What sort of information?'

'I'd agreed to look into his case again.'

McKittrick raised her eyebrows. Mills looked into his lap and shook his head.

'Raymond Dixon did not kill Sandra Stockwell. That much I know.' Tate stared at Mills, but he wouldn't look at her. 'I failed to help him thirty-three years ago when he needed me, this was my chance to make amends.' An image of Dixon's grey, clammy face wormed its way into her head. 'Only I was too late.'

'You've been helping him, even though he sent you a threatening note?' Mills finally met her gaze.

'It was hardly threatening. He just wanted to get my attention.'

'Why didn't you inform us after he made contact with you again?' McKittrick asked.

'Why should I? What did it have to do with the police?'

'You came to us with the note,' Mills reminded her.

'Let's just say Raymond pointed out the error of my ways.'

'He threatened you again?' McKittrick sat bolt upright.

'He hadn't threatened me in the first place. Aren't you listening to me?'

'How often have you been in contact with the deceased?' McKittrick again.

Tate closed her eyes. Deceased. Why were the police wasting time questioning her when they should be out searching for his killer? The hard plastic seat was becoming more uncomfortable as each moment passed. Tate shifted her weight, uncrossed and recrossed her legs. 'Twice – if you count today.'

'And what form did that contact take?'

'He came to speak to me in my flat.'

'How did he know where you lived?' Mills asked.

Tate shrugged. 'I have no idea.'

'What was the nature of the enquiries you've been making on his behalf?' McKittrick leaned forward, planting her elbows on the table.

Tate wondered whether she should reveal the details. What if she told them about the private investigator's discovery and more evidence mysteriously disappeared?

'I've been trying to contact the detectives who worked on the original investigation. With no luck so far. Maybe they're all suffering from some twisted sense of loyalty to Charlie Mills. What do you think, constable?'

Tensing at the mention of his father's name, Mills folded his arms and said nothing.

McKittrick ignored him. 'Why did you agree to help Dixon after all this time?'

Tate sighed. The question she'd been asking herself for the past two days wasn't why she had agreed to help him now, but rather, what had prevented her helping him in the last three decades. Out of sight, out of mind. It was the only reason she'd managed to come up with. It was no excuse at all.

'I've already said. I failed him before. I thought it was the least I could do for him now. After thirty-one years in prison.' Tate scraped her chair closer to the table. 'You want to know why? Guilt. Plain and simple.'

'Why not help him before now, if your conscience was that bad?'

'Do you think I could get some other clothes? I feel like a serial killer in this get up.' She pinched at the sleeve of the blue paper suit.

'Please answer the question, Ms Tate.'

McKittrick was certainly dogged.

Tate took a sip of water. 'I'd managed to forget about him. Without even trying. Once my career took off I didn't give Raymond Dixon a second thought.' She swallowed. This was turning into a group therapy session. She glanced at the red light on the digital recorder and closed her eyes.

'Ms Tate?' McKittrick said.

'I was too wrapped up in my own success.' She sucked in a long breath. 'There – will that do you? Is that enough contrition?'

'I'm only interested in finding out what you know about Ray Dixon's death,' McKittrick said. 'Did Mr Dixon say anything to you before he died?'

Tate looked from McKittrick to Mills, wondering how long they had been standing in the doorway of Dixon's living room. How much they might have overheard. 'No. Not really. Nothing that made any sense,' she said eventually.

'Tell us exactly what he said to you.'

'I don't really remember.'

'Perhaps you could try,' McKittrick coaxed.

'Really – he was just making noises, moaning. No real words as such.'

There was a knock on the door. Tate let out a breath. Mills paused the recording while McKittrick spoke to a uniformed female officer in the doorway. When she returned she pressed her knuckles onto the table and leaned over Tate. 'We'll leave it there for the time being. You can have a break. Someone will bring you a cup of tea and a sandwich.'

'Leave it?' Tate rose, the paper suit crackling noisily. 'You can't expect me to stay here any longer. You don't seriously believe I had anything to do with Raymond's death?'

'Sit down. We'll be back later.'

'You might want to start by rounding up the usual suspects,' Tate said.

'What do you mean by that?' McKittrick snapped.

'I know what happened at Beryl Dixon's funeral. About the mob that turned up. Why aren't you interrogating them?'

'There's no need to concern yourself with our methods of investigation, Ms Tate.'

'You've at least got to bring in the ringleader. Surely he must be your prime suspect.'

'Who?'

'Don't pretend you don't know. Gary Benson's had it in for Dixon from the beginning.'

McKittrick scrutinised her face. 'What makes you say that?'

'Christ – it's not particle physics. It was Benson's testimony that got Dixon convicted in the first place – no doubt with a lot of coaching from your old man.' She glared at Mills until he looked away.

'Did Mr Dixon mention Gary Benson before he died?'

'Why don't you arrest Benson, instead of keeping up this bloody charade?'

'As I say, we'll be back later to resume the interview.'

'For Christ's sake!'

'Constable?' McKittrick nodded to her colleague and he followed her to the door like a faithful Labrador.

'What's happened?' Tate said. 'What did that WPC just tell you?'

'As I said before, there's no need for you to worry yourself—'

'No need? Don't you think I have a vested interest? What did she tell you?'

McKittrick glanced at Mills. 'Let's just say you may have to reassess your unstinting faith in the innocence of Raymond Dixon.'

FORTY-SIX

Manisha Kapoor met Ralph Mills at the door. She snibbed the latch, slipped onto the landing and closed the door behind her. 'Trisha's already in a bad way,' she said. 'I'm not sure how she'll cope with this.'

Mills looked down at the folder he was clutching. It contained just one item. 'It's got to be done.'

'Would you like me to do it?'

'You've got to be good cop. Let me take any flak that comes. At least I can leave again. Should I line up the other FLO from Lewisham to relieve you?'

'No – the family knows me better. I've got to stay. I owe Trisha that much.'

Mills nodded and pushed open the door. 'Do you want to lead the way? She is expecting me?'

'I told Trisha you wanted a word – I didn't tell her why.'

'News about Dixon's death hasn't leaked out to the media yet?'

'I don't think so – I've got them all watching a *Little Mermaid* DVD, so I can't say for sure – you might want to check.' She let out a long and anguished sigh. 'At least Trisha's talking to Chelsea now. I get the impression she wants to keep her kids close to her.'

'Could you take them somewhere while I do this?'

'Sure. Will you be OK on your own?'

'Course.'

Kapoor closed the front door behind them and hurried into the living room. She paused the DVD and scooped Lola into her arms before the little girl could object. She told Ryan and Chelsea to come with her and carried the toddler out of the room. Ryan seemed eager to escape, but Chelsea stayed where she was, sitting next to her mum on the sofa.

Mills stood awkwardly in front of them, gearing up to explain what he'd come here for. 'Can you leave us, please, Chelsea?' he said, his voice shaky.

Collins looked up at him, took one look at his face and said, 'You've found her.'

'No. No we haven't.'

'When Nisha said you'd be coming over I just expected that's what you were going to say.' She struggled to catch her breath. 'So I didn't ask her anything else. I didn't want to know.'

'We don't know where Casey is. But I do have something I'd like you to take a look at. I need to speak to you privately.'

'I want to stay,' Chelsea said. She slipped her arm through her mother's and leaned her head against her shoulder.

Collins squeezed her arm tight. 'What have you got there?' She pointed to the folder in Mills' hands.

Very slowly Mills slipped a large colour photograph from the file and handed it to Collins. She snatched it from him. Chelsea frowned at the picture.

'Where did you find it?'

'Do you recognise it?'

'It's Casey's. Tell me where you found it.'

'You're sure it's hers?'

Collins studied the image of a pink, fur-trimmed cardigan for a few more moments. 'It's got a hole by the pocket on the left-hand side.' She pointed at the spot on the photograph. 'It's definitely hers. Why won't you tell me where you found it?'

Chelsea jumped to her feet – the tears falling freely, her face crumpling. She ran from the room.

'How comes you found her cardy but not Casey?' Collins continued to stare at the photograph, tracing a finger along the edges of the bright pink cardigan.

Mills was under strict instructions not to tell her anything about Dixon. The CSEs hadn't even finished searching the flat yet. 'Can you confirm she was wearing it when she went to school on Monday morning?'

Collins nodded. 'It's her favourite. She's never out of it. I can barely get her to take it off to wash it. She'd sleep in it if I'd let her.' She shook her head. Mills could see the tears ready to erupt from her eyes. 'What's that?' she said. 'On the sleeve there?' Collins swallowed. 'Jesus. Is that blood?'

Mills reached for the photograph. 'I'm sorry. I realise how upsetting it is seeing something like this. Thank you for identifying it for us, we really appreciate it.' He tugged on a corner of the picture. Collins wouldn't release it.

'Can I keep it?' she said.

Mills chewed his lip. Why would she want to keep something like that? He looked into her face and realised she wasn't about to loosen her grip. He let go of the photo. He'd expected fireworks from her, fully prepared for her to lash out, directing all her anger and pain at him. It had happened to him before in similar situations: grieving relatives needing to hurt someone as much as they were hurting themselves. Compared to the way she might have reacted he supposed he should be grateful.

'Where did you find it?' she asked him.

Mills wished Kapoor had stayed in the room. 'I'm really sorry, Trisha, but I can't tell you anything until I have more information myself. It's policy, I'm afraid.' He was acutely aware just how pathetic his reply must have sounded, especially when all he wanted to do was tell her the sick bastard that had murdered her daughter was dead. That he wouldn't be able to hurt anyone else's child ever again.

'You'll let me know as soon as you have any more news?' Collins' voice trembled.

'I promise we'll keep you completely up to date.' He walked slowly to the door, controlling his urge to run out of there and just keep running. He turned back to face her. 'I'm so sorry.' There was nothing else he could say. She nodded back at him and he left the room.

As soon as he reached the front door Mills heard Trisha Collins let out a desperate animal wail.

Braving the cold in a small internal courtyard, Angela Tate stood shivering in her thin paper romper suit and finished her second cigarette. She drained what was left of her luke warm tea and stubbed out the cigarette in a fire bucket filled with sand. Two hours ago, unable to face even the notion of food, she had refused the offer of a limp tuna and cucumber sandwich and now she was ravenous.

The door to the courtyard swung open and the same WPC who had fetched her tea stood in the doorway. 'They're ready to restart your interview,' she said and waited for Tate to join her in the corridor.

Back in the aromatic interview room, Tate resumed her previous position. This time however, a junior solicitor from the famed legal firm sat next to her, notebook open on the table. He had pink cheeks and an optimistic expression. Tate couldn't decide whether his flushed face was the result of a late boozy Saturday afternoon lunch or ninety minutes on a freezing football pitch in his local park.

Once the preliminaries were completed, McKittrick continued as if she'd never been away. 'Please run me through this morning's sequence of events again.'

'You've got to be kidding me. How many more times do you want me to tell you?'

'Please, Ms Tate. What time did you arrive in Rotherhithe?'

After a tortuous recounting of her precise movements between nine-thirty and whatever time the police arrived on the scene, Tate turned to her solicitor. 'Get me out of here. I don't care what you have to do. Just earn your bloody money. I'm not answering any more of these stupid bloody questions.' She looked at McKittrick. 'So don't waste your breath asking me any.' She folded her arms for emphasis.

'Did you pass anyone coming out of Mrs Dixon's building on your way in?'

Tate sat up straighter. They hadn't asked her that question before. 'Does this mean you've finally decided to take on board what I've been telling you?'

'Please answer the question, Ms Tate. Did you see anyone?'

'No! Don't you think that would have been the first thing I told you? From the time the cab dropped me off right up until the moment I discovered Raymond Dixon bleeding to death on his mother's living room floor, I didn't see a soul.' She pushed the elasticated cuffs of the paper suit up her arms. 'Bloody well wish I had.'

'No one at all?'

'I've just told you. Have you picked up Gary Benson yet?'

'We can't discuss the continuing investigation with you.'

'Of course you can't. What was I thinking.'

McKittrick gave a brief nod to Mills who pronounced the end of the interview for the benefit of the machine and stopped the recording.

'What's happening now?' Tate said. 'Are you going to leave me to stew for another two hours?' She nudged the solicitor. 'What are you – mute? Say something for God's sake!'

McKittrick held up a hand before the lawyer had a chance to speak. 'Our crime scene examiners have now completed a thorough search of Mrs Dixon's flat,' she explained once the CDs had been removed from the machine and carefully labelled and sealed. 'And the surrounding area.'

'Why are you telling me this?'

'No murder weapon was found.'

'Why didn't you tell me that as soon as I sat down?'

'Thank you for your cooperation, Ms Tate. It is appreciated.'

'Does that mean I'm free to leave?'

'After we've completed a few formalities, certainly.'

Tate leaned in towards McKittrick and lowered her voice. 'Strictly off the record – *are* you pursuing Benson?'

McKittrick mirrored her position and her hushed tones. 'Strictly *on* the record – I have no intention of answering that question.' She stood up.

'When can I get my clothes back?'

'That won't be possible, I'm afraid.'

'But that suit's a Versace.'

McKittrick shrugged. 'Your assistant is waiting outside – she has a change of clothes for you.'

'My what?'

Mills checked his notebook. 'Ashley Montogomery. She turned up at the crime scene shortly after you left. She's been in the station waiting for you the whole day.'

Tate had completely forgotten she'd texted the intern asking her to call the police if she hadn't got in touch within thirty minutes. Yet again the girl had disobeyed instructions. She was supposed to call for help, not tip up at Dixon's flat herself. 'How did she get my clothes?'

'I didn't ask,' Mills said.

After she'd been processed, Tate was led to the ladies on the next floor by a female officer and found Ashley Montogomery waiting for her inside. The girl held up an Oxfam carrier bag. 'Before you say anything, it's really not as bad as it looks,' she said. 'It was the best I could do, in the circumstances. I'm sure you can put up with it for the duration of the cab ride home.'

'Who said anything about going home?'

The girl held on tight to the bag as her mouth fell open. 'You're not going home?' She glanced at the bag, a pained expression on her face.

'What have you got in there? A pair of Day-Glo dungarees?'

'I think you should probably go home first. You won't want to be seen out in this. Trust me.'

'There's no time.' Tate grabbed the bag and peered inside. Denim. Lace. Hesitantly she reached in and pulled out the charity shop garment. She held it up.

'I told you it was bad.'

'A onesie?' The denim jumpsuit reeked of mothballs.

'Everything else was much, much worse, I swear.'

'Christ.' Tate started to peel off the paper suit.

Clearly embarrassed, Ashley turned away. 'There's a bra and pants in the bag too.'

'You've got to be kidding.' Tate stepped out of one hideous all-in-one and into another. 'I'll just have to cope.'

'Do you want me to phone for a cab to take you home?'

'I've told you already - I don't have time.'

'Why? Where are we going?'

'*I* am going into the office. I have work to do.'

FORTY-SEVEN

As Tate reached down to the bottom drawer of her desk, she unfastened the top two buttons of the 1980s onesie, afraid they might fly off under the strain. The garment was at least two sizes too small. She carefully reached towards the back of the drawer and retrieved the spare mobile phone that was lurking beneath a pile of old issues of the *Evening News*, the police having held on to her iPhone. She quickly rebuttoned the onesie, remembering why she had fastened it right up to the neck in the first place.

The bra Ashley had purchased for her was so yellowed and limp that she couldn't even bring herself to touch it, much less encase her naked breasts inside. So she had been obliged to remain bra-less. She hadn't felt so unencumbered since infiltrating the Greenham Women's Peace Camp in 1981. Pendulous was not an adjective she warmed to. Thank God Frank wasn't here. She'd never hear the last of it.

From the middle drawer of her desk she retrieved the large brown envelope of newspaper cuttings and kicked the drawer shut with the toe of her new canvas and rubber gym shoe: presumably something the intern had picked up in the pound store next door to the charity shop. Thankfully the shoes were the right size, and she managed to make her way to Rita's office on the third floor without any painful pinching or chafing. She opened the door to the tiny room and forced a smile. 'Thanks for coming in at such short notice, Rita.'

Rita inspected her over the top of her spectacles. 'My God – what happened to you?'

'The police kept my clothes. Now I wish I'd held on to the paper forensics suit. I haven't had a chance to go home and change.'

Rita sniffed. Then coughed. 'What's that awful smell?'

'Mothballs.'

The librarian held a hand to her nose and looked at the brown envelope Tate was holding. 'Haven't I seen that somewhere before?'

Tate shook the cuttings onto the desk. She sifted through the pile, and attempted to organise the flimsy scraps of paper into some sort of order. Rita watched her struggling for a moment then batted her hands out of the way and took over.

'How do you want to me to sort them?' She stared gleefully at the clippings, quite clearly in her element. 'Date? Location? Type of story?'

Tate was mesmerised as she watched Rita's thin fingers moving expertly over the pile, shuffling the scraps of paper as deftly as a casino blackjack dealer might shuffle cards. 'Date,' Tate said firmly. 'No, wait – location.' She thought again. 'Can we do both?'

Less than ten minutes later, Rita had separated all the clippings into orderly piles, each one denoting an area of south London, stretching from Croydon on the left to Bexley on the right. Each individual pile was stacked in date order, most recent at the bottom.

The two women stared at the newsprint ranged across the desk. 'Just before he died,' Tate said, 'Raymond Dixon told me he'd discovered the girl's body.'

'Casey Collins?'

'No! Paula Jeffries.'

'I assumed you meant—'

'Ray Dixon had nothing to do with Casey's disappearance.'

'How can you be so sure?'

Tate blinked at Rita. It wasn't something she could put into words. 'Trust me on that.'

'But—'

'Rita, please.'

'Hang on a minute, it still doesn't make any sense – I thought everyone assumed Dixon killed Paula Jeffries.'

'He's spent the last two years trying to find out what happened to her.'

'Oh.' Rita raised an eyebrow, an auburn, pencilled-in crescent appearing above the frame of her glasses.

'It's not as unlikely as it sounds.'

'Did Dixon say where he'd found her?'

'Do you think I would be here now if I knew that?' She selected a cutting from one of the piles and scanned the text. 'He was getting closer to finding a man he met in prison. Dixon was convinced that man killed Paula. Find the ex-con, find Paula's body. That was Dixon's thinking.'

'Why did he want to do that?'

'He thought he might be able to find a link between Paula's death and Sandra Stockwell's. That way he could prove he was wrongly convicted.'

Rita looked at the neat piles of cuttings then at the one in Tate's hand. 'And you really think sorting through all these stories will lead you to the ex-con?'

'Short of organising a séance, this is all I have. I can't just sit back and do nothing. Not with the police thinking Dixon is responsible for killing three little girls.'

'Three? So the police do think he was behind Casey's disappearance? They actually told you that?'

'Not in so many words. But it's quite clear which direction their inquiry is heading.'

'And you've brought me in here on a Saturday evening to clutch at straws with you? I cancelled a date for this. On the phone you said it was urgent.'

'A date? Who with?'

'No one you'd know.' Rita looked away.

It was the first time in thirty years Tate had seen Rita embarrassed. Her jaw dropped. 'Not Frank Carter!'

A crimson bloom spread across Rita's cheeks. The librarian started tidying the piles of cuttings.

Tate blew out a breath. No time to get into that now. 'So… anyway… I need your help to piece together whatever it was Dixon managed to find out.' She shook her head. 'I can't walk away from this.' Not again.

'I don't hold out much hope, if this is all we have to work on.'

'Christ, Rita, cut me some slack. I have to do something.'

Rita prodded a pile of clippings with the rubber end of a pencil. 'The earliest story here is from July 1980. The anniversary of Paula Jeffries' disappearance.' She picked up the cutting and held it under the light. 'It's one of ours,' she said, a hint of pride in her tone. 'I recognise the leading and the font.'

'You can tell from that little scrap it was cut out of a copy of the *Evening News*?'

'Can't you? You started here only a few years after I did.' She studied the article more closely. 'Did you write it?'

Tate nodded slowly, reluctant to admit to the clumsily written prose. Rita flipped through the remainder of the pile then shoved it to one side. 'This is hopeless.'

'We haven't even started yet. With your brain and my… bloody-mindedness, we might come up with something.' Tate selected a story at random from the adjacent pile. It was a report of a ten-year-old boy's disappearance from Denmark Hill in 1982. She returned the clipping to its pile and picked up another, more recent story: the sentencing of a man found guilty of downloading illegal images from the internet. 'Let's concentrate on what we have, make connections where we can,' she said, slipping the cutting to the bottom of the pile.

'All right. But I can't stay here all night. I've got an early start in the morning. I'm going away for a few days.'

Tate said nothing.

Rita glanced at the piles ranged across the desk. 'Let's see what connections we can make. Pretty much all the reports feature south London. Majority of them either child-related or sex-related crimes. What else? Are any of the victims the same? What about the offenders?' She peered at the top left hand corner of the desk and scanned across, then back to the left and across again. 'Is this particular ex-con Dixon was telling you about likely to be mentioned in one of these stories?'

'That's what I'm hoping. Dixon's mother was collecting any stories about men Raymond had met inside. If this ex-con went on to commit another crime, a report of it could be here.'

Rita started to make a list. 'We might as well start with the names. It's as good a place as any.'

Tate grabbed a sheet of paper and started making a list of her own.

The librarian tapped a pile with her pencil. 'There's a story here about a speeding offence – it doesn't fit the pattern.'

'Dixon's mum collected any kind of story. If the name she was looking for cropped up, she snipped it out of the paper.'

They continued the task in silence until Tate reached the final clipping in the last pile. She turned to the librarian. 'How many on your list?'

'Thirty-seven. What about you?'

'Forty-two.' She let out a long breath. 'What do we do now?'

'We cross-reference – search for the names on the *Evening News* database. See if the names crop up in any other stories. We can build more of a profile of each one – serial offenders go onto a new list. That's the first step.'

'How long will that take?' The futility of the task was starting to dawn on her. Meanwhile Rita seemed to be relishing it.

'It'll take as long as it takes.' She tapped something into her keyboard.

Tate was about to suggest she shouldn't bother when the door opened with a crash. Ashley Montgomery stood in the doorway, a carrier bag in each hand.

'You took your time,' Tate said.

'When did you last try to find a takeaway round here?'

Tate stared at the twelve-inch square boxes bulging through one of the bags. 'Pizza? Is that the best you could do?'

'There wasn't a lot of choice. I thought you'd prefer that to a kebab. I bought a bottle of wine too.' She reached into one of the bags and waved a pack of plastic disposable cups at Tate.

Rita reached into a drawer and retrieved two long-stemmed wine glasses. 'I think we can do better than that.'

'How's it going?' Ashley hurried to the librarian's desk and dumped the pizza bag on the floor. 'What do you want me to do next?'

'You… are going home.' Tate grabbed her keys from her handbag and pressed them into the intern's hand. 'You'll find a grey trouser suit in a dry cleaning bag on the left hand side of my wardrobe. Chest of drawers for bra and knickers. Top drawer.'

'But I want to help here.'

'Getting me out of this *Prisoner Cell Block H* uniform is the most useful thing you can do. Believe me.'

The intern opened her mouth, doubtless to protest again, when the phone on Rita's desk started to ring. Rita answered it and immediately passed the handset to Tate.

'Who even knows I'm here?' Tate whispered.

'It's possible I mentioned it to Clive on reception,' Ashley said, apologetically.

'Hello?'

'Ms Tate – at last!'

'Who is this?'

'Malcolm Denby – the private investigator? I've been leaving messages on your mobile all day.'

'It's… out of action at the moment. Do you have something for me?'

'I think I might. As you know, I've been going through the evidence boxes from the Camberwell Green police station for the period from 1979 to 1985. I started by cross referencing the original list of exhibits from the Sandra Stockwell investigation with the items still stored on site. It's been slow going.'

'And?'

'I've found two exhibits from that investigation. Both of them mislabelled. I'm hopeful I'll find more. It's just a question of sifting through the remaining boxes.'

Tate felt her legs weaken. She slumped onto the edge of Rita's desk. 'What have you found?'

'A blue cotton shirt and a school tie, both presumably belonging to the defendant.'

Tate exhaled the breath she'd held in. It was too much to hope he'd found Sandra Stockwell's missing shoes.

'You're sure they're from the Stockwell case?'

'Absolutely no doubt in my mind. The list is quite precise in detail.' He let out a little snort. 'It's actually quite ironic.'

'What is?'

'If they'd been labelled correctly, they would have been destroyed a couple of years ago – thirty years after the original case closed. These were labelled March 1983 – they were due to go to the incinerator next month.' He let out a satisfied breath.

'And you think you'll find the other missing exhibits?'

'As I say, I'm hopeful. I'll let you know as soon as anything else tips up.'

'Thank you.'

'Oh it's all in a day's work. I'm just relieved to have discovered them in time. Saved them from a fiery fate.' Another little snort.

Tate gave him the number of her spare mobile, thanked him again and passed the phone back to Rita, her hand shaking. She inhaled deeply.

'Everything all right?' Rita asked her.

Tate couldn't answer. The image of Raymond Dixon dying on his mother's floor pushed its way into her head. As far as Raymond was concerned, the private investigator had made his discovery about eight hours too late.

FORTY-EIGHT

Natasha McKittrick flipped down the passenger sun visor and checked her make-up in the mirror. Mascara and eyeliner had merged into a muddy mess. She found an old tissue in her pocket, dabbed a clean corner of it on her tongue and attempted to repair the damage under her eyes.

'I don't mind waiting with the team from Bromley BOCU, if you want to get off home,' Mills said.

'Why would I want to do that?' McKittrick glanced over her shoulder at the two vans of very bored looking uniforms.

'It's been a long day.'

'For all of us.'

McKittrick had been amazed by the swift response DCI Barrow had made to her request to pick up Gary Benson in connection with the murder of Ray Dixon. To his credit, Barrow contacted the senior commanding officer at Bromley Borough Command Unit himself to arrange for back up, while McKittrick, Mills and Murray made their way from Camberwell to Gary Benson's home in Beckenham.

Mills' phone started to chirrup. He took one look at the screen and rejected the call.

'Someone you're trying to avoid?' she asked him.

'For the time being.'

'Anyone I should know about?'

'Not really – it's the woman who ID'd Dixon this morning. She's a bit… demanding. Can't deal with that right now. I'll call her back later.' He shoved the phone back in his pocket.

McKittrick wondered if that was the way he treated every 'demanding' individual he encountered: ignore them for long enough in the hope they would give up and go away. It occurred to her he might be thinking about her in much the same way.

One of the back doors opened and Cath Murray climbed into the unmarked BMW, slumping heavily onto the seat.

'Any joy with the neighbours?' McKittrick asked her.

'Nothing worthwhile.' Murray buzzed down her window and took a breath. 'I get the impression it's not that kind of neighbourhood. Everyone keeping themselves to themselves. No one even seems to know Benson by name – there's certainly no popping next door for a cup of sugar.'

'Have you ever lived anywhere where that actually happens?' McKittrick made eye contact with Murray in the mirror of the sun visor.

The DC thought for a moment and shook her head. 'No. Thank God.' She smiled at McKittrick. 'You heard anything back from the team at old Ma Benson's place?'

'She says she hasn't seen him for days,' Mills said.

'That I don't believe.'

McKittrick turned to face her. 'What makes you say that?'

'Blokes like Benson love their mums more than anyone else in the world. I bet she still does his laundry for him.'

'Of course, we could be wrong about Benson. Anyone might have got to Dixon,' Mills said. 'Enough people probably wanted him dead.'

'Who would have known about his mother's flat in Rotherhithe?' Murray wriggled forward and shoved her face through the gap between the front seats.

'Any number of people,' Mills replied.

'I suppose Benson did find out about the funeral pretty quickly – even before we did,' Murray added. 'I'm guessing he's getting his information from his mum. I expect not much gets past her.'

A hundred yards up the street a white Ford Transit stopped in the middle of the road.

'Can you make out the number plate?' McKittrick asked Mills.

Mills squinted towards the van, but before he could say anything, with a squeal of spinning tyres it reversed suddenly and swung around, accelerating back out of the street.

'Shit!' McKittrick fastened her seatbelt. 'He must have spotted us.'

'Boss?'

'It has to be Benson. Get after him.'

'What?'

'Start the car!' She reached over and flipped on the lights and siren.

Mills pulled out quickly and floored the gas. The BMW lurched forward and bounced over a speed hump, the front bumper scraping noisily along the tarmac when it landed on the other side. McKittrick gripped the dashboard. Behind her Murray was requesting assistance, shouting instructions into her radio.

They took another speed hump even faster than the first, the car landing so heavily it shuddered. The siren let out a strangled wail then died completely.

'Do I have permission to request chopper back-up?' Murray asked McKittrick.

'Yes – and get traffic in pursuit. We can't chase him in this.' McKittrick craned her neck and peered into the wing mirror. The police van and patrol car were following thirty yards behind, blue lights flashing. She turned back to Mills. 'Have you had advanced driver training?'

Mills ignored her, gripped the steering wheel tighter and negotiated the final speed hump, with the inevitable grinding of metal against road surface. When they reached the end of the road he swerved onto the busy intersection in third gear, barely slowing, the rear of the car swinging wildly into the middle of the road as it turned. Benson's van had already reached the junction, fifty or so yards away, accelerating through as the lights changed from amber to red. Mills floored the gas again and McKittrick lurched backwards in her seat, her heart banging.

'How many vehicles have traffic dispatched?' she turned awkwardly to speak to Murray above the wail of the sirens of the chasing vehicles.

'Still waiting to hear.'

'Jesus.' She radioed the speeding convoy behind, ordering them to stand down, as traffic would be taking over. She glanced at Mills, his white knuckled hands wrapped around the steering wheel. They crossed the junction with the traffic lights still on red, almost clipping a car crossing in front of them.

'Have we lost the lights too?' McKittrick asked him. Mills didn't reply. He was too busy gritting his teeth.

The road ahead curved sharply to the left and Benson's van disappeared around the bend.

'Come on, Mills!' McKittrick shouted.

'Shhh!' Murray hissed from the back seat then hollered into the radio. After a burst of static she reported back. 'Three bikes and two cars leaving the Catford garage now.' She leaned forward, gripping both sides of the front seat to steady herself. 'MetroComm will call me back as soon as they've picked up the van on the CCTV.'

'You mean they haven't yet?'

'Not many cameras round here, apparently.'

The BMW swerved round the bend and McKittrick watched Benson's tail lights disappear from view again. 'Is it my imagination, or are we going round in a big circle?'

'The junction for the A234 is coming up soon. He's probably heading for that,' Murray told her.

'How come you know the area?' McKittrick twisted round to look at Murray again.

'Did The Knowledge for a while. While I was waiting to get into the Met. Wanted to do something useful.'

They cleared the bend and McKittrick was relieved to see the white van still ahead of them. But it seemed to be pulling away. 'It's a Transit, Mills – I think a BMW trumps a Ford. Why are we not gaining on him?'

Mills put his foot down again and slipped the gearshift into fifth as the road opened out onto dual carriageway. He managed to shorten the gap by fifteen or twenty yards. Then the van seemed to pull away again. For another hundred or so yards McKittrick watched helplessly as the Transit edged away. She pointed through the windscreen. 'There are traffic cameras here. Why haven't Comms called you?'

Right on cue, Murray's radio crackled into life. 'This'll be them.'

'What the fuck have they been doing? Fucking—'

Mills took his eyes off the road and looked at her, his eyes wide with surprise.

'Do you have a problem, Constable?'

A moment later a car pulled out sharply from a side turning just a few yards ahead. Mills, his gaze only just returning to the road in front of them, saw it a split second after McKittrick. He yanked the steering wheel to the right and swerved into the next lane. The front driver-side fender of the BMW crashed against the bumper of the car in front. That car then banged into the central reservation, overcorrected and swerved back out again.

Right into their path.

Mills stamped on the brakes. The vehicle behind slammed into the back of the BMW, shunting them even further into the car in front.

McKittrick flew forward, the seatbelt pressing painfully into her chest as the passenger airbag exploded in her face.

FORTY-NINE

'Are you OK?' Rita asked. 'You haven't been right since that phone call.'

'I'm fine.'

'Can I help?' Ashley threw open a pizza box and tore off a segment of quattro formaggio.

'Are you still here?' Tate asked her. 'I thought you were fetching my suit.'

'I'm ravenous – you've got to let me eat something before I go anywhere.'

Tate struck through one of the names on her list: the man in question had died three years ago. As far as she was concerned, the more deaths she discovered the better. At least it narrowed the field. She shifted position. Perched on the edge of a chair peering at a laptop balanced on a corner of Rita's desk was uncomfortable enough. Doing it dressed in a jumpsuit two sizes too small was agony.

Ashley wandered over to stand beside Rita, a floppy slice of greasy cheese pizza in her hand. 'Give me a list – it'll speed things up. I can grab a spare laptop from downstairs.' She glanced at the sheet of names sitting next to Rita's keyboard. 'What are you checking? Just tell me what you want done and I'll get straight onto it.'

Rita tore off a page from her pad and started to copy out some of the names as Ashley popped the last of the pizza slice into her mouth and shuffled towards Tate. 'I am supposed to be shadowing you, after all. I need to be doing whatever you're doing.' She ran a greasy finger down Tate's list. 'Who's Thomas Williams?'

'Why?' Tate snapped.

'What's he done to make him so important?' The intern licked her messy fingers.

Rita squinted down at the notes she'd been making. 'Failed to pay a speeding fine. Got a suspended sentence for it.'

'No – I mean what makes him so special he's on both lists?'

Tate and Rita turned and stared at the girl. Then at the other's list of names. Tate shook her head. 'Christ – why didn't we check that first?'

Rita snatched both lists from the desk and compared them. 'It's the only name that appears more than once.'

'Didn't I just say that?' Ashley whined. 'What does it mean? Him being on both lists?'

'Here we are,' Tate waved a scrap of newsprint in the air. 'He was the *victim* of a mugging. 1988.'

'Is that it?' Ashley asked. 'An unpaid speeding fine and a mugging? I thought he had to be some criminal mastermind or something.'

'Two stories, neither of them sex crimes, yet important enough for Beryl Dixon to cut them from the newspaper and keep for over twenty years,' Rita said.

'He has to be someone Raymond did time with – otherwise she wouldn't have cut out the stories in the first place. So we know he must have been in prison for a sexual offence – to be on the same wing.'

Rita tapped something into her keyboard, staring earnestly at the screen. 'Come on. Come on.'

Tate got up and looked over Rita's shoulder. A spinning egg timer the only clue that something was actually happening. Finally the screen refreshed and a dozen or so summaries of *Evening News* stories featuring the name

'Thomas Williams' were returned. Rita scrolled down the page.

'This is it.' Rita pointed at a snippet second from the bottom then clicked on the link for the full story.

A man called Thomas Williams was convicted of sexually assaulting an eleven-year-old girl in 1995. Rita scrolled down again until she found another reference to him. He was sentenced to seven years and sent down to do his time in Wormwood Scrubs.

'So he must have come into contact with Ray Dixon there,' Tate said, wondering why mention of that particular prison felt like it should mean something. She scanned the whole story. It would have been too much to ask to expect an address for the man.

'Shall we concentrate our efforts on him?' Rita asked her. 'I suppose he's as good a straw to clutch at as any other.'

Tate was only half listening to her, still wondering why Wormwood Scrubs seemed significant.

'Angela?'

Then it dawned on her. Her police contact had told her Dixon had violently attacked someone in the Scrubs. Dixon had a blemish-free prison record apart from that one incident. Someone had given him reason to act completely out of character. Dixon told her the man he'd been looking for had refused to speak to him about Paula Jeffries. Was that reason enough for Dixon to beat him up?

'This has to be our man,' Tate declared, sounding more hopeful than she felt.

Rita quickly reached into her bottom drawer and pulled out a laptop. She flipped open the lid and switched it on. 'In that case, we're going to need all the help we can get.' She looked over her glasses at the intern. 'Clean your hands first.' She handed the girl a tissue. 'Sorry, Angela – you'll have to survive a bit longer in that hideous jumpsuit. It's all hands to the pump.'

Tate watched as the librarian quickly typed 'Thomas Williams, UK' into Google. She then switched to 192.com and instructed the intern to do the same, just as soon as her computer came to life. Two hundred and thirty-six entries were returned for 'Thomas Williams' in London alone. Rita narrowed the search to Camberwell, which seemed to return results for the whole of the borough of Southwark.

'OK,' Rita said, turning to Ashley. 'You start from the top and I'll go from the bottom of the list and work up. Angela, you hit the middle. Ignore any entry that gives a current age less than…' Rita started counting on her fingers, 'thirty-three.'

'What's your thinking?' Tate asked her as she returned to her seat.

'He would have been too young to get done for speeding in 1997 otherwise. If the driver had been underage, that would have been the main focus of the story, not the fact he failed to pay his fine.'

'There's no age mentioned in either article?' Ashley asked. 'I thought that was one of the first things reporters are supposed to find out.'

'Freesheets,' Tate said, to explain the shoddy reporting. 'No attention to detail.'

'If there's a phone number included in any listing, try calling,' Rita instructed.

'And say what?' The intern looked perplexed.

'Use your initiative,' Tate and Rita answered together.

Ashley was just settling herself cross-legged on the floor when Rita's phone started ringing. 'Do you want me to get it?'

'I'm sure it'll be for you,' Rita told Tate. 'No one would call me at work on a Saturday.'

Tate snatched up the phone, irritated at being taken away from her task. 'Hello – Angela Tate speaking.'

'Thank God.' A woman's voice. 'The man who answered my call just now wasn't sure you were still in the building. You're my last hope. If you can't help me, I don't know where else to turn. You *have* to take me seriously. Promise me you will.' The woman finally paused to take a breath.

'Who's calling?'

'I'm sorry – I thought I just said.'

Tate removed the receiver from her ear an inch and pointed at it, shrugging at Rita. What was this woman on?

'My name's Fiona Wells.'

'I'm in the middle of something at the moment. Could you call back another time?'

'No – it's urgent!'

Tate grabbed her glass from Rita's desk and drained it.

'I keep trying the police incident room, but it rings and rings. Though I'm sure even if I did get through they wouldn't listen to what I have to say. The police seem to have made up their minds about him.'

Tate rolled her eyes. 'Can you slow down? Go back to the beginning and start again.'

'The man I told the police about this morning – he's all over the news now. But I think they've made a mistake.'

'What man?'

'They're linking him to the missing girl.'

'Who is?'

'The police – not officially – they're refusing to confirm the reports. But you read through the lines don't you? If it wasn't what they really thought, the BBC wouldn't be reporting it at all.'

'Reporting what?'

'Raymond Dixon – they're saying he abducted Casey Collins.'

Tate jabbed a hand towards a flat screen television bolted to the wall. Rita quickly located the remote and, after a moment, the *BBC News* channel appeared. An old picture of Ray Dixon took up half the screen, a reporter standing outside his mother's block in Rotherhithe filled the other.

The news ticker at the bottom confirmed that Dixon was believed to be the chief suspect in the Casey Collins investigation.

'Hello? Are you still there?' the woman shouted at the other end of the line.

Tate shoved a hand over the mouthpiece of the phone. 'How did that story get leaked?' She glared at Ashley. 'There was supposed to be a news blackout.'

'Don't look at me – I wouldn't do something like that – I swear.'

'You were an awfully long time picking up those pizzas,' Tate said.

'Honestly – I just wouldn't.'

'Are you still there?' Wells asked again.

'Sorry, Mrs Wells – I was just looking at the news report myself.'

'You didn't know about it?'

'I didn't know it had been made public.' She continued to scowl at the intern.

'I keep trying to get hold of the policeman I spoke to this morning, DC Mills – I have his mobile number. But he's ignoring my calls. I've left dozens of messages.'

Dozens? The woman was obviously exaggerating, Tate thought Mills probably had the right idea. 'You still haven't told me why you're calling me.'

'Haven't I?'

'Perhaps you should call back when you're a little more… composed?'

'I'm perfectly composed. Dear God, the police have already labelled me a neurotic time-waster, I don't need you to do the same.'

Then stop behaving like one, Tate felt like saying.

'The press are reporting Dixon killed the little girl. He can't have. It's impossible.'

Tate sat up. 'Go on.'

'I've seen her.'

'What?'

'I've seen Casey Collins.'

'When was this?'

'About an hour ago. I've been trying to get hold of the detective or the incident room ever since.'

'Why didn't you call 999?'

'I was going to – by the time I'd got the phone from the kitchen she was gone.'

'You saw her from *inside* your house?'

'She was getting out of a van, not forty feet from my front door.'

'What was she wearing?'

'I'm not making this up. You have to believe me – I saw her. She was wearing a jean jacket and a short ra-ra skirt.'

'Is the van still there?'

'Don't you think I would have called 999 if it was?'

'You should still do that.'

'I can't – I...' She let out a sharp breath. 'I've done it before, called the police, I mean – I was... mistaken last time. They won't believe me now.'

'How sure are you that you're not *mistaken* this time?'

'What do you want me to do – give you a percentage? A mark out of ten? I saw a little blonde girl. I'm almost sure it was Casey Collins. Isn't that enough?'

Tate was staring at the *BBC News* archive footage of a teenaged Raymond Dixon being manhandled by uniformed policemen between the Old Bailey and the waiting Black Maria. Why *would* the police believe this woman? They'd already decided what had happened to Casey. 'I still don't understand why you're contacting me.'

'If I can convince you, perhaps you can speak to the police for me.'

'What makes you think they're any more likely to listen to me?'

'You've been reporting on the case from the beginning. You thought Trisha Collins was innocent all along. You were proved right. The police will take you seriously. They have to.'

Tate let out a sigh, certain she had no more chance of convincing the police what this woman was telling her was true than getting them to believe in fairies at the bottom of her garden. 'I really don't think I can help.'

'Please – come here yourself – let me show you where I saw her. Then decide whether or not I'm a raving lunatic.'

Against her better judgement, Tate quickly took down the woman's details and hung up. As soon as she'd filled in the blanks for Rita and Ashley, the intern was pulling out her mobile from her bag.

'What are you doing?' Tate asked.

'We've got to at least try the police.' Ashley started to tap the screen. 'What if that woman's right?'

Tate held a hand over Ashley's. 'Stop. There's no need to get yourself labelled a time-waster too. I'll go and speak to her.'

Ashley stood up. 'Then I'm coming with you.'

'You stay here and help Rita – it's more important that we find an address for Thomas Williams.'

'What if she is a loon? You need me there for back up.'

'That really isn't necessary.'

'After what happened in Dixon's flat this morning, there is no way you can stop me.'

'You think I can't look after myself?'

'I'm coming whether you want me to or not.'

Tate turned to Rita. 'We shouldn't be long.'

Rita held up her hands and shooed them away. 'I'll probably get more done without you two distracting me. Just make sure you bring back a decent bottle of red.'

'If you turn up anything about Williams, you will call me straightaway?'

'You shouldn't need to ask.'

They were halfway down the corridor when Rita called to them from the door. Tate turned to see the librarian waving a raincoat at her.

'You might want to cover yourself up.'

FIFTY

Ralph Mills held up a hand to his face and stepped away from the flames, the intense heat forcing him back. 'Why has no one put it out yet?' He glanced up at the two firemen standing on the other side of the blazing van, fire extinguishers lying on the ground. They seemed as mesmerised by the flames as Mills was.

'The crew can't get the engine down here – the path through the trees is too narrow,' one of the uniformed officers from Bromley BOCU shouted over the roar of the flames. 'Fire extinguishers seem to do the trick for a while, but then it catches again. Whumf!' He nodded towards the two firemen. 'They've said there must be something highly flammable in the back of the van.'

'You think?'

McKittrick joined them. She watched the fire for a few moments before she spoke. 'Traffic said they've got no sightings of anyone leaving the park on foot,' she told him. 'No CCTV at all. Shame the chopper wasn't available – it might have picked Benson up on the infrared.' She rubbed a hand along her jaw. Even in the dark Mills could see a bruise forming on her cheek.

'You should get that looked at, boss.' He tapped his own face in the same place.

'When I want your medical opinion, I'll ask for it.' She shook her head. 'It's bloody ridiculous. How can a man just disappear?'

'Has anyone checked the CCTV from the railway station? It's possible he jumped on a train.'

McKittrick nodded. 'I'm waiting to hear back. The staff knock off every day at lunch time, so there's no one there to talk to.'

'We should check at Peckham Rye and Denmark Hill railway stations too – they're the closest to his mum's flat.'

'We've got them both covered.'

Mills looked up at the starless sky, the thick clouds illuminated orange by distant street lamps and the glow of the blazing van. 'We could really do with a downpour right about now.'

McKittrick started walking towards the van and Mills felt obliged to follow. 'Given Benson torched it,' she said, 'we've got to assume there's something inside he really didn't want us to find.'

'Seems a bit extreme – just to get rid of a knife. Assuming that's what he used to kill Dixon.' The flames cracked suddenly and Mills automatically stepped between McKittrick and the van. 'He had all day to do that.'

'He'd need to dispose of his clothes too.'

'Even so.' Mills scuffed a tuft of grass with the toe of his shoe. 'Has the search in Rotherhithe come up with anything?'

'Nothing so far. Apart from her cardigan there's no other sign of Casey in Dixon's mother's flat or in the immediate vicinity. I think it's pretty safe to assume she was never actually there.'

'Why take the cardigan there, then? He must have done it in the last day or so. It wasn't there when we took a look around.'

'We can't be sure of that. We didn't make a thorough search.'

The fire popped again and the two firemen shouted at them to stand back. When they didn't move straightaway, they were bundled clear by hands grabbing them from behind, both of them roughly dragged to the line of trees forty yards from the blaze.

'It's going up,' one fireman shouted and pushed McKittrick further into the wooded area.

A deafening boom echoed around the common. After a moment Mills turned to face the clearing to see Benson's van crashing back to the ground, acrid smoke billowing from the wreckage.

'Jesus,' a fireman standing next to him said, staring at the blackened hulk of metal. 'I've never seen anything go up like that.' He turned back to Mills. 'What was inside the van anyway?'

'Looks like we're not going to find out.'

'There won't he much for us to investigate, that's for sure. Though I can tell you the fire was started deliberately.' Behind his protective visor, the fireman's face broke into a wide grin. 'If that helps at all.'

'Cheers, mate – your input has been invaluable.' Mills turned back to McKittrick. 'Have you heard anything from the CSEs at Benson's place? Anything to link Benson to Dixon?'

'They've not turned up anything interesting yet. But I haven't given up hope – there's still the floorboards to rip up.'

'I don't suppose Benson's mum is cooperating?'

'Do you really expect her to? Grass up her only boy to the filth? It's not likely is it?' McKittrick grabbed her side as they started walking back towards the car. 'We've got two uniforms on her door. An unmarked car at each entry point to the estate. If Benson gets anywhere near her place, we'll have him.' She took a long look back at the smoking wreck.

'No more news from the hospital, I suppose?' Mills asked her.

'Cath's stable. That's all they'll tell me at present.' McKittrick lightly touched his arm. 'I'm sure she'll be fine.'

Mills didn't know how to react. It was the first time McKittrick had shown any sign of compassion. 'She wouldn't be in the hospital at all if I hadn't driven like a bloody idiot,' he said.

'Bringing Benson in is the one sure way to make you feel better.' She gripped his arm hard. 'OK?'

He looked down at her hand and nodded. 'OK, boss,' he said quietly and glanced up for a moment to meet her gaze. He held it a beat longer. There was something in her expression that suggested she was feeling just as shitty as he was. He took a deep breath. 'Right,' he said more firmly. 'Where to next?'

'Back to Camberwell. We'll head for the estate. See how the situation develops on the way. I want to speak to his sister as well as his mum.' She pulled up suddenly and clutched her side, gasping. Then let out a slow breath through her mouth.

'Quick visit to A&E on the way maybe?' Mills said. 'Check in on Cath at the same time?'

'It's just a stitch.' She started walking again and picked up speed, presumably trying to prove just how OK she was.

Mills wasn't convinced. She seemed to have developed a slight limp as well.

'We still haven't located any business premises for Benson. He's supposed to be running a maintenance company. You'd think there would at least be a lock-up somewhere,' she said, pausing every few words to snatch a breath. 'He doesn't even have a home office at his place.'

'Maybe he runs everything from his phone.'

'He's not a city trader. Where's he keep his tools?'

'Something to ask Lorraine and his mum about, maybe.'

'We just have to hope they start talking.'

FIFTY-ONE

A woman Angela Tate presumed was Fiona Wells was pacing up and down the driveway of a large red brick house as she and Ashley climbed out of the cab.

'Thank you so much for coming,' Wells said, sounding for all the world as if she'd invited them over for a spot of late supper. She extended her hand, then spent a moment scrutinising both women.

Tate was glad she'd borrowed Rita's raincoat.

'I don't have long,' Wells said. 'I've decided to take my children to stay at my mother's – I just want to get them away from here. It doesn't feel safe.' She was trembling.

Tate watched as Mrs Wells nervously flicked her hair and stamped her feet against the cold. She wondered again just how reliable the woman's story was.

'So – we'll get on shall we?' Tate turned on her heels and headed back to the kerb. 'Where did you see the van?'

Wells joined her on the pavement. 'Right here – where your cab stopped just now.'

'And what were you doing when you spotted her?'

'You do believe me, don't you?'

Tate dipped her head, not wanting to commit to a full nod. 'You said you were inside your house at the time?'

'In the hall – just inside the front door. I was expecting my husband. When I heard the sound of the engine I thought it was him, so I went to the door. He'd been to the wine shop – I was going to help him bring in the boxes. That's when I saw her get out of the back of the van.'

'Who was with her?'

'A man, I think. He had his back to me – he was holding the door open.'

'And the little girl didn't try to run away?'

'No – I think she may even have been smiling.'

Tate drew down a noisy breath.

'I can guess what you're thinking – it makes no sense to me either. But I know what I saw.'

'You mentioned on the phone you'd been mistaken before about seeing a little girl? Is it possible it's happened again?'

Mrs Wells gaze fell to her feet. 'There was no girl before – I got the police out under false pretences. But I promise you this time it's absolutely genuine.'

False pretences? No wonder Wells thought the police wouldn't take her seriously. They'd just wasted the last twenty minutes. They could have been helping Rita search for Thomas Williams.

'What I don't understand,' Wells went on, 'is if Dixon abducted the girl, and now he's dead… who's looking after her? When I saw him before, I don't think he had a van.'

'You saw Raymond Dixon?'

'I told you that on the phone.'

'I'm not sure you did.' Tate glanced at Ashley who shrugged back at her.

'I saw him this morning – just across the road there.' She pointed vaguely to the other side of the street. 'He was just standing there – looking over at my house. I told the policeman, Mills. At least he took me seriously about that.' She stared at the empty pavement across the road. 'So either Dixon wasn't working alone. Or he never took her in the first place. But then why would he be here the same day I saw her?'

'You're certain it was Dixon?'

'The police showed me his photograph. I identified him from it.'

'What was he wearing?'

'You don't believe me, do you?' She peered down at her watch. 'Look I have to go. It's a long drive and I don't want to arrive at my mother's in the early hours. I obviously can't say anything that will convince you.' She turned away and Tate watched her disappear inside her house.

'What do you think?' Ashley asked.

'Does she seem credible to you?'

Ashley shrugged. 'What's your gut instinct?'

Before Tate could answer, her phone started ringing. She glanced at the screen. It was the *Evening News* main switchboard number. As she hit the answer button she noticed the battery was down to a single bar. 'Make it quick, Rita.'

'Charming. Hello to you too.'

'Really – my phone could run out of juice any moment.'

'Should I call back on Ashley's phone?'

'No – you should bloody well tell me why you're calling. What have you found out?'

'I've located a Thomas Williams you might be interested in.'

'OK…' Tate held up a finger to Ashley who was bouncing up and down, desperate not to be left out.

'It took a long time to track him down – I managed to find a marriage certificate from 1972 online. Thomas Henry Williams, born 1947.'

Tate did some quick maths. 'So potentially the right age. Anything else?'

'Naturally – I would have waited until you got back here to tell you otherwise.' Rita cleared her throat theatrically. 'As it is, I thought you needed to know right away – given your location.'

'What are you getting at?' Why did Rita insist on drawing everything out? It was so irritating. Tate closed her eyes.

That was precisely why she did it. Just to wind her up. She let out a breath and waited for Rita to get to the point.

'There's an address on the marriage certificate. In 1972 Thomas Williams lived in Camberwell Grove. At the address right next door to your Mrs Wells.'

The breath stalled in Tate's throat. Rita gave her the house number and hung up.

'What is it?' Ashley had finally stopped bouncing.

Tate ran to the neighbouring house and peered through the metal gate to try to make out the number on the front door beyond. It was the number Rita had given her. In the gloom she saw the overgrown and weed-infested front garden seemed to be a dumping ground for old electrical appliances.

'Looks derelict to me,' Ashley declared.

'Well done. Top marks for observation. Anything else to add?'

'Make a great place to hide something… Or bury someone.' The girl shuddered.

'Precisely.'

'Should we ask Mrs Wells what she knows about it?'

Tate pictured the woman in her house fussing over her children, packing their cases, getting herself worked up into even more of a lather. 'Let's keep Mrs Wells out of it, shall we? I'll take a look around first. If I need her for background, I'll catch her before she leaves.'

'Background? Are you already planning a story?'

'I'm keeping my options open.' Tate rattled the gate on its hinges. It was firmly padlocked. She walked along the dense front hedge that separated the garden from the street until she reached the end. There was a narrow gap between the hedge and the brick wall marking the perimeter of the next garden. 'Side return,' she explained to Ashley. She pressed herself flat against the wall and slid sideways into the gap, snagging the sleeve of Rita's coat on a sharp twig protruding from the hedge. Ashley was right on her heels.

'You're staying out here.'

'No way – not after what happened this morning.'

'If I'm not back out in ten minutes, feel free to call the police.'

'What are you expecting to find?'

'I'm not *expecting* anything. First rule of journalism: keep an open mind. Flexibility is key,' Tate said as she twisted awkwardly and pushed further into the slim gap.

'I get it – you want the story for yourself.'

'We don't even know if there is a story. Not yet.' Tate steadied herself against the rush of adrenalin coursing through her veins. She could taste it in her mouth. What if Dixon had been on the right track? What if Paula Jeffries' body was buried here? Mrs Wells' account of seeing a man fitting Dixon's description seemed only too plausible now. He'd finally found what he'd been looking for these past two years.

'OK,' Ashley reluctantly agreed. 'Ten minutes. But then I'm calling for help.'

Tate found the torch app on her phone. A narrow beam of light illuminated the ground a couple of feet ahead of her as she picked her way over rubble and broken bricks, old paint cans and smashed glass. After inching forward for twenty feet or so, she reached a high wooden gate, the wood cracked and split along the lengths of its boards. The light on the phone went out, the battery finally exhausted. She shoved the phone into a pocket and felt for the latch on the gate, quickly discovering there wasn't one. Instead, her fingers traced the cold metal hunk of a padlock. She heard a noise. She froze and held her breath. A definite scraping sound, like metal dragging across concrete. She listened for a moment longer, hearing nothing except the distant rumble of a train and the faint wail of a police siren.

Had the noise come from this house or further away?

She quickly ran her fingers along the other side of the wooden gate. It was attached to a post that felt rotten in places. Her fingertips reached a rusty upper hinge, its surface gnarled and pitted. She gave it a hard tug and heard a couple of screws ping out of their moorings. She tugged again and the whole hinge plate freed itself from the post. She repeated the process with the bottom hinge, feeling her way in the dark, stopping every few seconds to listen for any sign of life in the garden beyond.

With both hinges free, Tate took a deep breath and pushed gently at the gate. It creaked and groaned, wood splintering on the padlock side as she forced it open wide enough to squeeze through. On the other side she made her way slowly along an unevenly paved path, her hand trailing lightly against the side of the house as she went. Loose mortar crumbled beneath her fingertips.

After about ten feet the paving gave way to soft ground, almost spongy underfoot. Tate trod carefully into the darkness, hands outstretched to feel for obstacles in her path. The ground rose slightly beneath her feet, then dipped again. She slowed even more and navigated up and over another mound of tightly packed soil. Her stomach lurched as she considered what might be buried in the ground.

She continued forward, eyes wide open, seeing nothing in the pitch-blackness. The air was moist and thick with a musty ripeness, like fermenting fruit. Stopping for a moment, she tilted her face towards the black sky. Shouldn't she be able to see some trace of light? London skies were never this dark.

Nearby trees rustled as the wind picked up suddenly and she heard a flapping overhead. Then she realised. Stretched from one side of the garden to the other was some kind of covering, by the noise, she'd guess a plastic tarpaulin. She was inside an enormous makeshift marquee.

Tate considered whether she should continue to explore the garden or make her way back towards the house. There was nothing to see out here, so she swung around a hundred and eighty degrees. Her foot caught against something. She stumbled. Sticking her arms out in an attempt to stay upright, she overbalanced and thumped awkwardly onto the ground. She managed to scramble to her feet again, but as soon as she was upright couldn't be sure which direction she was facing. She started walking forwards as slowly as before, hoping she was heading back towards the house.

A noise sounded behind her. Ashley? Tate stopped. Held her breath and listened. Something dropped over her head. A bag? Then a weight pressed against her throat as a hand covered her mouth. The pressure on her windpipe squeezed tighter and tighter, making it impossible to breathe. Her arms were pinned to her sides by a strong grip. She struggled, kicking back at her attacker. Her foot made contact with something solid, but the flimsy rubber gym shoe made no impact. She kicked again, as the grip across her throat tightened.

After a few moments her head started to buzz. A moment later her knees buckled. She dropped to the ground.

FIFTY-TWO

'And where exactly is your son's place of business, Mrs Benson?' McKittrick had asked the question before, but she still hoped the stubborn old woman sitting in front of her, Jack Russell curled up in her lap, would decide it was in her best interests to start talking. 'I know you think you're helping Gary by refusing to answer my questions, but in the long run it'll only make things worse for him.'

Mrs Benson pursed her lips and stared blankly at her.

There was a knock on the living room door and a uniformed officer appeared, Lorraine O'Donnell standing behind him in the hall. O'Donnell barged past him into the room. 'What do you think you're doing?' she said. 'She's seventy-two years old! Why don't you go and bully somebody else?' She stood behind her mother's armchair. The dog lifted its head, looked at her for a moment, then resumed its original position.

'Please – join us, Lorraine.' McKittrick said. At least now she didn't have to make the trip to O'Donnell's flat. 'Perhaps you can help? Do you have any idea where your brother might be?'

'How would I? I'm not his keeper. What's he supposed to have done, anyway?'

'We'd just like to ask him a few questions in connection with an incident that occurred earlier today.' She smiled. 'Quite routine.'

'Routine? Then why are your lot all over the estate? I counted three policemen on the landing. Isn't that a bit heavy-handed?' She sank onto the wide arm of her mother's chair. Immediately the dog started to growl at her and she jumped to her feet again. 'We can't help you – we haven't seen him.'

'Can you give us the address of your brother's business premises, Lorraine?' McKittrick kept her tone light.

'He's not likely to be there is he? This time of night.'

Maureen Benson shot out a hand and gripped O'Donnell's wrist tight in her fist. 'Fetch me my pills, will you, love. I feel a bit off colour. They're in the bathroom cabinet.'

O'Donnell swallowed hard, looked down at the gnarled fingers wrapped around her wrist.

'We might as well take a look.' McKittrick pulled out her notebook. 'It's no bother.'

'I was forgetting,' O'Donnell said, not taking her eyes from her mother's hand. 'Gary got rid of the lock-up a couple of years back.' She tugged on her arm until her mother eventually released it. 'I need to get Mum's tablets.'

'Obstructing the police is a criminal offence, Lorraine. You do know that?' McKittrick shouted after her as O'Donnell ran from the room. She turned back to Maureen Benson. 'The sooner we can speak to Gary, eliminate him from our enquiries, the better for all of us – wouldn't you say? Where is he, Mrs Benson?'

'He's a grown man – I don't know where he goes. Why would he tell me?'

'Where would he go if he needed help? Apart from here, of course.'

'Gary doesn't need anybody's help. Never has, never will.'

'According to the phone provider's records, Gary phoned you two hours ago. What did you speak to him about?'

'I don't remember. It couldn't have been important, else I wouldn't have forgot – would I?'

'He didn't mention to you where he was?'

Mrs Benson looked away without answering. 'When can I have my phone back? You've no right to take it away.'

'You have the receipt – it'll be quite safe with us.'

'What if someone wants to get in touch with me?'

McKittrick glanced at the landline sitting on a table next to the door. 'Sorry for the inconvenience.'

O'Donnell returned to the room empty-handed. 'Couldn't find your pills – you erm… need to get your prescription renewed.'

'Not to worry, love. I'll manage. Shouldn't you be getting back to Alfie?'

'I'd like you to stay here, Lorraine,' McKittrick said and blocked the doorway. 'I've a few questions I need to ask.'

'It's not convenient.'

'Would the police station be easier for you both, then?'

O'Donnell shot a glance at her mother, who glared back at her.

'Why don't you sit down and I'll get one of the PCs to make us all a cup of tea?' McKittrick stepped into the hall and found the uniform coming back in through the front door from the outside landing.

'Ma'am, we've just heard from DC Kapoor,' he said. 'She'd like to have a word.'

'Tell her to phone me.'

'Apparently she needs to show you something. Urgently, she said.'

McKittrick blew out a sigh. 'Don't let either of them out of your sight until I get back – understand?'

'Of course, ma'am.'

'No excuses from O'Donnell – she's staying right here until I've finished with her. If you have to, arrest them both and I'll continue the interviews back at the station. Clear?'

The PC nodded and took up a sentry position at the living room door.

McKittrick ran from the Essex onto the Shakespeare Estate, arriving at Montague House in two minutes flat. Kapoor was waiting for her at Trisha Collins' front door. 'This better be important,' she said as the FLO led her through to the living room.

'I couldn't leave the kids, boss. Trisha's taken a sedative. I don't think she's safe to look after them at the moment.' She pulled out a chair at the dining table and gestured for McKittrick to sit down. A laptop sat on the table, a blurred image filling the screen. 'Have you heard any more from the hospital about Cath?' Kapoor asked.

'Not as yet. I'm sure she's fine.' McKittrick hadn't checked on Cath's condition for over two hours, but what else could she say? She stared at the laptop in front of her. 'What am I supposed to be looking at?'

Kapoor clicked the mouse and the blurry image resolved into a street scene: two figures getting into a van parked in an otherwise empty road. 'I've been trawling through the CCTV for the area around the pharmacy burglary on Camberwell New Road.'

'Why? It's not your case.'

'There's not really anything to do here most of the time. I'm not much more than a glorified babysitter. I feel a bit useless. I thought I could kill two birds with one stone. This case hasn't been reallocated yet. I didn't want it falling through the cracks.' She took a breath. 'Besides – I've had the feeling there's something about the pharmacy case that…' She looked away.

'What is it?'

'Something about it has been nagging at me. I haven't been able to let it go.'

'This footage should never have been removed from the station. You do know that?' McKittrick applauded Kapoor's work ethic, but there was a line between dedication and obsession. She should know – she'd crossed it enough times herself.

Kapoor winced and defensively pulled up her shoulders, as if she was expecting a bollocking. 'I know, boss. I'm really sorry.' She dropped her chin. 'But when you see this you'll understand why I couldn't just walk away.'

The video continued to play, the van accelerated from the kerb and out of camera shot.

'What am I looking at now?'

'Those are the two pharmacy burglars.'

'And that's it? They drive away?'

'It's the bit coming up next.'

An image from another camera, presumably from a neighbouring street, appeared on the screen. Kapoor hit the pause button. 'See?' She pointed at a dark shape on the side of the white van.

'I still don't know what it is I'm supposed to be seeing.'

'I've watched this dozens of times now. Until I finally worked it out. This area here…' She tapped the screen again. 'Used to be a logo – it's been peeled off, but it's left an impression behind. Like those bright yellow old BT vans you used to see all the time. You could still see the branding, even though it was supposed to have been removed.'

'I can't make it out.'

'It took me ages. Then I realised that I'd seen the shape before. It's the same logo as the one on Gary Benson's van. He parks it right outside the building when he's visiting Trisha – even though the only bays downstairs are for disability badge holders. It winds me up every time I see it.'

'You're sure it's the same logo?'

'As much as I can be.'

McKittrick stared at the frozen image on the laptop. Even if it was Benson's old van. So what? 'How does this help us find Gary Benson?'

'He must have sold it to someone local – wouldn't you say? So I was thinking it's possible they know him. Could even be harbouring him right now.' She handed McKittrick a scrap of paper with a registration number written on it.

'That's very tenuous, Manisha. They might have just seen a 'for sale' card in the window of the newsagents and not known him at all. Is that what you called me over for?'

McKittrick wondered if the FLO duties might be proving too stressful for Kapoor. If she was taking such desperate leaps in the dark, making connections where there were none, perhaps she should be removed from the investigation. She decided she'd have a word with the DCI. 'They may just have nicked the van,' McKittrick said, in an attempt to drag Kapoor back to reality.

'I thought that too, but when have you ever heard of burglars hanging on to the same stolen vehicle for more than one job? Especially when those jobs are over four months apart?'

'OK.' She was humouring her now. 'Go on.'

Kapoor pointed at the piece of paper. 'We've never had the number for the van before – the plates have been obscured on every CCTV image I've seen. The DVLA records for Gary Benson produced this one.'

'How did you—?'

'I got someone at the station to run a check for me on any vehicle Benson's owned in the last fifteen years. This one is for the right make and model.' She sucked down another breath. 'So anyway, I was thinking: great – at least we can get the address of the new registered owner and pick up the people responsible for the chemist break-in.'

McKittrick needed to wrap this up. She had to get back to O'Donnell and her mother. She got to her feet. 'That's great, Manisha – good work. You know I can't authorise the manpower for that, though? You'll have to speak to DCI Taylor in CID.'

'No boss – that's not what I'm getting at. I know now there *has* to be a connection between these two and Benson.'

McKittrick was starting to lose her patience. 'How?'

'According to DVLA records, he never sold the van. Gary Benson is still the legal owner.'

FIFTY-THREE

The smell of damp was overpowering. Angela Tate opened her eyes. She blinked. Little by little, as her eyes adjusted to the dark, her surroundings started to materialise. A faint rectangular outline of light suggested a doorway immediately in front of her. The walls were bare brick, the floor beneath her a rough concrete. She tried to raise her head and immediately the room began to swim.

'Thank God!'

Tate jerked at the unexpected sound. She had presumed she was alone in her damp little cell. She heard shuffling across the concrete floor and a moment later Ashley Montogomery was looming over her.

'I thought you were dead,' the girl said. 'I couldn't hear you breathing.' Her voice caught. 'I was so scared.'

'Where are we?'

'I'm not sure. Someone threw a hood or something over my head and dragged me down into this room. I think we're in some sort of cellar.'

'Who grabbed you?'

'They came at me from behind. I didn't see.'

'More than one person?'

'I suppose so… I think I might have had a chance to fight them off if it had only been one.'

Tate tried to move her head again, more slowly this time. She surveyed the room as best she could. Her temples throbbed.

'I've already felt for a light switch,' the intern said. 'There isn't one.'

'How long have we been in here?'

'I don't know. Ten minutes? Twenty?'

'You were supposed to call the police after ten.'

The girl let out a long hissing breath. 'Sorry. I got curious. I just wanted to see for myself.'

'See what?'

'Whatever it was you were looking at. I was just reaching into my bag for my phone when they grabbed me – I swear.'

'I don't suppose you still have it?'

'They took my bag and emptied my pockets before they shoved me in here.'

Very tentatively, Tate propped herself up on her elbows. Her head screamed in protest. If she'd been unconscious for more than ten minutes that might mean she had concussion. She wondered if she should be worried. 'Did you hear their voices? Men or women? English or foreign?'

'Only the occasional grunt – I couldn't really tell. Maybe men with high voices or women with deep ones?'

'Could one of them have been Thomas Williams? According to Rita's research he'd be about sixty-five by now.'

'I really couldn't tell. Sorry.' She pressed her face closer to Tate's. 'I'm so glad you're all right. What happened out there?'

Tate suddenly remembered the mound of earth she'd stumbled over in the garden. 'Someone grabbed me by the throat. Cut off my air supply. I must have blacked out.'

'What did you see before they grabbed you?'

Tate told her about the mounds of earth.

'You think they were graves?'

She shuddered. 'It's certainly likely, wouldn't you think?'

Holding on to Ashley's arm, Tate managed to get to her feet. Unsteadily, she shuffled over to the door. There was no handle.

'So – what are we going to do?' The intern was suddenly standing beside her, fidgeting. 'We've got to get out of here.'

'I've just regained consciousness. Do you really think I've had the chance to come up with a plan?'

'We've got to do something.'

Tate thumped her fist against the wooden door. Then both fists.

'What are you doing!' Ashley grabbed her hands. 'What if they come back?'

'We'll never get out of here if they don't.'

'But we mustn't make them angry. What if they hurt us?'

Tate shrugged. She'd rather force the situation than wait around for something to happen. She thumped the door again. 'Hello!' she hollered. 'Is there anybody there?' She hit the door four, five times. Ashley joined in. They both hollered. After a minute or so Tate stopped and jabbed the intern sharply in the ribs. They listened. Nothing. She thumped the door again. Hollered again. They kept it up for longer this time. Then stopped and listened. Still no response. They repeated the routine for a few minutes. Then, in a lull, Tate was sure she heard distant footsteps. Retreating.

'Hello!' Tate yelled. 'Please – don't go! I just want to talk to you.'

A few seconds later a light flickered overhead. Moments after that the room was flooded in fluorescent light.

Tate blinked rapidly in the brightness. 'Well at least we got someone's attention.'

Ashley's mouth dropped open, her eyes wide circles. 'You're bleeding,' she whispered urgently and pointed at Tate's hairline.

Tate raised a hand to her head and felt something wet.

At that moment the door flew open. Tate and Ashley stumbled backwards, Tate almost losing her balance, grabbing on to the intern in an attempt to stay upright.

In the doorway stood a middle-aged woman with long, wild, almost colourless hair. She was dressed in peculiarly old-fashioned clothes: a shapeless cardigan covering an old lady's floral pinafore dress.

'What do you think you're doing? Making all that racket?' she barked at them.

Tate took a long hard look at the woman's face. Although her forehead was a corrugated mass of angry lines, the skin around her nose and mouth was almost wrinkle-free. It was impossible to gauge how old she was. Could she be Williams' wife?

'You've woken up my granddaughter,' she snapped. 'It'll take hours to get her back to sleep.'

Granddaughter? Was this the child Wells had seen climbing out of the van earlier? 'I'm so sorry.' Tate took a step forward.

'Stay where you are!' the woman screamed.

Tate held up her hands in apology while edging forward a couple more inches.

'I said stay!' The woman dug her hand into the folds of her dress and retrieved a knife, the blade glinting in the harsh light of the fluorescent strip in the ceiling. 'I don't want any trouble. Do you understand?'

Tate nodded and moved back, banging into Ashley as she did so. The intern yelped.

'I wouldn't dream of waking up your… granddaughter, did you say?'

The woman nodded.

'I had no idea there were any children living here. What's her name?'

'What's it to you?'

'Just making conversation.' She smiled weakly. 'Thank you for turning on the light just now. It was so horrible and dark in here. Cold too. And damp. Do you think we could have a couple of blankets? Or a hot drink maybe?'

'No.'

'Really? What about a glass of water?'

'You must think I'm stupid.' She jabbed the knife at Tate. 'Why would I give you a glass?'

'A beaker then – a paper cup. I need to bathe my head.' Tate pointed to the wound at her left temple. 'I think I must have hit my head on something.'

'That was an accident. You shouldn't have struggled so much. What were you doing in the garden?'

Tate hesitated, struggling to invent a plausible excuse. 'My dog ran into your garden. From the road. I came in to retrieve her. She's only little. She must have squeezed under the gate. Have you seen her?'

'You're lying. There's no dog.'

'Why would I lie?'

'What kind of dog is it?'

'Oh… just a mongrel. Little white and brown thing.'

'I shouldn't even be talking to you.' She glanced at Ashley. 'Either of you.' She started to close the door. 'You must be quiet now. I can't have my granddaughter disturbed again.'

'Wait – please. Don't lock us up. I panic in small spaces.'

'Too bad.'

'Mum?' a second, gentler voice called.

Over their captor's shoulder, Tate spotted a young woman. She too was dressed in shabby old ladies' clothes. The woman hesitated in a doorway on the other side of a square outer room. The walls on both sides of the room were lined with cardboard boxes. A flight of stairs led up from the doorway to an upper floor. The only way out.

'What are you doing down here?' the woman with the knife demanded.

'I thought you might need some help.'

'I'm all right.' She jabbed the knife towards Tate again, by way of demonstration. 'I told you not to leave Olivia on her own. She'll get frightened. Do you want that?'

The younger woman shook her head meekly.

'Hello,' Tate said. 'I'm Angela – what's your name?' She smiled at the new arrival.

The young woman simply stared at her, breathing noisily through her mouth.

'Don't tell her! Just get back to Olivia.'

'I do like your dress,' Tate said.

'I made it myself,' the younger woman said, the hint of a smile brightening her grave face.

'Oh I wish I had that sort of skill – all fingers and thumbs, me. You really are very talented.'

The younger woman looked Tate up and down.

'Oh this old thing, I know – I've got the world's worst taste in clothes. You should see what else is lurking in my wardrobe!'

'Shut up!' The older woman said. 'I know what you're doing. I was warned you'd try something like this. I won't fall for it. You're not my friend. You're not my daughter's friend. So don't act as if you are.'

The younger woman's smile quickly faded and she started to cough, quietly at first then more violently. Her chest heaved as she struggled to breathe. She leaned forward and gripped her knees, gulping down air.

'You shouldn't be here with all this damp,' the older woman said. 'I told you to go upstairs.'

Tate took a step forward. 'Perhaps I can help? I've had first aid training,' she lied.

The knife flashed inches from her face.

'Get back inside.'

Finally, the choking fit subsided and the young woman retrieved a small bottle and handkerchief from her pocket.

She dripped liquid onto the cotton square then lifted it to her nose, filling her lungs as best she could.

'Go now – go back to Olivia. Try to get her back to sleep.'

'That's your daughter is it?' Tate said to the younger woman. 'Olivia? It's a lovely name. She must be a baby – you're still so young.'

'She's not. She'll be—'

'Shut up! Don't speak to her, do you hear me?'

'What are we going to do with them?' the younger woman said quietly, her voice cracking.

'That's none of your concern. Or mine.' She looked both her prisoners up and down, contempt on her face. 'Daddy will decide what's best.'

FIFTY-FOUR

Natasha McKittrick closed the door of interview room five and exhaled. If she stayed a moment longer in the company of Mrs Benson she was sure she would end up nutting the woman. Tight-lipped was an expression invented for her. She suspected if she'd asked her for the right time, Maureen Benson would have refused to divulge it. Arresting mother and daughter and hauling them down to the station had been a last resort. McKittrick had hoped it would persuade one of them to start talking, but on the evidence so far, Mrs Benson would frustrate an expert team of rendition trained CIA operatives. But without her mother providing cues from across the room, it was just possible O'Donnell would let something slip.

After a swift visit to the ladies, armed with a can of Diet Coke and another of Trisha Collins' Temazepams, McKittrick dropped in on the incident room, which was currently doubling up as the nerve centre for the Raymond Dixon murder investigation. DCI Barrow had made some noises about getting another MIT in to take over, but McKittrick was determined to hang on to the case for as long as she could. She wanted to at least bring Benson in. Even if her team didn't get to take him all the way to court.

She flipped on her computer and scrolled through the latest emails. So far the licence plate recognition software hadn't come up with any sightings of Benson's old van, but then that was hardly surprising – according to Kapoor its new owners had been very careful to obscure the number plates. At least the CCTV footage collected from cameras situated around Dixon's mother's tower block in Rotherhithe had confirmed an unidentified hooded figure, probably male, had entered the building at 9.02 a.m. that morning and exited again just ten minutes before Angela Tate arrived. The height and build matched Benson. At the moment, it was all they had to connect him to the murder. As evidence the footage didn't even qualify as flimsy, but right now she'd take anything she could get. She drank the remainder of the Diet Coke and headed back downstairs to start on Lorraine O'Donnell.

Mills scrambled to his feet when she entered the interview room.

'Now, Lorraine,' McKittrick said, before she'd even pulled out a chair. 'I do hope you're going to do your brother a favour and tell us where we can find him.'

'Why are you keeping me here? I've got to get back to Alfie,' O'Donnell snapped. 'Mick's useless – he won't even get him to bed. Christ knows what he's given him for his tea.'

'The sooner you answer our questions, the faster we can get you out of here. It's completely up to you.' McKittrick flashed a brief smile at her.

'Whatever it is you think Gary's done, I can tell you right now he didn't. Couldn't have. He was with me since before lunchtime. Then for the rest of the afternoon.'

'Where?' McKittrick asked.

'What?'

'Where were you both?'

'At mine. Gary came round to… erm…'

McKittrick wondered if Mrs Benson had advised O'Donnell to come up with an alibi for her brother.

'He was fixing my washing machine. Yeah – that was it.'

'Can anyone else confirm Gary was with you?'

'I'm telling you – I'm confirming it.'

'Mr O'Donnell perhaps? Or your son?'

'I'm not having you getting my Alfie dragged into all of this. He's only a kid.'

'What time did Gary arrive at your flat?'

'Well before dinnertime.'

'An approximate time would really help us.'

'Eleven.'

'Did he tell you where he'd been before that time?'

'Ten – I mean ten o'clock.'

McKittrick sighed. It was clear Maureen Benson hadn't had a chance to coach her daughter through the story she was attempting to spin them.

'How did he seem when he arrived?'

'Fine – why wouldn't he be?'

'Not flustered in any way? On edge? Distracted perhaps?'

'Nope – he was just his usual self.'

'You're sure it was ten o'clock?'

A flash of panic crossed O'Donnell's face. 'No – wait a minute. Now I come to think about it, it was closer to nine.'

'Nine o'clock?'

'That's right.'

'What time did he leave?'

O'Donnell looked up towards the ceiling. McKittrick couldn't decide whether it was for divine inspiration or the woman somehow knew her mother was installed in the room directly above this one.

'He gave me a lift to the park – to pick Alfie up from football. Brockwell Park. That would have been after dinnertime – one o'clockish?' She looked at Mills, as if he would be able help her with the details of her story.

'Gary used his van?'

O'Donnell took a deep breath. More details she hadn't prepared. 'Yeah.' She nodded tentatively.

'Which one?'

'What do you mean, which one?'

'According to our records, your brother currently owns two vehicles.'

'He's only got one.'

'He never uses his old one?'

'He sold that a couple of years back.'

'Not according to our records.'

'Can't help you there. Your records must be wrong.'

'So, if we check the CCTV footage, we'll be able to confirm that Gary arrived at your flat around nine, drove to the park at one, and returned when?'

'Two-thirty, maybe.'

'And your son will be able to confirm that too?'

'I've told you – I'm not having my Alfie involved.'

McKittrick leaned on the table. She lowered her voice. 'You do understand how serious it is to pervert the course of justice? If we find out later you're not telling us the truth, you could face prosecution yourself?'

'Gary was with me all day.' She exhaled and gripped her hands together on the tabletop.

'OK… moving on. Your brother's business premises.'

'What?'

'You said he used to have premises a while ago. Where were they?'

'I never knew the address.'

'Where, approximately?'

'I forget.'

Mills cleared his throat and looked at McKittrick, his eyebrows raised. She nodded back at him.

'The boxes I saw Gary taking from your mum's place,' he said. 'Where was he storing those?'

'Don't know anything about that.'

'Big cardboard boxes, eighteen inches high. Heavy, by the expression on Gary's face. Where was he taking them?'

'You've got that all wrong.' O'Donnell started scratching at her forearm with stubby fingernails. 'I've never seen any boxes at Mum's.'

'Upstairs back bedroom – I counted at least a dozen on one visit. My colleague and I saw Gary carrying one down the stairs only moments before we spoke to you there. There was no way you couldn't know about them.'

O'Donnell shrugged. 'You'd have to ask Mum about that.'

'Does Gary store anything in *your* flat?'

'No!'

'So when we search it later, we won't find anything you're holding on to for him?'

The panicked expression had returned to O'Donnell's face. 'I don't know what Gary gets up to. He never talks to me about anything. As far as he's concerned, I'm just his stupid little sister. It's not like he shares his secrets with me.'

'Does he have many secrets, then?' McKittrick asked.

'No! It's just a figure of speech. If he talks to anyone, it's Mum. I don't know why you're wasting your time speaking to me – it's her you should be grilling.'

McKittrick stared into O'Donnell's face. Her eyes were darting this way and that, she was chewing the inside of her mouth. Why was she suggesting they interrogate her mother? Why the sudden disloyalty?

'So, if Gary did have any secrets – hypothetically speaking of course,' McKittrick said, 'your mother would be the one he'd confide in?'

O'Donnell nodded then glanced at Mills. 'Yeah. Why don't you ask Mum? And let me get off home.' She sniffed out a breath.

An urgent knock on the door made their interviewee jump. She clutched at her chest. 'Any chance I could have a ciggie? My nerves are shot right through.'

McKittrick ignored her and hurried to the door.

'Sorry to interrupt, ma'am.' The PC standing in the corridor was beaming at her, his expression anything but apologetic.

McKittrick closed the door behind her.

'Only you did say I should tell you of any developments straightaway.'

'Well come on then, spit it out.'

'The search team have come across an old invoice at Benson's house. There's a business address on it for him – an industrial unit on Wyndham Road.'

Ralph Mills stepped out of the unmarked car and tightened the stab-resistant vest around his waist. The uniforms were piling through the metal door of Benson's premises, having prised off the heavy padlocks with crowbars.

McKittrick had wanted to join them, just in case Benson was actually holed up inside, but instead she let Mills coordinate the operation, deciding to have another crack at Maureen Benson.

The first wave of officers made a preliminary search, established the building was empty and set about sifting through the items stored inside. Mills snapped on a pair of nitrile gloves and joined them.

Lit by two long fluorescent strips suspended from chains attached to the ceiling, the fifteen feet square space was remarkably clean and tidy for the headquarters of a maintenance firm. A blue tarpaulin covered a narrow workbench that ran the length of one of the walls. Together with a uniformed officer, Mills carefully lifted off the tarpaulin to reveal a bank of DVD recorders stacked five high and four wide along the worktop. At the back of the room Mills spotted a collection of cardboard boxes identical to the ones he'd seen at Mrs Benson's flat. He tore away the top flap of the first box. Inside were dozens of boxes of DVDs, the jewel cases still wrapped in their factory cellophane.

'Keep looking,' Mills instructed the team. 'Let's find out what kind of stuff Benson's been copying. I'm guessing it's not the latest Hollywood blockbuster.' He scanned the room. 'It's possible the murder weapon is concealed somewhere in here too.'

He stepped outside to call McKittrick.

McKittrick hung up on Mills more abruptly than she'd meant. It wasn't his fault they were no further forward in locating Benson. She could quiz Mrs Benson and O'Donnell about the DVD duplicating factory, but she was pretty sure she'd get nothing out of them. Even O'Donnell had stopped talking now, and both women were demanding to leave the station. She wanted to speak to Barrow about threatening to charge the pair with perverting the course of justice, but when she'd tried calling the DCI, she'd been diverted straight to voicemail. Would he actually turn off his phone in the middle of an operation? She stared down at her mobile, wondering whether to try him again, when it started vibrating in her hand.

'McKittrick.'

'Evening, ma'am. This is Easton – duty desk sergeant.'

A name that meant nothing to her. They must have changed shifts on the front desk.

'I hope I'm not interrupting anything—'

'What is it, sergeant?'

'There's a man in reception insisting he speaks to you. Won't take no for an answer.'

'Who is he?'

'He's refusing to give me his name.'

'Then get rid of him.' Why was he even bothering her with this?

'I would do, ma'am, only he says he has something to tell you, in confidence. Insists it's important.'

McKittrick puffed out her cheeks. What was another wasted ten minutes to her, the day she was having? 'I'll be down shortly.'

She thundered down the stairs, rehearsing the bollocking she'd give the desk sergeant on the way. As soon as she reached the reception area, the uniform behind the desk pointed towards a man taking a keen interest in the posters stuck to the notice board at the opposite end of the room. The man turned towards her.

It was Gary Benson.

'Hello, inspector,' he said, smiling. 'I'm glad I caught you.' He strode towards her, the smile still plastered across his face. 'I'd like to report a stolen vehicle.'

FIFTY-FIVE

Much to Tate's relief, the strange woman in the floral pinafore dress left the light on after she closed the door.

'What now?' Ashley's voice was quavering.

'We wait. What else is there?'

'I'm thirsty. And I really need to pee.'

Tate glanced around the small rectangular room. 'There's nowhere to go in here. You'll just have to cross your legs.'

'I'm getting desperate.'

'Try to think about something else.'

Ashley let out a long breath. 'I'm scared. What are they going to do to us?'

'It'll be fine. Let's just play it by ear shall we? I'm sure I'll think of something.' Tate hoped she sounded more confident than she felt. The house was completely cut off from its neighbours. Mrs Wells would be long gone. She prayed Rita would think to raise the alarm when they didn't return to her with the promised bottle of wine. But how long might Rita leave it before she did anything? Tate had no real sense of how long they'd been gone.

After what seemed like minutes, Tate heard footsteps coming from the outer room.

'Stand back from the door!' A voice yelled.

Tate dragged Ashley to her feet and the two women tensed as the door swung open to reveal a short, wiry man standing next to the woman in the pinafore. She was gripping the knife tightly in her hand. Tate tried to peer around them. There was no sign of the younger woman. She looked more closely at the man's face. A grizzly white beard covered most of it, thinning grey hair fell in a greasy slick over his forehead. This, presumably was 'daddy'. But was it Thomas Williams? He appeared to be the right age.

'Angela Tate.' Tate held out her hand. 'And you are?'

'No need for you to know that.'

'I can hardly call you "Daddy". What about Mr Williams?'

The man stiffened.

'Or is that too formal? Thomas then? Or Tom? It's completely up to you.'

His nostrils twitched. Tate could see his top lip curling beneath the straggly beard.

'Don't know who you're talking about,' he said. 'Never heard the name before.' He narrowed his watery eyes and nudged the woman in the floral dress with an elbow.

'I suppose you've heard the news. Must have come as a great shock to you,' Tate continued, undeterred by his denial. 'How long ago was it you met Raymond? It's got to be over twenty years now, hasn't it?'

She detected a definite tightening in his neck muscles. She turned to the woman. 'Did your *daddy* go away in 1995? How old were you then? Twenty or so? Younger?'

The woman glanced at the stooping old man, switched the knife from one hand to the other.

'Where did he tell you he was? Working abroad?' Tate stared into her face and saw confusion creep into her expression. 'Only you weren't abroad, were you, Tom?' She leaned forward. 'Your daddy was in prison all that time.'

The woman's jaw slackened. She looked again at the old man. Tate took her chance. She lunged at the knife and managed to make contact with the woman's arm, but her grip on the knife held firm. She swiped the blade towards Tate. The tip caught the back of her hand.

'Get back!' the woman hollered. 'Stop saying wicked things!'

Tate lifted her hand to her mouth and sucked on the wound. Ashley had slipped behind her. She could feel the intern trembling.

'They may be wicked,' Tate said. 'But nevertheless one hundred per cent true. Why don't you ask him what he was in prison for?'

The woman didn't take her eyes off Tate, learning quickly from her previous mistake. 'Why is she saying these things?'

'Because she's an evil lying whore. Pay no attention to her.'

'All right – if you don't want to tell her… I will.' Tate inched forward once again, watching the blade all the while. '*Daddy* was sentenced to seven years in jail for abusing an eleven-year-old girl.' She glanced up at the woman's face to gauge her reaction. There was barely a flicker. She already *knew*? Why wasn't it a revelation? 'Did he used to hurt you too?'

'That's enough!' Williams held up a hand.

'How old is your granddaughter? Olivia, isn't it? Are you worried he might start hurting her?'

'Shut up!' She jabbed the knife at Tate. 'I won't listen to you.'

'Because you know it's true, don't you? I suppose he hurt your daughter too?'

The woman swallowed, started biting her bottom lip.

'Why don't you leave him? We could…' She glanced Ashley, who was staring at her wild-eyed. *Hold it together, Ashley*. 'We could help you. We could help all three of you. You, your daughter and Olivia. We can make sure you're all safe. But we need to get you out of here.'

'I'm not listening to any more of this.' The old man started to shut the door.

'Wait!' the woman shouted. 'How did you know about Daddy going away?'

'We can help you. I promise.' Tate smiled sympathetically. 'I was speaking to a woman just the other day – her daughter was hurt just like yours. Her little girl went missing when she was only nine-years-old. That woman never got over it. Her life stopped the day Paula disappeared.'

Williams tensed. Tate pressed on.

'Do you know, she still keeps a room for her daughter in her flat, just in case she ever goes back home?' Tate stared at Williams. 'Only she'll never go home again, will she, Tom?

He stared right back at her defiantly.

'What did you say the girl's name was?' the woman asked.

'Paula. Paula Jeffries. Did you know her? She used to live not far from here.'

She stared at Tate for a long moment, unblinking.

Tate faced Williams. 'Only we know Paula will never return home, don't we, Tom?'

'Shut up.'

'Raymond tracked you down. Then he told me what was buried in your garden.'

'Lies!'

If only Dixon had told her. She could have helped him. He might still be alive now. 'He told me everything. How else would I have found you?'

The old man lunged at her. Tate didn't see his fist until it was inches from her face. She tried to duck, but his knuckles struck her hard on the jaw.

'Lying whore! Don't listen to her, Rosie. She's just lying to turn you against me. You wouldn't want to leave Daddy all on his own, would you?'

The woman shook her head meekly, like a small child, her eyes wide as plates.

'There's a good girl. Are you going to help me then? Like I told you?'

'Why's she saying those things?'

'Because she's evil. You mustn't take any notice of her. Do you hear me?'

'Rosie, listen to me – you don't have to be frightened anymore.' Tate risked a small step forward towards the door. She felt Ashley tug on her coat. She ignored her. 'He doesn't care about you. Or Olivia. Or – what's your daughter's name?'

'Mary,' the woman said quietly.

Tate was surprised she'd told her. Perhaps she was starting to get through to her. 'He only cares about himself.' Another baby step.

'She's lying,' Williams said. 'She doesn't really want to help you.'

'I'm not, Rosie. You can trust me. Why don't you go and fetch Mary and Olivia and we can all leave right now?'

The woman seemed to consider Tate's suggestion for a moment. Tate edged forward a fraction more. Too much.

'Get back!' Rosie jabbed the knife at her, forcing her back into the room.

'That's it, Rosie – you help Daddy like you promised.'

The woman reached out towards Ashley and grabbed her arm. She hauled her from the room, spun her round and suddenly the knife was at the intern's throat. She whimpered.

'Stay clear!' the woman warned. 'Or I'll slice her throat.'

Tate held up her hands and took a step backwards. A moment later Williams was in the room standing beside her. 'Keep still and your friend won't get hurt,' he said, forcing her arms behind her back. He wrapped something around her wrists, pulling tight until her hands were bound together. 'We're going upstairs now. You first.'

He prodded and poked at Tate until they were through the door and crossing the outer room, heading towards the doorway on the other side.

'Don't try anything,' he said as they passed through the door and onto the stairs.

Williams pushed her up to the next floor where they waited in a large gloomy vestibule, newspaper and sheets of cardboard stuck to the windows at the front and back. No wonder the place looked derelict from the outside. Tate remembered what Mrs Wells had told her about seeing Ray Dixon in the street. She imagined him standing on the other side of the road, looking over at this house, wondering if Thomas Williams still lived inside.

Ashley and Rosie appeared at the top of the stairs, the woman pressing the blade against Ashley's perfect skin.

'That lady I was telling you about?' Tate said, desperate to keep talking, to try to get through to the woman with the knife. 'The one whose daughter disappeared? Can you imagine what she's been going through, Rosie? All these years? You're a mother yourself – I'm sure you can.'

'Stop talking! Daddy doesn't want you to speak.'

'I'm just appealing to you, as a mother. And grandmother. Don't you think it's right that Mrs Jeffries should get a chance to have a proper funeral for her daughter? Instead of her being buried in an unmarked grave in your garden.' She drew a breath, trying to ascertain if what she was saying was having any impact. 'Because that's where Paula Jeffries is, Rosie. Your Daddy dug a big hole and threw her in.'

'Shut. Up! Liar!' Rosie said.

Ashley gasped. Tate watched as a line of dark red blood appeared along the length of the knife.

'Why did you make me do that?' Rosie snapped.

Tate tried to move closer to the intern, but Williams held on firmly to her wrists. He shoved her towards an open door and bundled her into a large stone-flagged kitchen. The temperature seemed to drop as soon as they crossed the threshold. Williams thumped a fist into her back and drove her forward, towards the back door. Tate peered through the glass at the blackness beyond.

'She's out there, Rosie,' Tate said. 'Paula Jeffries is buried in the cold ground.' She glanced over her shoulder to see the intern shuffling across the room, Rosie behind her, the knife still pressed against her bloody throat. *Stay calm, Ashley.*

'I told you to shut up,' Rosie said. 'Why do you keep talking when everything you say is lies?'

Tate took a breath. 'Not me. It's Daddy who's been lying to you.'

Rosie hesitated halfway across the kitchen.

'Don't listen to her, Rosie.' Williams unlocked the back door and pushed it open.

'I haven't lied to you once.'

Rosie took a deep, shuddering breath. 'You haven't stopped lying.'

'Enough, Rosie. That's enough.' Williams shoved Tate through the door and into the dark garden.

Tate watched helplessly as the woman manoeuvred Ashley to the back door step. In the dark, she couldn't tell how serious the gash across her neck was.

Still with a firm hold on Tate's arms, Williams moved quickly towards a low brick wall. He stuck the torch in a pocket and grabbed a shovel from the ground. He shoved it under his arm and retrieved the torch. He trained it on Tate's face. She screwed up her eyes against the glare.

'We've wasted enough time already. Chat chat chat.' He let go of Tate's wrists and waved the shovel at her. 'These graves won't dig themselves.'

FIFTY-SIX

'As I say – you've made a terrible mistake.' Gary Benson was sitting in the chair Angela Tate had vacated only a few hours before. He too was wearing a Tyvek forensic suit. He had spent the first fifteen minutes of the interview declaring his innocence and going to great lengths to describe the building site in Dulwich where he'd been working all day.

'Not with your sister then?' McKittrick asked as Mills took notes.

'No…' Benson narrowed his eyes and glanced from one detective to the other. 'What makes you think that?'

'According to Lorraine you were with her all day.'

'Today? What's she on? Silly cow.' He didn't miss a beat. 'Must have got her days mixed up. You can ask anyone on the site. They'll vouch for me.' He spread his recently swabbed fingers on the table, the nails cut short. Manicured hands that had been nowhere near a building site. 'Now – what are you going to do about my stolen van?'

McKittrick clenched her jaw and started to count to ten very slowly.

'You haven't asked me anything about it yet. That is why I came in, after all.'

'Why did you flee when you saw us outside your house?'

'Me? Flee from the police? Not likely. Law abiding citizen, I am. You must have seen whoever nicked my van. Get a good look at his face, did you?'

'What would this person be doing driving to your home address? In fact, how would they even know where you live?'

'Not a clue – you'd have to ask them that.'

'When did you notice your van was missing?'

He smiled his cocky little smile at her. 'That's easy – about twenty minutes before I came in here.'

'Where was it parked?'

'Outside the pub on the corner of East Street and Walworth Road.'

'Drinking and driving?'

'It's the only place I could find a space. Murder parking round there.' He smiled again. 'I wouldn't dream of drinking and driving. You've got me all wrong. As I say – model citizen, me. I'm the *victim* of a crime.' He looked down at the Tyvek suit. 'Though you would never guess it looking at me.'

'So these builder friends of yours – all working on a Saturday were they?'

'Times are hard – these fellas work whenever they get the chance.'

'And what were you doing there?' McKittrick looked down at Benson's perfect nails once again, at the soft skin around his knuckles.

He saw her looking. 'Project management. I'm a fixer. I make things happen. I'm your go-to man. Anything you need – I can sort it.' He grinned, flashing his teeth at her. 'I'd give you my card.' He made a show of patting down the Tyvek suit. 'Only they're in my other jacket.

'Sort anything?'

'Mr Fixit.'

'So if someone needed some… dodgy DVDs for example, you'd be their first stop? Is that how it works?'

His grin vanished. McKittrick could see the muscles in his cheeks bulge for just a moment as he ground his teeth.

Then he relaxed again. It was only a flicker of tension. But it was unmistakable.

'Now – that all depends on what you mean by "dodgy". Never get involved with anything illegal. That's a rule of mine.'

'Really?'

'Straight up.'

'We found a lot of duplicating equipment and boxes of blank DVDs all neatly tucked away in the lock-up you rent on Wyndham Road.' McKittrick scrutinised his expression.

The smile returned.

'Not me. I don't rent a lock-up. On Wyndham Road or anywhere else.'

'We found an invoice in your house requesting payment for three months' rent in advance.'

'Did you?' He scratched his chin, looked up at the ceiling. 'Oh yeah, now I come to think about it, I did rent a unit. But not for the last year or so. Must be an old invoice. What's the date on it? Don't know anything about any DVDs. You want to speak to the current tenant. Ask them about it.'

'We'll be speaking to the landlord in due course.'

Another definite flicker of stress. A darkening of his expression. But again he quickly recovered.

'The boxes found in the lock-up were identical to those DC Mills saw in your mother's flat.'

Benson looked at Mills for the first time. 'Well you've got that wrong. What would Mum be doing with a lot of boxes?'

'My colleague and I saw you removing one of them a week ago. When we met you on the stairs of your mother's block.'

More chin scratching. 'Now let me think… A week ago, you say?'

Mills flipped though his notebook. 'Saturday, February the eleventh. Ten-fifteen.'

'Oh Saturday – right. You should have said. That'd be the jumble I took down to the charity shop for her. You know, old clothes and that. Just a load of old rubbish. One cardboard box must look pretty much the same as any other I suppose.'

McKittrick pushed back her chair and stood up. They'd be at this into the early hours. She needed to get out of the room before she throttled him.

'That it, then?'

'An officer will be in shortly with some paper and a pen. We need that list of builders from you.'

'What about my van?' Benson called after them as McKittrick and Mills exited the room.

McKittrick marched down the corridor, keeping her arms firmly folded, fearing she might punch something, or someone, if she loosened her grip. Mills caught up with her by the time she'd reached the double doors leading to the stairwell. 'Cocky fucking bastard,' she said through gritted teeth. 'How I'd love to wipe that smile off his face.'

'Early days yet, boss. He can't keep that up. We know he was driving the van in Beckenham – it might take a while, but we'll get the CCTV to prove it.'

'Time's not on our side.'

Mills checked his watch. 'We've got another thirty-four hours to find something.'

'Assuming the chief super agrees to the extension.'

'He will. No danger. Then we can ask the magistrates to do the same. Fast track the forensics.'

'You don't think Benson would have disposed of the clothes he was wearing this morning? He set his van alight.'

'There'll be a trace of Dixon's blood on him somewhere. There's got to be.'

They walked back to the incident room in silence, McKittrick wondering at Mills' optimism. She hated the idea of seeing Benson walk out of the station. But there wasn't much she could do. When she reached her desk she found a message asking her to call Kapoor. She sent Mills out for coffees, made a quick trip to the ladies – her nerves were shot – then called the FLO back.

'Manisha – what is it?'

'I've just had a long chat with Chelsea. She was very upset. It took a while to get any sense out of her. But I think she's telling the truth.'

McKittrick could hear shouting at the other end of the line. 'What's going on there?'

'Trisha's just found out what Chelsea told me. I should probably call you back.'

'What's happened? What has Chelsea said?'

'According to Chelsea, and I really do think she's being honest this time, there's no reason for her to lie… Please Trisha, can you hang on just a sec…'

For God's sake, get on with it, McKittrick wanted to yell, her nerves still jangling.

The noises in the background subsided.

'Sorry, boss, I've just stepped out of the room.' She lowered her voice. 'Chelsea has just told me that the cardigan we found at Dixon's mother's flat wasn't the one Casey was wearing when she went to school the morning she disappeared. She says she told Casey to take it off because it had a big Ribena stain on the sleeve. She had a row with Casey about it. Had to practically drag it off her.'

'Wait a minute…' Something didn't ring true, but McKittrick couldn't put her finger on it. Then it came to her. 'This was Monday morning?'

'Yes.'

'Collins would have been there – she would have got Casey ready for school herself. So she would have known about the cardigan.'

'Casey didn't want her mum to know she spilled the blackcurrant over it. Chelsea promised her she wouldn't tell.'

'It still doesn't make any sense. Why didn't Chelsea tell us about it as soon as we showed the picture to her mother?'

'Chelsea won't tell me – but I get the impression she's feeling bad about fighting with her sister over it.'

The shouting ratcheted up again.

'If what she's saying is true, then how did the cardigan get into Mrs Dixon's flat?'

'Sorry boss, I really have to go,' Kapoor said. 'I'll call you back when I can.'

Kapoor hung up and McKittrick pulled the phone from her ear. She stared at the screen as it faded into sleep mode, taking a moment to process the new information. Mills arrived with the coffees, took one look at her face and told her to sit down.

'Christ, boss – what's happened?'

'I need to speak to the DCI. There's been… a development.' The phone vibrated in her hand. It was Kapoor calling back. 'Manisha. Before I go to DCI Barrow with this, are you absolutely sure Chelsea's telling you the truth?'

'I'm even surer than I was five minutes ago.'

'What's happened?'

'It all came out just now – Chelsea was arguing with Trisha. She said she didn't say anything about the cardigan before because she was too scared to. She didn't want to cause any more trouble.' Kapoor took a breath and swallowed noisily. 'One minute, Trish.'

McKittrick started pacing the room, unable to keep still. 'Manisha?'

'Sorry, boss.' Kapoor lowered her voice to a whisper. 'Chelsea saw Gary Benson take the cardigan from her sister's wardrobe two days ago.'

FIFTY-SEVEN

Angela Tate leaned heavily on the handle of the shovel, a sharp pain burning across her shoulders. She'd been digging for a while, trying to formulate some plan to get them out of there. With Ashley being held at knife point there weren't many options open. All she could do was continue to try to engage Rosie in conversation. Drive a wedge, however slight, between her and Williams. She knew time was running out.

'Don't stop digging,' Rosie snapped at her. 'Who said you could stop?'

Tate was standing in the six feet by eighteen-inch hole, the dirt halfway up to her shins, a lantern flickering at one end providing a meagre light for her to dig by. 'You know I haven't been lying to you,' she said. 'I swear on Ashley's life, everything I've told you tonight is true.'

'Stop talking. I'm sick of the sound of your voice.' Rosie shifted impatiently. Ashley let out a moan.

'Why don't you let me swap places with Ashley? My arms are getting so tired.'

'Daddy wants you to do the digging. So dig!'

Tate let out a long breath and drove the shovel into the ground again. She was getting nowhere. She peered into the gloom at the far end of the garden where Williams was smoking a cigarette, the glowing tip dancing around in the darkness like a firefly, the torch angled towards the ground.

Tate saw another light flash in the gloom and realised Williams was holding a mobile phone. She took another rest and stretched her arms over her head, all the while straining to hear what he was saying.

'Where are you?' he said. 'I was expecting you at five. I'm not taking another delivery. I've had enough. And I want you to collect all your… merchandise. I don't want it here anymore. Call me back as soon as you get this message.' The bluish glow of the phone disappeared as the orange cigarette tip burned more brightly.

Delivery of what? What had got him so rattled?

Tate scooped up another pitiful amount of soil and deposited it on the low ridge that was slowly forming along the length of the trench. 'My offer still stands,' she said as she collected another small clump of claggy London clay on the end of the shovel. 'I can get you out of here and take you somewhere safe.'

'How many times do I have to tell you to shut up?'

'What are you talking about?' Williams started towards them, the torch beam lighting his path from the rear of the garden. When he reached Tate he peered at the pit. 'You want to put your back into it. Or you'll never get it done. I've decided there's no need to dig two holes. One will be sufficient. As long as it's deep enough.'

Tate weighed the shovel in her hands and glanced over at Ashley. The knife was still poised at her throat. There was no way she could take out Williams with the spade without risking serious injury to the intern.

'Why don't you keep me entertained while I work, Tom? Rosie here isn't interested in talking to me.'

He flicked the glowing butt of his cigarette into the hole.

'Tell me about your time inside with Raymond Dixon.'

'Don't know who you're talking about.'

'Come on, Tom. What's the point in pretending? I know I'm not digging this hole for you to plant a crop of new potatoes. You could at least keep me entertained while I dig my own grave.' She forced a smile. 'How long were you inside with him?'

He looked at the woman with the knife. 'I've never been in prison in my life and I don't know any Raymond Dixon.'

'Have it your own way.' Tate shoved the next clump of soil at Williams' feet. 'Only Raymond remembered you very clearly. You might almost call it an obsession.'

'Stop making up stories.'

'I just write them down. Fiction's not really my thing.' She smiled. 'I only call it an obsession because it had to be, didn't it? Trying to track you down for so many years.'

'Why don't you shut your evil mouth?' Williams hissed at her.

'It'll be shut permanently in just a little while, so I'll ignore that suggestion if you don't mind.' Another lump of soil landed on Williams' shoes. 'It paid off, his dogged determination. He found you didn't he? I have no idea how many other people he told about this place. I suppose I was just one of many. I'd expect a few visitors if I were you, Tom.'

'Enough!' He kicked out at her. She only just managed to duck out of the way of his muddy shoe.

'Who's buried in the garden Tom?' Tate whispered. 'I mean, as well as Paula? Why not tell me? What difference does it make now?'

'What's she saying, Daddy?' Rosie moved closer, the knife still pressed against Ashley's throat.

'Don't pay her any attention. She's a liar. And a whore.'

'Really, Tom – we've only just met. That's quite an assumption to make.' Tate reached along the handle of the shovel with her left hand, to even the weight distribution. 'Is Mrs Williams somewhere in here?' In the gloom she saw Williams throw a glance towards Rosie. What *did* you do to Rosie's mum?'

'My mum's dead,' Rosie said quietly.

'That's enough, Rosie.' Williams' face contorted.

'So you shouldn't keep saying she's alive,' the woman muttered.

Ashley let out another moan. In the dim light coming from the lantern, Tate could see the dark stain on her neck getting bigger.

'Why don't you let Ashley go,' Tate said and started to climb out of the hole. Williams shoved her back in.

'You keep digging.' His voice was getting louder. 'Why did you have to come here upsetting everybody?' He shoved Tate again. She stumbled backwards and landed awkwardly on her arm.

'Yes - why keep saying you went to see her, when she's dead?' Rosie said. 'Why would you want to do that?'

Ashley let out a stifled scream.

Tate struggled to her feet and grabbed the shovel. She edged towards Ashley. 'Why don't you put the knife down, Rosie? You're hurting Ashley. And she's not done anything to hurt you, has she?'

Rosie looked at Williams.

'Don't listen to her!' Williams yelled. He jumped into the hole, knocking the shovel from Tate's hands. He threw down the torch and grabbed her by the throat, his bony hands clamping tight around her neck. Tate thrust up her knee, but he dodged sideways and she only managed to graze the side of his thigh.

'Stop it!' a voice called from the back of the house.

Williams turned, his hands still gripping Tate's throat.

The backdoor was open, a flickering light coming from the kitchen. Tate could just make out Rosie's daughter standing in the doorway, carrying a large child in her arms.

She started to walk towards them. 'Olivia's had a nightmare. Stop shouting or you'll frighten her even more.'

While Williams was distracted, Tate lifted her knee again, faster and harder this time. She made direct contact with Williams' crotch. He shrieked and let go of her, grabbing his balls as he staggered sideways.

'Put the knife down, Rosie,' Tate yelled. 'He can't hurt you now. Put down the knife and let Ashley go.'

Ashley's throat was slick with blood.

Tate moved slowly towards them, raising her arms as she crept forward.

'Why do you keep lying about seeing my mum? It's a wicked thing to do.'

'Your mum?'

'My mum's dead.'

'Did she die here?' Tate peered into the gloom, wondering where Mrs Williams was buried. She saw Williams roll over, still clutching his balls. He let out a high-pitched wine.

'Of course she didn't!'

'All right.' Tate held up her hands. 'I'm sorry.'

'My mum died a little while after Daddy brought me here to live with him.'

'Brought you here? What do you mean?'

Williams let out another whine.

'So I know you're lying. You didn't see her "just the other day".'

'Are you talking about Pamela Jeffries?'

'She died years and years ago.'

'Paula?'

The woman flinched.

'Paula! Put down the knife. I'm not lying, I promise you. I did see her. She loves you. She's waiting for you to come home.'

'My name's Rosie.' She started to sob. 'My mum died a long time ago.'

'No. No she didn't. You have to believe me. She'll be so pleased to see you. And meet your daughter and Olivia too. She's waited so long. She'll be absolutely thrilled.' Tate was close enough to reach out and touch the knife. She lifted her right hand, palm upwards. 'Give me the knife, Paula.'

Tears were streaming down the woman's face.

'Just give it to me, nice and gently.'

Paula Jeffries started to pull the blade away from Ashley's throat. She stared into Tate's face. 'I've missed her too.'

'Of course you have.' Tate extended her arm.

Ashley dropped to her knees. Gasping.

Paula's expression changed. She looked over Tate's shoulder. 'No!'

Tate turned to see Williams coming at her with the shovel. She ducked to one side. The shovel caught Paula's arm.

The knife flew out of her hand.

Williams turned and raised the shovel again.

Tate drove a rubber-clad foot into his shin. He tottered for a moment, the spade slipping from his grasp. Paula shoved him in the back. He wheeled around and slapped her hard across the face.

Tate reached out for the shovel. Williams got there first, stamping on her hand. He turned back to Paula and grabbed her by the hair.

'Daddy! Stop!' Mary started running towards them, the child in her arms wailing, kicking out her legs, struggling to be released.

Williams slapped Paula again.

The young woman had almost reached them when the struggling child squirmed out of her arms and ran into the darkness. 'Olivia! Come back here!'

'Leave her,' Williams said, raising his arm again, ready to strike Paula.

'Don't touch her!' Mary ran at him, throwing herself onto his back, wrapping her arms around his throat.

Tate sank to her knees and started grappling in the gloom, feeling her way along the ground, desperate to locate the knife. She looked up and saw Williams staggering backwards, trying to shake off Mary. A faint glint of metal flashed in his hand. As he spun around he held up the knife.

He hesitated.

Tate didn't notice the shovel until it swung down across his right arm, forcing the knife from his hand.

Ashley was bent double, the exertion of wielding the shovel too much for her. Paula jumped forward and snatched the spade from Ashley, driving it hard against Williams' legs. He dropped to the ground, taking Mary down with him.

Tate spotted the knife. But not before Williams. He scooped it up and lashed out. First at Paula. Then Ashley. The shovel came down again. This time hitting the side of his head. He collapsed sideways. Mary pulled herself from under him.

Tate scrambled out of the pit and ran towards the sound of the screaming child. 'Olivia!' She called into the dark. 'It's all right, sweetie. Everything's all right. Your mummy's OK.' She picked up speed, stumbling into the black, and found the child curled up in a tight ball at the back of the garden. She pulled the girl towards her and held her tight. 'It's all right.'

'I want my mummy!' the girl sobbed.

'Of course you do. Shhh. Everything's OK.' Tate put an arm around the girl's shoulders and led her towards the faint glimmer of light emanating from the back door. She reached the narrow trench and saw Paula standing over Williams, gripping the shovel tight in her hands. Mary was holding the knife. 'Here we are. Here's Mummy.'

The girl screamed and clung on to Tate. 'No! I want *my* mummy!'

'Shhh! It's all right.' Tate pulled the matted strands of hair from the girl's damp cheeks. She saw her face properly for the first time.

It was Casey Collins.

FIFTY-EIGHT

Dance music was thumping at such volume across the Camberwell North Community Centre, that Angela Tate could feel the fillings in her teeth vibrate. She watched as a beaming, and slightly drunk, Trisha Collins swung Casey off her feet, the nine-year-old chortling hard as tears streamed down her rosy cheeks. Behind them even Chelsea Collins was joining in. It seemed Trisha had forgiven the girl completely. Tate wondered abstractedly if Trisha would ever tell Chelsea that Gary Benson was her father. Not now, presumably, given Benson was in custody charged with the murder of Ray Dixon.

The room was jammed. Half the estate must have turned out to celebrate Casey's safe return to her family. No doubt attracted by the prospect of a free bar laid on courtesy of *The Herald*. It was the least the paper could do after their editorials had branded Trisha Collins first as an unfit mother then as a child abductor.

Trisha, panting and flush-faced, let go of Casey's hands and immediately Kiefer, her big brother, swooped the girl off her feet and onto his shoulders. Tate spotted Terence White appear from the crowd at the bar, a pint in one hand, a glass of something and Coke in the other. He handed the small glass to Trisha and then started patting her stomach with the flat of his hand. Trisha playfully batted his hand away and took a swig of her drink. She glanced across the room and noticed Tate looking at her. She raised her glass and Tate nodded back without smiling. White had slunk back into Trisha's life a couple of days after Casey's return. Tate was appalled Trisha had agreed to speak to him, much less take up where she'd left off. When she'd quizzed her about it, Trisha would only say she was giving him another chance 'for the sake of the baby.' What positive influence she thought White would have wasn't at all clear. Trisha took another swig and turned away from Tate, burying her head in White's chest.

Tate gave it two months at most.

Ashley Montgomery appeared on the opposite side of the makeshift dance floor. She waved cheerily at Tate, giving her the thumbs up. The intern had made a remarkable recovery following her ordeal. She was back at her desk less than forty-eight hours later, eager to get her personal account: *How I rescued Casey Collins* onto the front page of the *Evening News*. Tate had let her take the credit. Why not? She'd earned it.

The volume of the music suddenly ratcheted up and Tate decided a cigarette break was long overdue. She pushed through the heaving crowd towards the door, stopping every now and then to accept well wishers' congratulations and thanks. Even Lorraine O'Donnell raised a begrudging glass of cheap sparkling wine in her direction. It was amazing the woman had had the nerve to turn up at all, in the circumstances. Her brother was in Pentonville awaiting trial for not only the murder of Ray Dixon, but also the distribution of child pornography. Lorraine had given her own exclusive to *The Herald*, distancing herself from her brother. And her mother, who had been storing merchandise for Gary. Though of course Maureen Benson claimed vehemently she had no idea what was in the boxes he occasionally kept at her flat. It was possible that no one would ever have discovered the nature of Gary Benson's business if Thomas Williams hadn't been storing two dozen or so boxes for him in his basement.

Tate finally reached the exit and raised an eyebrow at Ryan Collins, who was loitering by the door with a few of his mates. He quickly hid a bottle of alcopop behind his back.

'I saw that,' Tate said. 'Don't be a moron. It'll rot your brain as well as your teeth.'

She opened the door and bumped into Frank Carter on his way in.

'I was just about to give you a call,' she said. You'd better get a move on – before it gets messy.'

'Will do.'

'How was your country break?'

Frank started fiddling with his camera case and couldn't look her in the eye.

'It's all right – I'll just grill Rita next time I see her.'

'It was lovely – thanks for asking.' He scanned the room. 'This feels just like a wedding reception. How long before a fight breaks out, do you reckon?'

'About thirty seconds after the free bar runs dry.'

'How are you, anyway?' He took a close look at her face.

'Barely bruised. An extra coat of foundation works wonders.'

'Maybe you should take off for a few days.'

'I haven't got time for that. I'm just starting to get somewhere with Paula Jeffries.'

'Have the police decided yet whether they're going to charge her with Casey's abduction?'

'Williams is still pointing the finger at Paula's daughter, Mary. Paula's insisting Mary had nothing to do with it. She's even talking about confessing to it herself, to keep Mary out of the frame.'

'And what does Casey say?'

'Not a word. Not so far.'

'Poor kid.' Frank shook his head. 'She must have been terrified.'

'I think she was well treated by Paula and Mary. As far as I can tell they made sure Williams never got anywhere near her. But there's evidence she was tranquillised, to keep her docile.'

Frank pointed at the nine-year-old, who was still in fits of giggles, riding high on her brother's shoulders. 'Looking at her now, you wouldn't think anything had happened at all.'

'It'll surface one way or another. It's only a matter of time. At least she's getting proper counselling.'

Frank started to get his camera out of its case. 'Has Paula Jeffries told you what happened in '79?'

'It's coming out gradually. I don't want to push anything.'

'Did she know what was buried in the garden?'

'That she won't talk about at all.'

'What's the latest body count?'

Tate shuddered as she remembered the mounds she'd stumbled over in the dark. 'Six. They've found the remains of a young girl. In addition to five infants under twelve months.'

'Five now?' Frank sucked in a breath. 'And was the girl Paula's granddaughter?'

Tate nodded. 'Olivia. Mary's daughter by Williams. Nothing from the police so far about the postmortem, but Paula's told me Olivia got very ill just after Christmas. Williams refused to allow her to go to hospital. After the girl died Williams promised to "fix everything". Paula says it was his idea to get a "replacement" for her. Another little blonde girl.'

'He managed to convince Paula and her daughter that was an OK thing to do?'

'He's been convincing them of God knows what for thirty-odd years.'

'Christ – the more I find out about it, the less I wish I knew.' Frank drew in a long breath. He touched Tate lightly on the arm. 'How are you, Ange, really?'

'I'm fine.'

'We've known each other too long – you can't fool me. Why don't you take a break?'

Tate shook her head. Frank did know her. And he knew perfectly well she couldn't just walk away. 'I've told you – I'm too busy. I want to organise a memorial service for Raymond.'

Frank pulled a face. 'Really?'

'I've got to do something.'

'I can't see that being very well attended.'

'I'm working on it.'

Frank raised his eyebrows.

'The PI I hired found more exhibits from the 1979 investigation. Including Sandra Stockwell's shoes. I've requested a DNA analysis of the blood on them. Ray Dixon will be exonerated just as soon as the results come back.'

'Don't get your hopes up, Ange.'

'I know I'm right.' And Gary Benson will finally be exposed, thirty-three years too late, she thought.

Frank pointed his camera towards the Collins family and fired off half a dozen shots.

'I'll see you later,' Tate said and pulled a pack of cigarettes from her bag.

Ralph Mills found Manisha Kapoor sitting on a low wall separating the Camberwell North Community Centre from the car park behind. She was staring into a glass of orange juice.

'Had enough?' he asked, and pointed towards the back of the building.

'Where have you been?'

'Just dropped the boss off at the station.'

'She didn't stay long.'

'She was only showing her face, deputising for the DCI.'

Kapoor put her glass on the wall. 'Thank God Barrow didn't decide to brazen it out. It would have caused a riot.'

Mills shoved his hands in his pockets. 'The boss told me the MIT will be decamping back to Lewisham next week.'

'I suppose they don't need our input anymore.'

'You're still staying with the Collinses, though?'

'No one's told me any different.'

Mills blew on his cold hands. 'Back to dealing with robberies and domestics for me.'

'Throw in the odd mugging and life's back to where it was before.' Kapoor breathed out a long breath, fogging the air. 'Talking of robberies, have you got anywhere questioning Paula Jeffries and her daughter about the pharmacy break-ins?'

'You were right to link them. Just got a call this morning about half a dozen other incidents.'

'Femodene?'

Mills nodded. 'Seems Paula Jeffries had insisted on contraceptives for her daughter. She didn't want any more miscarriages or…' He let out a breath. 'Dead babies.' The intense cold suddenly got to him and he shuddered violently.

'How could she be party to that? Her own daughter? Why didn't they just get away from Williams the first opportunity they had?'

Mills had been thinking much the same thing. 'They were with him for too long, he was their family. It's not unprecedented is it? Captives forming bonds with their abductors.'

'But you expect that sort of thing to happen somewhere else, not on your own patch.'

'Makes you wonder about all the cases we never find out about.' He shuddered again. 'You seen Cath since she was discharged from hospital?'

'I'm going to her place this evening, I said I'd do a bit of shopping for her. Maybe you should come?'

He nodded. 'Yeah – I'd like that.'

'She's itching to get back to work. It's driving her crazy being laid up.' Kapoor picked up the orange juice and put it down again. 'Has she mentioned anything to you about putting in for a transfer to HSCC?'

'No. Is she?'

'It's all she keeps talking about. Seems McKittrick made quite an impression.'

Mills said nothing. It was becoming a habit. It was too late now to mention Collins' stolen sleeping pills to anyone. But he didn't feel able to completely let it go. Maybe he should request a transfer to the Lewisham MIT himself. He was just about to mention it to Kapoor when he heard a familiar voice calling his name.

'Just the man I was after.' Tate hurried towards Mills and the FLO. 'Perishing out here isn't it?' she said when she reached them. 'As you were – don't let me interrupt your conversation.'

The two detectives exchanged a glance. Kapoor got to her feet.

'Confidential was it?' She stubbed out her half-smoked cigarette under a shoe.

'I can't tell you anything about our ongoing investigations. Not even off the record,' Mills told her.

'Oh I wouldn't dream of asking you to.' Tate smiled at him. 'But perhaps we should compare notes? Paula Jeffries has told me plenty. Be good to make sure we're all on the same page before my paper runs the story.'

'You can't print anything that will jeopardise—'

Tate held up a hand to stop him. 'You don't need to tell me that.' She stamped her cold feet to get some feeling back into them. 'I need to ask you a favour.'

Mills frowned at her.

'Could you have a word with someone about the DNA analysis I've requested? No one will taken any notice of me.

I promised Ray Dixon. Christ – it's the least I can do. After everything that's happened.'

Mills looked at his shoes.

'You were wrong about Dixon abducting Casey, just like your dad was wrong about him murdering Sandra Stockwell.'

'What difference will it make now?'

'How can you say that?' She thought she caught the two detectives exchange another glance. Kapoor was frowning at Mills. 'What is it?' Tate said. 'Do you know something?'

Kapoor continued to gaze intensely at her colleague. She seemed as much in the dark as Tate was.

Mills said nothing.

'What have you found out?' Tate asked him.

His nose twitched.

'Do you have the results?' Tate held on to his arm. She could feel his muscles tense under her fingers. 'If you know something you've got to tell me.'

'You should get a full report in the next couple of days,' he said finally.

'For God's sake – you can't leave me hanging. It's Gary Benson, isn't it?'

Mills drew in a deep breath.

'I knew it – all these years.'

'Even if it was Benson, he was only nine-years-old at the time – below the age of criminal responsibility. It's not as if he would be tried for it now,' Mills said.

'That's not the point. I promised Raymond. The blood wasn't his, was it? Can you at least tell me that.'

Mills blinked. He folded his arms, unable to look at Tate or his colleague.

'It was Benson, wasn't it?'

He shook his head.

'I don't believe you.'

He exhaled. 'It definitely wasn't Gary Benson.'

'There must be a mistake. I can't believe it was Raymond's.' Tate's head was spinning.

'It didn't match Dixon's DNA profile,' Mills said.

Tate puffed out a breath. *Thank God for that.* Unexpected tears sprang into her eyes. She shook her head. Poor Raymond. She took a moment to gather her thoughts. 'Have you run the results against your database? If it wasn't Benson… who… was it Williams?

Mills shook his head again.

'Christ – I'm not playing some guessing game with you. Have you found a match?'

'Yes!' Mills snapped back at her.

'Then who was it?'

He looked at Kapoor, an apologetic expression on his face. She was still frowning at him. 'What I said about Gary being too young, it still holds true,' he said.

'I don't understand – what are you saying?'

'Too young to be criminally responsible, I mean.'

'Will you please just spit it out? Give me a bloody name!'

'Trisha Collins.'

About the author

Eva was born and raised in south London. She's been a local government worker, singer and dot com entrepreneur.

She wrote her first novel in 2005, and in 2011 won the inaugural Lucy Cavendish fiction prize for *The Loyal Servant.*

For more information about Eva's other books, please visit her website at evahudson.com/books. You can also follow her on Twitter: @Eva_Hudson.

To keep up to date with new releases, you might like to join the mailing list at evahudson.com/newbookalert.

Printed in Great Britain
by Amazon

53660946R10239